**Advance praise for *Making Out with Blowfish***

"A five-star treat from a five-star author. *Making out with Blowfish* is a fast paced, easy to read story with characters that practically leap off the pages. Hank Fitzpatrick and his family and friends wade through issues that most of us can relate to. I laughed, I got angry, and I even cried. This flawless story will hold your attention from the first line in the prologue to the very last page. If you read only a few books a year, this should be one of them!"
 —Mary Monroe, *New York Times* bestselling author of *Lost Daughters*

"*Making Out with Blowfish* is a wonderful book for people lovers and animal lovers. Hank Fitzpatrick and his dog Chief are companions on the hero journey, they are on a roller-coaster of a ride through life together, and it is a pleasure to come along."
 —Jon Katz, *New York Times* bestselling author of *Second Chance Dog: A Love Story*

**Previous praise for *Exotic Music of the Belly Dancer*:**

"In the vein of David Sedaris or Chuck Palahniuk, Brian Sweany has written a tight satirical story that has you bent over with laughter one moment then wiping away the tears the next minute."
 —Frank Bill, author of *Crimes in Southern Indiana*

"Brian Sweany has re-invented the coming of age novel with *Exotic Music of the Belly Dancer*, a bawdy, unfiltered snapshot of adolescence. Hank Fitzpatrick, the hormonally challenged narrator of the story, has a remarkable capacity to be both nihilistic and tender—think *Fear and Loathing in Las Vegas* meets *Leave It to Beaver*—minus the literary pretense and relentless self-awareness of so many other protagonists in the canon."
 —William McKeen, author of *Outlaw Journalist: The Life and Times of Hunter S. Thompson*

"For anyone who ever wonders about that guy in school who has more fun, more girls, more drinks, more sex, drugs, and rock and roll, more luck (and bad luck) of the Irish, *Exotic Music of the Belly Dancer* tells all. But behind every party is the hidden truth: that the world, if given time, will break your heart."
 —Keith Donohue, *New York Times* bestselling author of *The Stolen Child*

"Exposing the belly of the male beast is a brave thing to do. Brian Sweany writes like an American Martin Amis, and that's a great thing."
 —Alexandra Fuller, *New York Times* bestselling author of *Don't Let's Go to the Dogs Tonight*

"*Exotic Music of the Belly Dancer* is funny and tragic, occasionally even a warm, homespun homage-to-me-familia, but it is the dark and subversive stretches that burned deeply into my psyche and kept me turning the page."
 –Sonny Brewer, author of *Cormac: The Tale of a Dog Gone Missing*

"Prepare yourself for a nostalgic, strikingly honest trip back to your yearning youth. *Exotic Music of the Belly Dancer* is more than a romp, and it will do more than jog your memory: it will run your memory over with a juggernaut of hormones, teen confusion and dawning awareness."
 –David L. Robbins, author of *War of the Rats*

# Making Out with Blowfish
## A Novel

By
Brian Sweany

First published by The Writer's Coffee Shop, 2014

Copyright © Brian Sweany, 2014

The right of Brian Sweany to be identified as the author of this work has been asserted by him under the *Copyright Amendment (Moral Rights) Act 2000*

This work is copyrighted. All rights are reserved. Apart from any use as permitted under the Copyright Act 1968, no part may be reproduced, copied, scanned, stored in a retrieval system, recorded or transmitted, in any form or by any means, without the prior written permission of the publisher.

All characters and events in this book—even those sharing the same name as (or based upon) real people—are entirely fictional. No person, brand or corporation mentioned in this book should be taken to have endorsed this book nor should the events surrounding them be considered in any way factual.
This book is a work of fiction and should be read as such.

The Writer's Coffee Shop
(Australia) PO Box 447 Cherrybrook NSW 2126
(USA) PO Box 2116 Waxahachie TX 75168

Paperback ISBN- 978-1-61213-218-1
E-book ISBN- 978-1-61213-219-8

A CIP catalogue record for this book is available from the US Congress Library.

Cover image by: © istockphoto.com / Sergey Kulikov
Cover design by: Jennifer McGuire

Author photograph by: Robin Loheide Sweany

www.thewriterscoffeeshop.com/bsweany

"Gird up now thy loins like a man;
for I will demand of thee, and answer thou me."

*–The Book of Job, 38:3*

"Men, when they turn out well, are wonderful. But being young and male is so vulnerable, so prone to disaster. When we see a boy born these days, we have our hearts in our mouths—how will he turn out?"

–Steve Biddulph, *Raising Boys: Why Boys Are Different—and How to Help Them Become Happy and Well-Balanced Men*

For Robin

# Prologue
# 2009

A nineteen-year-old girl is playing with my balls.

"Your shot," she says, handing me the wet Ping-Pong ball.

The game is called beer pong. It's played on a conventional table tennis surface, with ten cups lined up in an ascending triangle like bowling pins on opposing ends of the table. Each cup is filled halfway with beer, although I hear there's a variety of the game involving a quarter-cup of beer played by people who aren't binge drinkers. There are two players to a team, a turn comprising each player getting one shot at the cups on the opposing end of the table. Beyond these basics, everyone seems to have their own individual rules. My rules tend to err on the side of drinking more. Every time you make a lob shot, an opposing player has to chug that cup. A bounce shot into the cup is a double bonus, meaning two cups must be consumed; however, a bounce shot can be legally blocked by the opposing team. This is a rarely attempted shot, reserved only for those nights when you find an opponent who's already drunk, exceedingly chatty, easily distracted, or all of the above. First team to eliminate all ten cups wins the game.

An eleventh cup sits off to the side of the table. It's filled with water, to rinse your balls. The theory is not only does the water keep your balls clean, it cuts down on the drag from the beer. Like many theories—creationism, compassionate conservatism, a woman's sex drive peaking in her thirties—it's total bullshit.

Tonight I'm playing the game with three young women. Two of the women are nineteen, the other is twenty. They're dressed in matching black pants and white oxfords with black bow ties. I force myself to call them *young women* in the hopes of feeling a little less dirty-old-mannish about being twice their age and wanting to bone them. Plus calling them *girls* would be to imply they contextually belong in the same discussion as my thirteen-year-old daughter.

"Score!" I say, sinking the ball into the tenth and final cup. "Game, set, and match, bitches!"

The other nineteen-year-old, my teammate's twin sister, grabs the cup and lifts it to her lips. "Well, fuck me up the ass."

I half-consider responding, *That could be arranged,* if only because her ass is very fuckable. Aside from a small chicken pox scar on my teammate's forehead, the twins are identical: same dark, almost plum-colored hair, same light complexions, same gaunt but attractive figures, same fuckable Goth asses.

My wife's sudden appearance at the bottom of the staircase tempers my enthusiasm somewhat.

"Hank, what the hell are you doing?"

"Hi, honey," I say, trying not to slur. "Just playin' a li'l beer pong."

"With the caterers?"

We hired them on the recommendation of Beth's father. They had catered Dr. Burke's office Christmas party the night before. About fifty of our friends are upstairs right now insulting Obama, bitching about their jobs (or lack thereof), and trading pictures of their children. Which is why I'm down in the basement getting drunk with nineteen-year-olds.

I start toward the stairs. "You told them they were off the clock."

"Yeah," Beth says, glaring over my shoulder at the three caterers, especially the twenty-year-old, a petite blonde who looks a lot like a younger version of Beth. "That doesn't mean to go play drinking games with my husband."

"Lighten up, Beth," I say, walking alongside her up the stairs.

She stops and raises her hands in the air. "Sorry, Hank, but one of us has to be the responsible host."

"Come on. The kids are at your mom's house. Why don't you relax and live a little?"

She stabs me with her eyes. "I *am* living a little. I just don't need to pound twelve beers to do it."

"Twelve beers?" I shake my head unapologetically. "I've had maybe ten or eleven, tops."

My wife doesn't acknowledge my response and walks up the rest of the stairs. She walks away from me, slowly sinking into the mumbling crowd of low expectations and dead-end lives. I open a new bottle of Jim Beam.

Like most parties involving people in their late-thirties, this one loses its steam right around eleven thirty. The ice buckets of cheap white wine now filled with room-temperature water. The brie solidified. Beth's iPod *Party Time* playlist now on its third rotation. Our remaining few guests closing the night with their predictable excuses.

"The babysitter is going to cost me a fortune if I don't get out of here," Lisa says.

Lisa is our next-door neighbor. She's a divorced single mother, with long legs and unusually perky breasts sprouting from her tall, stick-thin figure. She's also a former Indianapolis Colts cheerleader. I was hoping to talk her into the hot tub with me and Beth tonight, holding on to that perpetual fantasy of all married men that one day, in a moment of weakness, curiosity, and one too many glasses of bad Riesling, my wife would dive face-first into another woman's snatch while I tagged her from behind.

As if somehow sensing my descent into heterosexual ecstasy, my gay neighbors, Oscar and Marshall, chime in unison. "Great party, Hank."

If you overlook their seven Chihuahuas, Oscar and Marshall are pretty damn cool. They drink cheap domestic beer and enjoy football and basketball as much as any guy with a properly oriented penis—plus they harbor my same burning hatred for Roy and Betty.

Roy and Betty, or "R&B" as we call them, are a retired empty-nester couple on our cul-de-sac who think being older than dirt and not having kids entitles them to never pay any taxes that go toward public schooling—a notion I'd concede if they were willing to refund the government every cent of social security they've collected over the last ten years.

They also think that Homeowners Association dues are more a suggestion than a mandate and have convinced enough neighbors to come along for the ride. Thanks to them and their brain-dead lemmings, the street lights in our neighborhood haven't been lit for three years because we don't have money to pay the electrical bill. Meanwhile, every school referendum has been met by an R&B remonstrance ensuring underfunded schools and plummeting enrollments to go with our dark streets.

I think Betty might be paranoid schizophrenic. Two or three mornings a week she comes outside in a faded aqua bathrobe. With an eye patch on her left eye, a surgical mask fastened snugly over her mouth, and a feather duster in her right hand, she proceeds to dust the boxwoods lining her front porch for a good fifteen to twenty minutes.

I've attempted to talk to Betty and Roy, her pathetically enabling wallflower of a husband, but they're just too far gone. They once tried to have my kids arrested for trespassing when they took three steps into their front yard to retrieve an errant kickball. If not consciously malicious, R&B are two of the more accidentally evil people I know.

"Got to get up early for church," Hatch says. "You know how it is, Hank."

"No, I don't," I say.

Elias Hatcher has to get up early . . . for fucking church? When the hell did everyone become such goddamn squares?

"Come on, buddy. Five minutes." I grab Hatch by the elbow. "Just give me that."

He starts to unfasten his trench coat before *buddy* is hardly out of my mouth. "Okay."

"Keep your coat on," I say, catching Beth leer at me one last time from across the room. "I need some fresh air."

"Suit yourself," Hatch says. "But I'll give you five minutes under one condition."

"What's that?"

"Turn this shitty music off."

In all fairness, Beth's playlist isn't that horrible. It just happens to be playing Owl City's "Fireflies" at the moment, quite possibly the most insipid song written in the last twenty years. And given that, with the exception of maybe the Black Keys, post-grunge rock and roll is the vinyl track housing of music, that's saying something.

"*Houses of the Holy* maybe?"

"Perfect."

I queue up the CD. Hatch and I love this Led Zeppelin album above all others. Well, actually, it might be a tie for me between *Houses of the Holy* and *Led Zeppelin II*—Zeppelin's loudest and therefore in my opinion best album—but at the very least we don't worship *ZoSo* just because everyone says we're supposed to.

"That better?"

"Go to the next track," Hatch says before stepping outside. "We need to chill out with some 'Rain Song.'"

We walk out onto the back porch. Jimmy Page's guitar and Robert Plant's vocals echo across the backyard from the outdoor speakers mounted on the back of my house. I have a glass of Jim Beam on the rocks in my left, a now half-empty bottle of bourbon in my right. I take a sip of the bourbon, inhaling the aroma. My nose burns a little. Just for a second, as the charred oak smell curls up my nose and down my throat, I miss being a smoker.

"Still drinking Beam, Hank?"

It's been at least fifteen years since Hatch started calling me Hank and stopped calling me Fitzy. I guess joining the Navy and more than a decade of sobriety made him put away childish things. He's gone from being my constant enabler to my constant rock: critical without being judgmental, supportive without being pandering, fun without being drunk.

"What's it to you, lightweight?" I like to make fun of his sobriety, only because it detracts from the more pathetic reality that I still drink Beam because its smell reminds me of high school. The smell of hard liquor on a girl's breath. The touch of her soft skin. The mostly awkward but always exhilarating sex.

"Just figured you would have upgraded after all these years to maybe a small batch bourbon or single malt."

"Oh yeah?" I shake my head. "And I just figured I wouldn't get lectured on my alcohol choices by a guy who's been sober since the Clinton administration."

"I'm just fucking with you, Hank."

"Yeah, I know."

"Then chill out."

"Sorry. Guess I'm just in a bad mood." I linger near the doorway between the house and the back porch, holding the door open for my other best friend. "Come on, Chief."

My big black dog sits by the back door just inside the house. Chief is a fourteen-year-old Lab mix. At age three he swallowed an oven mitt that had to be cut out of his stomach. At age six he had his left rear ACL repaired. At age nine he had his right rear ACL repaired. He's partially blind and mostly deaf. For the last year, he's had off-and-on seizures from Parkinson's disease.

"You need my help, old man?" I say to Chief.

"You should put him out of his misery," Hatch says just outside the doorway.

"And you should shut the fuck up." I hand Hatch my glass and bourbon bottle.

Hatch acts disgusted. "What do you want me to do with these things?"

"Hold them for a second, asshole."

Hatch reluctantly accepts my devil's water, and I walk back into the house. Chief can no longer stand up from a prone or even sitting position without assistance, his rear legs and hips now more atrophic than arthritic. I straddle him, reach under his chest like I'm about to perform a canine Heimlich, and raise Chief until he's steadied on all fours. We walk out the door side by side. I look down, Chief looks up at me, and I scratch him behind his ears. An understood alliance.

A lone black walnut tree canopies the porch, its limbs as stark and judgmental as the look on Beth's face tonight. My childhood home in Clematis Gardens had a black walnut tree much like the one in my yard now. It stood near the back of our property, fighting for space with the gnarled, parasitic ash trees along an old farmer's fence line.

"How long is the wife going to be out of town?"

"Another week or so," Hatch says.

"She still with US Airways?"

"Did you really bring me out here to talk about my hot flight attendant wife?" Hatch hands back my glass of bourbon but holds on to the bottle.

I take a swallow as opposed to a sip. Exhaling, I let the caramelly bourbon warm my insides. "Somebody called me 'sir' today."

"What do you mean?"

"I mean Beth and I went to the mall to do some last-minute shopping for the kids. We were walking through the front doors at Macy's, and some teenage girls were trailing behind us. I opened the door for Beth, and then I held the door open for the teenagers. One of the girls turned and looked at me, and I swear she was about to wink."

"I guess you still got it, Hank."

I wave him off with my glass of Beam. "Wait, I'm not finished. I smiled back at her, and she said to me, 'Thank you . . . sir.'"

"So?"

"So, Hatch? She called me 'sir.' I'm not a sir. I'm not even a mister. I'm a

Hank. I'm a Fitzy."

"Fitzy," Hatch says. "When's the last time anyone called you by—"

"The point is I was fucking despondent. Beth noticed, asked me what was wrong, and said I looked like I was going to pass out."

"And what did you say?"

"I said, 'That girl might as well have just punched me in the nuts.'"

"Man," Hatch says, shaking his head. "I don't envy Beth."

"Why do you say that?"

Hatch points the bottle of Beam at me. "Because for the next ten years you're going to be one shitty fucking husband."

"When did you get to be so insightful?"

"When I stopped depending on brewed hops and distilled corn for insight," Hatch says, patting me on the back. "But speaking of shitty fucking husbands, how's your mother doing?"

"Fine," I say, trying not to grimace in disgust at the mention of my mother.

"I'm still trying to wrap my head around how Debbie ended up marrying a Mormon."

I take another sip of Beam. "He's not that bad."

"Plus that daughter of his is one fine piece of ass."

"Lay off Lila. That's my stepsister you're talking about."

"Oh, it's 'Lila' now?"

"It's always been Lila. She hates being called Delilah."

"Of course she hates it."

"What do you mean by that?"

"Let's see, a hot half-Armenian Mormon in her late thirties, who likes to drink, and isn't married."

"To be honest, I don't think she's even dating."

"Exactly!" Hatch says. "That's total LDA right there."

"Okay, now you've officially lost me."

"What I'm saying is, your stepsister is not a Latter-Day *Saint*. She's a Latter-Day *Ain't*."

"I seriously have no idea what you're talking about."

"Don't be dense, Hank. If she's LDS, she's dyed-in-the-wool. No caffeine, no swearing, no sex, Jesus talked to the Indians, beam me up to the planet Kolob, all that crazy shit."

"And if she's LDA?"

"Then she's probably one freaky-ass slut."

"Fuck you, Hatch."

"You remember Maeve, right?"

"Sure," I say. "You dated her for quite a while, right before you enlisted."

"We didn't date that long—six or seven months maybe—and we didn't *date* so much as screw each other's brains out."

"And I suppose you're going to tell me Maeve is Mormon?"

"Born and raised."

"And she's a Latter-Day Ain't?"

"Well, not anymore. Thirty days after I was deployed she got married to a Mormon named Babe, proceeded to squeeze out four kids in three years, and I suspect she's not living in Salt Lake City for the beachside vistas."

"Babe?"

"It's his nickname," Hatch says. "He's the youngest of six Abrahams. His grandfather is called Senior, his dad is called Junior, and his four brothers are Abraham, Abe, and Bram."

"So he's Babe, literally the baby Abe?"

"Awesome, right?"

"If by 'awesome' you mean the dumbest fucking thing I've ever heard of. But I mourn your loss."

"You and me both." Hatch looks up to the sky and rubs his chin, his face practically glowing in the winter night. A memory. And a good one at that.

"Cat got your tongue?"

"You could say that," Hatch says. "Maeve loved her sex two ways. Dirty and filthy-stinking dirty."

"And on that note . . ." I offer my glass to Hatch. "How about a refill?"

Hatch unscrews the cap off the bottle, tilts the bottle down toward my empty glass. "No more ice?"

"Nah," I say. "At this point water would just be getting in the way of my buzz."

"That's the spirit. Now, as I was saying about Maeve."

"Your Mormon girlfriend who was into weird sex."

"I didn't say *weird*." Hatch screws the cap back on the bottle of bourbon. "I said *dirty*."

I take another sip of Beam and fight off another compulsion to smoke a cigarette. Chief has already collapsed on the back porch, tail still wagging. "Correct me if I'm wrong, but weren't you stationed in Thailand?"

"Technically I was stationed in Hawaii, but we went to Thailand all the time."

"And that's the place where pimps used to sell you two girls and a beer for how much?"

" 'Two-girl, one-beer . . . ten-dallah.' "

"Exactly. And didn't you meet a prostitute in Bangkok who stuffed her vagina with colored Ping-Pong balls and could eject each individual color upon request?"

"I may have met a woman with that particular skill set, yes."

"I can't imagine Maeve being any dirtier than Ms. Ping-Pong Pussy."

"Ms. Ping-Pong Pussy wasn't addicted to butt sex like Maeve."

"Excuse me?"

"Maeve put the *A* in *LDA*. I mean, I don't know, maybe it's a Mormon thing. But that girl loved anal."

"Oh Jesus."

"And I'm not just talking your standard ramming the penis up the poop shoot."

"I think I get the picture."

"I mean any foreign object that was within a ten yard radius of her asshole. Anal beads, fists, mason jars, large vegetables, tennis balls."

"I got it, Hatch."

"In fact, she was fairly ambivalent about her vagina. It got to where she didn't even let me go down on her because she'd much rather have me lick her assho—"

"I said I get the fucking picture!"

"It's not all that bad. It's kind of like making out with blowfish."

"And now I think I might throw up."

"It's just a phrase my submarine captain used to use whenever we got into a dicey situation. 'Men, it's time to make out with the blowfish,' he'd say."

"Meaning?"

"Meaning you choose your battles. Blowfish are the second most poisonous vertebrate in the world—two-hundred times more deadly than cyanide—but they're also a culinary delicacy. The choice is yours whether to die or have a good dinner."

"And somewhere in there is a metaphor for giving your Mormon ex-girlfriend a rim job?"

"You're the English major," Hatch says.

"Yeah . . ." I say, finishing the last of my Beam. "You can show yourself out."

Hatch tries to muffle a laugh. He pats me on the back again as he turns to leave. "Good talk, Hank."

It's been almost an hour since Hatch left, the now-empty bottle of Jim Beam my only companion. The winter cold is starting to seep through my overcoat. I trip hard over a root of the black walnut tree. Trip even harder over a memory.

When I was five years old, Dad ordered an aluminum swing set out of the Sears catalog, back when Sears actually printed catalogs and I viewed the toy section in their Christmas edition as the most sacred tome on Earth. Dad and Uncle Mitch put the swing set together. It was painted blue with diagonal green and white stripes on the bars. The directions said, "Assembly time approximately sixty minutes."

It took them four hours to build it. They moved the swing set directly underneath the black walnut tree, hoping the tree would afford some shade. I used to have a picture of Uncle Mitch pushing me, me and my fake grin pretending as always to love him.

The swing set teased me with illusions of childhood, my naïve bare feet bruised and cut by the jagged walnut shells that littered the ground. It was a vicious cycle, my feet building up just enough calluses through the summer only to go soft and vulnerable over the winter months. Later, in college—in a botany class I took as an elective because the teacher was a smoking hot

Carolina blonde who quit her job as a weather girl in Charlotte to get a fucking doctorate in plants—I found out black walnut trees were poisonous. They give off a toxin that causes certain plants to exhibit symptoms such as —and I can still remember watching the teacher's walnut-hard ass as she wrote this on the chalkboard—"foliar yellowing, wilting, and eventual death."

I miss those illusions. I miss being a smoker. I miss being called Fitzy. I miss the walnut shells. I miss discovering, after one too many drinks on penny beer night, the same smoking hot Carolina blond botany professor wasn't *really* a blonde after all. I miss carpets that don't match the drapes.

The music stops, right in the middle of "The Ocean" of all places.

"What the fuck?" I say to no one. "That's the last song!"

"Oh, don't get your panties in a bunch!" Beth shouts from inside the house.

Jessie James's "Wanted" starts up on the outdoor speakers.

"Come on, Beth. You cut Zeppelin off for this?"

"No . . ." my wife says. "For this."

Beth walks outside wearing nothing but my #18 Peyton Manning jersey. She starts dancing, shimmying her hips in rhythm with the song. She straddles my lap.

"Am I forgiven?" I say.

"No," Beth says. "But the Lexapro is making me horny."

I force a smile. For whatever reason, Lexapro has had the exact opposite effect on wife that it does on most people. Give her a placebo, she doesn't want me to touch her. Give her any competing antidepressants, and it's months of cold showers and masturbation. But give her Lexapro, and it's game on.

Is this what I've become? A husband dependent upon prescription antidepressants to turn on his wife and gloss over his bad behavior? Still, she loves me. Excepting my drunken dalliance with the caterers tonight, we're more happily than unhappily married. Not to mention, I have three kids who find me tolerable if not passably cool, and I have a great fucking dog.

This is the part in our hero's story where he looks back and reflects upon the man he is today, but the truth is I'm still searching for him. I am still lost. Not the guy who thought I had found my way out of the wilderness when I started dating Beth some fifteen-odd years ago. Not the guy I wanted to become.

# Part I
# 1995

# Chapter 1

Hatch chatters his teeth from beneath an old blanket. "You b-bought B-Beth a wh-what?"

"A ring," I say. "I bought her a ring." I hand him a plastic bottle of orange Pedialyte. I procured it from Dr. Burke's pediatric office. Short of running an actual saline IV, it's the best cure for dehydration or a hangover.

Hatch unscrews the cap, sips the bottle reluctantly. He gasps, licking his teeth. "That shit tastes awful."

"Serves you right."

Hatch and I only took five and a half years to graduate from IU, forever counting ourselves among the Indiana University Class of '94.5. We moved up to Indianapolis in January, signing a lease on an American Foursquare in Broad Ripple. Our house is directly across the street from the Red Key Tavern, Kurt Vonnegut's old watering hole, and a few blocks south of Atlas Grocery, which is where David Letterman once worked as a teenage bagger.

"M-moving a little fast, aren't we, F-Fitzy?"

Hatch is sick. He's feverish and severely dehydrated but refuses to go to the doctor. He's shivering even though he's running a one-hundred-and-three-degree temperature. He's running a temperature because he has food poisoning. Yesterday during a Patrick Swayze marathon—*Red Dawn, Next of Kin, Point Break*, and of course the one hundred fourteen minutes of cinematic perfection that is *Road House*—we each drank five forties of Crazy Horse malt liquor. I passed out and pissed the bed. Hatch got the munchies, mistook a half-pound of raw bacon in the fridge for lunchmeat, and made himself a sandwich. He's been shitting blood for the past hour, insisting he's turned the corner, but the truth is his dad kicked him off his health insurance last week.

"Fast? We've been dating for almost two years." I swallow down a burp. I'm still a little drunk. A lot drunk actually. About half of *Road House* still sits unwatched on the laser disc player I appropriated from Dad's office right before Mom sold the dealership.

Speaking of my dead father, Hatch has managed to appropriate him as his own excuse to blow off life and drink himself into oblivion. After he downed his third forty of Crazy Horse last night, Hatch confessed he couldn't recall the last day he hadn't been drunk. Over the last year, he's held multiple jobs. Just out of school he worked the early morning shift at an indoor playground on Indy's northeast side called Leaps & Bounds. His responsibilities included dusting the entire four-story jungle gym, washing the balls in the ball pit, waxing the floors, and smoking blunts with a gangbanger who was there on a work-release program. When a Pizzeria Uno opened next door the same week his coworker got thrown back in jail for failing a drug test, Hatch quit Leaps & Bounds to become a waiter, sobered up for almost three months before they offered him a management position, then proceeded to get fired after every bottle of Chianti in the Uno's bar somehow ended up at a Delta Gamma sorority party at Butler University. Hatch went back to being a waiter at the Beef & Boards dinner theater on the north side of Indy, worked there just long enough to meet B.B. King, then quit the day after he touched Lucille.

I just convinced Dr. Burke to hire Hatch to paint the interior of his house, which should keep him busy through the spring and part of the summer, but at present, Hatch's monthly contribution to our rent check is somewhere between ten dollars and a half-dozen late-night burritos. He disputes this number by claiming he makes up the difference by paying for most of our booze, a dubious claim seeing as (a) he drinks most of our booze, and (b) nearly all the liquor we still have in our house is the remaining contraband from Uno. Fortunately, about a month after we moved in here, I answered an open advertisement to IU grads for "Eager and Earnest Hoosiers with English Degrees." I got on the ground floor of a start-up independent publisher all of five blocks from my house called College Avenue Press. My title is assistant editorial director. My gross income is twenty-two thousand dollars.

Hatch's affinity for the sauce has nothing to do with me or my dad. The apple doesn't fall far from the tree, and Hatch is a drunk hanging from a fucking sequoia of alcoholics—his father, his mom, his grandfather. Since I started dating Beth, I feel like I've turned a corner. Hatch still seems stuck in the straightaway.

"Beth is the best thing that's happened to me, probably ever," I say. "Besides, this ring was the one my dad gave my mom, so it's not like I paid for it or anything. I don't know what I'm going to do with it."

Hatch sits up and rewraps himself in the old blanket. "Oh, you know *exactly* what you're going to do with it."

"Can't you just be happy for me?"

Hatch smiles, but I think it's probably the food poisoning doing the talking. "Always, buddy." He grabs a cup off the coffee table that has a swallow of malt liquor left in it. And the bastard fucking drinks it! He reaches in between the couch cushions and pulls out an unopened forty of room temperature Crazy Horse. He says, "Now Qualms, motherfucker."

Qualms is another one of Hatch's stupid drinking games, *Qualms* being the code word for "finish your entire fucking drink." Even sick, Hatch can find time for a drinking game. Originally intended as a power-drinking variant of the more universal "Social!" toast that allows for the occasional harmless chug with a friend, Hatch has turned Qualms into a weapon, a way to pummel people into inebriated comas. See, the loophole in Qualms is that you simply must finish your current drink in hand. So Hatch drinks down his drink—in this example, a solitary swallow of cheap malt liquor. Meanwhile, he hands you a fresh drink—in this example, an unopened forty-ounce bottle of cheap malt liquor—and proceeds to immediately yell, "Qualms!" Then, while casually burping up a mere drop of backwash, he sits back and waits to see if the foam first comes shooting out your mouth or your nose.

This time, it's my nose. My stomach is okay, though. Money being as tight as it is, the only thing I've had in the last twenty-four hours is a bag of Cool Ranch Doritos and a large Diet Coke, both purchased with my mom's Unocal 76 gas card. Forty ounces is surprisingly easy to keep down on an empty stomach.

I wipe traces of malt liquor off my mouth. "You really are a fucking dickhead."

Hatch is laughing. "Just trying to lighten the mood, Fitzy."

"Consider it lightened," I say. The ring is sitting in its open case on the coffee table. I grab the case and take one last look at it—a 1.85-carat princess-cut diamond ring set in yellow gold that my dad spent five years saving up for. I close the case and stuff it in my pocket.

Hatch follows the ring with his eyes all the way to my pocket. "You sure you know what you're doing, Hank?"

"No, but this is the first relationship I can see me being in over the long term."

"The long term?"

"Two years this July. But we've been on-again, off-again friends for six years. You know this."

"I know you were on-again, off-again fucking Laura for most of the eighties."

"Not true," I say. "I dated Laura in high school and then accidentally had sex with her one time in college."

"Oh, you *accidentally* tripped and fell into her vagina?" Hatch snaps his fingers. "God, I hate it when that happens."

"Don't go there, Hatch."

"Don't go where?"

"I'm pretty sure Laura had it coming."

"How do you figure?" Hatch sounds more earnest than he's usually capable of being.

"Never mind," I say, catching myself. No one save Laura and my mother know my secret. The faked abortion. The chain of lies. The brother who turned out to be my son.

Fortunately, Hatch's ADHD bails me out. "You ever find out what happened to the Tool?"

After we started dating, Beth and I agreed to keep things nonexclusive when she left for the '93 fall semester at the University of Illinois. She told me she wanted to take things slow. What she didn't tell me was her summer fling, "the Tool," quit his bartending job in Empire Ridge and followed her to Champaign. He lived in her house for most of the semester. Beth said she felt sorry for him and that he slept on the couch. I didn't believe her. Although by Christmas of that year we started dating exclusively, I know that tanned, white-teethed, square-jawed smile that used to stare at me from a picture frame on Beth's nightstand didn't sleep on any goddamn couch. This July will be our two-year anniversary, and any mention of the Tool still pisses me off, which is why Hatch is mentioning him.

"The Tool has been out of the picture for a while."

"Define 'out of the picture,'" Hatch says. "Does he still call her?"

"Don't care."

"He still live in Champaign?"

"Still don't care."

"Has he bought Beth a ring yet?"

I grab Hatch's hand and try to shove the bottle of Pedialyte in his mouth. "Shut up and drink your baby formula, asshole."

Hatch pushes my hand away. He secures the cap to the Pedialyte and throws the bottle off to the side. "So when are you going to tell her?"

"I was thinking spring break."

"It doesn't get any more romantic than beer bongs and wet T-shirt contests."

"It's not that kind of spring break, asshole. We're staying at Beth's parents' place down in the Southern Outer Banks."

"North Carolina isn't exactly balmy this time of year."

"But it's quiet and isolated. "

"Yeah, right . . ." Hatch winces. I can hear his stomach gurgling. "At least until you two superfreaks get there."

# Chapter 2

Sophie B. Hawkins's "Damn I Wish I Was Your Lover" plays from the boom box on the back deck of the beach house. Beth sits on the bottom step of the deck, a cigarette in one hand, a beer in the other. She's wearing a black bikini. She flexes her bare toes in the sand, winking at me as she sings the lyrics.

Beth is set to graduate from Illinois in a little over a month. Dr. Burke decided to reward his daughter with a free spring break at the family's beach house in the Southern Outer Banks of North Carolina. Stan told Beth to invite all her friends, but she only invited me. I'm not complaining.

The beach house is one of the older houses on this stretch of sand. It's a one-story cedar-shake bungalow Stan painted pink as an ode to John Mellencamp, but it has an intimate salty charm compared to all the "mansions on stilts" popping up like weeds from Emerald Isle on the west side of the SOBX all the way to Fort Macon in the east. The mansions notwithstanding, the area still maintains a quirky vibe, with its mix of trailer-park locals and older professionals from the Triangle. Just last night we attended a barbecue cohosted by a tenured, gay art professor from East Carolina University and a champion marlin fisherman out of Morehead City. While an "SOBX" bumper sticker doesn't have the cache of the "OBX" logo seemingly engraved into the rear bumpers of every Land Rover, the upside to vacationing far south of places like Cape Hatteras and Duck can be summed up in four words: *no fucking New Yorkers.*

"Still can't believe we're here," I say, handing her a bottle of Kalik.

"Believe it." Beth lifts the overpriced beer to her lips, swallows once, then twice. She pulls the bottle away, licking her lips. "Needs more lime."

I start to get up. "I can get you a bigger slice."

"Stay here." Beth pulls me down. "It's our first day on the beach together. I think I can manage without the lime."

I smile and clink her beer with mine. "Thanks for getting me Kalik, by the way. I know you wanted Corona."

Beth kisses me on the cheek. "Beer is beer. And how could I not get Kalik after you told me it was the beer you drank the only time you and your dad got drunk together?"

A gust of salty air rolls off the beach. I watch Beth's hair blow back and down the small of her tanned back. Beth notices me staring.

"What are you in the mood for?" she says.

I roll my eyes. "Do you have to ask?"

"For dinner, perv."

"Oh," I say. "Shrimp burgers maybe?"

We shared the bathroom when we changed out of our swimsuits. She told me not to peek, so I peeked. We went over to Big Oak Drive-In for dinner and ate a couple of shrimp burgers with french fries, then split a six-pack of Yuengling—Indiana is a lesser state for not allowing the sale and distribution of this amber deliciousness—while walking down the beach.

When we got back to the beach house we argued over what movie to watch. The videos were stacked on top of the television. Beth suggested *When Harry Met Sally*. I suggested *Field of Dreams*. Somehow we decided *The Cutting Edge* was a good compromise.

The movie wasn't half bad. Beth had evidently seen it a few hundred times, repeating the movie's signature quote—"Toe pick!"—each and every instance Moira Kelly's character, Kate Moseley, said these words to the fallen hockey star turned rebellious figure skater, Doug Dorsey. Doug, D.B. Sweeney's character, reminded me of Han Solo. In the seconds before Han Solo was frozen in carbonite in *The Empire Strikes Back*, Princess Leia told him, "I love you," prompting the greatest single line in moviemaking history, Han's cooler-than-cool comeback, "I know." Not to be outdone, when Kate Moseley finally proclaimed "I love you" to Doug Dorsey, he replied, "Just remember who said it first."

I like Doug Dorsey.

Beth and I grabbed a smoke on the back porch after the movie ended. The weather in April in the SOBX is your basic crapshoot—as likely to be forty degrees on any given day as it is eighty—but we still threw on our swimsuits and jumped in the ocean again for a late-night dip. Beth is scared of sharks.

"Come on," I say, grabbing Beth's hand and pulling her up out of the water. "No more shark jokes."

"Promise?" Beth says.

"I promise."

"What do you want to do now?"

I try to be sweet but obvious with my intentions. "How about a shower?"

Beth kisses me on the lips. She stands on her tiptoes in the sand, reaches around and squeezes my ass, pulling me in to her. She steps back. "How about a nightcap first?"

I wrap a towel around my waist. Beth throws on her Illini Gymnastics sweatshirt. We walk back into the beach house. A bottle of cheap wine sits on the table, flanked by two empty glasses.

"What's the special occasion?" I say.

"Don't start thinking you're too special," Beth says. "I picked it up while you were jogging on the beach earlier today. I asked the guy at the liquor store what's the best cheap drunk he could recommend. He gave me this."

I pick up the bottle, drag my thumb over the label. "Cisco? Isn't this the stuff that sent a bunch of sorority girls to the hospital because they pounded them like wine coolers?"

"That it is," Beth says, retrieving the bottle from me. She unscrews the cap. "The liquor store guy told me one of the big bottles should be enough for both of us."

"So I assume you bought two of the big bottles?"

"You assume correctly, Mr. Fitzpatrick." Beth drinks the cheap wine straight from the bottle.

"How is it?" I ask.

She licks her lips. "Tolerable."

"Terrible?"

"Tall-ur-uh-bull."

Beth puts on Aerosmith's *Toys in the Attic,* pours me a glass of Cisco.

"Fancy," I say. Beth laughs.

As of five minutes ago, we've opened the second bottle of Cisco. I pour Beth a full glass from the new bottle. "You feeling this?"

"Yeah," Beth says. "Quite a bit actually."

"Me, too."

Beth's eyes rotate to the right. She grinds her teeth, like she has something on her mind. "You remember senior year spring break?"

"In high school?"

"Yeah."

"Pretty drunk week. Not a whole lot that I do remember."

"Oh, come on," Beth says, punching me in the arm. "Play along with me."

"Okay, there was you and Claire with those parking signs."

"I gotta pee!"

"Exactly," I say.

It was late in the week in Panama City Beach, at which point Beth and Claire's blood supply had been replaced by pure Southern Comfort. They stole our condo unit's parking signs, two metal plaques with a block letter *P* on them. For the remainder of the vacation they'd hold them up whenever they had to go to the bathroom and announce to the room, "I gotta pee. Get it? I got a *P*?"

"You know what I remember about you, Hank?"

"What?"

"I remember interrupting you having sex with Laura in the bathroom."

"Was that before or after Claire kicked Laura's ass?"

"Definitely before, but not by much." Beth tries to disguise her sigh, a muffled sound of disappointment tinged with jealousy around the edges. "How long did you two end up dating anyway?"

I don't like where this line of questioning is going. Beth isn't in on my little secret, at least not yet. I proceed with cautious ambivalence. "Can't really remember exactly. A year and a half maybe?"

"You sure about that?"

"I think I just established that I'm not sure."

"I could've sworn I heard that you two hooked up occasionally in college."

"Not *occasionally*," I say. "Once."

"When was that?"

"Doesn't matter."

"I want to know."

"You're going to make a bigger deal out of this than it needs to be."

"When?"

I put my Cisco down. "About two years ago."

"*About* two years?"

"Fuck, Beth. It was April 22, 1993. Is that what you want to hear? It was about three in the morning the day after my birthday at Sheila Fleming's apartment."

"So it was before we started dating?"

"Of course. A little less than three months, actually. She was the last girl I had sex with before I started dating you. There, you happy?'"

"Wait a second," Beth says. "Laura was the last girl you had sex with before me?"

"Isn't that what I said?"

"But that was in April of '93, and we started dating in July of '93."

"Yes, three months. We just went over this."

"And you're sure Laura was the last girl you had sex with before me?"

"Why would I fucking make that up?"

"But we didn't even start dating exclusively for another five months after that, in December."

"Yes, over winter break," I say. "I was there, you know."

"Yeah, I know." Beth has many facial expressions: sad, happy, pouty, coy, seductive. I've never seen guilty, until this second. An unspoken affirmation hangs in the air.

"Fuck me!" I say.

Beth gets up from her seat, walks around to my side of the table. "Hank, please. What's past is past."

"Who was it?" I'm shouting now. "When was it?"

Beth is crying. "It was the fall semester at Illinois, when Jordan came to Champaign and I—"

"The Tool? The fucking Tool?"

"But Hank, you told me you were still dating around."

"Guess what, Beth? I was lying!"

"Seeing other people was what you and I both decided was best at the time."

"Nice to see you embraced the concept with such enthusiasm. So you fucked the Tool in September . . ."

"And once in October."

"What the fuck, Beth?"

"But you and I weren't even dating exclusively un—"

"Until after you made sure you got in a few more good fucks with the Tool. Yes, thanks so much for pointing out this technicality to me. Man, that's a load off my fucking mind."

"Baby, wait," Beth says, grabbing my elbow.

I wrench my arm from her hand, grab my glass of Cisco. "I'm going for a walk on the beach. Do not follow me."

I down my glass of Cisco. The breezy spring night hits me in the face as I step outside. A part of me wants to be the old Hank. He wants to jump in the car, head to the nearest strip club, and make a bad night even worse. Beth owes me that, right? This is what relationships are: tit-for-tat ledgers in which every kindness or transgression is returned with interest. Accountability is measured only by checkmarks on an internal grocery list of mistakes. Why was I promiscuous as a young man? Because my godfather made me that way. My therapist even told me so. It wasn't immoral. It wasn't personal. It was just me getting even.

Getting even. Is that what this is all about? Really? Here's a thought, Hank. Why not tear up that fucking grocery list? Maybe there is something to the Golden Rule. The difference between happiness and despair, between love and hate, could just be the difference between a mistake forgiven and a mistake avenged.

If life can be distilled into a formula that simple, I've wasted a lot of years being an asshole.

I walk back into the house. Beth sits at the kitchen table. She's crying.

"Beth . . ." I say, my tone purposely measured. I sit down next to her at the table. "I'm sorry for yelling at you like that. It's not like you violated my trust. You just hurt my pride."

Beth stands up, wipes her eyes with the sleeve of her sweatshirt. She walks over to me and pushes my chair out, sitting on my lap. "I love you, Henry David Fitzpatrick, and I'm sorry for hurting you. I just wanted everything out in the open. Nothing else before us matters to me anymore."

I kiss her, my lips lingering on hers. "Do me a favor, Beth?"

"Anything," she says.

"Look down at your left hand."

Beth's eyes open wide. She looks like she might pass out.

I hadn't planned on slipping the 1.85-carat princess-cut diamond ring set in yellow gold onto her finger. It just sort of happened.

"Wait, what?"

I drop to one knee. "Beth, you're the best thing that's ever happened to me. We're moving too fast and everyone will say we're insane, but I say we prove them all wrong and live happily ever after. Elisabeth Alison Burke, will you marry me?"

The tears return to Beth's face. She drops to her knees and kisses me. "Yes, yes, a thousand times yes."

"You sure?" I say, wiping her tears off my face.

"Henry David Fitzpatrick . . ." Beth says. "I've been in love with you since I was sixteen years old."

We start to undress one other right there at the kitchen table. I undo her bikini top from behind, watching her reflection in the sliding glass door as I cup her small breasts in my hand. She turns to face me, pulls my shirt over my head.

"You ready for that shower now?" Beth says. We kiss a little longer in the bathroom, awkwardly reluctant to cross the threshold. With some encouragement from Beth, I finally slide my hands down the back of her bikini bottoms, squeezing her butt and sliding her bottoms off in one fluid motion. She returns the favor. I open the shower curtain.

"Uh, Beth."

"Yeah, babe?"

I point inside the shower. It's one of those three-by-three fiberglass stalls tacked into a bathroom as an afterthought. Barely large enough to fit both of us standing motionless, hands at our sides, let alone what we're envisioning.

"I know you're a tiny girl and all, but—"

"Hey." Beth laughs. "I'm game if you're game."

From Casanova to the latest paperback smut, there are a myriad of sordid tales of young lovers in the throes of passion. The story of the girl bent over in a shower stall while her fiancé tries to tag her from behind while propping his foot on the edge of a toilet seat and untangling his penis from a shower curtain is probably not among these accounts.

"This isn't working," I say.

Beth looks like a baseball infielder waiting for the next pitch, her hands on her knees. She says to me over her shoulder, "I realize that, Hank."

We give up on the shower and towel each other off. Beth's hair is wet, much longer than it usually looks. It falls all the way down to just above her bare nipples. Beth grabs me by the back of the head and brings my lips to her breasts. She grabs my hand, turning away from me, her breasts leaving my mouth.

"Hey," I say. "I was just getting started."

"I know you were," Beth says. "So let's go out back and finish."

I lead us out to the beach. Beth follows close behind with a blanket. She unfurls it on the sand.

"Lie down," she says.

I lie down. Beth straddles me, the ocean at low tide gently humming in the background. She leans in to kiss me on the lips, pulls away. She leans in again, her hair falling over her shoulders and onto my face. She moves down, her hair and her breasts grazing my throat, my chest, my stomach. She takes me in her mouth.

I've always struggled to be both sexual and emotional at the same time. That's just how I'm wired. Sex fills a physical need in me, like eating. Hunger more than desire. It's a release. Clinical in its coldness.

Not now. Tonight I am electric. The hair stands on the back of my neck. Goose pimples. The salty fishiness of the ocean in my nose. Beth's skin on my skin.

A few minutes pass. I push her away.

"What?" Beth says, raising her head. "That doesn't feel good?"

"Too good, actually."

Beth crawls back up my body, spiderlike, straddling me again. She runs her thumb across my cheek. "Are you crying?"

"No," I say, embarrassed.

"It's okay if you are," Beth says.

"Doesn't feel okay," I say.

"It's actually kind of a turn-on." Beth kisses me softly on the lips. She reaches down with her left hand, her right hand propping her up. She executes a quick shimmy motion with her hips and guides me inside her.

I tell Beth not to peek when I tiptoe naked across the back deck to retrieve the remaining Cisco, so she peeks. I'm too lazy to go inside to retrieve the glasses. I hand her the bottle.

"That was some crazy sex," I say.

Beth tilts the bottle up to her lips, swallows. She hands the bottle back to me. "Babe, I've never had an orgasm like that before."

I hold up two fingers. "I think I counted two of them."

"That you did."

"When you started playing with yourself and you did that thing—"

"You liked that?"

"Hell yeah I did!"

"What about when you used your tongue—"

"Didn't see that coming, but I dug it, too."

"You sure?"

"Positive, Ms. Burke."

"That's Mrs. Fitzpatrick to you."

"It is?"

"Why wouldn't it be?"

"Beth Fitzpatrick," I say. "The name doesn't exactly roll off the tongue. Beth Burke is a cool name, and calling up the credit card companies and all that stuff sounds like a big hassle to me. If you want to keep your name, go for it."

I wait for her smile. For her gratitude. For her admiration for a boy raised in a fairly conservative Catholic household who stood before her now as this enlightened hunk of a man and shining beacon of gender equality. Instead, Beth kicks me in the shin.

I crumple to the deck in a naked heap.

"Well, thanks for giving me fucking permission!" Beth says, storming into the beach house with her fists clinched.

I compose myself and follow her inside the house. "What is wrong with you?"

"Nothing, dickhead." She kicks me in the shin again, although not quite as hard. She fumes across the family room and slams the bathroom door in my face.

Uh, what the hell just happened?

The bottle of Cisco laughs at me on the table. I grab the bottle, walk into the kitchen, and pour the remaining half bottle down the drain. My apologies to the bacteria in the sink, for they will soon be trying to kick the living shit out of each other.

# Chapter 3

Harper Donovan and I stand in the front room of my American Foursquare. I hand her the keys. "She's yours now," I say.

"Thanks, Hank."

Hatch and I moved out of the Broad Ripple house a month after Beth accepted my proposal. To save up for the wedding, I'm living with my mother in Empire Ridge and commuting to my job at College Avenue Press. Hatch didn't seem to care. He just packed up his shit and moved into a small loft apartment with Mack along the Broad Ripple canal that Mack has already nicknamed "Crack House" after the vagrants who mill around the canal looking for a score. My landowner waived the penalty for breaking our rental contract, because I convinced Harper to take over the lease.

Since we were eighteen up until two summers ago when I started dating Beth, Harper Donovan and I had been friends with benefits. We never dated or anything like that. We were simply the unspoken asterisks in each other's life. She'd get in a fight with her boyfriend, come over to my place, and we'd have sex. When I recall relationships with other women, I don't necessarily recall having sex with Harper during that time, though we may indeed have had sex. The sex just happened. It was like eating or breathing. The arrangement made perfect sense to us, but it offended almost every other girl I knew. The guys of course wanted to know my secret. They wanted me to write a book, give seminars, but mostly just introduce them to Harper.

Harper and I almost hooked up as sophomores in high school. Harper transferred from Prep after winter break and flirted with me for weeks. Half the sophomore class met at the theater for the premiere of *Police Academy 4: Citizens on Patrol*. Harper offered me the seat beside her. I said, "No thanks," and shot her down before a young and mop-headed Sharon Stone even made it onscreen.

Sitting next to me, Hatch said out loud, "Hell, Harper, I'll take you up on the offer if Hank is too stupid not to." Later that week, my driver's license only three days old, I totaled a brand-new Oldsmobile Custom Cruiser just off Dad's lot while Harper and Hatch were actually making out in the backseat. They were a couple for most of the summer.

Harper and I fooled around a little in high school, nothing major. In fact, the only significant encounter was when we didn't do something. We were seniors. It was Grad Night at Kings Island. I smuggled a pint of Beam and a couple of joints into the park. Laura was back at Bucknell. Hatch and Harper smuggled my near-catatonic butt out of the park. The party followed us to our hotel room, at which point Hatch laid me in bed, tucked me in, then proceeded to have sex on the floor with his girlfriend. Harper passed out next to me, in my arms. Maybe I thought Harper was Laura. Then again, maybe I didn't.

There was nothing dramatic or even memorable about the first time we had sex. It happened in college, freshman year. I ran into Harper one random Thursday night in downtown Bloomington. Penny beer night at Jake's—penny beers, quarter pitchers, dollar well drinks. It got ugly fast. After some suggestive dancing on the dance floor, I took Harper back to my apartment, and we just did it.

Whether by accident or fate, Harper and I continued to keep in touch—the occasional run-in at a bar, a phone call every now and again to check in on each other—but our relationship, or whatever you want to call it, was long over. Though we didn't know it at the time, it ended about two years ago under the vigilant watch of Batman and Robin—actually, a mural of Batman and Robin I painted on Jack's wall back when he was still my youngest brother instead of my oldest son.

I had painted the life-size mural after Mom moved into her new house. The Dynamic Duo watched me have sex with Harper Donovan in Jack's bed. I still remember that night. It was early 1993, February or thereabouts, a few months after Dad died. She was on top the entire time.

I tried to hook up with her once more later that summer, right before Beth and I started dating. It was Skinemax night at Sandford & Son. I was watching soft-core porn and got struck by a fit of nostalgia. I called Harper, invited myself over to her place on Pennsylvania Avenue. She let me in, but she didn't let me *in*. She was in a long-distance relationship with some guy from New Jersey. We watched a movie. She went to bed. I showed myself out of Harper's apartment, and out of her life.

"You getting some roommates?"

"Yeah," Harper says, swinging the keys around her index finger. "Peter's going to move in with me. Maybe Lila, too."

Peter was a high school classmate of ours. A little on the odd side. Bad hair. Glasses that don't go with his face. Not the best dresser, just came out of the closet, but a good guy as far as unfashionable homosexuals go. Delilah Prestwich, or "Lila" as we all call her, is Harper's half-Armenian best friend. Olive skin, dark hair, big breasts, a gorgeous body hovering between the athletic and the voluptuous. She and her parents moved to

Empire Ridge right after high school. Lila went to college up in Indianapolis, so outside of me and Harper, she's largely steered clear of the Prep and Ridge social circles. She says she's Mormon, but I've seen Lila drunk enough times to know she's just going through the motions. In an alternate bachelor universe, I'd have hit on her years ago.

I make a motion for the door. "Tell Peter and Lila I said hello."

Harper looks at her watch. "They'll be here in about an hour. Why don't you tell them yourself?"

"Sorry," I say. "I'm already late meeting a couple friends out in Broad Ripple for dinner. We're going to hit the bars after that."

"Anyone I know?"

"Claire Sullivan and Derek Candela."

"Claire and Beth are pretty good friends, right?"

"Best friends."

"Speaking of whom, where is your new fiancée?"

"On vacation with her family."

"Still hard to believe you're getting married."

"Most of the time I don't believe it."

"When's the big date again?"

"August 12."

"So you still got a good year and a half to screw things up?"

"No, Harper. August 12, 1995."

"You mean this year?"

"Yep," I nod. "About four months from now."

"I suppose I can't talk you out of it."

"Correct me if I'm wrong, but your ship sailed to Jersey a long time ago." I say these words with a shameless, almost expectant flirtatiousness.

Harper leans in and kisses me on the cheek. "That it did, Hank."

I'm still attracted to Harper, and a tiny rush of hormones courses through my body and reminds me of that fact. She's a pretty girl: light brown hair that curves in at the base of her neck, large eyes, odd but strangely attractive conical breasts, and a trim if not athletic body with thin arms. She has the beginnings of a potbelly and thin legs. She could have better posture, as she has a tendency to hunch forward.

I open the front door. "You guys think you'll make it up to Broad Ripple tonight?"

Harper shakes her head. "Probably not. I have a lot of unpacking to do. We might sit around and have a few cocktails, nothing too crazy."

"We'll be dancing at Mineshaft if you change your mind."

"I doubt I'll change my mind, but thanks for the invite."

"See ya, Harper."

"See ya, Hank."

I walk down the steps of my former porch. The front door swings open.

"I forget something?" I say.

"No," Harper answers. "Just wanted to extend my own personal invite if you get too drunk tonight."

"Your own *personal* invite?" I smirk.

"For a place to crash," Harper says. "Get your mind out of the gutter."

"I should be okay, but thanks again." I walk to my car, step on the street, and circle around to the driver's side door. Harper follows me part of the way, stopping at the curb.

"It's a long drive back to Empire Ridge. And you are prone to doing stupid-ass stunts, the least of which would be driving drunk. I've got photos, you know."

"That's not my gig anymore." I open my door and say over the roof of my car, "That's not *me* anymore."

"Nevertheless," Harper says, "the invitation still stands."

Claire and Derek are already drinking and halfway into a basket of garlic cheese bread when I show up at Bazbeaux. Turns out Claire and Derek don't like cheese as much as I do, so we pass on the Pizza Alla Quattro Formaggio and go with the barbecue chicken. We devour the pizza. Claire is the designated driver and drinks only two beers, but Derek and I still make it through the two buckets of Rolling Rock by the time we're out the door on our way to Mineshaft.

Mineshaft is a confection of loud music, bright lights, smoke machines, drink specials, and wannabe pickup artists. We carve out a spot near the end of the bar, close to the dance floor. I order a round of tequila for me and Derek. We are well on our way to a night of suspect music and even more suspect decisions.

"Come on, Derek," Claire says, holding out her hand. "Dance with me."

"Hold up," Derek says, turning to me. "Cheers, Hank."

We do our tequila shots. Derek and Claire disappear. I pull up a stool to the bar. Two hands side around my face and cup my eyes.

"Guess who," a female voice says from behind me.

I play along. "Blonde or brunette?"

"Brunette."

"Crotchless panties or magic underwear?"

Her hands slide off my face. "There's no need to be gross, Hank."

I turn just to catch Lila's round ass walking away from me, scolding me almost. I reach out and grab her hand. "Come on now, Lila. You know I'm kidding."

Lila turns. "Make it up to me, then. Buy me a drink."

A quick glance over to Claire. She and Derek are already on the opposite end of the dance floor. Already mangling the lyrics to Alanis Morissette's "You Oughta Know."

"Sure, why not." I say, giving Lila the once-over. Her straight dark hair hangs loose over a short white dress that extends just below—and I do mean *just below*—her hips. "What's your potion?"

"Two kamikaze shots."

"Two?"

"One for me, one for you."

"Look, Lila. I probably shouldn't be—"

"Drinking with a friend?" Lila grabs another barstool, scoots up next to me.

"A friend who I'm attracted to."

"You're attracted to me? Since when?"

"Since Harper introduced us like three years ago."

"So why have you never hit on me?"

"Blame it on Harper. She's pretty much posted the 'No Fishing' sign around you. She doesn't want me corrupting you."

"Corrupting me?" Lila eyes the pack of Marlboro Lights on the bar, points to them. "Yours?"

"Nope," I say. "I quit a few months ago. I think they're the bartender's."

On cue, the bartender slides toward Lila. He grabs the hard pack, flips open the lid, and offers her a cigarette in one deft motion.

Lila pulls out one cigarette with her long fingers. The bartender immediately reaches out and lights the cigarette with a Zippo and a loaded smile. Lila inhales long and deep, then exhales the smoke through her nose. She leans her elbow on the bar. "Seriously, Hank. I'm a little disappointed here."

"Disappointed?" I hold two fingers in the air, nodding at the bartender. "Two kamikazes, please."

"Yeah."

"Why?"

"That you didn't try harder."

"Like I said, Harper didn't want me—"

"Oh, don't give me that bullshit." Lila exhales a puff of smoke. "You had your chance."

"When?"

"That night you showed up at the dorms for sex with Harper and she ended up being snowed in at her fiancé's house and couldn't make it."

"That night you and I watched a movie together?"

"So you do remember?"

"I remember it being pretty innocent."

"Innocent? We watched the unrated version of *Wild Orchid,* and I wore a pink negligee."

"And I didn't hit on that?"

"No," Lila says. "You didn't."

"Sorry about that."

"You should be."

"How can I make it up to you?"

"You can help me set our parents up on a date."

If I didn't know Lila, I would think she's batshit crazy. But really, she's just a dreamer who believes in true love and in fate. Her mother was a nurse who fell asleep at the wheel driving home after a twenty-four-hour shift, and ever since Harper told Lila how my father died, she believes our parents, both widowed by automobile accidents, are destined to be together. There's one flaw in Lila's master plan: Her father is Mormon, and my mother is Catholic.

"Yeah, Lila. I'll get right on that."

"You just need to give my dad a chance."

"No I don't."

"Two kamikaze shots," the bartender says, rescuing us from ourselves. He sets down two large glasses of vodka, Triple Sec, and Rose's Lime Juice that are clearly doubles.

Lila is the first to raise her glass. "To the soon-to-be-married man."

I nod, raise my glass. "To great friends."

We drink our shots, slam our glasses down on the bar. I wipe my mouth. "So you're living with Harper now?"

"Just for the summer," Lila says. "Heading for New York in the fall."

"Work?"

"Postgraduate studies at NYU."

"What are you studying?"

"Getting my MFA in Creative Writing."

"I'm jealous."

"You're jealous of someone overpaying for a worthless post-graduate degree just for the privilege of not making any money?"

I shouldn't grab Lila's hand, but I do it anyway. I shouldn't rub my thumb up and down her hand and then give it an affirming squeeze, but I do it anyway. I shouldn't wink and say, "Something tells me you of all people will find a way to make it work," but I do it anyway. An attention whore? A guy who likes the smell of a pretty girl? A glutton for punishment? All of the above.

The DJ spins Alanis into Salt-N-Pepa's "Whatta Man." Lila grabs my hands. "Dance with me, Hank?"

"No way," I say, almost too quickly.

"Oh come on, you party pooper. This is my jam! Just one dance?"

Claire and Derek have disappeared in the crowd, so I let the half-dozen Rolling Rock and two kamikaze shots do my talking for me. "Okay, one dance, but under one condition."

"What's that?"

"Get your story straight." I grab Lila by the waist, pulling her off her bar stool and onto the dance floor. "You were wearing a peach negligee."

One dance leads to two. Two dances leads to three. We're about halfway into Boyz II Men's "I'll Make Love to You" when Lila Prestwich and I start making out. I don't know if Lila instigated the kiss or if I instigated the kiss. But that's not important.

The fact Claire is watching me kiss her? Yeah, that's probably important.

# Chapter 4

I wake up with a monster hangover.

I'm in my old bedroom on College Avenue.

And I'm in bed with Harper and Lila.

"Morning," Harper says to my right, her head resting on my chest. "How's the head treating you today?"

Lila rolls toward me on my left side. Still asleep, she lifts her arm around me.

"Harper . . . what did I . . . what did you . . . what did we do? I don't know what happened last night, but I—"

"But you need to relax is what you need to do."

"Relax?" I say.

"Look under the covers," Harper says. "See anything unusual?"

I lift up the covers. "No."

"Exactly. You're fully clothed from head to toe."

"Wh-what happened to me?"

"Apparently you stumbled the entire ten blocks from Broad Ripple at two in the morning. I'm surprised your ass didn't get mugged. You stormed into the house crying about kissing Lila, and then you passed out on my bed. In lieu of sleeping on stacks of cardboard boxes, Lila and I slept here with you. And I do mean *slept*."

"I wish I could say that comes as a relief." I jump up out of the bed. Fuck, my head hurts.

Harper says, "What's the big deal, Hank?"

"The big deal is that I'm a ticking time bomb. I'm a ticking time bomb with a penis hardwired to fuck things up."

"You and your penis time bomb are being a tad melodramatic."

I grab Harper's hand with an exaggerated shake. "Hi, have we met? My name's Hank Fitzpatrick, the guy you had consensual sex with for three years *while* we were dating other people."

"But that's not you anymore. You said so yourself."

"Yeah, and last night I kissed Lila, and then I slept in the same bed with two girls I am extremely attracted to while miraculously not fooling around with either of them. The law of averages says I don't have too many of those miracles in my pocket."

"You're *extremely* attracted to me?" Lila says, apparently awake.

"Go back to sleep, Lila," I say.

# Chapter 5

"Hank, this is Leon Ramsey. Leon, this is my son, Henry David."

Leon extends his hand. "Hello, Henry. If you don't mind, I prefer Mr. Ramsey."

So much for first impressions. I take his hand in mine, squeezing a little too hard. The tops of his hands are exceedingly hairy, sticking out of his plaid oxford shirt in brown tufts like Michael J. Fox after he transformed into Teen Wolf.

"Well, Mr. Ramsey, you can just call me Hank."

Mom invited me down to Empire Ridge tonight to meet her latest and not-so-greatest boyfriend, Leon Ramsey. This clown makes me miss even Tom the Spandex Love Machine, although he might be better than Marky Mark, the corporate pilot who was only three years older than me. I had a soft spot for Robert Ware, the assistant football coach from Prep who insisted Jeanine and I call him "B-ware."

Where to begin with Leon? For one thing, he's one ugly son of a bitch. He has these unstylish oversized glasses that look like they're from the 1970s, and his hair is a sad grayish-brown color, like a dead carp. Instead of a tangible chin, he has folds of skin covered in a patchy beard that runs from his upper lip to his chest and makes his face look like a big vagina. Mom told me he teaches economics at IU, that he's an atheist, and that he doesn't like kids but he loves his two Siamese cats, Ayn and Rand. Fucking perfect.

Leon, Mom, Jack, and I sit down for dinner. Mom cooks everyone chicken, save for Leon. He doesn't eat chicken because the smell of white meats—chicken, pork, and fish, but not turkey burgers—makes him gag. Mom grills him a large filet cut that costs more than the rest of our meal put together.

I don't like Leon and can feel myself itching for a fight, so I turn to face the only person in the room whose company I can tolerate. "How's my big and bad first grader?"

"Good," Jack says to me.
"You like school?"
"Yep."
"You like your teachers?"
"Yep."
"You have a girlfriend yet?"
"Noooo!"
"You like anybody?"
"Noooo!"
"What's your favorite class?"
"Recess."

"Recess?" Leon says, dropping his fork and knife on his plate in mid-cut. "As stimulating as this conversation is, could we kindly have a little peace and quiet during our meal?"

Jack look downs at his plate, as if he's been scolded by Leon before. I wipe my mouth with my napkin and turn to face him. "Excuse me, *Leon*?"

"Hank, what he's trying to say is—"

"Debbie," Leon interrupts. "I can fight my own battles, thank you very much."

"Then do it," I say.

"All I'm asking is to come home from a long day of work and not have to —"

"Home? This isn't your fuhh-freaking home."

"Good job saying 'freaking,' Hank," Jack says.

His squeaky voice is like a good fart joke, an irresistible force that disarms me instantly. How can I possibly stay mad with those dimples staring at me? I ruffle his hair. "Thanks for the support, little buddy."

"You're welcome."

I look down at Jack's plate. "Why don't you eat your asparagus?"

"I hate asparagus," Jack says. "It makes my pee smell like the water in the janitor's mop bucket at school."

"You'll eat it and like it," Leon says.

"Yeah," I say. "This conversation is over. Jack, give me your plate."

I stand up from the dining room table and take Jack's plate to the kitchen. I rinse off his dish and put it in the sink. Like a miniature shadow, Jack follows me into the entryway.

"And just what do you think you're doing?" Leon says. Mom sits beside him quietly, her usual straight-lipped and vacant-eyed self.

"I'm taking Jack for some pizza," I say, opening the front door. "And getting the freak out of this freaked-up house."

"You will not—"

"The hell I will, Leon." I notice Jack arch his eyebrows.

"Hank, you said H-E-L-L."

"Head outside, little buddy, and I'll catch up. I need to have a grown-up talk with Leon."

I shut the door behind Jack, turning back to the room. Mom still sits at the kitchen table in silence. Leon is standing, red-faced.

"What's wrong, Leon?" I say.

"I have never been disrespected like that."

"I find that hard to believe. Someone as miserable and as unlikable as you?"

"Hank, please," Debbie says under her breath.

I bow. "Oh, welcome to the party, Mom."

"You just need to get to know Leon."

"No, what I need is a strong mother. What I need is someone who doesn't whore herself out to the first man who shows her affection. What I need is someone who doesn't waltz into our lives and presume to be a patriarch. Newsflash, Leon—the position is filled, you stupid fucking cocksucker."

Leon steps around the table and makes a move toward me. I raise my finger, pointing at him. "Better be sure, asshole. You lay a hand on me, and I will thoroughly enjoy driving my fist through the back of your head."

# Chapter 6

Claire never told my fiancée about Lila. With the notable exceptions of my slipping my tongue down a half-Armenian Mormon's throat and Vagina Head's continued courtship of my mother, it's been a blissful few months.

Beth graduated from Illinois at the end of May, and that same month, we signed a lease on a house in Rocky Ripple, an incorporated river town of hipsters just northeast of Butler's campus. I was promoted last month from assistant editorial director to editorial director at College Avenue Press, and Beth got a job teaching gymnastics at a private club after her first day at the hospital confirmed everything she hated about clinicals: being around death isn't for her. Beth's Dad still isn't over the quitting nursing thing, but her Mom is so supportive of the whole living-in-sin arrangement she helped us move. Being the devout, condoms-and-cohabitation-for-everyone, Vatican II Catholic that she is—not to mention too hopped up on narcotics to give a shit—my mother of course gave us the hearty thumbs up.

Beth has her face buried in one of her five hundred wedding magazines. I'm trying to wrap up a phone conversation with Hatch, about a third of which Beth hears thanks to Hatch's booming voice that dominates conversations even from the other end of a telephone line.

"If you need anything, call me," I say.

Beth puts down her magazine. "Don't know what you were talking about, but it sounded ominous. What's up with Hatch?"

I hang up the phone. "You don't want to know."

"Sure I do," Beth says, her curiosity genuine. Somehow, she and Hatch have become civil acquaintances if not friends.

"Apparently Hatch went on a bender after we got engaged and I broke the lease on our apartment. He said he pretty much bottomed out the night he went bar-hopping in downtown Indy and woke up the next day in Buckhead not knowing how he got there."

"Buckhead? As in Atlanta, Georgia?"

"He woke up in a strange woman's bed, went out for some air, and actually said to her, 'When did Indianapolis get so fucking humid?'"

"Jesus."

"But wait, it gets better. Hatch gets in his car and then drives back to Indy and straight into rehab."

"Rehab?" Beth says. "What kind of rehab?"

"AA," I answer. "He's been clean and sober for six months."

"Six months? And this is the first you've heard of it?"

"I told you he and I hadn't been keeping in touch."

Beth puts down her wedding magazine. "You know what? Good for Hatch. We should throw a party for him to celebrate."

"Uh, yeah. That's not gonna happen."

"It'll be fun, Hank. No booze. Just some good movies and good friends."

"I can already tell you Hatch won't be able to make it," I say.

"Why?" Beth says.

"Hatch enlisted in the Navy."

"You're pulling my leg."

"Finished the twelve-step program and then went straight to boot camp. Says he's hoping to get sent to Bangkok and check out some Thai hookers."

"Now that sounds more like Hatch," Beth says, sorting through the pounds of wedding-related parcels on our coffee table.

"How many invites we get back?"

"Most of them," Beth says.

"How many are coming?"

"Most of them." Beth holds a nearly square envelope up to the ceiling lights, trying to see through it. "Hey, what's this?"

"What's what?"

"A letter addressed to you," Beth says. "No return address. Looks like a wedding invitation or something. Anyone we know getting married?"

"I don't think so," I say. "Open it."

Beth opens the envelope. She removes the card, reads it aloud. "Dear Mr. Fitzpatrick, thank you for your condolences. Regards, Tammy Elliot and Laura Powell."

"What?" I say. "That's all it says?"

"Who are Tammy Elliot and Laura Powell?"

"That's fucking bullshit!"

"Uh, Hank?" Beth raises her hand. "Remember me? Your fiancée here, a little concerned about her soon-to-be husband being all cryptic about a card from two mystery women."

"Sorry," I say, I grabbing the card from Beth in disbelief. "No mystery here. Powell is Laura's married name. Tammy is her mother."

"Laura Elliot? Your ex-girlfriend?"

"Whatever," I say, handing Beth the note. "It's no big deal."

"Condolences?"

"Arthur died of a heart attack a couple weeks ago."

"Laura's father?"

"Yep."

"I'm sorry."

"Me too, Beth. And I wrote her what I thought was a pretty nice letter. I told her I knew what she was going through and said she could call me anytime to talk about it. I told her what a good man Arthur was and how I thought he would have been an awesome grand . . ."

"What's that?"

"Nothing," I say, catching myself. "You're not mad?"

"Why would I be mad?"

"Because I didn't tell you about the letter. I sure as hell felt guilty about it."

"She used to be an important part of your life, Hank. And now she's going through something you have a uniquely personal perspective on. I'd be disappointed if you *didn't* write her a thoughtful letter."

"Really?"

"Hank, your ex-girlfriend sent you a generic thank you card. So what? Where was your head at when your dad died?"

"There's more to it than that, Beth."

"Then what is it about?"

I want to tell Beth that Laura is more than an ex-girlfriend. She was more than just my first love. She's the spurned mother of my first-born son, like that Virgin Mary statue all Catholic boys treasure for the first decade of their lives only to stash away once they hit puberty and religion becomes spectacularly uncool. In the two years since Laura and Mom told me I was my brother's father, I've mailed Laura three large envelopes stuffed with pictures of Jack and some of his drawings from school. She never wrote me back until today. Laura has always worn guilt well.

"Can we sit down for a second?" I say. "I need to tell you something. You deserve to know before we get married."

"Sure," Beth says.

We walk into the living room and sit down on the couch. Beth reaches over and grabs my hand. "Hank, I—"

"Please, let me finish before I chicken out."

"But I—"

"I told Laura in the letter that I always thought Arthur would have been an awesome grandfather."

"That's a sweet to thing to say, given what you and Laura went through."

"You mean the abortion?"

"Should I mean anything else?"

"Yeah, about that. See, the thing is, that's not exactly how it all went down. When I talk about Arthur being an awesome grandfather, I'm not speaking metaphorically. There's no easy way for me to say this, so here it goes . . ."

Beth is still holding my hand. I look at the analog clock on the wall. The second hand ticks menacingly. My throat starts to close.

"Laura faked her abortion," I say, finally. "She carried her baby to term, and then my mother secretly adopted the baby. My brother, Jack, is actually—"

"Your son," Beth says. "I know."

I stand up, shake her hand loose. "Excuse me?"

"A part of me has always known, or at least suspected. The way you look at him, the way you act around him. Your paternal instinct just kicks in. You can't help yourself."

"Beth, being fatherly is a long way from being *a father*. There's no way you could have known unless—"

"Your mom told me."

"She didn't."

"She did and she didn't."

"Huh?"

"Remember last fall when you were at the book fair in New York?"

"Vaguely."

"And I called telling you I went out to dinner with your mother and she had a bad reaction to her medication."

"Rings a bell," I say. "Was that the time she slammed a Bass Ale after taking three Class IV Narcotics?"

Beth nods. "Bingo."

"You said she signed her home address instead of her name on her credit card bill and that she started—"

"Speaking in tongues. Exactly."

"And I take it you understood at least some of what she was saying?"

"It was all slurred gibberish at first. The restaurant manager almost called an ambulance. But eventually I got her stabilized with a little food and water. I got her back home, put her in bed, and that's when she started becoming a little more lucid. When I was tucking her in she said to me, 'Beth, I always knew you'd be a better mother for Jack.' "

"What did you say?"

"What do you think I said? I told her I could never replace her as Jack's mother. And then she put her hand on my face and said, 'I'm not talking about me. I'm talking about Jack's real mother, Laura.' "

"And then what happened?"

"She passed out."

"I'm so sorry, Beth." I sit back down on the couch, grab my fiancée's hands. I raise them to my lips and kiss them. "Why didn't you say anything to me after you found out?"

"I had no way of knowing."

"Knowing what?"

"If you even knew," Beth says. "And I sure as hell wasn't going to be the one who told you."

"So you're not mad at me?"

"Well, of course I'm a little upset you didn't trust me enough to tell me earlier, but I can't fault you for keeping it from me. The fewer people who know, especially in a gossipy town like Empire Ridge, the less chance there is it gets back to Jack. You need to tell him on your terms. I get that."

"And if the day comes when he lives under our roof as my son?"

"Then I'll welcome *our* son into *our* home with open arms. Hell, I'd do the same for Jack even if he were your brother. That's what you do for people you lo—"

I cut her last sentence off. When all else fails, kissing a girl shuts her up faster than anything else.

Beth's lips purse around my own. She relaxes, backs away. "Like I said, I don't want you feeling guilty about writing a letter to Laura. This is the type of crap married couples or very nearly married couples are supposed to talk to each other about."

"So you're giving me permission to write letters to ex-girlfriends behind your back?"

"I didn't say that." Beth puts her wine down, points to our bedroom door.

"What?" I say.

"Get in that room right now, smartass!"

"Why?"

"Because I'm going to tie you up, rip your clothes off, and then proceed to punch you in the balls a few hundred times."

"If you don't mind," I say, "I'd just settle for a cold, dispassionate grudge fuck at my expense."

"I'm sure you would."

Like I said, with the notable exceptions of my slipping my tongue down a half-Armenian Mormon's throat, Vagina Head's continued courtship of my mother, and telling my fiancée I have a secret love child, it's been a blissful few months. As Beth throws me on the bed, strips me naked, ties me up with four silk scarves, and drizzles hot candle wax onto my nipples, I think everything is going to be okay.

One thing is for sure: I'm not fucking things up.

# Chapter 7

I'm fucking things up.

The guys at work decided this morning to take me out for "lingerie lunch" at Legzz, a seedy strip club down on Meridian Street. A mini-bachelor party, they called it. We left the office at noon. It's now three o'clock. All of us—me, Aaron, Chuck, and Hector—are anywhere from slightly tipsy (Aaron, he's Jewish, and a lightweight) to quite nearly tanked (that would be yours truly, the bachelor).

Aaron Rosner is the publisher of College Avenue Press. An import from West Bloomfield, Michigan, with eyes too small for his face and a head of tight curls, he's the only Jew I know in Indianapolis. His close relationship with the Borders corporate office up in Ann Arbor—I think he's sleeping with the fiction buyer—has almost singlehandedly kept us in the black. Aaron's real claim to fame is that he was the high school classmate (confirmed) and childhood friend (alleged) of Elizabeth Berkley from *Saved by the Bell*. He reminds me of this incessantly, to the point where I've started calling him "Jessie" or "Spano" as the mood suits me. Rounding out the trio are College Avenue's sales and marketing director, Chuck Gill, and Chuck's dark-haired, vaguely George Clooney-looking roommate, Hector Rush.

"A toast to Jimmy Chitwood," Hector says. That's his nickname for me. It's an ironic reference to my lack of basketball skills. Hector never fucking shuts up. He's the media relations director at the US Hardcourt Championships in downtown Indianapolis, and over the last half hour I've learned more than I have ever wanted to know about professional men's tennis. In no particular order: Jim Courier generally keeps to himself, Bud Collins drinks beer during rain delays, Goran Ivanisevic loves to go clubbing, and Stefan Edberg is a nice guy who practices perpetually with his shirt off in front of the ladies.

"How about just a toast to bachelors?" Chuck says.

We hold our beers up. "To bachelors!" we shout.

Hector slaps a ten-dollar bill on the table. I eye it skeptically. I've avoided the customary lap dance up until now. "I thought you said you didn't have any tens?"

Hector smiles. "I saved one for you, Chitwood." He signals a dancer to approach.

The lunch crowd at Legzz is comprised of escapist truckers and second-shift factory workers getting a buzz on before they clock in. The clientele is reflected in the dancers, a cast of toothless, stringy-haired drug addicts with bad skin. The one who approaches me has no breasts, no ass, and even worse, no calves. She's wearing a cowboy hat and cowboy boots along with G-string panties, all of which suit the song, Bon Jovi's "Wanted Dead or Alive."

"A dance for the bachelor?" she asks, straddling me.

"If you'd be so kind," Hector says. He reaches over, stuffs the ten-dollar bill down the front of her panties.

Aaron, Chuck, and Hector are laughing their asses off. I can honestly say this is one of those rare times I'm not enjoying a mostly naked woman writhing on top of me. She's ugly, but not as ugly as we are. I miss Beth, but I don't miss being this guy.

I pull into my driveway. It's six o'clock, and I'm mostly sobered up. Beth is standing on the front porch smoking a cigarette. She smells of cheap wine and belligerence.

"How was work?"

"Work," I say. "Work was good."

"What'd you do today?"

"Nothing."

"You sure about that?"

"Yes."

"So, if I happened to run into one of your coworkers at Target earlier today, and if she happened to tell me, 'I can't believe you're letting those guys take Hank to a strip club,' you'd deny that, too?"

"Shit," I say.

"Yeah, shit is right. *You're* a shit."

Beth hates strip clubs. *Hates* them. I think it all goes back to my "I fooled around with a stripper last night" comment right before we started dating, which thereafter planted this notion in Beth's head that (a) all strippers fool around with their customers and (b) I possess some kind of preternatural attraction to strippers, neither of which is remotely true. Last month, when Mack orchestrated a weekend rafting trip in West Virginia for my bachelor party, Beth told me the wedding was off if she heard there were strippers. Mack had wanted to get a couple of West Virginia's finest to show up at our campsite, but that fell through—thankfully—at the last second.

"The wedding's off," Beth says.

"What?"

"You heard me."

"It was the guys' idea. I didn't know about it until today."

"And I assume they knocked you unconscious and dragged you to the strip club?"

"No."

"That's the only acceptable excuse in my book."

"It was no big deal."

"You know how I feel about those places."

"It was a joke. The women are grotesque there."

"I bet they are."

"No, really. The place is called Legzz. It's a dump. I'll take you there. If you can find me one attractive girl in the place, I'll give you a hundred bucks."

"That's not the point."

"Then what *is* the point?"

"For one, you think tucking dollar bills in ugly women's G-strings is funny. What's that say about your respect for women overall?"

"Oh, come on, Beth."

Beth starts to cry. "But more importantly, you just stood in front of me, five days before our fucking wedding day, and lied straight to my face."

Beth grabs her keys and makes like she's leaving.

"Where you think you're going?" I say.

"Out."

"Out where?"

"To get drunk maybe. Maybe I'll even hook up with the Tool."

"Beth, please." I grab her hand, take her keys away from her. "I messed up, and I'm sorry. I'm sorry I went there. I'm sorry I lied to you about it."

"Why *now*, Hank? Why *today*? You know what I did today? I started packing for our wedding and our honeymoon. There isn't a day that goes by where I'm not messing with some detail about this wedding. It's all I think about. *You* are all I think about."

"And you're all I think about, too," I say, but it comes across as reactive rather than heartfelt.

"Evidently not," Beth says. She grabs the door with her free hand, opens it.

"Where are you going to go without your car keys?" I ask.

"I'll fucking walk."

"No you won't."

"Watch me."

I slam the door shut with my forearm, squeeze Beth's hand hard. Maybe a little too hard. "Beth, this is what couples who've been together for a while do. They fuck things up sometimes. And they don't leave to avoid confrontation, or go crying to Mommy, or kick their significant other in the shin. They work it out. I didn't want to be there. Yes, I could've said no, but I didn't, and that's all on me. But the whole time I was there, I was . . ."

"You were what?" Beth says.

"I don't know . . . sad, I guess."

"How much of a fool do you think I am, Hank?"

"I'm being dead serious. I was sad for me, sad for the girls on stage, sad for letting you down."

"But you didn't know I had found out yet."

"Just me knowing was enough." I point back and forth between us. "I signed up for the long haul with us."

Beth's arm goes noticeably slack. "So these girls were grotesque?"

"Hideous."

Beth lets go of the doorknob, turns around. "I still would really like to kick you in the shin right now."

I reach down, raise my pants leg. "Go ahead. One free shot."

"I have a better idea."

"What's that?"

"I got a list of follow-up calls to make for the wedding." Beth reaches down to the veneer desk just to the right of the door. She picks up a piece of paper, hands it to me. "Why don't you make the calls?"

I grab the list. I bite my lip, wincing. "Sure you don't want to just kick me or have some angry makeup sex?"

"You and your libido."

"I'd like to think I'm pretty normal."

"Normal?" Beth says.

"Yeah."

"Since when is a compulsively masturbating sex addict who lies to his fiancée about going to strip clubs classified as 'normal?'"

I raise my hand. "I'll take hyperbole for eight hundred dollars, Alex."

"What did you say to me the very first time I told you I wasn't in the mood?"

"You remember that?"

"Well, you've said it a few times since then."

"Well, you've not been in the mood a few times since—"

"Just answer the question, Hank."

"I said, 'I'm going to have an orgasm every day with or without you, so you might as well be along for the ride.'"

"Okay then, if you could have only one superpower, what would it be?"

"That's not fair, Beth. The last time we had this discussion, we weren't even dating yet."

"*What* superpower?"

"Invisibility," I say, sighing. "I would want to be invisible."

"And why is that?"

"So I could spend my days hanging out in the showers of hot chicks."

"And when you board an airplane, what's the one thing you look for?"

"Now you're just taking stuff out of context."

"It's a simple question, dear fiancé. What's the one thing you hope for when you get on a plane?"

I shake my head, powerless. "I hope there's an attractive woman sitting next to me."

"And why oh why would you do that?"

"Because I want to know that if the plane starts to crash, there's a chance I might have sex with her right before I die."

"That's not normal, Hank."

"I'll tell you what's not normal," I say. "The fact I can't even fantasize about other women anymore besides you is not normal."

"You're just saying that. I'm willing to bet you have plenty of fantasies about other women."

"Oh, sure I do. I dream about threesomes and foursomes and fivesomes all the time, but you're always there in the starring role."

Beth starts to laugh. "In your own uniquely perverted way, that just might be the sweetest thing you've ever said to me. I think I even trust you now."

"Good to know." I hold my watch to my face. "Considering we'll be husband and wife in, oh, less than one hundred and twenty hours."

Beth also raises her wrist to her face, looks at her watch. "Wow!"

"Assuming the wedding is back on, of course."

Beth shuffles her feet toward me. She slides her arms inside mine, rests her head on my chest. "Of course it's on."

"Good to know," I say again.

Beth lifts her head up off my chest, looks up at me. "Fivesomes?"

I smile. "If you like, I could draw up a diagram for you."

# Chapter 8

While Mom again felt there was a certain grandeur lacking in a thirty-year-old church that looked like a limestone IHOP, we nonetheless decided to have the wedding at St. Benjamin. St. Isadore downtown is where I buried my father, and I intend to give it that lone distinction. I will never again step inside that church.

Our wedding photographer is a dead ringer for Kenny Rogers. He was Dad's roommate at Notre Dame. At this precise moment, I think I hate him.

"And we're done, gentlemen," Kenny says. "See you inside."

The pre-wedding photos are done roughly ninety minutes after they started. Even by Indiana standards, the humidity is withering. The heat index is pushing one hundred degrees. The groomsmen head into the air-conditioned confines of St. Benjamin. In need of a moment to myself, I decide to hang outside for a few minutes.

"Hank, can I talk to you?"

It's Uncle Mitch. He approaches me from the bushes, lying in wait. He looks awful, a good twenty pounds lighter since I last saw him. His once salt and pepper hair has faded into a washed-out gray. He's wearing a faded gray T-shirt with blue jeans torn on one knee. As always, he smells of cheap aftershave and cigarettes.

"What in God's name are you doing here?" I say.

"Nervous?" he says, reaching for my arm.

I take a step back. "Why would I be nervous? The people I can trust in my life are few and far between. Being able to give myself to one of these rare individuals is a gift."

"I suppose I deserved that."

"This isn't about deserving anything, Uncle Mitch. Now is not the time for us to have this conversation. This is my wedding day. Are you really that delusional and self-absorbed to think you can presume to wash away your sins on today of all days?"

"You just called me 'uncle' again. I like that, Hank. I like that a lot."

Mitch smiles. He reaches to me again, but this time I don't back away. I let him grab my arm. He squeezes, smiles even bigger. A part of me is afraid of him. A part of me feels sorry for him. A part of me hates him. A part of me loves him. I start to smile.

Really? A smile? Fuck that! I tug my arm loose. I back away from him. "Again, why are you here?"

"Ask me, Hank."

"Ask you what?"

"Ask me why I did it."

"I don't want to know why you did it."

"It's my penance," Uncle Mitch says, his eyes moistening with tears. "I have to tell you. I have to acknowledge my moral weakness to those whom I've aggrieved and accept your anger and hopefully your forgiveness."

My fist connects with his nose before I realize I'm even throwing it. Uncle Mitch falls to one knee. The years of repression and guilt channeled into the hardest punch I've ever thrown.

"There's my anger," I say. "Your forgiveness is waiting for you in hell, you goddamn motherfucker. This is still about you and your satisfaction. You're not looking for penance. You're just looking for another fucking orgasm."

I turn. Uncle Mitch reaches out and grabs my hand. Just as I raise my opposing closed fist for another blow to his face, he places something in my palm. It's a familiar gold Tissot watch with a brown alligator leather band. My father's watch.

"Your mom gave this to me when John died," Uncle Mitch says. "But it belongs to you."

I take the watch in my hand. I walk away without acknowledging his gesture.

# Chapter 9

I'm petrified. The pre-ceremony pint of blackberry brandy that Mack made me drink served only to make me tipsy and petrified. Two blackberry-smelling beads of sweat roll parallel down my body from each armpit. My stomach isn't helping. I try to concentrate on bending my knees. If they lock up on me, I'm dropping hard.

The groomsmen fan out behind Father. With Beth being an only child and me only having one sibling, we struggled to fill out the wedding party. My groomsmen are Aaron Rosner and Mack, while Beth's bridesmaids are Claire and my sister Jeanine. Mack is best man, serving as Hatch's stand-in while he's doing God-knows-what to a Thai prostitute. Claire is the maid of honor, and still uncomfortably attractive. The groomsmen and I stand at attention, hands clasped behind our backs, just like we practiced at rehearsal last night. True to form, Mack forgets and folds his hands in front. I elbow him, eyeing his hands.

*What?* Mack mouths.

"Your hands," I say through gritted teeth and a half smile.

"Oh," Mack says, gritting his teeth and wincing. "I forgot."

Aaron meets Jeanine halfway down the aisle, escorting my sister to her seat. Kenny Rogers snaps a shot of both bridesmaids as they enter the church. The best man and maid of honor, Mack and Claire, are next. Mack meets Claire halfway down the aisle, escorting her all the way to the altar. They separate to leave room for Father Fish, the bride, and yours truly.

Jack is up. He's the ring bearer. We don't have a flower girl, not that it seems to faze this six-year-old. *"Walk slowly,"* we all told him last night. *"This isn't a race."*

He listens to our advice. I'm guessing he covers the length of the church in about twice the time it took the entire wedding party. Jack gets to me and smiles. I smile back. As I give him the thumbs up, I look at my father's watch on my wrist. I'm proud of Jack and maybe even a little proud of myself.

The trumpets go silent.

The rustling of wedding programs.
Someone coughs.
Wagner explodes out of the pipe organ.
Everyone stands.

The double doors at the back of the church open wide. I see Beth on her father's arm. The hairs on the back of my neck stand on end. But I'm not nervous. I don't feel sick or even faint anymore.

Usually when a moment is bigger than me, it involves someone getting hurt, someone dying, someone getting buried. But not today. This is living. This is me rising up, spitting the dirt out of my mouth, and telling my demons to kiss my ass. I'm not one for religious moments, but if this is what true grace feels like, sign me the fuck up.

Beth looks radiant. Her dress is what she's wanted all along: simple but elegant. The top of the dress is off the shoulders, slowly dipping to a vee in the front with a hint of embroidery and beading. Her bouquet is made of white and peach roses to tie in to the color of the bridal party's dresses.

Did I mention she looks radiant?

Father Fish steps forward into the aisle. I follow him. We meet Beth and her father just as the music stops. Mom stands in the pew next to us. I'm the only one who seems to notice her wobbling.

Mom is intoxicated. She's wearing an inappropriately white dress of course, accessorized by an oversized strand of pearls that gives her a flapper throwback look—and not in a good way. Beth caught her this morning chasing a couple Darvocet down with a pitcher of mimosas. Several people have asked me why Leon decided not to come to the wedding. My answer to all of them has been, "Because he's a dick."

Father folds his arms, careful not to bump his cordless microphone. "Deborah," he says to my mother, "you and . . ."

The pause we all know would come.

". . . your husband, John Fitzpatrick, gave life and love to your son Hank. You watched him grow into manhood. Today, he's chosen to marry. I ask that you accept his choice of a bride into your own family, that you give your blessing to him as he continues life now in a very different way, that you give consent to this marriage."

Father extends his hand, palm up, and bows his head. Mom says, "We do."

Father Fish smiles when Mom says "we." He turns to his right, walks a couple steps until he's halfway between Beth's parents. "Joan and Stan," he says, "you gave Beth life and love. You taught her how to get along in this world. And also, today, she has chosen to marry Hank. I ask that you now give your blessing of her choice of a husband, and that your home will always be open to your daughter and your future son-in-law."

Joan and Dr. Burke say, "We do."

Father steps back toward the center of the aisle. "And now, Stan, I ask that you offer your daughter's hand in marriage."

Dr. Burke kisses his daughter. He turns to me, nods. We hug.

The gesture is scripted. Dr. Burke and I had been working on it since last night. He came up with the idea at the rehearsal dinner, saying to me, *"A hug instead of a handshake would add something special to the moment, don't you think?"*

I said, "Sounds like a plan to me, Dr. Burke," if only because it seemed more appropriate than *I'm a not-so-closet narcissist about to experience a day in which I'll be overshadowed to an almost obscene degree, and you're asking me if I'd mind making a play for the spotlight?*

The hug is perfectly executed: a firm backslapper in which we each buried our head in the other's opposite shoulder. I can even hear the muffled *awwwwwww*s in the crowd.

Stan puts his daughter's hand in mine.

Beth smiles at me, her hand shaking a little. I look into her eyes, but of course stray down to her cleavage. A single strand of pearls and two matching pearl teardrop earrings offset her tanning bed-bronze skin. I give her hand a squeeze. I look back into her eyes, winking at her.

There's a pause. A brief moment of silence. I can hear my father's watch ticking.

# Chapter 10

The wedding party pulls up to the reception in the limousine, a stretch Cadillac Deville. I help Beth out of the limo. A guy wearing a white oxford with rolled-up sleeves, a black tie, and earphones walks up to us. I guess him to be the DJ.

The ceremony was a blur. What did I say? What did Beth say? I remembered Jeanine serenading us with a stirring rendition of "Edelweiss," but that's only because I heard her practicing the song at the rehearsal. Didn't Beth's cousin give one of the readings? Yeah, that's right. The unemployed thespian cousin as opposed to the heavily medicated celebrity vegan chef cousin who introduced me to Woody Harrelson.

Woody had come back to his alma mater, Hanover College, to star in a play called *The Diviners*. I cornered him at the cast party at the buffet table. He was wearing a tall cowboy hat to compensate for the fact he was much shorter (and much balder) in person than he appeared to be on camera. We talked while shoving handfuls of pan-fried tofu in our mouths. I couldn't recall a word I said to Woody. Much like my own fucking wedding.

All I genuinely recall is looking into Beth's eyes and putting things on cruise control for about an hour. In the limousine ride to the reception I asked Mack—*three times*—if he and I remembered to sign the wedding license.

"Yep, we signed it . . ." Mack said. "Still."

Beth and I decided to have the reception at Beaver Stick Golf Club, a refined but understated club overlooking "one of America's premier public golf courses." I don't golf, so I'm impressed merely to the degree Beaver Stick affords Beth and our wedding guests a nice backdrop for getting hammered. The clubhouse is a contemporary design—clean lines, a gray-shingled roof broken up by white columns, and walls of glass surrounded on three sides by an expansive redwood deck pitted by golf spikes.

"Just count to sixty and then come inside," the DJ says to us, his pocket already lined with a fifty I spotted him in exchange for a promise that he not play "The Chicken Dance" under any circumstance, in-law requests included.

The glass walls of Beaver Stick, an anemic air conditioning system, and a guest list thirty percent longer than the fire department legally mandates for this particular building conspires with the one hundred-degree heat index to turn our reception into an oven. My mother-in-law walks around with a linen napkin filled with ice cubes, massaging the necks of the older folks. The younger folks—well, they're just drinking themselves into an oblivious stupor.

"Again, I apologize," I say to the manager as he walks away from me

"What was that about?" Beth asks.

"No big deal," I say, sipping on my third or fourth beer in the last half hour. "Somebody got busted peeing off the balcony."

"Already?" Beth swipes my beer, tilts the pint glass into her mouth. She hands the glass back to me. "That's not a good sign."

I set my beer down, take her hand in mine. "You ready?" I ask.

"Does my answer really matter at this point?" Beth says.

We thought long and hard about what our first dance together would be. We thought about being sentimental old fools. But honestly, how do multiple generations of newlywed couples continue latching on to "Unforgettable," "What a Wonderful World," and "Unchained Melody" and still with a straight face call their wedding song *special*?

Beth and I had no recourse. I escort her to the dance floor. The DJ pops the CD in the player.

*With a little love, and some tenderness . . .*

Damn straight. Hootie and the fucking Blowfish, baby!

For seemingly as long as Beth and I've been dating, there's been Hootie. We loved Hootie before anyone else loved Hootie. We never get tired of Hootie. I pledge to get some Hootie from Beth while she's still wearing her wedding dress. It's an hour's drive up to the airport hotel. We'll have a couple glasses of champagne, feed each other chocolate-covered strawberries. I'll casually raise the privacy window between us and the limo driver. Then I will slip my hands beneath her dress and—

"What are you thinking about?" Beth asks.

"Hootie," I say.

In the wake of the BoDeans's breakout hit "Closer to Free," people forget that Hootie and the Blowfish's "Hold My Hand" was the actual theme music of the *Party of Five* pilot episode. Granted, gliding across the dance floor with my wife lacks the dramatic flair of Bailey Salinger playing air guitar or the Salinger brothers doing a synchronized sanding routine, but Beth and I do our best. I dust off some of the old cotillion standbys.

"Debbie, I think Hank's doing the foxtrot," Grandma Louise says to Mom. Grandma is here with her nurse after we secured her a day pass from the Franklin Community Alzheimer's & Dementia Care Center, so this will likely constitute her solitary coherent sentence of the afternoon.

I dip Beth again.

"Easy there," Beth says, blowing a few stray curls out of her face. "This champagne's kind of getting to me."

I furrow my brow, give Beth my close-mouthed I'm-up-to-something smile while grinding my pelvis into her. "Isn't that the idea, honey?"

Beth pokes me in the chest. "Someone needs to hose you down."

I take note of the guests surrounding the dance floor, none of the men wearing their coats, all of the women barefoot and wrapped in dresses so drenched with sweat they look glued on. Jeanine crouches in the corner of the dance floor capturing the moment with her camera and her black-and-white film. One of Beth's Illinois friends quietly dry humps his date, a raven-haired minx in a tight-fitting, snakeskin-patterned dress with a slit that goes halfway up her thigh.

"Someone needs to hose all of us down," I say.

"Good point," Beth says. "Still, it's been a good reception."

"Mack's speech was funny. Claire rambled a bit."

"That's what Claire does when she's nervous."

"Then she must have been terrified."

"Hey, be nice."

"I'm just teasing you."

"Thanks by the way," Beth says.

"For what?"

"Not stuffing the cake in my face."

"Oh, you're welcome, I guess."

"You guess?"

"I thought you were going to say something romantic like, 'Thanks for being my husband' or 'Thanks for saying yes.'"

"Do you want me to say that?" Beth says.

"No, at least not now that I've prompted you to say it." Contemplative pause. "Okay, go ahead and say it."

The song ends. Beth leans in, kisses me. She whispers in my ear, "Thanks for being my husband."

I kiss her back. "You're welcome."

I lost Beth after our dance together. First she danced with her father, then I danced with my mother, apparently thereafter Beth snuck out for a cigarette —to the extent a five-foot mound of billowing white could "sneak" at anything. The party felt like it was starting to wind down, although Dr. Burke was still trying to strong-arm the Beaver Stick manager into tapping into a fourth keg.

"I miss anything?" Beth says.

"Where'd you come from?"

"The ladies' room."

I sniff, detecting a generic floral air freshener and a whiff of spearmint all but subsumed by tobacco. "That's not what it smells like to me."

Beth and I are "mostly" nonsmokers now, both of us still in that post-college transition phase in which we have to teach ourselves how to drink without smoking. We've tried using straws for a few months, pretzel rods after that, but sometimes there's just no stopping that first cigarette once you have three or four cocktails in you.

"Cut a bride some slack." Beth chews furiously on a stick of spearmint gum. "It's been a stressful day."

"Sure has," I say. "You and your dad have a good dance together?"

"It was nice," Beth says. "How about you and your mother?"

"It was good, all things considered."

"What's that supposed to mean?"

"Oh, I don't know. Maybe that given a choice between hitting me in the face with a frying pan for three and a half minutes or dancing to an unbelievably heartbreaking song, my mother went with the more painful option."

"The song?"

"Yep."

"Dan Fogelberg was pretty rough."

" 'Leader of the Band'?" I shrug my shoulders. "Rough? Hell, how about borderline incestuous? Mom was glued to me like a second suit."

"Her desperation on full display."

"Debbie unfiltered."

"You should really help her."

My mother isn't equipped to be by herself. I realize that, but at this point in my life I have better things to do than babysit a fifty-year-old woman. She is the most tragic of widows, the kind who goes from high school to college to marriage to family without breaking stride and so never learns to discern between being *alone* and being *lonely*. The kind whose happiness will forever labor beneath the yoke of lost love.

"Why do I need to help her, Beth? She's got her mimosa pitchers, narcotics, and Leon to get her through the day."

"Leon came?"

"He's out in the parking lot in the car listening to a Cubs game. He told Mom he'd drive her home, but he doesn't want to come into the reception."

"What a dick," Beth says. She rests her head on my shoulder. "But at least Jack is eating all this up."

"You think?"

"Being his big brother's ring bearer is the biggest day of his life. He told me so. Your mom said he tried that tux on yesterday morning and hasn't taken it off since. The kid is over the moon for you."

"His *brother's* ring bearer, huh?"

Beth smiles, brings her head into my chest. "Like I said, you need to tell him on your terms. I get that."

I continue to live a lie with Jack—my brother, my son, my whatever. He's happy. Isn't that enough? With a mother teetering on the precipice of abject despair, who am I to push her over the edge?

I reach down, straighten Beth's dress. "After we finished dancing, Mom said to 'make sure to ask Jack where babies come from.'"

Beth giggles, more than a little tipsy. "Well, have you asked him?"

"Not yet. But speaking of the place where babies come from, one of the Kornatowski boys tried to feel up Callie."

Grandma Louise's sister, Great Aunt Joy, married into the Cleveland-based Kornatowskis. Kornatowski is a surname that evidently in Polish means "he who fucks like rabbits." They have ten kids, separated by fourteen years, and an exponentially larger number of grandkids. Six of the ten Kornatowski brood had been the reception's main entertainment for the last few songs, assaulting the dance floor—and some of the female guests—with moves and gesticulations more Miller Lite than measured.

"My cousin Callie?" Beth says.

"No, honey, the Kornatowski boys tried to feel up the entire state of California."

And there you have it: the first recorded smartass remark as husband and wife.

"Ouch!" I say, reeling from the first recorded physical reprisal in response to said smartass remark as husband and wife.

"Callie probably had it coming," Beth says.

"I highly doubt it."

"What makes you say that?"

"Because the Kornatowski boys are so drunk I caught one trying to hit on my mom."

"Isn't Aunt Joy your grandmother's sister?"

"Yep."

"So that means your mom and Aunt Joy's sons are—"

"First cousins."

"That's gross."

"Nope," I say. "That's a Catholic wedding reception."

The DJ transitions into Meatloaf's "Paradise by the Dashboard Light." What am I saying? Of course the DJ transitions into Meatloaf's "Paradise by the Dashboard Light."

The dance floor divides in accordance with proper Meatloaf etiquette—boys on one side, girls on the other.

Thanks to Meatloaf, the reception finds its second wind. The song's fadeout is interrupted by the high-pitched feedback of a microphone being switched on.

"I'd like to take this moment to congratulate Hank and Beth," Mack says. The big man is sporting a full-on lather. Pools of sweat rim his shirt at the armpits and chest. He holds the microphone in his right hand, a sweat-drenched towel and a pint of light beer in his left.

Mack continues. "Darndest thing, Hank. I was sitting on the toilet just a few seconds ago, about ready to pass out, when I looked underneath the stall next to me and saw a pair of rhinestone shoes. DJ, if you wouldn't mind cuing the music up for me. Ladies and gentlemen, it's my pleasure to introduce, all the way from Memphis, Tennessee, THE KING!"

The back door flies open, and in walks Derek Candela dressed from head-to-toe in his authentic replica "Vegas Elvis" costume—a white polyester jumpsuit covered in gold and silver costume jewelry topped off by Derek's exposed hairy chest, a butterfly collar, multiple Hawaiian leis hanging from his neck, and a white cape extending down his back.

Elvis grabs the microphone from Mack. "Hey, cameraman," he says to Kenny Rogers, "you mind taking a picture of me and the lucky lady?"

Elvis takes a knee, offering Beth a seat on his other knee. She accepts the invitation. Kenny Rogers snaps the photo while Elvis keeps playing to the crowd.

"Oh man, oh man," he says. "This is one pretty lady. I-I-I-I could see me leaving Priscilla for this hot number. You hear that, Hank . . . *HUGHHH*!"

Beth stands up, laughing. Everyone is either (a) laughing, (b) screaming, or (c) drunk, with most of us more like (d) all of the above.

I'm thinking Elvis might be close to a *(d)* himself.

"So I'm down in Memphis with Mickey Gilley and the Gatlin Brothers. Hey, can somebody get the King a beer? These peanuts here are making me thirsty. Anyway, like I was saying, I-I-I-I was hanging with Mickey and the Gatlin Brothers, about halfway through a fried peanut butter and banana sandwich. Oh man, oh man, those things are so good . . . *HUGHHH*! And I said, Mickey, I need to make it up to Empire Ridge, Indiana, to see my friends Hank and Beth get hitched. And I gotta tell you, now that I'm here, I-I-I-I feel a lot of love in this room. Put your hands together if you feel it, too."

The crowd responds with applause, shouts, and random song requests.

The King stands between me and Beth. "I-I-I-I just want to introduce the lovely couple here. I met Mr. Fitzpatrick during my '68 comeback album. This guy was one of the greatest bodyguards the King ever had, and he could go into a bar and pick up women left and right. It even made the King jealous."

This is one of those offhand comments meant to be funny but inevitably misinterpreted by half the audience as inappropriate. Fortunately the drunken half of the audience is loud enough to overcome the uncomfortable handclaps of the reasonably sober half. Unfortunately, the tribute to my pickup skills elicits a brief but obvious straight face from Beth.

Elvis picks up the vibe.

"What's even more impressive," he says, "is not only how Hank managed to steal away my biggest groupie, Beth here, but how this lovely lady managed to wrap him around her finger. I-I-I-I'd like to therefore dedicate my first song today . . . to the crowd."

The girls in the audience scream like inebriated, sexed-up groupies, which is cool to me in a nostalgic, perverse sort of way. I think it's their bare, pedicured feet getting to me. I like good feet almost as much as good calves.

"And of course," Elvis adds, "I-I-I-I dedicate the song after that to the happy couple. Hit it, Jimmy."

The King strikes the pose, his hand in the air, knees bent.

*You ain't nuthin' but a hound dog . . .*

Elvis grabs Beth out of the crowd, twirls her a few times. The King escorts Beth back to me as the procession begins.

Callie jumps onto the middle of the dance floor. For someone so recently victimized by my Polish cousins, she seems to have recovered to the point where she can hump the King's leg. She stands and backs up into the crowd.

Elvis gives the ladies what they want: more pelvic thrusts. Aunt Joy is the next to respond. It's the first and hopefully last time I ever see dirty dancing by a couple separated by a half century.

Aunt Joy cedes the floor . . . to my mother. The screaming is deafening. I shield my eyes for fear of reopening the psychological scars of a son still holding fast to the image of his mother as an asexual being.

The song ends. The girls can't get enough.

"It's been a long time since I've done a live show," Elvis says. "I-i-i-i was screamin' for that teleprompter. But I'm going to do a romantic number to close things out today. I'd like the women to all come gather around me."

Per the King's instructions, all the women at the reception surround him.

"Okay, Jimmy," Elvis says. The DJ cues up the song.

*Wise Men say*
*only fools rush in . . .*

"Why aren't you out there?" I say to Beth, her head leaning on my shoulder.

"I got my king right here."

I shake my head, somewhere between embarrassed and appreciative of the compliment. I push her onto the dance floor. "Get out there!"

Kenny Rogers stands with his camera between me and the King. "Wait for the bride!" someone shouts.

Beth lifts up her skirt. Her eyes scan for an opening in the King's harem. She shrugs her shoulders, saying, "Here goes nothing." She slides in front of the group while flashing the peace sign and doing the splits.

Again, the screams are deafening. Beth smiles as the cameras flash. It's the best picture of the day, no doubt destined for a shelf in the Fitzpatrick household for years to come. But the picture will only tell half the story. The picture won't tell you a third of the girls in the photo are under twenty-one and sauced out of their heads. The picture won't tell you the girl to the left of Jeanine and right above Beth is the only twenty-year-old I know with double-F breasts and that she planned to get a breast reduction in eight weeks. The picture won't tell you that even though Claire is on the King's arm and laughing out loud, she just wishes Derek would propose to her already.

Someone grabs at my shirtsleeve. I turn around. No one is there.

"Down here!" the voice says.

"Hey, little bro," I say.

Even covered in a layer of sweat, Jack is the cutest person in the room. People call him Dad's tanned and tow-headed clone, but only because they don't know any better.

The fact Jack even comes out of his room is a minor miracle, let alone the fact he's as well-adjusted as any six-year-old on the planet. After the accident, Mom held him back for another year of kindergarten. The teachers said "he couldn't concentrate" and that "he lacked focus." On behalf of all the sons in the world whose fathers were gored by a Ford Bronco's front bumper, allow me to say to those kindergarten teachers, go fuck yourself.

"Hank," Jack says, "I wanted to tell you something."

"Go for it, buddy."

"Uhhh . . ." He rolls his eyes, like he's lost the words and is trying to find them. In one breath, lacking any inflection or pause between words, he says, "I-just-wanted-to-say-congratulations-I-love-you-and-I-hope-you-have-fun-on-your-honeymoon."

Rehearsed? Probably. Prompted by Mom? Undoubtedly. But the tears start to well up in my eyes nonetheless.

Let's get one thing straight. I have not been a second father to Jack, not by any stretch of the imagination. But I've done my best. I lift him in the air and pull him into my chest. I give him a big wet kiss on the cheek that he of course immediately wipes off. I set him down, ruffle his blond mop with my hand.

"Hey, Jack, I want to ask you a question."

"Okay," Jack says, his face flushed with the typical embarrassment of a kid who realizes he's about to have a conversation with an adult.

"Where do babies come from?"

"That's an easy question."

"Then tell me," I say. I grab a random full beer off the table next to me and take a sip.

"Babies start in the mommy's esophagus, then they grow in the Eucharist, then they come out the mommy's butthole . . . as an egg."

The beer shoots out my nose. I laugh. I laugh hard. So hard that I nearly miss seeing my mother-in-law being held upside down by Mack over the newly opened fourth keg of beer.

Aside from our parents and the Kornatowski boys, there are maybe a handful of people left at the reception over the age of twenty-four. The DJ cues up "Oh What a Night" by the Four Seasons. I stand up, pulling my wife out of her chair and back onto the dance floor.

"One more dance?" I say.

She takes my hand in hers. "How about we keep that number a little more open-ended?"

"Forever then?"

"Forever it is," Beth says.

# Chapter 11

"These things are good," Beth says with her mouth full. She's wearing a bright yellow bikini and picking brownie crumbs out of her navel.

"Probably my favorite wedding present," I say, my mouth also full.

My sister Jeanine made me a batch of fun brownies for the honeymoon. We baked them together the night before the wedding. She had held court in my kitchen, channeling the illegitimate daughter of Julia Child and Jerry Garcia.

"The key is to mix your weed in with the butter reduction," she said while stirring the pot of melted butter and marijuana with her right hand and chain-smoking Marlboro Lights with her left hand. "Too many people just mix the weed in with the brownie mix and throw it in the oven. You know what that does, right?"

"Uh, sure?" I said to her, not having a fucking clue.

Jeanine pointed at me, smiling. "You'll thank me for these tips someday."

"If you say so," I said. "But just for kicks and giggles, remind me again what's wrong with mixing the dope into the mix."

"Pretty basic knowledge, really." Jeanine poured the green gelatinous ooze in a mixing bowl. She grabbed the dry brownie mix and dumped it into the bowl. She added an egg and about a third of a cup of water, and stirred the mix with a wooden spoon. "You only get a fraction of the THC if you just cook the weed into the mix."

"Basic knowledge indeed," I said. "What's THC again?"

"Come on now, Hank," Jeanine said. "Tetrahydrocannabinol. It's the shit that gets you high."

"Oh, so you're saying cooking the weed in the brownies gets you less high?"

"Bingo."

"We don't want that."

"Hell no, we don't!"

Beth and I couldn't afford a honeymoon. We were up to our eyeballs in student loans, and Dr. Burke's beach house was booked through the end of the summer. At the last minute, Dr. Burke's partner offered us a three-day weekend on his houseboat on Lake Cumberland free of charge. The eighty-foot-long houseboat is more like a condo on water, with six bedrooms, plus a full wet bar and hot tub on the roof and a two-story curly slide extending off the stern of the boat.

With over twelve hundred miles of shoreline and a maximum depth of two hundred fifty feet, Lake Cumberland in southern Kentucky is the largest lake east of the Mississippi. The great thing about Cumberland is that no one west of the Mississippi or east of the Appalachians seems to know it exists. The man-made reservoir is a vast flooded valley, surrounded on all sides by public parkland. Dr. Burke's partner told us we could quite possibly go all three days without seeing another boat on the water.

It's a theory I'm prepared to put to the test.

We finish our last bites of brownies. I smile. Beth is lying on a sun lounger. I'm sitting at her feet. The Divinyls's "I Touch Myself" starts up on the houseboat sound system, which immediately compels me to massage her calves.

"Freak," Beth says.

I give her calves a good squeeze. "How stoned are you right now?"

My bride giggles. "Way stoned."

Beth and I have spent the past half hour taking turns coating one another from head to toe with Palmolive—softens hands while you're doing your wife—and sliding down the curly slide. Montell Jordan reminds us both that "This Is How We Do It," although I can't imagine many people in South Central do it this way.

"I'm over the slide," Beth says, climbing out of the water. She grabs a towel, wraps it around her hair.

"What do you want to do now?" I say, stepping aboard the boat's aft deck.

Beth removes her towel from her head, throws it at me. "I want to fool around."

"Uh . . ." I wipe my face off with the towel. "Isn't that what we've been doing?"

"No, I mean *really* fool around."

"If you insist." I throw the towel on the ground. I rush Beth, my left hand on her right breast. My free hand, seemingly of its own volition, reaches between her legs.

Beth pushes me away. "Easy, tiger."

"But I thought you said—"

"How about a little foreplay before you go stampeding toward the clitoris?"

"I can do that, too," I say, sprouting a full tripod at this point.

"Then go up top," Beth says, pointing at the aluminum stairs next to the slide. "I have a surprise for you."

Montell Jordan defers to TLC. Beth walks downstairs. She turns up "Waterfalls." I peer down the steps. "Can I come?"

"You stay up there," Beth shouts back. TLC is cut off in midstream, replaced by the beginning of Van Halen's "Summer Nights."

Fuck yeah! Beth just put on the *Super Sexy Six Metal Mega Mix*.

It's a six-song "boner block" of music that gets me going: Van Halen's "Summer Nights," Mötley Crüe's "Girls, Girls, Girls," Def Leppard's "Pour Some Sugar on Me," Led Zeppelin's "Whole Lotta Love," Jackyl's "Dirty Little Mind," and the Scorpions's "Tease Me, Please Me." Beth made the mixtape for my twenty-fourth birthday back in April and proceeded to do an eighteen-minute striptease that quite nearly made my dick explode.

"Close your eyes," Beth says.

I close my eyes. I can hear her coming up the steps to Sammy Hagar's scratchy serenade.

"Okay, you can open them."

I open my eyes. Beth is standing in front of me. In place of her bikini, she's wearing silver pasties on her nipples and a thin red shimmy skirt.

"Oh my God," I say. "Are you a . . . a belly dancer?"

# Chapter 12

The conservation officer seems like a nice guy. He speaks with a lazy southern drawl. And he keeps the back of his squad car exceedingly clean.
"That there wuz sumthin' I ain't uh never seen."
His name is Don. He arrested us on charges of indecent exposure. Our houseboat was tucked away in a fairly isolated cove, but our music had attracted his attention. I was having sex with Beth—still wearing her belly dancer costume and the Scorpions's "Tease Me, Please Me" echoing in my ears—when Officer Don tapped me on the shoulder.
Beth sits in the front passenger seat, trying to talk Officer Don out of taking us to jail. For being eternally mortified, she's amazingly composed. She asks Don about the fishing on Cumberland, about where he's from—the disarming Beth charm at work. She looks like she's getting somewhere. It's time for me to step in and close the deal.
"Flossie!" I blurt out, less sober than I expected to sound.
" 'Scuse me, son?" Officer Don says.
"Aunt Flossie," I say. "She lives, or should I say lived, in these parts. Campbellsville, or was it Mannsville?"
Officer Don nods. "Both those towns ur in this county."
I pretend not to notice Beth shaking her head. "My aunt Flossie lived there her whole life. We used to come down and stay on her farm. There was this huge barn across the street where they'd hang tobacco leaves to dry."
"Makes sense," Officer Don says. "Tobacco's a big crop 'round here."
"Yeah," I say. "Big crop."
"Son?"
"Yes sir."
"Your aunt Flossie. She got a last name?"
"Last name?"
"That's whut I said."
"She was my great-aunt, my dad's aunt."
"Great-aunts don't have last names?"

"I'm sure they do," I say. "I just can't remember mine."

For all my earnestness, my name dropping goes about as well as if I had told Officer Don that Jesus was a black homosexual democrat who hated Adolph Rupp. He escorts us into the Columbia County Jail.

Beth and I had to wait to be processed after a three-hundred-pound bald man who was arrested for a DUI on a riding lawn mower. The lady who books me, an old, haggard, Bea Arthur look-alike, speaks with an accent bordering on indecipherable. "Have uh seat," she says, nodding to the chair beside her desk. "Nye-eem?"

"Hank Fitzpatrick," I answer.

"Birth-dye?"

"Four, twenty-one, seventy-one."

"White?"

"Huh?"

"White?"

"One more time."

"White?"

"Uh, yeah, I'm white."

"*Weight*, Hank," Beth says from the other side of the room. "What's your weight?"

"Oh, sorry," I say. "One seventy-five."

I haven't been one seventy-five since the eighth grade, and Bea Arthur notices. "You show 'bout that?"

I throw my thumb over my shoulder. "If John Deere over there can get away with saying he's two forty, I can get away with one seventy-five."

I swear Bea Arthur smiles. "Y'all kin go now," she says.

"What?" I say, looking at Beth. She shrugs her shoulders. I look back at Bea Arthur.

"Your bail's posted," she says, enunciating for my benefit. "Wuz only five bucks uh piece. Officer Don went easy on y'all."

"Define 'easy,' " Beth says.

"You two ain't hurtin' nobody, so we're giving you deferrals. Long as y'all pay a seventy-five-dollar fine within the next sixty days, we'll just say today never happened."

"And that's it?" I say.

Bea Arthur shakes her head. "Not exactly. Y'all are on probation. Best keep your noses clean for the next eighteen months, and *then* we'll forget about today."

"Sounds good to me." I stand up. "Now, do we pay you the ten dollars for bail, or do we pay it on the way out?"

Bea Arthur shakes her head. "Like I said, your bail was posted. Paid for a half hour ago."

"By who?"

"He's outside uh waitin' for y'all. Says he's your uncle."

# Chapter 13

"What the fuck are you doing here?"

"Please, Hank, let me explain."

I stand in the middle of the Columbia County Jail in my swimsuit and flip-flops, my fists clenched. Uncle Mitch stands opposite me, unshaven and smelling like body odor, still in the same polo and torn blue jeans from two days ago.

Beth grabs my elbow. "Hank, let's just leave."

I yank my arm free of my wife. "Answer me, Mitch. What the fuck are you doing here?"

He steps tentatively toward me, his outreached hand nearly touching my arm. "I couldn't let things end like they did the other day. I had to see you. I overheard someone going into your wedding say where you were going for your honeymoon, so I got a room at a motel down here and just waited things out. The moment just kind of presented itself when I was having a cup of coffee on the town square and saw you being taken in handcuffs into the police station. Indecent exposure? I can only imagine what you were—"

I poke him in the chest. "You can only imagine *what*, Mitch? Being there with me, just like old times, so you can grab hold of my little pecker?"

Uncle Mitch stumbles backward. "Hank, I—"

"You *what*?"

"I only want your forgiveness."

"Never."

"You don't mean that."

"I don't?"

"You are your father's son. His capacity to forgive is inside you. I know it is."

"And what the fuck is that supposed to mean?"

"You don't think he knew?"

"Knew what?"

"About me?"

"Fuck you!" I shout. Officer Don walks back into the station just as I pin Uncle Mitch against the wall, my elbow in his throat.

Beth is crying. Uncle Mitch gasps for air. "W-we were teenagers. He caught me with another guy, one of his bandmates. I swore to him it was a one-time thing. He promised to never tell anyone, but he had to have known. He just had to have known, Hank."

I knee Uncle Mitch in the groin. He falls like a sack of potatoes. I reel back my foot for another blow. Just as my foot connects with his exposed ribs, Officer Don checks me into the wall.

He spins me around, pins my arm behind me, immobilizing me. "Mr. Fitzpatrick, that's enough. There'll be none of that in my station, yuh hear?"

Both of our backs are turned away from Uncle Mitch. Beth is the one who sees him reach into his pocket.

"Gun!" she screams.

Bea Arthur is already on the com in the other room. *"We have a four-seventeen in progress at the Columbia County Jail. I repeat, a four-seventeen. Officer on the scene. Request backup."*

Beth drops to the floor. Officer Don lets go of my wrist. We both turn to the assailant. "Sir, I'm going to have to ask you to put that gun down," Officer Don says. "We don't want to see anyone get hurt here."

"Spare me your bullshit, officer," Uncle Mitch says, waving the handgun in our faces. "I know how this works. I just pulled a loaded gun inside a fucking police station, plus I'm a convicted sex offender. The math just isn't working in my favor on this one."

I reach out to my godfather. "Uncle Mitch, please . . ."

"Going with *Uncle* Mitch again, huh? Smart boy." He motions toward me with the handgun. "Come here."

I walk toward him. "This is just between you and me, so let's have it out, then."

"Yes, Hank," Uncle Mitch says. He places the barrel of the gun directly on my heart. "Let's have it out."

I recognize the gun. I'm suddenly short of breath. The room goes black for a split second. When I open my eyes I feel like a part of me is outside my own body, hovering above the scene, watching Uncle Mitch force me to undo his life, to absolve his sin. But I'm not afraid anymore. I'm pissed off.

"Humor me, *Uncle* Mitch," I say, trying not to sneer. "How can we make this right?"

"It's simple, really. Say you forgive me."

"And that's all?" My hands are raised. Beth is sobbing now.

"Yes, Hank," Uncle Mitch says. "That's all. I need your mercy. I need your father's mercy. Please, set me free."

"No," I say.

"What?" Uncle Mitch pushes the handgun harder into my chest.

"You heard me. I know you're a monster, but I also know there's a small part of you who was my godfather and Dad's best friend. You're a sick fuck. But you're not a killer."

He steps closer to me, pushes the barrel of the handgun beneath my chin. "You don't think I'm a killer, huh? What if you're wrong?"

"If I'm wrong, then I'd rather die knowing I never forgave you than live knowing I offered you even an ounce of hope for your miserable existence."

Uncle Mitch's eyes open wide, manic-like. He grabs me by the shirt with his free hand, pushes the handgun even deeper into my chin. The room is spinning. We're both sweating. His three-packs-a-day breath is stifling.

Then, as suddenly as he grabbed me, Uncle Mitch just backs away.

"You aren't your father's boy, Hank."

"What?"

"You heard me," he says. "John Fitzpatrick forgave everyone, but forgiveness doesn't come easy to you. Your dad was always too busy being humane to be human. You're tougher. And in a weird way, I feel like I had something to do with that. Thank you."

"For what?"

"For setting me free . . . *son.*"

Uncle Mitch turns the gun on himself. The bullet is through the back of his head before Officer Don can even raise his sidearm.

A godfather's love measured by the diameter of his exploded brain matter.

They've moved us to another wing of the building, away from the carnage. Beth and I sit in Officer Don's office.

"You okay, honey?" Beth says, squeezing my hands.

I squeeze back. "Some honeymoon, eh?"

Officer Don enters the office. "You two can go now. Paperwork is pretty much done here. We have to hold the assailant's gun until the investigation is officially closed, but I assume you'll eventually want it back."

I stand up. Beth follows my lead. "Want it back?" I ask.

"Yeah," Officer Don says. "The gun is nice, all things considered. It's a Smith & Wesson three fifty-seven Magnum. We did a trace on it, and records show it's still registered to—"

"John Fitzpatrick," I say.

"You knew?"

I rub my mouth. "I knew it the moment he pulled the gun on me. That's why I didn't do it."

"Didn't do what?"

"Forgive him."

"You didn't forgive your uncle because he had your father's gun in his hand?"

I open the door to Officer Don's office. Beth walks out of the room. "I didn't forgive Uncle Mitch because I knew my father was about to kill him."

On cue, my wife vomits in the hallway of the police station.

# Part II
# 1996

# Chapter 14

Most of my friends growing up would tell you I had the picture-perfect childhood—that the Fitzpatrick family was ripped wholesale out of a Norman Rockwell painting. For sure, I had a nice roof over my head, a younger sibling I wanted to kill only some of the time, and parents who aspired to nothing less than the world's greatest love affair. But in truth, I had a dark secret that belied the painting, a secret darker even than my boy-loving godfather.

My mother, you see, she hates animals. In my first eighteen years of life, various people—no fewer than three babysitters, Aunt Claudia, even Laura once—conspired to get me a dog. And each time, Mom was steadfast in her opposition. *"As long as you live under my roof . . ."* she'd say, *"fish are the only pets you'll ever get."*

I told myself the moment I was on my own, I'd get a dog, and I'd train it to hate my mother right back.

Then life happened. Through the first part of college I was too drunk and self-absorbed to care about a dog. Through the second part of college, after Dad was killed, I couldn't be trusted with my own welfare, let alone a dog's. Regardless, in a rare moment of nearly genuine but ultimately misguided sympathy, Hatch brought a puppy into our apartment at IU. She was a shar-pei bitch. We named her Moosehead. Ironically, she had a taste for cheap beer—four-dollars-a-case Drummond Brothers was her favorite—and pissed on every inch of our carpeting. We lost our damage deposit and our lease. Hatch's mom took in Moosehead, renamed her "Musette," and gave her the run of the free-range ostrich farm in Oklahoma. She sent me a Christmas card last year with Musette and her dressed in matching elf costumes, the attached note thanking me for uniting her with her "canine soul mate." Two weeks later, Musette took an ostrich foot to the head and was buried at a pet cemetery near Norman.

"Hurry up, Hank!" Beth says.

It was my wife's idea to come to the Empire Ridge Humane Society today. After we got back from the honeymoon and found out she was pregnant, she said to me, "A family has got to have a family dog." A few months later, after a couple false starts—a litter of inbred Yorkies at a trailer park that quickly dissuaded her from yippy dogs (thank God) and a brief impulse to adopt a retired racing greyhound that had a manic fear of staircases and a taste for guinea pigs (don't ask)—here we are.

The animals are subdivided into three separate rooms: Cats, Dogs, and Puppies. Ever the sucker for lost causes, I've already tried talking Beth into adopting an adult dog, but she wants no part of it. "We're adopting a puppy," she told me. "We're adopting a little fella who we'll watch grow up and grow old, just like a member of the family."

Beth grabs my hand, leads me straight to the puppies. Turns out she was already here yesterday and has her mind set on a liver-spotted American bulldog mix. His shelter name is Moxie. He looks like Chance, the dog from *Homeward Bound*.

I reach down to pet him. His puppy teeth stab me like dozens of little needles. He attacks my hand and forearm, chewing on me as if I'm lathered up with bacon grease.

"Moxie is just teething, Hank."

"I realize that, honey."

"He'll settle down eventually."

"And until that time comes, imagine our baby's face in his mouth instead of my hand."

Beth lets out an uncomfortable exhale, turns away from Moxie's cage. Just like that, he's off the list.

As was the norm in late spring and early summer, the kennels at the Humane Society are bursting with litters, a tableau of flavor-of-the-month purebreds and crossbreds—chow mixes, rottweiler mixes, even a litter of full-blooded pit bulls—now exiled to lonely corners smelling of excrement and human cruelty. Distracted by Moxie, we had initially just walked by the cage of eight-week old Lab mix puppies in the center of the room.

Their collective date of birth is listed as April 1, 1996—April Fool's Day. The puppies are all jet black, save for one. He has a white dot on his head, white paws, and a bold splash of white on his chest. Beth picks him up, his brothers and sisters yelping after him, starved for attention.

"This little guy is adorable," she says.

And with those words, seemingly on cue, the puppy lays his head on my wife's shoulder.

I pull out of the Humane Society parking lot. The puppy is curled up in Beth's lap. "What do we name him?" she asks.

"I was thinking Knute, Rockne, or Gipper."

"Triple veto," Beth says.

"How many vetoes do you get?"

"As many as I want."

"How about Clashmore Mike?"

"Clashmore who?"

"Clashmore Mike," I say. "Most people don't realize Notre Dame's original mascot in the 1920s was not a fighting Irish leprechaun. Back then the team was called the Notre Dame Ramblers, and their mascot was an Irish terrier named Clashmore Mike."

"Uh, no offense, Mr. Master of Useless Trivia, but that name sucks."

"Well, what would you suggest?"

Beth strokes the puppy's square, slightly pointed head. "I wouldn't mind something Irish, as in *Ireland* Irish as opposed to *Notre Dame* Irish."

"You mean like Angus or Chieftain?"

"Oh, I like that."

"Angus?"

"He's a dog, Hank, not a side of beef."

"Chieftain, then?"

"Yes," Beth says. "He looks like a Chieftain. He looks like a Chief."

# Chapter 15

"I can see the head, Beth. I can see our baby's head."
"Blond?"
"Dark hair," I say. "And a lot of it."

My wife is propped about a third of the way up in her bed, her legs spread. Beth's ob-gyn Dr. Martha Florio sits on a chair between Beth's legs, exhorting her to push. Dr. Florio is short, thick but not fat. Dark hair. Always smiling. She has the look of a Greek mother, always ready to smother you in kisses and oddly pronounced pastries. I stand just behind and to the left of Dr. Florio, looking over her shoulder. Bob Marley's *Legend* CD plays in the background. We're coming up on 8:00 p.m., nearly twenty-seven hours after my wife's first major contraction.

"It's not coming," the doctor says under her breath.
"What?" I say.

We're not calling the baby "it" by accident. Beth and I decided to bring our first into the world the old-fashioned way. Even after four ultrasounds—which Beth insisted upon, convinced she had drunk and smoked the baby stupid on our honeymoon—we refused to know the gender of our child, hamstringing the grandmothers into buying an almost exclusively yellow wardrobe.

"The baby," the doctor says. "It doesn't want to come out this way."

Dr. Florio is from the new school of childbirth and delivery. She doesn't believe in using suction or even forceps. That is unfortunate for Beth. After all these years of self-deprecation in regards to her wide "birthing hips," it turns out Beth has an extremely narrow pelvis. "I see it a lot in gymnasts," Dr. Florio tells us, as if that makes what she's about to say any easier.

"Hey kiddo," the doctor says. Since the day Beth had her first ultrasound, Dr. Florio has addressed her as "kiddo." Her informality and comfort with the word makes me think it's a catchall nickname she uses with most of her patients.

Beth is exhausted. "Yes, doctor?" she says.

"We're going to need to deliver your baby via C-section. The combination of your narrow pelvis and the baby's large head makes a vaginal delivery problematic."

I adjust my fitted seven-and-five-eighths-inch Notre Dame ball cap, silently cursing the long line of massive Fitzpatrick craniums. *"We have fiveheads as opposed to foreheads,"* Dad would say.

"Whatever you need to do to get my baby out happy and healthy, do it," Beth says. She accepts the news better than I expected. Must be the drugs talking.

I smile at my wife. I lean down next to her face. "Everything's going to be okay, honey," I whisper. I pat her belly. Her hospital gown barely contains the seventy-plus pounds she's put on during pregnancy. Twenty pounds of that weight gain is in her formerly A-cup now D-cup breasts, which is one of nature's cruel jokes on men. As suckable as they might look, milk-swollen breasts are rendered too sensitive to even think about fondling, let alone the full-on pearl necklace you fantasize about roughly twenty-seven hours a day.

I kiss Beth on her sweaty, oily forehead. I run my hand through her unwashed hair. She is dirty. She smells like body odor. I just saw her take a crap in the bed when she tried to push the baby out.

All in all, Beth is as beautiful as I've ever seen her.

Dr. Florio instructs two nurses to "prepare for an emergency C-section." *Emergency?* I have to stay calm, for Beth's sake. God, I fucking hate hospitals.

Beth reaches up, squeezes my hand. "Do you think we should tell everyone what's up?"

"I guess so," I answer. "But I don't want to leave you."

Dr. Florio looks at me. "It'll be a few minutes until the operating room is prepped, kiddo. We have some time."

I still don't want to leave Beth. But she nods, pushes me. I kiss her again, this time on the lips. I've been spoon-feeding her ice chips for the better part of a day, but her lips are still horribly chapped. "I'll be right back," I say.

An episode of *Beverly Hills 90210* plays on the waiting room television. It's a repeat of this season's two-part finale. Steve Sanders is having a twenty-first birthday party on the Queen Mary with the Goo Goo Dolls as the house band. David Silver and Donna Martin are getting back together, which is predictable. Brandon Walsh is dumping Susan Keats, which is unfortunate given how insane Emma Caulfield looks in a bikini.

Stan and Joan are seated in the waiting room across from Mom, my sister Jeanine, and Jack. To borrow some of Hatch's AA-speak, Jeanine has been Beth's enabler over these last nine months. After we moved back to Empire Ridge last year, she had a front-row seat to most of the pregnancy, living with me and Beth while completing clinicals toward her physical therapy certification. She has a PT job lined up in Portland, Oregon, but she got her start date deferred six months so she could help out during Beth's maternity leave. The two have put on an ice cream-eating display, the likes of which I have never seen nor will ever see again. I'm almost surprised there's any Edy's French Silk Light ice cream left in the greater southern Indiana area, given that they've been going through the stuff at a gallon-per-week clip.

I say all the right things to everyone—"The baby is okay . . . Beth is going to be fine . . . It's a very routine procedure"—but that doesn't stop Dr. Burke from insisting on being in the operating room. The hospital's on-call pediatrician isn't doing rounds until tomorrow morning, so Dr. Florio welcomes the company. I don't tell Dr. Burke this, but I welcome the company, too. I'm scared.

The nurse hands Dr. Burke and me our gear. Together we suit up: scrubs, surgical gowns, caps, masks, and shoe coverings. The nurse shows us to the operating room. My surgical mask doesn't seem to fit, positioned just so on the bridge of my nose that it deflects all exhaled air out the top of the mask and straight into my eyes.

"Here," Dr. Burke says. He reaches over and pinches the metal band running along the ridge of my mask, sealing the mask to my face.

"Thanks . . . Stan." My voice cracks a little.

"It'll be okay, Hank." My father-in-law pats me on the back. I don't know if I've earned his love yet, but he's giving it to me anyway.

I hand Stan the video camera. "Sure you don't mind filming?"

"Not at all," Stan says. "You worry about Beth. I'll worry about saving the moment for posterity. Besides, the more things to keep me distracted and out of the way in there, the better."

I read somewhere that C-sections were formerly only used to save the baby's life. The survival of the mother wasn't even considered until the early 1800s, at which time they figured out you could stitch the mother back up as opposed to leaving her to die from infection or massive hemorrhaging. As much as I know Beth appreciates my grasp of random useless trivia, I think it's best not to bring up this factoid.

Stan and I enter the operating room. Beth is lying on a table in the middle of the room, her swollen belly exposed to the bright surgical lights overhead. Dr. Florio and a nurse stand to the left of her belly, a second nurse stands to the right. The second nurse is swabbing Beth's belly with what I assume to be some kind of antiseptic. A tray of gleaming surgical instruments hovers over Beth's chest: various scalpels, scissors, and clamps. A light blue screen is raised just below Beth's chin, preventing her from seeing the actual procedure. I take a seat on a stool beside Beth's head. Stan positions himself just beyond the screen with the camcorder.

Ten minutes pass, maybe fifteen. Scalpels and scissors are constantly exchanged just above the rim of the blue screen. A stream of instructions pass between Dr. Florio and the nurses. Their words are drowned out by the ambient noises of an operating room. The classical music on the PA system. The beeping of the heart monitor. That high-pitched whistling coming from the suction machine, a noise that haunts me with images of multiple cavities, pulled permanent teeth, root canals, and five years of braces, retainers, rubber bands and headgear.

Dr. Florio asks Beth, "How you feeling?"

Beth blinks, looks at me. She has that powerless look on her face, like the look my Grandpa Fitzpatrick had after he had a stroke.

"Beth?" I say.

She closes her eyes, inhales. "Having . . . trouble . . . breathing," she stammers.

"You need to relax, kiddo," Dr. Florio instructs. "That's just your epidural doing its job, maybe a little too well. It's numbed you to where you can't feel yourself breathe."

"I'm here, honey," I say. "So's your father. And pretty soon our baby will be here, too. Just stay calm and focused, feel yourself breathing in . . . and out."

I repeat this mantra over and over—*in . . . and out, in . . . and out*—until I can feel her breathing steady itself. "Thanks, Hank," she says.

"They're just getting the head out now," Stan says.

I turn to my wife. "Can I watch?"

A moment of clarity from Beth. "Can you witness the birth of your first born? What the hell kind of question is that?"

I stand up, an expectant father not expecting . . . *this*.

Of course, there's the tattoo: a dainty daisy-like flower to the left of Beth's navel that has long since been stretched to the general size of a hockey puck. But it's her stomach that gets me. It's peeled back in layers of skin and muscle. The hypodermis layer is most pronounced, like a line of tapioca pudding set against a backdrop of blood and amniotic fluid. I want to be disgusted. But I'm not.

"Look at all that hair," Dr. Florio says. She and the two nurses are wrenching the skin around the baby's head, trying to dislodge it from Beth's uterus. One of the nurses sticks a tube in the baby's mouth. The baby chokes, coughs up some fluid, and begins to cry.

"Hear that?" Stan says from behind the camcorder. "That's what you want to hear."

Dr. Florio gives the baby one hard tug, and then it's out. And it's purple. And its head looks like an eggplant.

"Now comes the verdict," Dr. Florio says, turning the front of the baby toward us.

The moment of truth. Five sets of eyes all trained on one baby's genitalia.

"I was right!" Stan exclaims.

"What?" Beth says.

I walk behind the screen, lean down and tell my wife the news.

*It's a girl.*

Like Stan, I always knew it would be a girl. Some people would even go so far to suggest if there's any justice in this world I will have nothing but daughters.

Some people? Who am I kidding? *A lot* of people would go so far to suggest this. The birth of a daughter is a father's great reality check, the giant "fuck you" to guys like me who look back at their formative years with shamelessly wistful naivety. Newsflash, Hank: Every girl you've ever been with is someone's daughter. And about fourteen years from now, your daughter is going to be dealing with pricks just like you.

Taking cues from great-grandmothers on both sides of the family, we name her Sasha Grace. It's been about five minutes since they wiped her down, drained the fluids from her nose and mouth, and placed her in an incubator. Sasha is already pinking up. Stan is still recording. Still crying, Sasha opens her eyes for the first time.

"She's looking all around, Beth," Stan says. "Sasha is looking for her mommy."

Stan appears restless. Dr. Florio is still busy on the south side of my wife sewing things up. I say, "How about we wheel the incubator to where Beth can see her baby girl?"

"Good idea," Stan says.

I reach for the camcorder, starting to pull it off Stan's shoulder. "I'll take this off your hands and go update the troops. Why don't you give your granddaughter her first checkup?"

Stan pulls the camcorder shoulder strap over his head, thrusts the camcorder at me. "That's an even better idea."

I kiss Beth on the lips. She's still a little drugged, trying to maintain consciousness on the off chance the hospital might change its policy regarding the handling of newborns by catatonic patients.

"You did it, sweetie," I say. "Get some rest. I love you."

She musters a response through her haze. "I love you, too, Hank."

I hand the camcorder to the throng of new grandparents, aunts, and uncles. They huddle around the small view screen for a first glimpse of Sasha.

I sneak outside for a smoke. Neither Beth nor I smoke anymore, so I bummed one off Jeanine.

"Got one for me?"

Mom stands there, tears streaming down her face in mauve tentacles.

"You don't smoke," I say.

"Neither do you."

"I needed a cigarette today." I flick my cigarette into the parking lot. The embers glow as the cigarette bursts on the asphalt.

"Yeah," Mom says. "I'm sorry, son."

"Sorry for what?"

"I'm sorry he couldn't be here."

Leon refused to come tonight. Married six months to my mom, and he's still the same old dick.

"I'm actually happier that Leon isn't here."

"Not Leon." Mom buries her head in my shoulder. "Your father. I'm sorry he couldn't be here to see the birth of his first grandchild."

"But technically didn't he get to see the birth of his first grandchild?"

"Not really."

"But you and he were there when Laura—"

"No, don't you remember? Your father was up at Notre Dame for his reunion."

"Oh, that's right."

"I drove to Pennsylvania and back by myself in a rental car, and then I dropped off the car in northern Indiana. Your dad picked me up in Angola. When he saw Jack for that first time, the look in his eyes made all my guilt and fear about our deception just go away. I saw that look in Stan's eyes tonight. I just wish I could have seen it one more time in John's."

It's the first time I've heard her talk about Dad since she started dating Leon. My tears follow hers. I want to tell Mom how I feel. I want to tell her about my dreams about Dad. Not the ones in which I used to imagine him in a witness protection program or the ones where I took his place in the accident. But the new dream.

I'm somehow transported back in time. I wake up in my apartment on October 1, 1992 knowing my father is going to die. The skinny girl with the bony ass, long legs and high-arched feet is still in my bed. My bedside alarm clock reads 7:30 a.m. There's still time! I rush to the automobile auction. I get there minutes before the accident. I find Dad by the coffee machine. I hug him.

*Hank, is everything all right?* he asks. I tell him how desperately I've missed him, and he says to me, *I just saw you on Tuesday.*

*Don't ask any questions, Dad,* I say. *Just come here, stand with me, and watch.*

We stand there, tucked safely in the office, separated from the auction by a half wall of cinder blocks and a thick pane of glass.

I look up at the clock, then point into the garage. *You're thinking about buying that Sonoma, right?*

Dad nods. I put my arm around my father, securing him next to me. We watch the white Ford Bronco careen into the garage and crush the rear end of the GMC pickup.

My father stutters, *H-how, d-did you know that was going to happen?*

*I love you, Dad,* I say, pulling my wallet out of my back pocket. *And there are some people I'd like you to meet.* I reach into my wallet. I pull out three pictures: one of Beth on our wedding day, one of Jack, now seven years old, and one of his grandchildren.

Just as my father reaches out to grab them, the pictures dissolve in my hand.

"Mom," I say.

I stare at her so fiercely I feel like I'm staring through her.
"Yes, Hank?"
"I wish Dad were here, too."

It's nearly dawn now. Beth is sleeping. I stand at the window of our room, looking east. Sasha's head rests on my shoulder. I hold her tight with both arms. I lean my nose into her soft, innocent-smelling skin—that spot just behind the ear on a baby's neck. I hold this seven-pound-fourteen-ounce glimmer of hope against my chest, and all I can think to whisper are three lonely words.

*"Dad, I'm sorry."*

"Hey, don't hog her," Beth says. Her voice is like a lifeline to me. As she's done so many times before, often without even knowing it, my wife saves me from myself.

"You awake?"

Beth reaches her arms out. "Yes, now give her here."

"Patience, Mommy," I say.

Beth sits up. She pulls down a flap on the left side of her shirt, revealing her bare chest. I position our newborn daughter in the crook of her right arm. Beth squeezes her nipple between her left index and middle fingers as I help guide Sasha's head toward her mother. Beth is still weak from the C-section, so I help support Sasha with my left hand. With my right hand I help Beth squeeze her nipple to get the colostrum going. The fact I'm massaging a woman's swollen breast without being the least bit turned-on is a big step for me.

# Part III
# 1997-1999

# Chapter 16

The dirty little secret about life is that it speeds up as you grow older. You put things in cruise control and watch the miles tick by without stopping to look at the scenery. It's a secret no one bothers to tell you until you've actually succumbed to the time warp, feckless and coma-like, as people younger than you have "retro" eighties parties and DJs label your favorite songs as "classic" rock. Why is it an eternity between Christmases for a child? Because the time between Christmases is half of a two-year-old's life, a third of a three-year-old's life, a fourth of a four-year-old's life, and downward it goes until you can't distinguish one holiday from the next. Hell, I'm twenty-eight years old, so my next Christmas is a mere thirty-six hundredths of my life away. Think about thirty-six hundredths of a second. It's an eye blink, a flash of light, an impulse. Time is all about context. Years become days. Miles become inches. Life becomes death. Can somebody prescribe me a fucking pill to slow this shit down?

Like Rip Van Winkle, I feel like I've missed a significant part of my life—or at the very least 1997 and 1998. Sasha turned three today. I don't believe it, but that's what Beth keeps telling me. Jack played her "Happy Birthday" on his recorder. Jack turned ten in February. I don't believe it, but that's what Mom keeps telling me. Chief celebrated the occasion by swallowing a cake-covered oven mitt. The vet charged us eight hundred dollars to cut open his stomach and extract the goddamn thing. He asked me if I wanted to keep the oven mitt.

Speaking of playing the recorder, is there a reason school systems still insist on imposing this archaic form of recreational entertainment on our troubled youth? Throw in square dancing, and I'd rather take my chances with methamphetamines, bullying, and hate crimes.

Mom called me today to say the divorce was final. It started when Leon tried to get Mom to sign all her financial assets over to him after we won the wrongful death lawsuit against the Indianapolis Auto Auction. He told Mom that he was "just better at moving money around" than she was. Then Leon's mother died, and he sued his siblings for their inheritance—at the funeral. But I think the last straw was when she caught him not only hitting up Jeanine for some weed, but hitting on her with a four-hour erection powered by Canadian pharmaceuticals.

Mom and Leon were married, and then they weren't. Vagina Head just disappeared. Yesterday he hopped on a plane to Amsterdam with a cashier's check for one-point-five million dollars, roughly half of my father's estate. I'm trying not to be too hard on myself, but I keep thinking that my ambivalence and hostility toward Mom cost our family half of Dad's blood money.

Sorry, Dad. I let you down again.

# Chapter 17

Beth pushes open the door to the restroom. She looks at me over her shoulder. "I have to pee. Wait for me?"
"Sure," I say.
The door swings behind her. A whiff of her perfume wafts out in the hallway, that same subtle lavender scent she's worn since I first met her. I close my eyes and inhale deeply, like I always do when a pretty woman who smells good walks by me. I leave my foot just inside the door, cracking it open. I can hear the faint trickle of my wife's urine.
I think I've got a thing for women urinating. Not in a sick way. I'm not talking I want a golden shower or anything like that. But the image of a woman's pale cheeks on cold porcelain makes me yearn to be a toilet seat. I picture the goose bumps starting to rise on Beth's bare ass. The toilet flushes. I listen close to hear the elastic snap as she pulls up her panties.
Okay, maybe it's a little sick.
"All done," Beth says.
We're attending our ten-year high school reunion. Beth had the idea to have a combined Ridge-Prep reunion. As Empire Ridge High School Class of '89 president, I was tasked with doing much of the field work.
"Pretty big turnout," I say.
"See," Beth says. "I told you Prepsters weren't snobs. We Ridgies are the ones with the chips on our shoulders and the inferiority complexes."
Beth and I approach the bar. I raise two fingers. "Got High Life?"
"Nope," the bartender says.
"Miller Lite?"
"Just Bud and Bud Light."
Beth shakes her head. "I can't do straight-up Budweiser."
"Not in the mood for the Heavy, huh?"
"The Heavy" is a popular nickname for Budweiser. The judges will also accept "Diesel" and of course the standard "Bud."
Beth places her hand on her waist and strikes a pose. "I have to watch my girlish figure, you know."

"Is this the part where I'm supposed to say, 'Beth, your butt's not that big'?"

"No, Hank." She smacks me on the arm. "This is the part where you make an innocuous statement that has nothing to do with my butt, because by specifically singling out my butt, you reinforce my insecurities and subconscious belief that my butt is in fact big."

"Uh, come again?"

"We've been married for four years," Beth says.

"I realize that."

"So you should realize when to talk or not talk about my ass."

"There are times when I can't talk about your ass?"

"Sir," the bartender interrupts. "You know what you want yet?"

I place a ten-dollar bill on the bar top. "I guess make it two Butt Lights, then."

"Excuse me?" the bartender replies.

At some point over the last decade Bud Light eclipsed Miller Lite in popularity, which is unfortunate because Bud Light tastes like plastic and gives me diarrhea to the point where I've taken to calling it Butt Light. The joke escapes the bartender, but the allusion doesn't escape my wife.

"Bud Light is fine, and keep the change." I slide the ten-dollar bill across the bar. The bartender slides two amber bottles back at me.

I hand Beth hers. She sips the beer, nursing the bottle and her ass-driven self-esteem. "Anybody interesting on the walk-in list yet?"

"Chip Funke is here," I say. "You just have to get past his groupies."

"Really?" Beth says, starstruck.

I'm still amazed at Chip Funke's meteoric rise from McDonald's third shift manager to teenage weekend warrior to NASCAR phenom. For about eighty years Empire Ridge has been home to the limestone quarries that built the Empire State Building, the Pentagon, the Biltmore Estate, the St. Anthony Society Chapter House at Yale, the entire University of Chicago campus, and the Washington National Cathedral—and yet the city was finally put on the map because one of its citizens possessed a high aptitude for making left turns.

"Chip had to attend a friend's wedding in North Carolina this afternoon, but a friend of a friend of a friend told me he was going to bust his ass to get here."

"Not bad for the bandie who always talked about his go-karts."

"The what?" I say.

"Your words, not mine, when I said we should invite him to the reunion."

"I never called him that."

"You most certainly did call him that," Beth says. "I asked if you knew Chip Funke in high school, and you said that he was quiet, pretty much kept to himself."

"That's not the same as calling him a—"

"And then you added, 'I really just remember him as being a bandie who always talked about his go-karts.' "

"Fucking bandies."

"Wasn't your father a bandie?"

"Yeah," I say. "But Dad didn't cost me prom king."

"After ten years you're still sore about that?"

"I couldn't get the hood or bandie vote to save my fucking life."

"You're a pretty boy, Hank. Always have been, always will be."

"But I went to pig roasts, I got in fights with Prepsters for no reason. I had street cred."

"Street cred," a disembodied voice says from across the room. "That's fucking hilarious."

Like the parting of the Red Sea, the crowd separates, cleaved neatly in half by Elias Hatcher's booming voice.

"What's a guy got to do to get a ginger ale around here?" Hatch grabs me and Beth in a full bear hug. We haven't seen each other in four years. His cutlass bangs against my leg. I can feel his hardened, sinewy body underneath his Full Dress Navy Whites, and I'm more than a little envious.

"Nice uniform," I say.

"And how," Beth adds.

Hatch stands at attention, salutes. "Petty Officer Third Class Elias Hatcher at your service."

I grab Hatch by the shoulder. "Color me fucking impressed."

"But wait, there's more," Hatch says. "Claire, you can come out now."

The Hottest Girl I Never Tried to Sleep With comes around the corner. Beth screams, runs to Claire, and about knocks her over. They hug, scream a little more, make a couple quick excuses for why they haven't kept in touch.

Claire comes up to me, winks, and gives me a big kiss on the lips. "I've missed you, Hank."

Maybe it's because I'm standing in a room of former classmates whose bald heads and multiple chins don't seem to give a shit about life, but I think Claire looks better than she did in high school. A silver sequined cocktail dress accentuates legs I don't remember being that long and an ass that's as exactly as tight as I remember. I wink back, and I mean it. "Feeling's mutual, Claire."

"What the hell is that on your ring finger?" Beth says. "Is that what I think it is?"

Claire looks down at her left hand, smiles. "Yes, it is."

"We got hitched in Vegas last night," Hatch says.

Beth, Claire, and I have spent the last hour doing tequila shots. Not our best decision. I tried to talk Chip Funke into being our designated driver, but he said he needed to fly back that night to Charlotte. Something about wrecking his car in practice and being on "Bill Junior's shit list." Apparently Bill Junior is someone I should know, so I nodded and said,

"That's the last guy you want to piss off." I had Beth take at least five pictures of us together. I'm pretty sure I was a total ass.

Depeche Mode's "Somebody" starts playing on the dance floor.

"Where the hell is my husband?" Claire says.

"He's walking around being Hatch," I say. "You can take the guy out of Empire Ridge, but you can't take the Empire Ridge out of the guy."

"Still the social fucking butterfly, isn't he?"

"Always," I say.

"I love this song." Claire grabs my hand. "How about a twirl with the new bride?"

I look to Beth. She nods. "Go on. I'm in no shape to dance."

Claire and I are reasonably hip people. And given that we spent our formative years as drinking buddies in the late eighties and early nineties, it's written in stone that we must worship Depeche Mode. "Somebody" is an awkwardly intimate song, a point of fact I fail to remember until I get on the dance floor.

Claire runs her hands through my hair, because she's Claire. "You surprised?"

"That's an understatement. You and Hatch? When did it start?"

"About six months ago. I had a layover in Heathrow. Hatch was in London on leave. We kinda just hit it off."

"Kinda? What happened to Derek?"

"You know and I know he was never going to settle down."

"True. But Hatch?"

"What's wrong with Hatch?"

"Nothing. I just always thought of you two more as siblings than lovers."

"Me, too."

"Then what gives?"

"Things change. Feelings change. Plus, neither of us wants kids, and with him being a naval officer and me being a flight attendant, our hectic schedules just somehow fit together."

"That doesn't sound like love to me."

"It'll get there," Claire says. "I'm sure you know what I mean."

"No, I don't know what you mean."

"Don't play dumb with me, Hank. I remember that night at Mineshaft."

"I wondered how long you were going to hold that over me."

"Hold it over you? You know that's not my style."

"But Beth is your best friend."

"And so are you. I knew the day you two got engaged you weren't fucking ready. I figured you'd mess up along the way, but with a little luck you'd get there. Nobody's perfect, except for maybe your father."

The DJ grabs the microphone, stumbles through a contrived segue into Richard Marx's "Right Here Waiting." It's another overly personal love song, but Claire and I keep dancing, unfazed.

"Claire, my dad was far from per—"

"What's it been now, six years?"

"Seven years in October."

"I miss him, Hank."

"Take a number."

"I sense a little resentment. You okay?"

"My dad had his faults. Why can't people just love him without fucking canonizing him? Did you know he was a draft dodger?"

"What?"

"Back in the late sixties, Dad got his draft notice for Vietnam right after he and Mom got engaged. He ended up failing his physical for the military."

"Flat feet?" Claire looks down at my feet, remembering my own personal deformity.

"No, smart gal." I roll my eyes. "A hernia."

"Easily fixable."

"Exactly! But guess what? The government can't order you to have the surgery. Dad refused to get the operation until he was too old for the draft."

"So you have your dad's weak groin to thank for being alive?"

"I guess you could say that." I laugh, but only a little. I'm struck by the role Dad's balls have played in my life. A cough here, a snip there. Gaming the system. Learning how to be a man after someone has lost the instructions or else read them to you in fucking Spanish.

"Speaking of fathers, congratulations. Sasha, right?"

"That's right," I say. "Sasha Grace."

"Two years old?"

"Just turned three."

"Any sisters or brothers planned?"

"One or two more, depending on what Beth can handle. Sasha was a C-section."

"Ouch."

"And my wife might be the meanest pregnant woman on Earth."

"On behalf of all past, present, or future pregnant women, go suck a dick."

"I'm not kidding. Hitting, screaming, cursing—you name it. If my wife were a dude, I could've had her arrested."

"And yet you kept coming back for more."

"Of course I did."

"Why?"

"Because I love her, Claire."

"I can see that, Hank." A wistful, almost envious look from the ever-guarded Claire Sullivan Hatcher. She runs her hands through my hair again. "You're very sexy when you're in love—have I ever told you that?"

I smile at Claire. She positions herself closer to me, my knee now firmly between her legs. I place my hand on the small of her back, maybe even a little lower than that. Low enough to know she's not wearing any panties. If her hemline were any higher, my knee would be buried in her bush right now. Tanned a soft gold and rock-hard, Claire's calves flex with every step she makes.

Claire and I have always had great chemistry. But in lieu of attempting anything that could be deemed a relationship—sexual, casual, or otherwise—we long ago settled into a flirty but harmless cat-and-mouse game.

At least this is what I keep telling myself. What Claire and I engage in is definitely flirty, but hardly harmless. A failed relationship or lost love is a maypole of life, for a brief moment the absolute unyielding center of everything but in time dismissed as something not worth getting that excited about. Far harder to escape the semipermanent shadows of an affair that never was.

"Mind if we dance with yo' dates?"

The combination of the *Animal House* reference and Richard Marx giving way to Poison's "Every Rose Has Its Thorn" snaps me back to reality.

"What?" I say.

Hatch and Beth stand in front of us on the dance floor. "May we cut in?" Hatch says.

I step back, bow. "Be my guest."

Claire winks at me again. "Thanks for the dance, Hank."

Not only do I not wink back, I don't even make eye contact. "You're welcome."

Beth reclaims my empty hand. She straddles my leg, more obvious with her dry humping than Claire was, being my wife and all. "You two looked pretty cozy," she says.

"You know Claire is like a sister to me."

Beth shakes her head. "In West Virginia maybe."

"She's your best friend."

"That's never stopped her from hitting on my boyfriends—or my husband apparently."

"What do you want me to say, Beth?"

"How about 'I love you, honey'?"

"I love y—"

Beth puts her hand on my mouth. "It doesn't count if I have to prompt you."

I take her hand away. "It seems like it doesn't count regardless."

"And what's that supposed to mean?"

"It means that maybe I'd enjoy dancing with Claire a little less if you showed more interest in me."

"More interest? We had sex last night."

"Yeah, for the first time in eight weeks."

"I'm sorry. Apparently you've been living in a cave for the last three years. Have you seen my stomach? Ever since the C-section, my abs look like a fat old person's ass. I don't feel pretty."

"But you *are* pretty. You're fucking hot. We've had this conversation before. I'm a very vain guy. If you get ugly and fat, I'm divorcing you."

"You really know how to make a gal feel special, Hank."

"That's what you don't seem to get. You're still in twice as good a shape as almost any twenty-eight-year-old woman I know, let alone tonight's episode of *The Bald and the Bloated*."

"Except for Claire."

"Fuck Claire! She's got her high school body because she's never been pregnant, and she's too self-absorbed to ever get pregnant."

Beth leans in, kisses me on the lips. "You really think that?"

"Hell yes, I think that." I lick my lips, tasting both Claire's and Beth's lipstick on my tongue. I'm pretty fucking turned on right now.

"You're just buttering me up."

"No I'm not," I say. "The butter comes later tonight."

# Chapter 18

I hold my open hand in front of my dog's face. "Stay, Chief, stay."

Whatever else Chief has in him besides Labrador retriever—German shepherd, English setter, collie—all I know is genetics has conspired to make him one kick-ass dog. Chief is pushing four years old, in the prime of his life. It's hard to believe that my big, black bear of a dog was ever small, but he used to fit in the crook of my arm. His favorite place to sleep was on top of the air vent in the kitchen, which he barely covered even with his body fully extended. We took him to doggy daycare as a puppy. His favorite companions were a wolf hybrid and a Greater Swiss mountain dog, both twice his size, who always let Chief push them around.

Chief is a member of the family, and Sasha is the eternal object of his affection. When she passes by him, Chief never misses an opportunity to shellac her in the face with his oversized pink tongue. And whenever Sasha decides to stuff her hands in his feeding bowl while he's eating, Chief simply backs away and either waits until she's done or allows Sasha to hand-feed him one piece of kibble at a time.

Chief starts to move at the sound of the whistle. I raise my hand again, my eyebrows furrowed. "I said *stay*, dog!"

"You don't need to be so hard on him, Hank."

Jack is staying with me for the weekend while Mom is up in Indianapolis with Aunt Claudia getting all of Grandma Louise's affairs in order. Grandma died last week. I tried to cry at the funeral and play the part of the heartbroken grandson, but it's hard to get past the fact she was such a psychotic, racist bitch. Jeanine brought her fiancé, Marcus, to the funeral. They met in Portland when Jeanine was his physical therapist. Marcus is a professional basketball player for the Idaho Stampede of the Continental Basketball Association, and he's black as coal. Grandma would have hated him, and I loved Jeanine for bringing him.

With Beth and I working full-time, and Sasha taking up seemingly every other spare moment of our waking existence, Chief has been largely left on his own over the last year or so, and it's starting to show. He's tipping the scales at one hundred ten pounds, when he should be closer to eighty. He's pushing boundaries to get attention—eating shoes and cell phones, stealing food off the kitchen counter. He's partial to Oreos and entire loaves of bread, plastic wrap included.

I blame myself. I've started taking him to the park and running him through some of his old obedience training. It seems to center Chief, calm him down a little. Right now he's in a sit-stay position. Jack is tossing a tennis ball up in the air about ten yards away, purposely trying to make him break his position.

"This is so unfair," Jack says. "Why do you have to tease him like this?"

"I'm not teasing him."

"But look at him." Jack points at Chief's face. "He's sad."

"We've been over this before," I say. "Dogs aren't wired like people. They're dominant or submissive, not happy or sad. I'm Chief's pack leader, not his friend."

"But I thought you loved Chief?" Jack throws the tennis ball. Chief flinches but barely.

"Free dog!" I shout. Chief sprints after the ball. "I do love him. But it's not like what I feel for Beth or Sasha or . . ."

"Or Mom?"

"Or Mom," I repeat reluctantly.

"What's the difference?"

"The difference?"

"Between how you love Chief and how you love everybody else."

"Have you ever heard of the word anthropomorphizing?"

"Anthro*what*?"

I sometimes forget Jack is only ten years old. The circumstances of his birth and his life give him an old-soul quality, at least in my eyes. "Anthropomorphizing is when pet owners treat their dogs like people. They pretend dogs think and feel the same way people do. They love novels and movies in which dogs not only save Timmy from the well, they talk, crack jokes, are relentlessly ironic, and have extensive backgrounds in forensics. They obsess over dog food labels as if their wild canine cousins don't subsist on rotting deer entrails, and they dress their dogs in those gay outfits."

"Umm, Hank?"

I'm suddenly aware that I'm ranting and that Jack probably has no idea what I'm talking about. "Yeah, buddy?"

"You shouldn't say *gay*."

I shrug, angry at myself. Being Sasha's father comes naturally and effortlessly to me. My relationship with Jack is still uncomfortable, still forced—my sibling and paternal instincts always at a stand-off.

"You're right, Jack. Sorry about that."

"No big deal. I say it all the time at school and on the bus."

"Well, knock it off, okay?"

"Okay."

Chief brings me the tennis ball, soaked through with his salvia. I grab it from his mouth, throw it a good fifty yards.

"Nice throw," Jack says.

"Thanks."

"You have a pretty good arm for an old dude."

I stop walking, reach my arm across Jack's chest as if to stop him from falling forward. "An old dude? Just how old do you think I am?"

"Like fifty or something?"

"What?"

"Ha!" Jack smiles, points at me. "I totally got you."

"Yeah, Jack," I say. "You got me, all right."

We race back to the car. I let Jack win.

# Part IV
# 2000

# Chapter 19

Beth and I sit in Dr. Florio's office. My wife flips through the March 2000 issue of *Parents* magazine. She's uneasy, rifling through the pages without looking at them.

I grab her hands, take the magazine away. "Will you just relax, honey?"

She inhales deeply, turns and looks at me. "Bite me."

We're here for the eighteen-week ultrasound. This time around we're finding out the baby's gender—that is, if my wife doesn't have a heart attack in her OB's waiting room.

There's a lot riding on today's visit. One girl and one boy is the master plan. This pregnancy has no other option but a boy.

Our new gay neighbors, Oscar and Marshall, told us to load up on red meat and salty snacks and for me to pound a pot of coffee before sex to get the Y-chromosome sperms swimming faster. Beth's thong-wearing aerobics instructor with the store-bought breasts—I think her name is Shena, but I might just have Tone Loc's "Wild Thing" in my head—told her to have "as much sex as humanly possible" because more boys are conceived during the honeymoon phase of a relationship. Needless to say, I'm a fan of Shena. Beth's hairdresser, Jodi, told her to let me initiate sex and focus on my pleasure because "if the man climaxes first, you almost always conceive a baby boy." I like Jodi, too. She's a dishwater blonde with sky-blue eyes. She has a hot, older-woman look to her, like Julie Christie in *Afterglow*. A lot of people say if they had a time machine, they'd go back two-thousand years and meet Jesus Christ; personally, I'd just go back to 1965 and fuck Julie Christie. Jodi has been pumping out kids since her teens and sneaks out for smokes every fifteen minutes. When she washes my hair, it feels so good I almost think I'm cheating on my wife.

Putting aside our friends' learned advice, and Beth's father being a pediatrician and all, we've done our homework on this one. There are fifty-one boys born for every forty-nine girls, so we know math is on our side. We flirted with trying the Shettles Method, which mandates "deep, penetrative intercourse no more than twenty-four hours before ovulation and no more than twelve hours past ovulation." The Chinese Conception Method showed some promise, right up until we realized all our dates were wrong because we were using the Gregorian calendar instead of the Chinese lunisolar calendar. Ultimately we settled on the Whelan Method—i.e., having sex at the beginning of Beth's cycle up until four-to-six days before ovulation. Whelan doesn't specify the level of depth or penetration like Shettles does, so I improvised. (I've narrowed it down to somewhere between "fuck me harder" and "fuck, that hurts.") All I know is the Whelan Method involves more sex than most any other approach, so I'm willing to make the sacrifice—you know, for the children.

The door to the waiting room opens. A nearly attractive nurse with pinned-back hair and comfortable shoes holds a clipboard and smiles at us. "Mrs. Fitzpatrick?"

Dr. Florio smiles at my wife, her hand on her belly. "How you feeling, kiddo?"

"Not so good, to tell you the truth," Beth says. "I've had a lot more nausea and a lot less sleep with this pregnancy."

"Interesting." Dr. Florio squirts the ultrasound gel onto my wife's already bulging abdomen with her right hand, follows up with the transducer in her left hand. "Let's take a look, shall we?"

We eye the black and white sonogram. There's only so much you can see four and a half months into a pregnancy, at least that's what I remember with our daughter. With her translucent spine and huge head, Sasha looked more like a cross between a baby dinosaur and Patrick Ewing.

"Whoa!" I say. "That popped up fast."

We see the back of our baby. It turns. We see a beating heart.

"Hmmm . . ." Dr. Florio says.

Beth turns to her. "What?"

"Your husband was right. He did pop up fast."

"*He* popped up fast?" I say.

Dr. Florio points to the baby's now-obvious phallus. "Oh, he's definitely a boy."

Beth raises her hand. I give her a high five. She notices Dr. Florio's pensive look. "Is there something you're not telling us, doctor?"

"There's a reason he popped up fast," Dr. Florio says. "I'm going to turn the probe ninety degrees here and let you see for yourself."

"Holy shit," Beth says.

"What? What am I looking at?"

Dr. Florio adjusts the transducer. "You're looking at two heartbeats, Hank."

"Come again."

Beth puts her hand over her face. "I'm pregnant with twins, Hank."

"That's why you poked out so quick at eighteen weeks," Dr. Florio says. "That's why you're sicker and not sleeping compared to when you were carrying Sasha."

"It certainly explains a lot," Beth says. "I got the hormones of two boys raging inside me."

"Exactly," Dr. Florio says.

I shake my head. "Are you sure, doc?"

She points to the video monitor. "There are clearly two babies, kiddo. The second one is just lying across the bottom, hiding almost. And they both look to be boys."

"And this would explain the abnormalities in my AFP tests a couple weeks ago?" Beth asks.

Dr. Florio nods. "It totally explains it."

I have no idea what the hell "AFP" means, but I give a confident, affirmative nod as if everything in the world now makes sense. I'm only on page twenty of *What to Expect When You're Expecting*. My interest always starts to lag in the middle of the Fibroids section, and I completely jump ship at Incompetent Cervix.

My wife is crying.

"Beth," I say. "You okay, honey?"

"I'm fine. Just a little scared is all."

"These two boys look perfectly healthy, kiddo."

"It's not that, doctor," Beth says. "It's just that I've been reading up on vaginal births after a cesarean. I was really hoping with this pregnancy that I could, you know, at least try to . . ."

"VBACs aren't for everyone."

"I know that."

"Least of all gymnasts and their narrow pelvises."

"As you've told me before."

"Let's just cross that bridge when we come to it," I say, running my hand through my wife's hair and brushing her bangs back. I kiss her on the forehead. "You'll be fine. I promise."

# Chapter 20

"I hear congratulations are in order."

Lila Prestwich stands at the entrance to the College Avenue Press office. She's wearing tight jeans and a sleeveless knit top that barely contains her always-ample bosom. Her hair is cropped just below her chin, her olive skin giving off the somewhat off-putting black currant scent of Ralph Lauren Safari perfume. A printed tote with a Strand Bookstore logo hangs over her right shoulder.

I walk over to Lila. She gives me a casual hug. "How long have you been standing there?"

"Long enough," Lila says.

"So you heard that phone call?"

"Was that Beth?"

"More like her evil doppelganger."

"Trouble in paradise?"

"That's an understatement. I once told someone that my wife might be the meanest pregnant woman on Earth. I take that back—she *is* the meanest pregnant woman on Earth."

"Sorry to hear about that. Still, congrats. Twin boys, huh?"

"Who told you?"

"Your boss."

"Fucking Rosner. When was that?"

"It was when he was in New York last month. He came by my apartment and took me out to celebrate."

"Yeah, celebrate."

"*College Avenue Press, an imprint of the Random House Publishing Group.* That isn't worth celebrating?"

"It's just 'College Ave' now, per an edict from some marketing department idiot who thinks branding means anything in publishing."

"I like College Ave," Lila says.

"Whatever. Aaron took the money and ran. Meanwhile, I'm afforded a slightly bigger paycheck with a lot less editorial freedom. Forgive me if I don't join in the merriment. But enough about me. To what do I owe this visit?"

"Just flew in today. I wanted to stop in and say hello before I drove down to Empire Ridge."

"Well, hello."

Lila reaches out and gives me a much improved hug followed up with a kiss on the cheek. "Hello, Hank."

"Here, have a seat." I smile, offering her a chair. "How's New York treating you?"

"Best city in the world."

I sit in the chair opposite her. "Still working for that literary agency?"

"Not anymore. I took a job with Little, Brown and Company just last month. I'm their new director of foreign rights."

"Nice."

"It sounds nicer than it pays."

"And who's the lucky guy in your life these days?"

"Chris."

"Next time I'm in New York you should introduce me to him."

"I'll introduce you to *her* if you'd like."

"Come again?"

"Hank . . ." Lila says, patting my hand. "I'm a single Mormon woman pushing thirty. You figure it out."

"I guess I just never figured you for a—"

"Lesbian?"

"Yeah."

"Chris is the hardcore lesbian. I'm still solidly in the bisexual camp. We're living together in one of her father's brownstone rentals on the Upper Westside. She's the lead singer of an all-girl band called Femshack."

"How very New York of you."

Lila nods, raised her eyebrows. "Yeah, Dad is *really* pleased."

"How is Papa Prestwich doing these days?"

"You'd know better than me, Hank."

"I doubt it."

Actually, I do know better. Mom and Gillman Prestwich have been dating for six weeks. After Mom's rogues' gallery of suitors, I figure a guy who doesn't drink, doesn't swear, and goes to church too much is probably a safe option.

"They're so cute together, Hank."

"I'll take your word for it. Now, I'm assuming you didn't come here just to chat about the Odd Couple and tell me you've started playing for the other team."

"Astute observation as always." Lila reaches down into her shoulder bag, pulls out a manuscript. She hands me the tightly bound pages. The first page is blank. The second page has a W.B. Yeats quote from the poem "The Second Coming" that says,

*The darkness drops again; but now I know*
*That twenty centuries of stony sleep*
*were vexed to nightmare by a rocking cradle,*
*And what rough beast, its hour come round at last,*
*Slouches towards Bethlehem to be born?*

"What is this?" I say.

"It's my book."

"That thing you've been working on for like five years that you won't tell anyone about?"

"All one hundred and twenty thousand words of it. The working title is *The Messiah Project*."

"Quick synopsis?"

"It's a near-future dystopian novel that asks the question, What would happen if someone traveled back in time, obtained the genetic material of Jesus of Nazareth, came back to the future, and foisted the Second Coming on the world by creating a cloned Christ?"

"Holy shit, Lila. I love it! It's very commercial. Plus you have this great angle as this attractive, well-connected, fall-away Mormon. I assume your agent is sending it out to the big boys—Random House, Simon and Schuster, Penguin, or at least your own people at Little Brown."

"He wants to, but I don't know."

"Lila, come on now. Bunts aren't your style. You need to swing for the fences on this one, babe."

"I don't know."

"What's to know?"

"I feel like the big New York houses just aren't for me. I work for one, so I have a pretty good idea how much they suck. My book has to pique the interest of an editor, who then submits the manuscript to an ed board meeting in which a room full of editors with disparate literary tastes must somehow come to a consensus that the book is publishable by spending an hour vetting the author's platform and sixty seconds vetting the author's actual writing acumen."

"Sounds about right," I say. "At some point in the last ten years, the word 'platform' went from meaning 'a raised horizontal surface' to 'the degree to which one manages to blow smoke up an editor's ass.' "

"Exactly," Lila says. "Which is why I've been trying to focus on the midsized New York independents—Norton, Houghton Mifflin, Harcourt, Bloomsbury."

"And what's the word?"

"Most editors seem to enjoy the book, to a point."

"What point is that?"

"The point at which the protagonist obtains Jesus Christ's *genetic material*. I've been told the scene is somewhat blasphemous."

"Oh, come on, seventy-five percent of your editor friends are Jews. How bad can it be?"

"Let me preface this by saying the protagonist is a theoretical physicist and recovering crack addict who discovers time travel at about the same time she becomes a born-again Christian."

"I love her already."

"An angel visits our protagonist in her sleep and tells her she must travel back to ancient Jerusalem to procure the seed of the Son of David and bring it back to the future to fulfill the prophecy of the Messiah's return."

"Procure the seed?"

Lila nods, points at me. "That's the tricky part. She drugs Jesus and gives him a handjob."

"Why not go all the way and have her give him a blowjob?"

"Well, she starts off doing just that but is worried her saliva might taint the semen."

"Fantastic! What happens next?"

"She travels back to the future intent on inseminating herself with Jesus's sperm, only to misplace the sample at a local sperm bank, and then—"

"Madcap hilarity ensues from there?"

"More or less."

"And you're telling me no publisher will touch this?"

"Are you really surprised, Hank? This is the new millennium. Clinton is out, Dubya is in, and the publishers see the writing on the wall. Like Moses's golden calf, Christian fiction is a huge cash cow just waiting to be suckled."

"And imagery like that is exactly why you should have a publishing deal."

"Oh, I signed with a publisher," Lila says.

I scratch the winter stubble on my face. "Who is it?"

"I'm looking at him right now."

"Huh?"

"Aaron and I had two things to celebrate. He signed with Random House, and then he signed me as College Ave's newest author, with you as my editor."

I grab Lila's shoulders and squeeze her tight. I kiss her right on the lips. "Well, hot damn!"

Lila looks flustered, and she never looks flustered. "So you're okay with this?"

"Why wouldn't I be?"

"Well, Aaron and I kind of took the decision out of your hands."

"Lila, it's not like I don't know you're a good writer. I've been asking to see your stuff for years."

"And now you're going to see probably too much of it. Just promise me you'll be brutally honest."

"I have no intention of patronizing you. The first step in becoming a good writer is allowing people to tell you you're a bad one."

"That's a good line, Hank."

"That's a *great* fucking line. But I do have one condition."

"What's that?"

"Change your name and the title."

"My name?"

"Delilah Prestwich is a mouthful."

Lila smiles. "That's what she said."

"You know what I mean. Even Lila Prestwich is a little too, I don't know, stodgy."

"Stodgy?"

"Your book has time travel. It has a crackhead giving Jesus a handjob. You need something simpler, something bolder."

"What do you have in mind?"

"I was thinking something like D.D. Preston."

"I could live with that. Sounds sort of J.R.R. Tolkien or George R.R. Martin-ish."

"Exactly!"

"Okay then, so what's wrong with *The Messiah Project*? It's an allusion to the Manhattan Project."

"Yeah, I get that, which is kind of my point."

"And what is your point exactly?"

"The title isn't subtle enough. Leave the hitting-the-reader-over-the-head allusions to C.S. Lewis."

"Any suggestions?"

"Just one."

"Lay it on me."

"*Sperm Bank Messiah.*"

# Chapter 21

The moment we got back from Beth's OB with the news of the twins, I started running, and I haven't stopped. I don't know why I'm running: excitement, fear, uncertainty. I'm running five, seven, sometimes ten miles a day, six days a week. Chief, my tireless running partner, is back down to eighty pounds. I'm at one eighty-four, down from my wedding peak of two fifteen. My wife passed me on the scales this morning. At one eighty-five, Beth has packed on nearly sixty-five pounds during the pregnancy.

I sip my coffee. "Would you stop crying already?"

Sasha is still sleeping. Beth sits at the kitchen table. She's wearing my robe because her robe doesn't fit her anymore. Her hair is wound tightly on top of her head beneath a white cotton towel. She's been crying for about twenty minutes straight.

This is pretty much our standard third-trimester breakfast. This morning in bed, I came at Beth with my 6:00 a.m. erection, assumed the spoons position, and squeezed her milk-sodden circus boobs. She rejected my advances, and then I went into my commensurate emotional shell and ignored her as she tried to explain how her lack of a sex drive had nothing to do with her feelings for me. I went downstairs, put on some coffee, and masturbated to Internet porn, which afforded Beth just enough time to shower, look at herself in the mirror after getting out of the shower, and crank up the self-loathing.

While I'm on the subject of porn, I simply couldn't imagine being a teenager in the Internet age. Instant gratification with the click of a mouse: Holy hell, I would've been blind and dead by age sixteen. Barring a cooler older brother or an oblivious father with a hidden stash, porn in the eighties was acquired through a mix of subterfuge and raw tenacity. Even then, it usually amounted to only bad soft-core videos and ten-year-old hand-me-down magazines.

"Fuck you, Hank!"

"Is this still about your weight?"

"I'm heavier than you!"

"It's just a number."

"Husbands are supposed to be supportive."

"I'd like to think I'm doing a pretty good job at that."

"You're not supportive. You're fucking one eighty-four!"

I shake my head in disbelief. I run my hands through my hair. "That's what's bothering you? The fact I'm not a goateed, pinheaded lard ass like most of your friends' husbands? Go ahead, call up your gal pals. Ask them if their husbands make a pass at them every morning and night, even when they weigh a hundred and eighty-five pounds."

"Having the libido of a sixteen-year-old boy doesn't make you a good husband."

"But it doesn't me make a bad one either."

"I didn't say that."

"Maybe not in so many words. What do you want me to do, Beth? Do you want me to apologize for being attracted to you?"

"No."

"Then what?"

"I want you to apologize for not being my friend."

"Oh Christ."

"Wanting me is the easy part for you."

"I got a thing for my wife," I say, shrugging my shoulders. "Guilty as charged."

"It's *liking* me that you struggle with."

"Well, I'm sure struggling with liking you right now."

"Stop being so fucking glib."

"Glib? Is that what I'm being?" I stand up too quickly, knocking my chair to the floor. I lean toward my wife. "I was going more for pissed off."

Chief barks, running into the room. He growls, positions himself between me and Beth. He shows me his teeth, the hair on his back standing on end.

I'm being overly demonstrative in my movements toward my wife, and Chief has had enough. He usually doesn't have an aggressive bone in his body—that is, unless you mess with his pack, especially Beth and Sasha. It's like he just knows.

"Easy, boy," I say.

Beth pats him on the head, dabs her eyes dry with a tissue. "It's okay, Chiefy."

Chief stands down, starts to stroll back to his favorite spot on the entryway rug near the front door. He stops, turns his head, and looks at me over his shoulder. I swear he's leering at me. He is still one kick-ass dog.

I walk across the kitchen, place my empty coffee cup in the sink. I approach my wife, maintaining a passive stance. I touch her shoulder. "I'm sorry, honey."

Beth looks at my hand, then down at the table. "Do you even know what you're apologizing for?"

I remove my hand from her shoulder. "Not a clue."

"Then why apologize?"

"Because I rarely know what I'm apologizing for."

"Fuck you, asshole!"

I step back, turn on my heel. The kitchen opens up to the family room. I walk to the side table along the far wall of the family room, grab the dog-eared copy of *What to Expect When You're Expecting*. I walk back to the kitchen, open the book, and slam it down in front of my wife.

"Show me," I say.

"What?"

"Just show me, Beth."

"I don't know what you want me to—"

"Maybe I missed a section. Maybe somewhere between gastrointestinal ills, rubella, toxoplasmosis, cytomegalovirus, fifth disease, group B strep, Lyme disease, measles, UTI, hepatitis, mumps, and chicken pox, I missed the part about abusive wife syndrome."

Beth is crying again. "Y-you just recited those diseases off the top of your head?"

"Of course I did." I grab my coat off the coat tree in the hallway leading to the garage door. The coat is an olive double-breasted London Fog trench that used to belong to my father. It's a little dated, but I'll wear it forever.

"How did you know all of them?"

"Because I read the goddamn book," I say, buttoning my coat. "Chapter fifteen lists all the shit that can go wrong with your body during pregnancy."

"But why did you read it?" Beth says.

I open the door to the garage. I turn to my wife. "I read it because you're my friend, because I like you." I turn away from her. I walk out into the garage, shutting the door behind without waiting for a response.

# Chapter 22

Mom is married again.

She and Gillman Prestwich dated for a whole twelve weeks before eloping. They got married in Nauvoo, Illinois, which I'm told holds some sort of sacred significance to Mormons, but to Mom's credit, she refuses to convert. Once a Catholic, always a Catholic, I guess, although I'm not allowed to swear or bring alcohol into her house.

Son of a bitch, that really fucking sucks a goddamn ass-ramming moose cock.

*Phew.* I feel better now.

# Chapter 23

>Basic Search
>>First Name
>>**Angelina**
>>Last Name
>>**Valerio**
>>City or ZIP/Postal
>>**Boston**
>>State/Prov
>>**MA**

What the fuck am I doing?

I've considered a lot of reasons as to why I've decided to contact my Spring Break '91 fling—the most meteorically intense but brief love of my life and, in fact, the only other woman besides Beth I had ever considered marrying—when my wife is nearly nine months pregnant with twins. Being in a sexless, emotionally abusive marriage for the last six months might have something to do with it, but the reason I seem to have settled on is actually a rhetorical question: What's wrong with a guy on the cusp of being a father again taking stock of his past and wanting closure with someone who used to be important to him? And by rhetorical, I mean I don't want anyone to answer that question, because the obvious answer is nothing's wrong with that if you're an insensitive douche pump.

"What are you doing, Hank?"

"Nothing, Urwa."

Urwa Mashwanis is College Ave's silver-haired, middle-aged Pakistani IT director. He's a nice guy, annoying as hell but forever well-intentioned. He constantly and too often graphically whines about his marital woes, a typical conversation with him going something like this: "How's Beth doing with her pregnancy? My wife put on a hundred pounds with our baby and never lost it, and now she refuses to have sex in the missionary position. Only doggie, only doggie. She doesn't even like the cunny-lingus. You want to grab lunch?"

Urwa looks at the top of my computer screen, reading aloud. "Whitepages.com? Who you looking for?"

"Nobody."

"Angelina Valerio doesn't sound like nobody to me."

Aaron Rosner tends to err on the side of apocalyptic—maybe it's a Jewish thing—so in anticipation of Y2K, he hired Urwa away from Eli Lilly's patent division for twice the salary. Predictably, Y2K amounted to a whole lot of nothing, but Urwa was retained at the same level of compensation. This pisses me off a little. While, yes, my family's seven-figure settlement with the Indianapolis Auto Auction has paid for three cars and half the mortgage on a quarter-million-dollar house, my actual salary still skirts IRS tax brackets with the reckless abandon of someone who, minus a dead father, would be flirting with abject poverty.

"You want to grab some lunch?"

"We've been through this before, Urwa. You don't eat lunch."

"Sure I do. Large fries. Best deal in town."

Urwa insists that the $1.75 the MCL Cafeteria down the street charges for a Styrofoam box filled to the rim with French fries is the steal of the century. "I figure I get about a thousand calories for less than two bucks," he is fond of saying.

I just need to stop arguing with Urwa and let the potato-addicted Pakistani face his maker—probably sooner than he's likely anticipating—on his own grease-laden terms. "Fine, Urwa, eat your damn fries."

"You still haven't answered my question."

"What question?"

Urwa points at my computer monitor. "Who's Angelina Valerio?"

"She's nobody."

"She's not nobody. I've seen the letters you typed to her."

"How about you get back to your desk and mind your own business? It wasn't multiple letters. There was just one."

"I counted at least four."

"Damn, Urwa," I say. "You are one nosy fucking Pakistani. There was only one letter. I sent copies of the same letter to four different people."

"Oh," Urwa says. "Why did you do that?"

"Angelina Valerio is an old friend who I lost track of is all."

"Friend?"

"Fine, an old *girl*friend. Beth and I have had a rough go of things the last couple months."

"Beth's body is going through lots of changes," Urwa says, empathetic apparently as long as it doesn't involve the prohibition of missionary sex and the cunny-lingus.

"Don't you think I know that?" I say. "It's not like I'm going to do anything stupid. I'm just real lonely and want to talk to an old friend. I've spent the last three weeks searching the Internet for any Angelina Valerios along the East Coast."

"The East Coast?"

"Angelina was from Boston."

"Got it."

"I found four Angelina Valerios in the greater Boston area and sent four duplicate letters out to these women."

"What if they call you back and Beth answers the phone?"

"Won't happen."

"How do you know?"

"I listed my office phone number and office return address on the letters."

"Smart thinking."

"I thought so."

"Deceitful thinking, but smart thinking."

"You can shut up and listen to my story, or you can be an asshole. Your choice."

"Sorry," Urwa says. "Go on."

"Three of these Angelina Valerios have returned my call, all of them telling me the same exact thing—'I'm not the Angelina you're looking for, but your letter was so beautiful I wish I was her.'"

"Some letter I take it."

"I thought so."

My phone rings. The caller ID on the phone flashes *Out of Area*.

"You going to answer that?"

"Nope," I say. "Probably just Cindy again."

"Aaron's former secretary?"

"Admin assistant," I say. "And yes."

"I thought Aaron fired her."

"He did."

"She still calls you a lot."

"That's because she still wants my dick."

"You have a highly inflated opinion of yourself, Hank."

"That's a fair comment," I say. "But in this case I'm not exaggerating. Remember when Aaron, Cindy, and I went to that Canadian bookseller convention in Windsor?"

"Vaguely."

"Well, the three of us went out on the town one night. We ended up at Jason's."

"Jason's?"

"A famous high-end strip club."

Urwah's face practically lights up. "Continue," he says.

"Cindy had never been to one, so we took her. She got really drunk."

"*Really* drunk?"

"Really drunk."

"What happened?"

"Aaron disappeared into one of the back rooms with three girls and a wad of hundred dollar bills, so Cindy and I took a cab back to the hotel. The moment we got back, Cindy stuck her tongue in my ear in the elevator, told me she was going to her room to draw a bath, and asked me to join her."

"So she didn't really come right out and say she wanted your dick."

I shake my head. "You're right, Urwa. She didn't say that. I guess she could have just been implying that my personal hygiene left something to be desired and that in the interest of being environmentally conscious we do some innocent tandem bathing."

The phone starts ringing again. Again the caller ID flashes *Out of Area*.

"Just pick it up, Hank."

"Fine," I say. I pick up the phone. "Hello, this is Hank."

"Hank Fitzpatrick?"

"Yes."

"Hank, how ah yuh?"

My chest hurts. Hearing that deep Boston inflection for the first time in nine years makes me dizzy, short of breath.

"Angelina?"

"You muss think I'm so wid callin' yuh like this."

"Weird?" I say. "I'm the one who wrote a letter and mailed it to four random Angelina Valerios in the greater Boston area."

"Foh-uh?"

"Yeah, Angelina." I close my eyes and smile, inhaling the memories. "Foh-uh."

"Yuh always knew how to sweep a gal off huh feet."

Urwah hovers over my desk. "Angelina, can I put you on hold for just one second?"

"Shu-uh."

I stare down Urwah. "What?" he says.

"Aaron coming in at all today?"

"Not that I'm aware of," Urwah says.

"I'm taking this in Aaron's office."

He swats his hand at me. "You're no fun."

# Chapter 24

*"Welcome to Indianapolis International Airport."*

I make my way through security to the Delta terminal. I take a peek at the arrivals listed on the video screen. Her plane landed at Gate A7 ten minutes ago.

*"Smoking is prohibited in the main concourse of Indianapolis International and is restricted to designated smoking areas."*

The automated voice over the PA sounds strangely familiar, but I'm too nervous to think about that right now.

*"I'd be nervous, too, if I were you."*

"Who said that?" I say, turning around. People are staring at me.

*"I think you know who this is, Hank."*

"Jesus?"

*"It's been a while. How about we go somewhere a little quieter so all these nice people don't get freaked out by the guy talking to himself?"*

I hold my cell phone up to my mouth. "I'll just pretend I'm talking to someone on the other end of the line."

*"Suit yourself. Before I forget, what's with that book Lila is writing?"*

"*Sperm Bank Messiah*?"

*"Yes. You really make it hard for me to like you sometimes."*

"Sounds like somebody needs to reread his Sermon on the Mount."

*"Don't throw that back in my face."*

"Hey, you're the pacifist."

*"What are you doing here, Hank?"*

"Relax, Jesus. Angelina has a short layover in Indy on her way to see some old college friends down in Tallahassee. She's here for an hour, and we're just having a coffee."

*"Boston to Tallahassee by way of Indianapolis? Help me out with that one."*

"It was like two hours out of her way, and we wanted to catch up."

*"And your nearly nine-months pregnant wife knows about this?"*

"I'm not hurting anyone."

*"Keep telling yourself that."*

"Look, these last few months with Beth have sucked. I don't have anything to feel guilty about."

*"You apparently feel guilty enough to imagine your conscience as the voice of Jesus Christ who's talking to you from the airport PA system although curiously no one else can hear me."*

"Hank, izzat you?"

"Uh, I gotta go." I hang up my phone.

Angelina drops her purse, runs over, and hugs me as if we just said goodbye yesterday as opposed to nine years ago. She steps back, smiles. "Look at yuh, Hank. Yuh haven't aged a day. Yuh might even be a little skinny-uh."

I smile as I listen to the *R* disappear off the end of her words. "I've been running lately."

"It shows."

"You're not so bad yourself." I wish I was just being nice, just as a part of me wished on the drive up here from Empire Ridge that Angelina had let herself go. I'm convinced the two main reasons old flames are rarely rekindled are time and gravity. The passage of years makes you forget why that beautiful young woman was special, while gravity conspires with bad eating habits and a sedentary middle-age lifestyle to distort her figure until you start believing she never was.

None of this has happened with Angelina Valerio. With the exception of some faint crow's-feet, she's still a knockout. Her hair is dark brown, nearly black. She's petite but not rail-thin, reminding me vaguely of Cynthia Gibb, Rob Lowe's love interest in *Youngblood,* but more reminiscent of Lisa Dean Ryan, aka Doogie Howser's high school sweetheart, Wanda.

"Want to grab a coffee?" I say.

Angelina looks at her watch. "I only have about forty-five minutes. How's about a Bloody Mary?"

"Twist my arm."

We sit down at the bar. We both order our Bloody Marys extra spicy.

Angelina clinks my glass. "Chih-uhs."

"Cheers," I reply.

And just like that, the forty-five minutes is over. We talked about our lives since we said our goodbyes. About how Dad died. About how she was my last girlfriend who really knew my father and that this fact had always stuck with me. She told me she'd saved every one of the letters and poems I wrote her in a shoebox beneath her bed. She told me she's been celibate for the better part of the last eight years for reasons I couldn't quite understand, but that now she was "in-tuh dudes again" and engaged to a "Bah-stun cahp." She told me about her fiancé. I told her about Beth, Sasha, and the twins.

I escort Angelina back to her gate. She leans in and hugs me again, kissing me on the cheek.

"You know, Hank, yo-uh writing still makes me cry."

"What part?" I say, always a sucker for validation.

"All of it." Angelina reaches into her purse and pulls out my letter. "'As I stand once mo-uh on the vudge of fathuhood, about to again become that which I miss so much in my life, I want to find closhuh with someone who was once close to my haht, someone who knew me as just the fehlessly precocious son of Hank Fitzpatrick, and not the flawed, insuhcuh man I've become.'"

"Did I write that?"

"Don't be so modest. Yo-uh one in a million, Hank. Yo-uh the one that got away."

"Right back at you, Angelina. But I have to say the new guy sounds like good people."

"Uh, yeah, Hank. He's good people."

We giggle, acknowledging a moment from our shared past. Myrtle Beach in just the early cusp of spring. Air temperatures still dropping into the thirties after the sun goes down. We ran naked out of the ice-cold ocean, and I gave her my towel even though I had lost all sensation in my extremities. As we warmed up in the hot tub, she kissed my shivering, purple lips and said, "Yo-uh good people, Hank." Never hearing this phrase before in my life, I of course looked around to see if my family had magically teleported into the tub with me.

"I read him yo-uh lettuh, you know," Angelina says. "Pulled out the shoe baw-ux and read a couple of 'em."

"Really?"

"Yo-uh not mad, ah yuh?"

"No, no," I say. "Not at all."

"You shuh-uh?"

"Yeah, I'm sure."

"Well, okay then. Call me outta the blue and let's do this again sometime."

"Sounds like a plan," I say.

I kiss Angelina on the cheek and watch her board the plane. The tone of our goodbye is too casual, both of us pretending like we'd talk again, maybe as soon as tomorrow. But I know better. As happy as I was for these forty-five minutes, this is all I'm entitled to. Angelina is like the autographed Notre Dame football I keep on my mantel—unblemished, tanned and oiled to a bright sheen, perfect. Never to fade in the sun. Never to be left out in the rain. Never to be thrown and bounced off blacktop until its dimples wore smooth. Never to be touched. Never to be carried to bed under the arm of an adoring child who dreamt of being the next Joe Montana.

Huh. Go figure.

I'm not jealous. I don't love Angelina Valerio, or even the idea of her.

*Making Out with Blowfish*

As it turns out, I'm still very much in love with my wife.

In all honesty, Beth probably doesn't give a fuck either way at that moment. Regardless of my long-overdue epiphany, she's two weeks from praying that modern medicine finds a way to stuff two watermelons inside her husband's bladder and make him shoot them out the end of his penis.

# Part V
# 2001-2002

# Chapter 25

Aisha adjusted the turban wound tightly to her head, her long hair bound up and dripping rivulets of sweat down the small of her back. She pulled the rough excess of her collar over her face, trying to shield herself from the drifting sand. The fake beard only added to her discomfort.

Sand snuck into the folds and various openings of her drafty garment—little more than a burlap toga, tied at the waist by a rope. It had been a birthday gift from her sister, years ago, back when their parents thought they were merely recreational hookah users and not the biggest marijuana dealers in Dearborn, Michigan. Aisha was happy she wore the thing, actually. She was far from home, in need of a touchstone.

She was six months clean, not that this helped her gain her bearings. It was just after daybreak. Strangers passed her on the streets of Jerusalem. A steady stream of Pesach pilgrims filtered into the city. A merchant towing along a caravan of camels laden with spices, fabrics, and dried figs. A peasant driving a small, curiously stoic flock of sheep—too hardy to die, too lean to ever make a profit. Three women balancing atop their heads baskets of donkey and camel dung to be later used as fuel for fires. Aisha rubbed shoulders with strangers dead two-thousand years in her world: Sadducees, Pharisees, Phoenicians, Babylonians, Arabians, Roman soldiers, tax collectors, merchants, craftsmen, peasants, beggars, slaves. Aramaic, Hebrew, Greek, and Latin were spoken intermittently, mixing in her head and rendering translation difficult.

While pursuing her doctorate in theoretical physics, Aisha had befriended an exiled seminarian—exiled presumably for being too deist and too heterosexual—who tutored her in Greek and was familiar with the colloquial, first-century dialect. In exchange for Ecstasy-fueled, exceedingly non-missionary sex, Aisha had mastered the language from the modern Greek all the way back to Mycenaean, plus a little Aramaic, Hebrew, and Latin.

The smell of incense, the sound of trumpets and Psalms, the oxen, sheep, kids, and doves being sold for sacrifice. All carried with them a poignancy she had never felt. The sun danced over the Mount of Olives, brighter than any sun she had ever seen. The Antonia Fortress and Herod's Temple veiled most of the city in their imposing shadows. Aisha reached down, pulling a weed from the ground outside the abandoned amphitheater. She smelled the weed, inhaling deeply and imagining troupes performing Homer, Aeschylus, Sophocles, or perhaps another even greater Greek tragedian history had forgotten. Two Jewish rabbis cursed at her in Hebrew, remembering the theater's more sinister raison d'être as a gladiatorial killing field for thousands of pious men.

"Shabot shalom," she said to them in a plaintive but consciously masculine tone.

Aisha made her way to the western edge of the city, keeping to herself as the day progressed. After the encounter with the rabbis she spoke aloud only once to buy a loaf of bread and some pressed olives. She waited outside Herod's palace for her cue from the Roman soldier. He was a handsome man, a well-muscled legionnaire in his early twenties with medium-length hair that curled out from under his helmet. His armor comprised overlapping strips of iron that hugged his torso in two halves and fastened on the front and back by a system of brass hooks and leather laces. He carried a shield and a short sword.

Late last night Aisha had bribed him with several gold pieces and a handjob. She needed the practice. The legionnaire unlocked the palace gate and walked away.

She checked inside her hip pocket for at least the tenth time in as many minutes. Everything was still there: the half-dozen empty vials, the cryoprotectant semen extender, the plastic gloves, the small bottle of mead laced with roofies. A hundred yards down the corridor, He sat in His prison cell . . .

I stack the pages neatly on my desk. Trimmed down from one hundred and twenty thousand words to an even seventy-five thousand, *Sperm Bank Messiah* has taken up most of my professional time these last few months. I'm late for my twin boys' first birthday party today. I assume Beth will understand, just like Beth assumes it's perfectly normal for a couple married seven years to have sex once every two months.

"Very nice," I say.

I can hear Lila breathing on the other end of the speakerphone. "You think?" she says.

"Yeah, I do. You have a way with character and setting. I felt like I had a front-row seat to Passover in ancient Jerusalem. Obviously, the handjob scene with Jesus needs some more work."

"Agreed, but the general setup is better?"

"Yeah, more or less."

"What do you mean by that?"

"I'm still torn overall on Aisha."

"But I thought you were into exotic olive-skinned women."

"That's beside the point," I say, trying not to smile or picture my stepsister in a peach negligee—failing at both. "Why did you give your protagonist, who's supposed to be a born-again Christian, an Islamic name?"

"Truthfully?" Lila says.

"No, just make something up. Yes, truthfully."

"I wanted to piss off all those misogynist fuckers in the Middle East."

"Okay, I'll buy that. But you couldn't come up with a better name than Aisha?"

"What's wrong with Aisha?"

"It makes me think of little black kids doing the running man in single-strap airbrushed overalls."

"Come again?"

"You know, Another Bad Creation, aka the boy band ABC? *Iesha, you are the girl that I neva had, and I want to get to know you bettah!*"

"Still nothing."

"You disappoint me, Lila."

"My profuse apologies, but other than my protagonist reminding you of early nineties hip-hop artists, what else don't you like?"

"Your setting."

"What's wrong with Indianapolis? You love Indy."

"If you want this book to make any kind of commercial or critical splash, at least move Aisha out of the Midwest."

"Why?"

"Because unless you're Jonathan Franzen or Jeffrey Eugenides, the Midwest just doesn't sell. It's the *Saved by the Bell* factor."

"The *what*?"

"The *Saved by the Bell* factor. Ever watch those old reruns of *Saved by the Bell*?"

"No, not really."

"Come on now, Lila. Either you have or you're lying to me. It's fucking *Saved by the Bell*."

"Okay, I've seen a few episodes."

"A few episodes?"

"And by that I mean every episode at least four times over. I guess I was just hoping we had reached our nostalgia quota with Another Bad Creation."

"That's better," I say. "You remember the first season?"

"Barely. It's been a while."

"The series actually debuted on the Disney Channel in 1988 under a different title, *Good Morning, Miss Bliss*. The focal point was Miss Bliss as opposed to the students, and the setting was John F. Kennedy Junior High School in Indianapolis, Indiana. After one season, the show was retooled as *Saved by the Bell* and quietly relocated to Los Angeles and the now-familiar

Bayside High School. The acting never got better. The stories never got better. There was always the laugh track and predictable 'ooos' and 'ahhhs' whenever Zack and Kelly kissed. But that one small tweak to the setting made a horrible show legendary."

"Well . . ." Lila says, clearly unimpressed. "That's sixty seconds of my life I'm never getting back."

"What do you mean?"

"I like the Midwest, Hank. It has an everyman quality that readers can relate to—like John Hughes's Illinois and Judd Apatow's Michigan."

"Readers don't want to relate anymore, they want to escape. Why the hell do you think *Freaks and Geeks* got cancelled after one season? Not to mention you have the critics to think about. And there's only one surefire setting for the preening literati."

"Cue the New York rant."

"It's been that way since Nick Carraway partied with Jay Gatsby in West Egg, and you know it, Lila. You make Aisha a Manhattanite, and critics will eat that shit up."

"How about Brooklyn?"

"Even better. Hell, go for the jugular and put her in Williamsburg, Bed-Stuy, or Dumbo—the more indie you can make the setting the better. And if you're thinking about working in a Midwest anecdote about basketball, change it to something completely esoteric that nobody west of the Hudson gives a shit about, like cricket or cribbage."

"What's cribbage?"

"My point exactly. And if you can get a critic thinking that only he will get your references, that's a guaranteed rave review."

"And by rave review you mean three pages of a pseudo-literary celebrity showing off before spending maybe three sentences actually talking about my book?"

I stand, grabbing my sport coat off the back of my chair. I extend my arms through my coat sleeves. "Is there any other kind of rave review?"

"You got somewhere to be?" Lila says from seven-hundred miles away, ever the prescient one.

"It's the twins' birthday."

"Give Burke and Johnny a kiss from their Aunt Lila."

"Give Chris a kiss from your brother Hank."

"Behave," Lila says. "Although Chis and I aren't really what I'd call 'a couple' at the moment."

"Trouble in paradise?"

"Trouble in paradise, trouble everywhere. I feel like I've lost control."

"I'm guessing a lot of people in New York don't feel like they have control over much of anything right now."

I can hear Lila start to tear up. She blows her nose into the phone. "It's been eight weeks since the towers fell, Hank. Eight weeks! And you can still smell it on the streets, on your clothes, on your soul. The city is just so . . . sad."

"Hang in there, Lila. My recommendation for you and Chris would be not to do anything rash."

"Are you my editor or my therapist?"

"Depends."

"On what?"

"Will you let me flirt with you or keep playing that stupid sister card?"

"Go to your boys' party, Hank."

The phone line goes dead, and I'm a little sad not to hear Lila's voice anymore.

# Chapter 26

Principal Denise Lobrano runs through the afternoon announcements at St. Benjamin Catholic School. She leads the school in a closing Hail Mary. I can hear the pious mumble of the two hundred or so students echoing her prayer down the musty hallway of 1970s carpet and 1870s ideals. She motions for Jack and me to enter her office.
"Good afternoon, Principal Lobrano," I say, shaking her hand.
"Please, Mr. Fitzpatrick, call me Denise."
Jack's principal is an obvious gym rat. She's in her forties and has that overly fit, emaciated look that belies her femininity: almost perfect half-spheres for breasts poking from a striated overly tanned chest, hollowed-out cheek bones, arms so lean I can make out every veined curve of her triceps and biceps. If her muscle tone was just a shade softer, she'd be hot. As it is, much like Demi Moore, Madonna, and the female cast of *Friends,* she's let her fear of aging scare her into looking like a starving triathlete.
"Okay, Denise," I say, trying not to ignore the painful, bony firmness of her handshake. "But only if you call me Hank."
"Deal," Denise says. She motions to the two curiously out of place floral-print wingback chairs across from her desk. "Please, have a seat."
"Look, I'm sorry our mother couldn't be here today."
"A belated honeymoon, I hear?"
"So she tells me."
"No big deal," Denise says. "You're listed as his emergency contact anyway. Quite a gap in age between you two."
Jack joins in on the conversation. "Eighteen years."
"He could be your father," Denise says.
"Wish he was."
"No you don't, little brother." I pause to quietly note the irony. I feel like my inflection on *little brother* was a little too loud and compensatory. How great would it be if I just ended the ruse here, Jack? Sitting in a floral-print wingback chair in your principal's office.
"You'd be better than Gillman," Jack says.

"That's not exactly a high bar you're setting there."

My brother—at least for a little while longer—can't help but chuckle. Once again, I've lived to fight another day.

"Hank," Denise says. "I don't mean to interrupt, but this is a fairly routine disciplinary issue. I'd like to get you in and out of here as painlessly as possible."

"Disciplinary?"

"Yes. See, the seventh graders went on a field trip up to the International Festival at the Indianapolis Convention Center today."

"I ate baklava for the first time," Jack chimes in again.

"Did you like it?" I say.

He shrugs his shoulders. "Not really. Too dry."

Denise sighs, shuffling her papers. "Jack, can you wait outside in the administration office lounge?"

"Be glad to." He gets up, leaves the office. I try to pretend I don't see him winking at me.

Denise closes the door and turns to me. "I didn't want to embarrass him, Hank."

"Uh-oh," I say. "This is going to be interesting."

"Apparently, Jack bought one of those water wiggler toys at the festival."

"Water wigglers?"

"They're those trick hoses filled with gel that are hard to hold on to because they keep rolling in on themselves."

"Oh yeah, I know what you're talking about. They kind of look like an artificial, uhhh, vagi—"

"Let's just say sex toy."

"Yes, let's say that. What was he doing with it?"

"He was in the hallway outside Mr. Winsome's seventh-period history class simulating, uhhh . . ."

"Masturbation?"

"Among other things, yes."

"I'll talk to him. What's the damage?"

"A slap on the wrist. Jack's a good kid. We've confiscated the item, and he'll have a week's detention."

"That's fair," I say, standing up. "Is there anything else you need from me?"

"Just keep an eye on your little brother. He seems lost."

"Thanks, Denise. Would I be a bad role model if I said, 'That makes two of us'?"

"Nah, Hank. You'd just be human."

I say my goodbyes to Denise. Jack is sitting in the administration office waiting room flirting with a redhead. And she's cute.

"Who's your friend?" I say.

"Oh, uh, this is, uhhh . . ."

The redhead offers me her hand. "My name is Brooke, Mr. Fitzpatrick."

"Please, Brooke." I shake her hand. "Mr. Hank, or just Hank, is fine."
She starts to back out of the room. "Anyway, call me, Jack?"
Jack nods. "Yeah, sure."
"Great," Brooke says, blushing. "Nice to meet you, Mr. Hank."
"Same here, Brooke."
I smack Jack on the shoulder. "Not bad."
"Shut up, Hank."
"Just teasing you, buddy. Let's get out of here."
Jack stands up from his chair. "How bad is it?"
"Detention for a week. You're lucky."
"You going to tell Mom?"
"Nope," I say. We walk down the hall to the front doors of the school. I open one of the doors, and we walk outside. "I have a better idea."
"What's that?"
"Let's leave the car here and take a walk."
"Where?"
"Home."
"But that's like three miles."
"And I feel like we're going to need all three of them."

We're about a mile from the school when I summon enough courage to broach *the* subject. "Okay Jack, let's do this. Has Mom ever had the talk with you?"
"What talk?"
"You know, the sex talk."
"Hell no!"
"What about Gillman?"
"Gillman needs to have the sex talk with himself."
"Good point, but all joking aside, have you ever talked with anyone about, you know, sex?"
"I had sex ed last year and the year before that, in fifth and sixth grade. I know how to do it."
"That's not what I asked. Have you ever sat down and talked with anyone about any questions you might have?"
"Questions? What kind of questions?"
"Anything," I say. "If you want to ask something, ask me. That's what I'm here for."
"Hank, this is really weird."
"We could always go back and have this chat with Principal Lobrano if that would make you feel more comfortable."
"Hell no!"
"Then talk to me. If my twelve-year-old brother gets caught simulating masturbation with a sex toy, I'm thinking he has some issues."
"I don't have issues."
"Are you masturbating?"

"Hank, shut up!"

"Well, are you?"

Even though we're at least a dozen blocks from school, Jack still looks around as if to make sure no one can hear him. "Yes, I masturbate."

"Good."

"Good?"

"Don't believe anything people tell you about the evils of masturbation—Mom, Gillman, Father Liam, or for that matter, anyone at St. Benjamin. It's going to keep you sane. Did you know that masturbating five times or more a week reduces your chances of getting prostate cancer by thirty percent?"

"Looks like I'm probably not getting prostate cancer, then."

"That's the spirit," I say. "When you can't stop thinking about a girl, masturbate. When you can't stop thinking about what you want to do with that girl, masturbate. If you're upset, if you can't concentrate, if you're anxious, if you're depressed, if you can't sleep . . ."

"Masturbate?"

"Exactly!"

"This is officially the grossest sex talk ever."

I haven't even skimmed the surface of gross, but I'll keep that to myself. I still remember the first time I masturbated. It took me three nights to muster the courage to go through with it. The first two nights, I would get just to the precipice of my climax and then chicken out because of the cramping. For a forty-eight hour period, I almost convinced myself masturbating *was* evil, otherwise why would it hurt so much? On that third night, I brought the album cover of *Exotic Music of the Belly Dancer* into my bedroom. I propped up the faceless beauty on my bed with two pillows and stood over her. The overhead lights cast a glare on her breasts, so I turned them off and used my desk lamp. I had planned on using Kleenex so I could flush the evidence, but the toilet paper was too rough, so I used the legs of my old teddy bear. I can still picture the teddy bear riding my cock and my ejaculate covering his face.

"Jack . . ." I say. "You have no idea what gross is."

"I bet I do."

"I bet you don't. But the bottom line is, don't be afraid of yourself, of what you're feeling. Masturbate as much as you want, and if you have any questions, just ask me."

"Really?" Jack looks around again, still convinced someone is eavesdropping. "Anything?"

"Yes, please. What are kids your age into these days?"

"Well, I haven't had sex, if that's what you're fishing for."

"You're twelve, Jack, so I'd hope not."

"You'd be surprised with what's going on with kids my age."

"Really?"

"Well, maybe not at St. Benjamin. But I hear stories, you know, about what they do at the junior high."

Ah yes, the dark specter of public schools. I'm guessing the stories Jack hears are overblown, if not complete bullshit. Vilifying public schools and their demonic minions is a time-honored Catholic school tradition. I think back to my parochial schooling, back to those Monday mornings we'd come into class and everyone would open their desks and summarily claim all their pencils had been stolen. They hadn't been stolen, of course, but we all knew the CCD kids had been in our classroom for Sunday school. CCD, aka the Confraternity of Christian Doctrine, or simply "Catechism," as it's more commonly called today, is the religious education program provided to kids who don't attend Catholic schools. In my childhood, CCD was basically the mark of Cain. It meant your parents were too poor to send you to Catholic school, and so you couldn't help it that you were a pencil thief or that you never showered, which was why our classroom stunk only on Monday mornings. Curiously enough, I don't recall any priests, nuns, or teachers trying that hard to correct our perceptions.

"I don't care about the stories you hear, Jack. What are *you* doing?"

"Nobody, I mean nothing. Nothing at all really."

"Good to hear," I say. "I assume you've kissed a girl."

"Well . . ."

"What?"

"When I say 'nothing,' I mean *nothing*."

"No kissing at all?"

"A little. The occasional game of kiss and tag at a birthday party. Lately I've kissed a few girls because somebody dared me to at the . . ."

"Skating rink?"

"Yeah, how'd you know?"

"Open skate night taught me a lot of things, too."

"Good, so you know where I'm coming from."

"Not exactly," I say. "My life wasn't quite as sheltered as yours. Just so we're clear, you've never French kissed a girl?"

"Nope."

"Okay then, time for your first lesson."

"What are you talking about?" Jack starts walking double time ahead of me.

"Come back here, you idiot! I'm not going to freaking kiss you."

Jack slows down. "Then what are you gonna do?"

"Teach you how to practice." I hold my right fist close to my mouth. "Raise your hand to your mouth like I'm doing."

"No way!"

"Do it!"

"Okay," Jack says, mimicking my motions. "Whatever."

"Now, you know when it's cold outside and you blow air through the opening in your hand to stay warm?"

"I guess so."

"That's basically the same principle we're going with here, only instead of blowing through your hand you'll be puckering up and sucking."

Jack drops his hand away from his mouth. "I was wrong, Hank."

"What?"

"*Now* this is officially the grossest sex talk ever."

I grab his hand and lift it back toward his face. "Do you or don't you want to learn how to kiss a girl?"

"I do," Jack says, rolling his eyes.

"Instead of a perfect circle like you'd normally use to warm up your hand, make it more of an oval so the opening in your hand is shaped like a mouth."

Jack shows me the lemon-shaped opening in his hand. "Like this?"

"Perfect." I press my mouth against the side of my hand. "Now, pucker your lips and kiss the opening of your hand like this."

Jack follows my directions to the letter. "Like this?"

"That's pretty good," I say. "Remember, it's all about balance. You're not trying to swallow your hand, but at the same time you don't want to stab the opening of your hand with your mouth. That's when you slip in the tongue. Just like your lips, there's a give and take to it. Imagine you're kissing a girl. Don't fight her tongue, but at the same time don't let your tongue just hang there limp in her mouth."

"How will I know if I'm being too aggressive or not aggressive enough with my tongue?"

"Believe me, you'll figure it out. And whatever you do, don't use your teeth. Don't bite her tongue, don't lick her teeth, just keep the teeth out of the whole equation."

"Why?"

"Because that just encourages her to keep biting. And biters are the worst kissers, among other things."

"What other things?" Jack asks.

I pat my naïve student on the shoulder. "That's not in today's lesson plan, buddy. I just want you to know one thing."

"What's that?

"No matter what situation you find yourself in, you can come to me. If things are getting too heavy or out of control—at a friend's house, at a party, wherever you are—I'm just a phone call away. I will come get you, no questions asked."

"No questions asked?"

"None," I say as we approach a busy intersection. I don't notice the "Do Not Walk" sign.

"Easy there, big bro." Jack holds his arm out to prevent me from stepping into the street. My protector. "So, we done with the sex talk?"

"Do you want to be done?" I ask.

"I didn't want to start."

"What do you want to talk about?"

"Music maybe?

"Perfect. What's everyone into right now?"

"Train, Matchbox Twenty, Destiny's Child."

"Yuck."

"Tell me about it," Jack says.

"No Staind or Incubus in there?"

"So you know what everyone is into right now?"

"I have a radio, fool."

"I don't listen to the radio." Jack smirks. "I'm pretty much all about the Dave Matthews Band."

"Still?"

"What's not to like?"

Jack spent two weeks with Jeanine in Portland last summer, and she effectively brainwashed him. Gone was our shared love and shared CD collection of Metallica, Scorpions, Guns N' Roses, and Mötley Crüe, and in its place were cassette bootlegs of various live Dave Matthews shows and mind-numbing deconstructions of the band's "transcendent visual imagery and musicianship." Jack's words, not mine.

"Do we really have to go over this again, Jack? There are three reasons I don't like the Dave Matthews Band. Reason number one, too many drunken frat boys at their concerts. Reason number two, they've become the fallback band for Deadheads who still haven't come to terms with Jerry Garcia's death, getting a job, or personal hygiene."

"I like the Grateful Dead."

"Of course you do."

"What's the third reason?"

"They don't rock."

"Don't rock? Have you even listened to them?"

"I've listened plenty, and I can't envision going to a Dave show and banging my head, pumping my fist, or feeling my heart about to explode out of my chest."

"That's your main criteria for music? Whether or not it makes you violent and gives you a heart attack?"

"When I want to rock, I want to rock, not do the stoner shuffle to safe, uninteresting folk music."

"I wouldn't call Carter Beauford safe or uninteresting."

"He's Dave's drummer, right?"

Jack nods. "And probably rock n' roll's greatest living percussionist."

I shake my head in a dissenting motion. "I'm never leaving you alone with our sister again."

"Name someone better."

"He's practically in our own backyard. Does the name Kenny Aronoff ring a bell?"

"Should it?"

"He's John Mellencamp's drummer."

"Is it possible for you to have a musical discussion without referencing

Mellencamp?"

"Okay then, what about Neil Pert?"

"Neil *who*?"

"Dear lord, I have failed you as a big brother."

"Relax, Hank." A car honks as it passes by us. Jack waves. "I know who Neil Pert is. I just don't think he's as good a drummer as Carter Beauford."

"Neil Pert could eat a bowl of drumsticks and crap a better solo than Carter Beauford."

Jack laughs at me. I laugh right back at him to spite myself. I'll never be a Dave Matthews fan, but if the guy can deliver me more of these moments with Jack, I might just jump on that Phish-wannabe frat-rock bandwagon. Talking about music is something I always wanted to do with Dad, but by the time I had formed an opinion one way or the other, he was gone forever. I think Dad would have been on Jack's side in this argument, but I don't tell him that. Blues harps, fiddles, a full horn section: That was John Fitzpatrick's kind of music.

Thank you, Dave Matthews. If somewhere in between smoking dragons with your girlfriend, getting stung by bumblebees, and wearing pineapple grass bracelets, you can make the world smile, who am I to disparage a twelve-year-old's cassette bootlegs?

# Chapter 27

With my late nights working at College Ave and Mom being an absentee parent to Jack in the midst of her newly wedded bliss, I feel like I'm neglecting my wife and children.

Well, I *know* I'm neglecting my wife.

Beth and I are struggling. It started after the twins were born. At first, I chalked it up to the same thing she went through with Sasha: another bout of post-partum depression. We talked through it, or pretended like we did, for about a year. Raising a toddler and two infants was a convenient distraction. I stopped counting the weeks and months that would go by without having sex with her. Beth stopped asking how my day was. The idea of even striking up a conversation intimidated me. I felt like a stranger in my own house.

Nothing prepares you for this in a marriage. For the doldrums. For those moments when your sails stall and the ship flounders. A part of you wants to look to the horizon, hoping for that wind that will carry you home or at least to kinder shores. But a part of you also just wants to jump off the boat.

"Hello again, Vanessa."

She bows her head. "Good morning, Hank."

Beth and I sit on the couch across from the old woman. Her name is Vanessa Sheed. She's our couples therapist. In her midfifties, soft in the middle, and pear-shaped, with auburn hair sprinkled with strands of gray and an authoritative, borderline-sneering Margaret Thatcher countenance. Beth, of course, corrected me this morning, saying the woman "isn't so much old as she is just older than us" and that my choice of adjectives is "further indication of your emotional immaturity."

Whatever. If I'm a kid masquerading as an adult, then Beth is counting the days until she can apply for an AARP card. The disapproving sneers. The constant rejections of her "sex ogre" of a husband. The lamentations about how she's lost her womanhood to motherhood. Beth didn't lose anything; she gave it away enthusiastically.

We agreed I should see Vanessa for a couple sessions on my own prior to meeting in a group setting. And by "we" I mean Beth ordered me to do it. All things considered, our conversations have gone pretty well. I started opening up. I uncorked a bottle of resentment about my sainted father. I talked about Jack in the context of being my son and not my brother. I wrote a letter to my dead godfather asking him why he felt compelled to massage my balls and stick his finger up my butthole. Great stuff all around. Turns out this last bit about my butthole was a repressed memory that my therapy only now brought to light. I can't say I'm particularly grateful or that I've become a better person for now having a conscious memory of my godfather knuckle-deep in my anus, but I leave that to the professionals to decide.

Barring the anus revelation, a part of me almost thinks the worst is behind us and that we might be turning things around. There's no way we're going to throw all this away, are we? Life with Sasha and the twins is pretty close to perfect. Beth and I even had sex twice, *in one week*! At one point, I almost went forty-eight hours without masturbating to Internet porn. My streak came to a crashing halt when the new neighbors moved in. The wife, this full-breasted half-Vietnamese woman named Lang who works in the healthcare industry, had me searching on the Internet for a few hours, dick in hand, for *Busty Asian Nurses*. There's a revelation for you, Vanessa: I didn't even know I was into Asians.

"Hank," Vanessa says. "Would you agree with your wife's assessment?"

"What?"

"My assessment of you," Beth says. "Do you agree with it?"

"I don't know." I shrug my shoulders. "What's this about anyway? I thought we've been in a good place lately, even in the bedroom. Haven't we?"

Beth shakes her head. "He wasn't listening, not that I'm surprised."

"Please, Beth," Vanessa says, holding her hand up. "Hank, your wife thinks you're in a state of arrested development. That the sexual abuse you suffered as a child was compounded by the sudden death of your father and essentially froze you, emotionally and psychologically, at twenty-one years old."

I turn to my wife. "So that's it? We're really all the way back to square one here?"

"Our problems aren't going to be solved simply by rolling around in the sheets a couple times."

"Did I say they were solved?"

Vanessa raises her hand to interrupt. "So you don't agree with your wife, Hank?"

"That's just it," I say. "A part of me agrees with her implicitly. My childhood, my boyhood, that brief period of my life in which I had a father, *is* a moment frozen in time for me. A part of me will always want to stay in that moment. But that doesn't mean I'm not working to be a better person, a better father . . ."

"A better husband?" Beth says.

"Of course, a better husband." I bite my bottom lip, my finger raised to my wife's face, almost touching her nose. "You didn't let me finish, and that's my problem with *you*, Beth."

"Let's assume a less aggressive posture, Hank," Vanessa says. "But I like where this is going. Keep talking to Beth, not me."

"Yeah, Hank, talk to me." She reaches for my hand as I lower it. I pull my hand away.

"My problem with you is that you don't want to fix things. You seem to take some sort of perverse pleasure in exposing my faults. I've never seen someone try so hard to dislike another person. I know I'm not the world's best listener. I know I'm not good with money and I don't think about the future enough. And I know I publish books instead of saving sick kids."

"What are you talking about?" Beth says.

"I'm not your fucking father, and you resent me because of it."

"That's absurd."

"Is it? You're here today to fix me, not us and certainly not you. You don't want me to be the man of the house, you want me to be *your idea of a man*. Your idea of a man balances the checkbook, watches the stock ticker all day, alphabetizes his family videos, and knows his children's vaccination schedules by heart."

"What's wrong with that?"

"Nothing, I guess. But your idea of a man has also spent the better part of the last thirty years as a glorified roommate to his spouse. Your idea of a man hasn't kissed his wife in public since Jimmy Carter was president."

"You've made your point, Hank," Vanessa says.

"Your idea of a man doesn't even hold his wife's hand, never mind have sex with her."

"I said that's enough."

"Don't worry, Vanessa." My wife reaches over and touches the therapist's knee. "I can handle this."

"Then handle it," I say.

"Do you like your life?" Beth asks me.

"What?"

"It's a simple question. Do you like your life?"

"I guess so."

"You guess so? Let's see. You have your perfect little family. You have a job you love. Meanwhile, I'm the one taking care of the kids. I'm the one who, on top of being a mom and a good housewife, goes to work in the evenings to take shit from entitled teenage gymnasts who reek of smelly feet and dirty tampons. Your life has turned out exactly the way you wanted it to turn out. And I'm just a stay-at-home mom with a worthless nursing degree and no marketable skills."

"You're being a little hard on yourself, Beth."

"Am I?"

"If you want to do more with your life, then do it. But don't sit here and act like I'm the bad guy or try to tell me that your parents raised you right."

"Better Stan or Joan than Debbie."

"Nice misdirection."

"How so?"

"My mom lost her reason for being a good partner to someone nine years ago when her husband got stabbed in the liver by a truck. What are your parents' excuses?"

"At some point you're going to have to start realizing there's an expiration date on grief."

"And at some point you're going to have to start fucking me more than once every three months."

"Okay, you two," Vanessa says, standing. She extends her arms between us, like a referee. "This session is no longer productive."

Beth sits in the car, still crying. I approach the driver's side door. Inhale. Exhale. I open the door, slide behind the wheel. I shut the door, forcing a half smile.

"That went well," I say. "Gotta love the Random House insurance."

"Hank . . ." Beth says.

"Unlimited ten-dollar co-pays for therapy. I confirmed our appointment for next month."

"Hank . . ." she repeats through a veil of mascara and tears. "I want a trial separation."

My wife's request is hardly shocking. She's played this card close to a dozen times in our seven years of marriage. My standard response is to grovel, say something about how "we need to think about the kids first," then spend the next thirty to ninety days working our relationship back to a semi-tolerable equilibrium. Lather, rinse, repeat.

But today, I just don't have anything left in the tank.

"Fine by me."

# Chapter 28

**From:** Fitzpatrick, Hank [mailto:hfitzpatrick@collegeavepress.com]
**Sent:** Tuesday, April 16, 2002 11:26 AM
**To:** Prestwich, Delilah [mailto:di_prestwich@yahoo.com]
**Subject:** Advance Praise for SPERM BANK MESSIAH

Dear Lila,

They love you! The last review is my personal favorite.

Hank

P.S. Until my situation with Beth gets settled, I'm working mostly in New York at my satellite office in the Bertelsmann Building. An author friend is letting me crash at his place on 42$^{nd}$ Street for free. I'll be here for the rest of the week. Come by for lunch?


"A sardonic yet endearing confection of Ian Frazier humor, Paul Theroux travelogue and Karen Armstrong theological progressivism."

   –*Publishers Weekly*

"Think Monty Python's *Life of Brian* by way of *Dr. Who,* its unbridled self-awareness, mordancy, and aleatoric narrative arc derailed only by the occasional and unfortunate homage to Anita Diamant's *Red Tent.*"

   –*Kirkus Reviews*

"Thank God for D.D. Preston! Other critics might take a few potshots at her almost consciously derivative protagonist, but I have to think

Dickens and John Irving would get a kick out of the baton being passed from Oliver to Garp to a time-traveling born-again crack whore. *Sperm Bank Messiah* is crass, vulgar and inappropriate. Needless to say, I loved it. Recommended for all serious fiction collections."

–Library Journal

"With American fiction heading into an inevitable post-9/11 morass, D.D. Preston reminds us of what the world used to be like, vacillating between willful enervation and ambivalent immurement. She dares to be contumelious, her ribald yet perspicuous prose challenging the reader on every page."

–The New York Times

"Modernism and its wicked doppelganger secularism have reached their zenith with *Sperm Bank Messiah*. Soon-to-be excommunicated Latter-Day Saint turned homosexual activist D.D. Preston piggybacks on the mainstream media's virulent hatred of all things Christian and masculine and gives us perhaps the most willfully offensive and wicked tome in the history of English (and I use this term loosely) literature."

–Salt Lake Tribune

# Chapter 29

**From:** Fitzpatrick, Hank [mailto:hfitzpatrick@collegeavepress.com]
**Sent:** Tuesday, April 30, 2002 8:14 AM
**To:** Prestwich, Delilah [mailto:di_prestwich@yahoo.com]
**Subject:** Young Lions Fiction Award Nominees Announced


Dear Lila,

What did I tell you about kissing New York's ass?

Hank

P.S. Dinner tonight?


**Young Lions Fiction Award Nominees Announced**
Posted Monday, Apr 29, 2002
The New York Public Library announced six nominees for its second annual Young Lions Fiction Award [YLFA], which recognizes the work of authors aged 35 or younger.

Nominated for the YLFA top six are: *The Muse Asylum* by David Czuchlewski (Putnam), *The Miracle Life of Edgar Mint* by Brady Udall (Norton), *John Henry Days* by Colson Whitehead (Doubleday), *Esther Stories* by Peter Orner (Mariner Books/Houghton Mifflin), *Paradise Park* by Allegra Goodman (Dial Press/Random House), and *Sperm Bank Messiah* by D.D. Preston (College Ave/Random House).

The ceremony will be held May 11 in the Celeste Bartos Forum at the New York Public Library's Humanities and Social Sciences Library. The winner will receive a $10,000 award.

"[YLFA] is run by avid readers and formidable writers who believe in, and are committed to, the cultural necessity of the written word," Mark Danielewski, last year's winner for the novel *House of Leaves*, said in a statement. "It's essential for writers in the early part of their publishing lives to have opportunities for support and ratification."

YLFA stemmed from the Young Lions group, a membership organization for library supporters in their 20s and 30s. The nominees for YLFA were selected by a Reading Committee of Young Lions members, writers, and librarians, including Rodney Phillips, director of the New York Public Library's Humanities and Social Sciences Library.

# Chapter 30

The bad news is Colson Whitehead's *John Henry Days* won the Young Lions Fiction Award. The good news is, on the heels of Lila's nomination, Michael Pietsch, publisher and executive vice president of Little, Brown and Company, outbid Random House's own paperback imprint Vintage for the trade paper rights to *Sperm Bank Messiah*, singlehandedly putting College Ave in the black for the rest of the year. Mr. Pietsch heard I was in town visiting Lila and asked that we both attend the party he was hosting for Alice Sebold, one of Little Brown's new authors. The party is being held at Flûte, a champagne bar on West 54th Street.

Lila and I emerge from the bowels of the subway. She had wanted to take a taxi from her apartment, where I've been crashing off and on since Beth kicked me out of the house. I wanted to take the One Train, seeing as it dumps you at 50th and Broadway, all of a five-minute walk from the bar. In a rare fit of acquiescence, Lila agreed to take the train.

"See, that wasn't so bad, was it?" I say.

Lila smiles. She straightens her cocktail dress, a black sleeveless number with a plunging neckline that dares me to stare at her cleavage. As usual, the sight of me walking down the street with her on my arm provokes multiple *How the fuck did he land her?* sideways glances.

"Loosen up, Hank."

"Easy for you to say. These are your coworkers."

"Can we at least go over this one more time?" Lila says.

"Sure," I say.

"This is a party for who?"

"Alice Sebold."

"And she wrote what?"

"*The Lovely Bones*, her debut novel and a follow-up to her memoir, *Lucky*. Alice is married to Glen David Gold, author of *Carter Beats the Devil*, an ambitious novel of Roaring Twenties pre-Depression era America that reads like *The Great Gatsby* as viewed through the lenses of Michael Chabon-slash-Daniel Wallace American postmodern fiction."

"Well done, Mr. Fitzpatrick. You've been studying."

"Maybe a little," I say.

"And what's *The Lovely Bones* about?"

I stop walking. "Uhh . . ."

"You mean to tell me you remembered all that about her husband, and you can't give me just a simple one- or two-sentence overview? You're a publisher, for God's sake."

"I don't read other people's books. I want to say there's a . . . murder?"

"Good guess."

"Of a little girl."

"Now you're getting somewhere."

"And her name is Eliza Naumann."

"No."

"No?"

"You're thinking of the protagonist from Myla Goldberg's *Bee Season*."

"Bone Boatwright, maybe?"

"And that's Dorothy Allison's *Bastard Out of Carolina*."

"Scout? Moby?"

"And now you're just being a smartass."

"Why am I picturing a fish?"

"Because her name is Susie Salmon."

"Susie, that's right. Now it's coming back to me. Susie is murdered, and then her skeleton narrates the book. Hence the title."

"Hank." Lila shakes her head, pulls on my arm. "Just leave the talking to me tonight, okay?"

If you didn't know the exact address of Flûte, you'd walk right by it. A former speakeasy, the bar is tucked down in the basement of a Theater District high-rise and by way of signage is afforded little more than a small marquee at the top of an unlit stairwell. The only giveaway tonight is a smartly dressed blond woman holding a clipboard and a muscular gentleman in a tight black tuxedo standing in front of a red velvet rope.

"Name?" the blond woman says.

Lila gives her a fake smile. "Delilah Prestwich and Hank Fitzpatrick."

The blonde nods at the muscular gentleman. He unclips the velvet rope, motions down the stairwell. "Ma'am, sir," he says.

As far as New York publishing parties go, the atmosphere at Flûte is predictable. The lights dimmed to the point of near-pitch. Cozy surrendering to indulgent. Too many conversations competing for floor space. Publishing executives who've been told to watch their bottom lines toasting to million-dollar deals with two-hundred-dollars-a-bottle champagne in lieu of paying their copy editors living wages.

Lila and I settle in quickly at two open seats at the far end of the bar.

"Who's your friend, Lila?" a voice says over my shoulder.

I turn. The voice belongs to a petite woman—thin and no more than five feet tall, about Beth's height. Her hair is cut short. There's no telling in this light, but I'm guessing it's some shade of brown. Standing next to her is a gentleman in dark-rimmed glasses with an ill-fitting, cheap charcoal suit but good skin and even better hair.

"Hi, Amber," Lila says. "Hank, this is Amber Pate, Director of Subrights for Little Brown. We're officemates."

I shake Amber's hand and proceed to lie. "Oh, *that* Amber Pate. I've heard a lot about you."

"Same here," Amber says. She hooks the arm of the gentleman standing next to her. "This is Joseph Mann, Director of Acquisitions for audiobook publisher Talk Hard Media."

"Joseph, Hank Fitzpatrick," I say, shaking his hand.

"Please, call me Joe."

"So, Joe," I say. "Audiobooks. Is that like, books on tape?"

"Uh-oh." Amber shakes her head.

"What?" I say.

"You said the three-letter word," Amber says.

"Books on tape?"

"Yeah." Joe jumps in. "It's a common mistake. In 1975, Books on Tape became the first company to produce and sell audiobooks to consumers and then to libraries and retailers. Talk Hard, my company, opened its doors three years later. *Books on tape* has since become the generic term for audiobooks, but saying *books on tape* to me is like telling a Puff sales rep to pass you a Kleenex or a Panasonic sales rep to go Xerox some copies."

"Gentlemen . . ." Lila says, grabbing my arm. "As fascinating as this topic is, I need to pull Hank away for a bit and work the room."

"Wait a second, Lila," Amber says. "I need your powers of persuasion."

"For what?"

Amber puts her hand on Joe's shoulder. "I'm trying to convince Joe here to buy the audio rights to *In the Hand of Dante*."

"The new Nick Tosches book?" I say.

"That's the one," Amber says.

"I thought you already had an audio deal," Lila says.

"That's the problem. A competing audiobook publisher paid me a lot of money for the rights, and then they spent even more money renting a recording studio in Paris and hiring Johnny Depp as the narrator."

"Johnny Depp?" I say. "That's pretty sweet."

Amber nods. "You would think so, right? Problem is, over the last month they've salvaged about an hour of usable audio at most. Apparently Depp and the author keep showing up at the studio blitzed out of their minds on red wine. The audio publisher wants out, and I'm trying to convince Joe to pick up the tab."

Off to the side of Amber, Joe shakes his head. "Let the record show I love both Depp's and Tosches's work and think the idea of these two characters pounding wine in Paris is cooler than anything I've ever been a part of." He finishes his glass of Dom, cutting himself off in mid-sentence. "And let the record also show that I'm not touching this project with a ten-foot fucking pole."

I tilt my head, raise my champagne flute. "You're a smart guy, Joe."

The party ended. I got to meet Alice Sebold and Glen David Gold. Alice was unbelievably nice, her husband generous with his time and quick with anecdotes that keenly played off my uninteresting stories. I can't imagine they cared too much about my life as a small-time editor, but I appreciated their efforts to suggest otherwise.

Michael Pietsch never spoke to me.

"Don't take it personally," Lila says. "Michael has a lot on his mind these days."

"I'm sure he does," I say. I slide my Metro Card through the subway turnstile, once for Lila, who walks through, and then for me.

"You're in publishing, you know how it is. Sales are flat across the board. Guys like Michael are under the gun to find new customers, new markets, new sources of revenue, the next big thing."

The One Train approaches the station. We take a seat in the middle of the second car.

"The next big thing," I say. "You mean like *The Lovely Bones*?"

"I'm talking bigger than just one author or one book," Lila says. "You didn't hear this from me, but Michael had some execs from Gemstar in the office today."

"Is that name supposed to mean something to me?"

"You don't know Gemstar?"

"Nope."

"It's the company that manufactures the Rocket Book."

"That electronic book reader thingy?"

"Yes," Lila says. "They want to format the entire Little Brown catalog for their Rocket Book."

"I think Michael is barking up the wrong tree with that one."

"How so?"

"Electronic books? I just don't get it. Books are something you touch, something you smell, something you hold in your hands—keepsakes, heirlooms. Reading a book on a computer screen is never going to catch on."

"You're probably right," Lila says.

"Trust me on this one."

We exit the subway at the southeast corner of 79th and Broadway, the closest station to Lila's place. I quickly tired of living on my friend's couch on 42nd Street and moved into the spare bedroom in her Upper Westside brownstone.

"Enough publishing talking," Lila says. "How about a nightcap?"

"Chris not waiting up for us?" I ask.

Lila hooks her arm in mine. "She left this afternoon for Georgia. Femshack is playing at a music festival down in Savannah. You knew that."

"I did?"

"You did."

"Well . . ." I say, pulling Lila's waist in to mine, "having you all to myself is really going to suck."

"Behave," Lila says, pushing me away.

"Hey now, you know no one is happier than me that you two worked it out."

"Nothing to work out, really. Chris and I never should have broken up in the first place. Last year was a weird time for everyone, I think. After 9/11, instead of holding on tight to those we loved, it seemed like a lot of us tried to just run away, myself included."

"I know the feeling."

"I'm glad I stopped running, Hank. She was just too perfect to let go."

"And I'm sure living rent-free in a brownstone within walking distance of Central Park doesn't exactly detract from Chris's perfection."

"Listen here, fucker." Lila smacks me in the ass. "You about ready to stop talking and start drinking?"

We cross the street to the Dublin House, a narrow taproom smelling of Guinness and mildew. The mustachioed bartender nods at Lila when she enters. "Billy Doyle, two rounds of the usual," Lila says. He slides us two pints of Guinness and two shots of Jameson in short order.

We toast, slamming our shots of Jameson in concert. I chase the shot with a small sip of Guinness, letting the creaminess of the head massage my tongue. I return my pint to its loyal coaster. "Great bar," I say.

"The best," Lila says. "Hasn't once shut its doors since the day Prohibition was lifted."

"Where'd Chris get the idea for the name of the band?"

"You really want to know?"

"What else do I have to do?"

"Chris started up her band right out of high school back in her hometown of La Plata."

"Where's that? California?"

"Rural southern Maryland. They used to play out of an old army barracks. They nicknamed the place 'the Femshack,' and it became kind of a hangout for all the hip DC lesbians. When they got their first real paying gig in Georgetown, the name Femshack came with them."

"And that's it?" I ask.

Lila nods. "That's it."

I grab my pint, holding it up to the lights tinged yellow by a century of cigarette smoke. "Did you know Guinness used to be prescribed to post-op patients, pregnant women, and nursing mothers, and that new research suggests a daily pint can lower your risk of a heart attack?"

"Okay, enough of that." Lila grabs my pint, sets it on the bar. "What's on your mind?"

"Nothing."

"My ass. When you start right in with the random useless trivia, that usually means you're trying to work up the courage to ask me something. Let's just dispense with the bullshit and get to it."

I grab my pint of Guinness, finishing it in three swallows. Billy Doyle seems less than impressed. I clear my throat.

"She's been calling you, hasn't she?"

"Who?" Lila asks, as if she doesn't know exactly who I'm talking about.

"Beth."

"She wants you back, Hank."

"Bullshit," I say.

Beth started talking divorce almost immediately after we were separated. I hear she might even be dating. Six months of trying to fast-track me out of her life, and now she has a change of heart? I'm not buying it.

"You've given people a second chance who deserved it a whole lot less than Beth."

"Maybe."

"At least just call her back, if only because I'm tired of being your fucking answering service."

"I think I'm going to tell Jack."

"Wait . . . what?"

"I'm going to tell Jack that I'm his father."

Lila has known for years. I can't remember when I told her, only that she didn't act surprised. No one seems to act surprised when I tell them. For someone who struggles mightily with being a father, I seem to at least wear it well.

"How'd we get on this subject?" Lila says.

"I'm drunk," I say. "Felt like talking about something else."

"I'll accept drunk as your excuse, then."

"My excuse for what?"

"For being out of your goddamn mind."

"The boy is thirteen years old, Lila. He's nearly in high school. I have Sasha and the twins, and apparently my wife again if I want her. Jack deserves to know."

"Your mother should be the one to tell him, Hank. Not you."

"But he needs a father."

"Jack *has* a father."

"Who, Gillman? That looney tune is no father to Jack."

Oh shit. Did I really just say that out loud? Lila's bottom lip is quivering. Her eyes well up with tears. "Lila, I'm sorry. I didn't mean it."

"Oh you meant it, dickhead!"

Billy Doyle approaches, his mustache leering at me menacingly. "You got uh problem here, laddie?"

"I'm fine," Lila says, waving him off. "I think you know by now I'm a big girl, Billy."

Billy Doyle leaves. I grab Lila's hand. "I'm sorry for what I said, really I am. I know Gillman means well."

Lila grabs a cocktail napkin, wipes her eyes. "Hank, he just comes from a totally different world than most people. His grandparents were polygamists, his parents were glorified drill instructors, and he thought the answer to undoing all their damage was to just seek out very atypical women—first my mother, a barely practicing LDS Armenian, and now your mother . . ."

"A loud, obnoxious Irish Catholic with a taste for narcotics-tinged melodrama?"

"Your words, not mine," Lila says. "Problem is, Gillman Prestwich is his father's son. Dad needs a passive woman. He needs a wife who doesn't laugh at him when he asks her to wear shirts with sleeves and Capri pants instead of shorts because it makes her look like a harlot."

"You have to admit that was pretty hilarious. He called her a harlot. I mean, come on, who uses that fucking word anymore? Hey, Gillman, the nineteenth century called, and it wants its thesaurus back."

Lila laughs, the last swallow of her pint shooting out her mouth. I raise two fingers. "Billy, a couple more Guinness here."

Billy Doyle stands at the other end of the bar, unmoving.

Lila leans into me. "Uh, you kinda have to earn your way up to calling him Billy." She raises her hand. "Hey Billy . . ." she says in her best fake Irish brogue, "two pints o' the black for me and Henry David Fitzpatrick."

"Fitzpatrick?" Billy Doyle says, his eyes and mustache perking up in unison. "Why didn't yuh say so?"

Lila struggles to find the lock with her house key. I'd offer to help her, but I see three doors to our apartment.

"Shhhhhhh," Lila says, putting her finger to her mouth.

"What?" I say.

"Weeft."

"Weeft?"

"Weef to be quiet."

"You're the only who's talking."

"Shhhhhhh," Lila says again.

The rounds of Guinness and Jameson blurred into one another. How many rounds did we have? Five? Six? Seven even? For good measure, Tony bought us a round of Tullamore Dew on our way out the door.

Lila opens the door, walks into the apartment. I follow her inside, shut the door behind us.

"Wuuna sleep inna yuroom or inna mine?" Lila says.

"In my room or yours?"

"Yeah, zwut I said."

As is customary with my constantly raging libido, my penis does a half-salute inside my pants as if to say, *Can we, pleeeeease?*

"My room is fine," I say.

"Zoot yerzelf," Lila says. She walks up to me, kisses me full on the lips, with tongue. She stumbles back. "Mmm, you taste good."

"You're not so bad either," I say.

Lila pats me on the chest. "Can I tell yuz one thing?"

"Sure, Lila."

"You do whateverz you thinks is best for Jack. Yours hiz dad. Gillman isn't."

I grab Lila by the hand, pull her into me. We kiss. I feel her pelvis lean into mine. My road to redemption deserves at least one tap on the snooze bar, doesn't it? Just as I start to slide my hands down the small of Lila's back, she appears.

*"What are you doing, Daddy?"*

Lila doesn't see her. Only I can see her. She's a figment of my imagination, but in every way that counts, she's very real. She is my six-year-old daughter, Sasha.

When I was a teenager, my father and I had precious few man-to-man conversations. But the one I remember most was the lecture on fidelity. I was twenty years old and had just screwed up my fourth relationship in as many months.

*"How do you do it?"* I remember saying to my father.

*"Do what?"*

*"Stay with one woman . . . forever."*

*"Masturbation and patience,"* Dad said. *"But mostly masturbation."*

His candor surprised me. Genuine off-color humor from John Fitzpatrick? I didn't know whether to congratulate him or run screaming to Mom. *"Uh, yeah . . ."* I said, still off balance. *"I think I got a pretty good handle on the masturbation, Dad."*

Dad grinned. *"Truthfully, Hank?"*

*"No, just make something up. Yes, truthfully."*

*"Jeanine helps me."*

*"Come again?"*

*"Your sister."*

*"Yeah, I know her name."*

*"Whenever I'm in a potentially compromising position, I picture myself with the compromising woman, and then I picture my daughter watching everything I'm doing. It's like a built-in monogamy kill switch."*

And so, here I stand, on the verge of quasi-incestuous, olive-skinned Armenian Mormon sex, when my daughter Sasha appears.

I unhinge my lips from Lila's face. "Good night," I say abruptly.

"What's wrong, Hank?"

"Nothing," I say, giving Sasha a quick smile. She smiles back.

"Sure about that?"

I reach into my pocket and pull out my cell phone. "You were right, Lila. I should call my wife."

# Chapter 31

I open the front door and walk into the house without knocking. Gillman and my mother are in the family room watching television.

"Hey, son," Mom says. "Back already? I thought you wanted to stick around and spy on Jack a little bit."

"It's an eighth-grade dance, Mom. He made me drop him off a block away from school. I'll live if I miss creeping on a bunch of thirteen-year-olds." I slap the application to Empire Ridge Preparatory Academy on the coffee table in front of Gillman and my mother. "Now, do either of you mind explaining this?"

"That's a Prep application," my stepfather says.

"No shit, Gillman."

"Hank, a little respect for your father, please."

"Gillman's not my fucking father. He's barely a father to his own daughter."

Gillman stands up. I move toward him until we're standing face-to-face. He's my exact height but outweighs me by a good seventy pounds. For a guy who abstains from alcohol and caffeine, you think he'd exhibit a modicum of temperance with sweets and fried food.

"Debbie," Gillman says, turning away from me. "I don't have to stay here and take this in my own house."

"Running away already?" I say. "Come on now, Gillman, I know you want this fight. I can see it in your eyes and that donut-stuffed face. You're ready to go all Mountain Meadows Massacre on me, aren't you?"

"Hank!" Mom shouts.

"It's okay, Debbie." Gillman waves my mother off. "I got this."

"Sure you do," I say.

"Why would you think I'd run away, Hank?"

"Everyone runs away."

"Open your eyes, son."

"Don't call me—"

"Spare me the martyr routine," Gillman says. "Look around you. I'm the only one who hasn't run away. Your sister, Jeanine, moved to Portland the day she graduated college. We're lucky to get a Christmas card from her. You're in and out of Jack's life when the mood suits you, teaching him how to masturbate and French kiss but not teaching him the difference between right and wrong or what it means to be a Christian. Meanwhile, your marriage is falling apart and you spend months at a time in New York away from your family just so you can flirt with my daughter."

"Excuse me?" Mom says.

"That's an oversimplification of things," I say. "And you know it."

"What exactly am I 'oversimplifying'?"

"First off, let's just leave Lila out of this. She confides in me more than she'll ever confide in you, and that's your problem, not mine. As for Jack, if I didn't have that talk with him, no one would. The kid was scared shitless. He was turning into an emotionally and socially dysfunctional freak. He was turning into *you*, Gillman."

"Give me a break, Hank."

"If you could only see yourself in social situations, Gillman."

"I am plenty social."

"No, I'm talking when you have to get down and dirty with us unwashed Gentiles. Seeing you with your fellow Mormons at a Catholic wedding reception is priceless. You guys all huddle together around one table with this panicked, bug-eyed look as if you're witnessing an orgy."

"To be fair, if it's anything to do with you Catholics, I usually am witnessing an orgy."

" 'You Catholics,' huh? Oh good, let's go there next. Let's talk about you teaching Jack what it means to be a Christian."

"What about it?"

"You fucking suck at it."

"Hank!" Mom shouts again.

"Debbie, I said I got this." Again Gillman waves her off. "Okay, Hank. Take your best shot."

"You don't want my best shot."

"Try me."

"Okay, Gill-man. I realize the Catholic Church is far from perfect, but an apostasy? My ass, you intellectually dishonest and morally hypocritical Mormon prick. Let's not forget for the first thousand years of Christianity my imperfect church was a goddamn one-man show. If not for that millennium of kicking ass and taking names, there wouldn't even be a Christianity for your church or anyone else's church to break away from. Hell, I got T-shirts older than your religion. Suck on that fucking revelation, Joseph Smith."

I'm short of breath. Face red. Pulse racing. Perspiration drenching my shirt. But I've won. I know it. I can see it in Gillman's eyes. I can taste it in the sweat dripping down into my mouth like liquid vindication.

Mom abruptly stands up and leaves the room. Strangely, Gillman hasn't budged.

"Have you said all you wanted to say, Hank?"

I wipe my brow with the sleeve of my shirt. "I guess so."

"Are you familiar with the term *putative father*?"

"Should I be?"

"I'd be if I were you. A putative father is defined as the presumed father of an illegitimate child."

*Gillman knows I'm Jack's father.* I guess the joke is on me, eh, Joseph Smith?

"When did Mom tell you?"

"The first night we went out on a date, and I didn't run away."

Fortunately, Mom's complete inability to engage in subterfuge has lessened the blunt force trauma of this revelation. There are only so many ways you can bring characters into the story, make them interesting and necessary to the narrative arc, and then find plausible ways to drop the big reveal on them. Quite frankly, I'm a little disappointed here. Mom telling Gillman over a basket of breadsticks at a shitty Italian restaurant is rather pedestrian.

"Well, go on," I say.

"You sure you want to hear this?"

"It's becoming increasingly clear that it doesn't matter what I want."

Gillman has practiced this speech. His words sound like they're being recited more than said. "A putative father registry is a state level legal requirement for all non-married males to document through a notary public with the state each female with whom they engage in heterosexual sexual intercourse in order to retain parental rights to any child they may father. The putative father registry is intended to provide legal recognition to the non-married putative father of a child, provided he registers within a limited timeframe, usually any time prior to the birth or from one to thirty-one days after a birth."

"But all bets are off if I never even knew he was my—"

"I'm not finished, Hank." Gillman's eyes roll up into his head and then back, as if he's scrolling down the page to the last sentence. "Lack of knowledge of the pregnancy or birth is not a legally acceptable reason for failure to file."

I bite my lip in disbelief. Gillman has won, big time. He's called my bluff. I won't say anything to Jack, at least not yet, and Gillman knows that. I've been Jack's age. The kid is an emotional and hormonal powder keg, and I refuse to be the one to light the trail of gunpowder.

"So that's it?" I say.

"Hank, I'm—"

"You're pulling the rug out from under me."

"I don't want to shut you out of Jack's life."

"Then don't!"

"Answer me this," Gillman says. "When's the last time your mother had a drink? When's the last time she took a sleeping pill? Where is Jack graduating in his class?"

"I don't know."

"Your mother hasn't had a sip of alcohol or so much as one narcotic in almost three years. Jack is graduating first in his class. First! Do you know how proud that makes me feel? I messed up with Lila. I know that, and I hope she can learn to forgive me. But with Jack, I have a chance to make things right. He and your mother are the lights of my life. I know I come across to you as old-fashioned and weird, but I'm a good man. I don't want to change your mother or your brother."

"Jack is not my brother, Gillman. He's my son."

"I know he is, and I can't begin to fathom what you've gone through. All I'm asking is for a little more time. You and I are never going to be father and son, and I think we're both fine with that. But I'm not going anywhere, and I hope for Jack's sake you don't go anywhere either. Just let me be his father for a little while longer. I promise you there will come a time when I won't stand in the way."

Several minutes pass in silence. Conveniently, Mom pokes her head around the corner and walks into the room. She and Gillman sit back down on the couch. I pick up the Empire Ridge Preparatory Academy application off the coffee table.

"Is he going to have friends there?" I ask, looking at just my mother.

"Yes, baby. Tons of friends. Almost half his eighth-grade class is going to Prep."

"That's good, I guess." I hand her the application. "I know you don't need my permission or anything, but I think he'll be okay there."

My stepfather grabs me by the crook of my arm. "We don't need your permission, Hank, but we want it."

A smile tries to fight its way through my straight-lipped visage, but it's not going to fucking happen. I jerk my elbow free of Gillman's fat, clammy hands. "Don't get to thinking we're picking out china patterns anytime soon, asshole."

# Chapter 32

I pull into the driveway in my blue Subaru Outback. The odometer is at one hundred seventy-five thousand miles. The engine rattles as I turn off the car, reminding me I'm about five thousand miles overdue for an oil change.

Beth sits barefoot and tanned on the front porch steps, just back from a girls' weekend in Las Vegas with Claire, Lila, and Chris. She's wearing a white tank top and her favorite old pair of cutoff jeans, a glass of red wine in her left hand and her right hand cocked just enough to suggest it might have recently been holding a cigarette.

I step out of the car.

"How were the kids?" Beth asks in between sips of wine.

"Fantastic," I say.

"I hate my brothers!" Sasha screams as she marches toward the house. She is her mother's six-year-old clone, right down to her blond hair, her high cheekbones, her obstinacy, and even the way she struts, her left foot extending farther out than her right.

"Fantastic, huh?" Beth finishes off her wine, sets the glass on the porch, stands up, and makes her way toward the car.

"We had a bit of an incident." I point to the two sleeping balls of fat known to the outside world as Johnny and Burke. "The boys kind of barfed on their big sister."

We named the boys after their grandfathers, the "Burke" name almost an inside joke in honor of the Cisco Affair of 1995. They are identical twins, their only distinguishing features being their moles: Johnny looks like a little Indian girl with a single pinprick mole in the middle of his forehead, while Burke has two moles appearing like a vampire bite on the right side of his neck.

Beth recovered nicely after her second C-section in four years. I would like to credit my bedside manner for her recovery, but as I haven't been in her life for the last six months, I'm indebted more so to the post-cesarean umbilical hernia that forced the insurance company to cover the entire cost of Beth's tummy tuck. She lost her tattoo along with a few inches of loose skin. She even lost her navel. The fake navel looks real enough, and I've caught Beth enough times staring at her bare stomach in the mirror to know she's pretty pleased with the results. The surgeon also gave her a breast lift at a reduced rate. Even though we're separated, Beth has caught me staring at her cleavage enough times to know I'm pretty pleased with the results.

"Both of them barfed on her?" Beth says.

"She wanted to take them on the merry-go-round. I advised against it, but you know Sasha when she gets an idea in her head. I sat the boys on each side of her and made sure to not spin them too fast, but it didn't take much for them to start spewing."

"Is it bad that I'm picturing our daughter covered in her brothers' vomit and wanting to laugh out loud?"

"Go for it," I say. "I sure as hell did when it happened."

"*Ruff!*"

Chief doesn't like being left out of the loop, least of all when there are adults carrying on a conversation ostensibly oblivious to the two small children in their arms. He stands on the front porch, uneasy, as if to say, *That's precious cargo, people. Now shut the fuck up and pay attention to what you're doing.*

A giant white cone, or "E-collar" as the vet calls it, extends from Chief's neck. A square patch on the side of his ribs is shaved almost down to the skin. His left rear leg is shaved bare all the way up to his hip. His left front paw is similarly trimmed, although just to the knee. A month ago he jumped the fence after some Fourth of July fireworks got him skittish. Beth got a call two days later from the elementary school barely a mile from her backyard. When she found Chief, he couldn't stand up. He had torn his left rear ACL and would need surgery. The vet said someone probably hit him with a car and just drove off.

Beth, the woman so frugal she had refused to go on any vacations since our honeymoon—save a three-day weekend in the Wisconsin Dells on our five-year wedding anniversary—wrote a check to the vet for five thousand dollars without even thinking about it.

"Good boy, Chief," I say, reaching down into the cone and ruffling his ears. I open the front door for Beth. "How much longer does he have to wear this stupid thing anyway?"

"Until his wounds heal enough that he won't be tempted to lick them," Beth says. She nods in acknowledgement of the open door. "Thanks, Hank."

"You're welcome." I follow her inside. "Now what's with the shaving?"

Beth looks down, flexes her calves for my benefit. "You like that? My legs were getting pretty disgusting. I figured it was time to not look like an ape."

"No, not *your* shaving." I laugh a little, then a little more. "What's up with all the bare spots on Chief? I mean, I know you explained the surgery to me and everything, but I thought he just hurt his leg."

*Making Out with Blowfish*

"Oh, that," Beth says, noticeably disappointed. "His rear leg is where they did the surgery, but his side is where they attached the post-op painkiller patch, and his front paw was where they ran the IV."

Beth walks into the study just off the front hallway. She places Johnny in one of the two cribs pushed up against the hardwood bookcases. She tucks Johnny in, points to the other crib. "You can just put Burke in here for now."

I lay Burke in his bed, swaddling him in a similar fashion to his brother. My eyes dart from one corner of the study to the other. A diaper pail vies for space with a fax machine. A changing pad sprawls over the antique mahogany desk I bought at an estate sale. My first-edition library of Fitzgeralds, Steinbecks, Hemingways, and Faulkners share space with Dr. Marc Weissbluth's *Healthy Sleep Habits, Happy Child*, Rachel Simmons's *Odd Girl Out: The Hidden Culture of Aggression in Girls*, Rosalind Wiseman's *Queen Bees and Wannabes: Helping Your Daughter Survive Cliques, Gossip, Boyfriends, and the New Realities of Girl World*, Dr. Dan Kindlon's and Dr. Michael Thompson's *Raising Cain: Protecting the Emotional Life of Boys*, Dr. William Pollack's *Real Boys: Rescuing Our Sons from the Myths of Boyhood*, and Steve Biddulph's *Raising Boys: Why Boys are Different—and How to Help Them Become Happy and Well-Balanced Men*.

"I like what you've done with the place."

"I thought you might," Beth says.

I grab the paperback copy of *Real Boys* off the shelf, cracking the spine. I read aloud the first few lines of the introduction: " 'Boys today are in serious trouble, including many who seem "normal" and to be doing just fine. Confused by society's mixed messages about what's expected of them as boys, and later as men, many feel a sadness and connection they cannot even name.' "

"Agree or disagree with the premise, Hank?"

I close the book, return it to the shelf. "Yeah, I'll buy that."

"Technically you did." Beth reaches over, squeezes my elbow.

I don't smile.

"Too soon for child support jokes?" Beth asks.

"Yeah . . ." I say. "Probably."

"Would you like to stay for dinner?"

She has asked me over for dinner at least once a week since I closed my satellite office in New York and started working full time again out of College Ave's Indianapolis headquarters. I've been promoted to publisher. Last month Aaron Rosner's father helped him secure a seat on the board of directors at Domino's Pizza in Ann Arbor. Aaron always hated Indiana anyway. "Too many goddamn Gentiles," he said. I've been sleeping on a cot in the copy room. My clothes smell perpetually of warm paper and ink.

I have yet to accept my estranged wife's invitation.

"I don't know, Beth."

"Where do you have to be today?"

"Nowhere really, but with you just getting back from Vegas, I thought you might like some quality decompression time with the kids."

"I do want some quality time, Hank . . . *with my family*."

"Your family?" Her words chase me to the front door, Beth trailing close behind. "Not to bust your bubble or anything, but I haven't been a part of this family equation for almost a year now."

Beth wheels around me, blocking my path to the front door. "Please, Hank. I want you to stay. I want you to want to stay. It's not like we're divorced."

"Legally separated, divorced—it's just semantics, isn't it?"

"Is it?"

"What is it you want from me?"

"It's not about what I want."

"Okay?"

"It's about what I don't want."

"Enough with the mind games, Beth. Just—"

"I don't want to be separated anymore." She reaches out, grabbing me in a desperate bear hug. She buries her head in my chest, tears welling up in her eyes. "I don't think I ever wanted it."

I try to push her away, my heart wanting both literal and metaphorical space. But she won't let go. "Where's all this coming from?"

"What do you mean?" Beth says.

"I know you've been dating."

"Who told you that?"

"People."

"Well, those people are full of shit. I've been thinking about us for a long time, and the Vegas trip pushed me over the edge. Those girls just move at a different speed than me."

"Let me guess," I say. "Claire, Lila, and Chris ended up in various states of undress with strippers and/or each other, and you sat in a dark corner thinking, 'What the fuck is going on?' "

Beth looks over both shoulders, then back at me. "How'd you know?"

"Chris and Lila will always be Chris and Lila, especially when you get some cocktails in them. As for Claire, she's the consummate attention whore. She'll latch on to the coolest guy in the room or stick her tongue down the hottest girl's throat without thinking for a second about Hatch. And why is that?"

"Don't know," Beth says.

I wipe the tears out of my wife's eyes. "Because Claire Hatcher would rather be noticed by a hundred men than loved by just one. You've always wanted to know why it is we never once fooled around in all those years. Well, there's your answer."

"Every guy has his one Hottest Girl I Never Tried to Sleep With, and Claire Sullivan has been your undisputed titleholder for as long as you've known her."

"Where did you hear that?"

"At a bar, from you, before we ever started dating." Beth pokes me playfully in the stomach. "My question to you, Henry David Fitzpatrick, is when did you get so fucking perceptive?"

"Let's just say I've had a lot of free time on my hands lately."

"So you'll stay for dinner?"

I shake my head. "I still don't think that's a good idea."

"Why not?" Beth says.

Holy Christ. Is she crying again?

"Look . . ." I say. "Just because I have keen insight into your girlfriends doesn't mean my insight when it comes to you has improved one iota."

"Can you let me be the judge of that?"

"How about a rain check?" I say in my best paternal voice, rubbing Beth's arms for good measure.

"Fuck you, Hank!" Beth says, punching me in the chest. "Fuck you!"

My instinct is to run away. But let's be honest here: lately, my instincts have sucked balls.

I wrap my arms tightly around my wife. I can feel her start to relax in my embrace. She fights me, but only for a second. "Beth," I whisper.

"Yes?" she whispers back.

"There's something else you're not telling me, isn't there?"

Silence.

The wall clock ticks off the tension one second at a time.

"My mom and dad got divorced," Beth says.

"They filed for divorce? When?"

"No, they *got* a divorce. It's over. They filed sixty days ago and didn't tell anybody about it. They were afraid I'd try to talk them out of it. They broke the news to me in a fucking e-mail!"

I stroke Beth's hair. "Honey, I'm so sorry."

"What are you apologizing for?" she says, wiping her nose with the back of her hand. "Being right?"

"No," I say. "I'm apologizing for not being a better husband."

Beth smiles. She leans in, kisses me on the cheek. "A wise man once told me, this is what couples who've been together for a while do. They fuck things up sometimes."

I accepted my wife's dinner invitation. Later that night, as I rolled off her naked body, sweating and spent, I accepted her breakfast invitation.

# Part VI
# 2003-2004

# Chapter 33

I open the door for my wife to the urologist's office. "Ladies first."

Beth pokes me in the ribs. "And soon-to-be-not-so-manly men last."

"Hey now . . ." I say, trailing off as I look at my watch. "I can always walk right back out this door."

My vasectomy is scheduled for 10:00 a.m., but this day began more than a year ago, back when Beth gave birth to the boys. The attending nurse came in and checked on her prior to the caesarian. The nurse was an exceedingly chatty woman with pendulous breasts who claimed to know Peyton Manning and who I remember as being named Jill. She talked Beth out of the tubal ligation. She said to her, *"Don't let the doctor feed you that 'while I'm down there I might as well' bullshit. If you want to be up and about tomorrow, tell them to kiss your ass. If you want to be bedridden for a week, get your tubes tied."* And then Nurse Jill looked at me and said, *"He looks like a tough guy. I think one small snip is a fair trade for cutting open a six-inch gash in your abdomen . . . twice."*

They sewed Beth up, her tubes intact. The vasectomy issue remained unsettled, largely because the state of our marriage remained unsettled. After we got back together, it became a once-a-month dance with us:

*"When you going to make an appointment with the urologist?"*

*"Soon."*

*"How soon?"*

*"As soon as I'm comfortable with the idea of my nutsack getting sliced open."*

I was prepared to do the vasectomy two-step for as long as she let me get away with it, which turned out to be about six months. She backed me into a corner with one simple gesture: She went off the pill.

Marriage is the toughest job in the world. It requires patience, compromise, and the humility to acknowledge there are very few nonnegotiable items when it comes to the marital covenant. A couple of my nonnegotiables are: one, nothing interrupts the Notre Dame game on Saturdays; and two, my immutable right to make love to my wife without ever wearing a condom. Some would call that a very shallow outlook, but I'm too busy having mind-blowing, latex-free sex with my wife—who for purposes of this analogy is doing a reverse cowboy wearing nothing but a tight Notre Dame polo and knee-highs—to give a shit.

Beth signs me in. The waiting room is unusually crowded—well, not so unusually, but I'll get to that later—so we stand shoulder to shoulder against a wall.

"Nervous?" Beth says, turning to me.

"No," I say, looking at my watch again.

"Why do you keep doing that?"

"Doing what?"

Beth nods at my watch. "We're ten minutes early. Relax."

"I'm kinda hoping we'll get in and out."

"Where you gotta be?"

"Nowhere," I say. "Just want to get it done and get home."

"And get on the couch with me waiting on you hand and foot?"

"Doctor's orders."

"Yeah, doctor's orders," Beth says. That's when her eye catches a glimpse of ESPN Sportscenter on the waiting room television. "Wait a second."

"What?" I say, fully aware I'm busted.

"Today is Thursday."

"That's right."

"As in the first day of the college basketball tournament."

"Really?" I say. "That's a weird coincidence."

"Is it?"

"Kind of funny how many guys are in here today, don't you think?"

"Hank, please don't tell me this is the reason you've procrastinated about this for six months."

"Well, it's not the *only* reason."

"You son of a—"

"Oh come on now, Beth. This is a once-in-a-lifetime opportunity. Four days and forty-eight games of basketball, during which time you're actually under strict doctor's orders to be at my beck and call. How could I not pass that up?"

There's a knock at the door between the waiting room and the examination rooms, a door we happen to be standing in front of. We move away from the door.

"You ready, Hank?"

The nurse's voice is casual, familiar even. Her jet-black hair is pulled back in a tight ponytail, but the perfect Asian bone structure and the slightly mushy lilt on the end of her voice are dead giveaways. Well, that and the familiar D-cup Asian boobs staring back at me.

It's Lang, my full-breasted, half-Vietnamese neighbor. She always wears shorts and never wears shoes. I make up excuses to go over to her house just to look at her tight calves and perfect bare feet.

*Making Out with Blowfish*

And I really need to move to a bigger fucking town than Empire Ridge.

Beth doesn't recognize Lang, partly because she looks distinctly different with her hair up, but mostly because Lang is part of that exclusive subset of pariahs in my insecure wife's social circle known as The Perfectly Nice Women Who Will Never Be My Friends Just Because They're Hotter Than Me Club. In a way, the club is a godsend, as it helps me behave, but it gets annoying when we're vetting the invite list for vacations and couples weekends and "Does she look better than me in a swimsuit?" is Beth's one nonnegotiable item. In recent years, it's also really cut down on the quality of the traffic in our hot tub.

My wife kisses me on the cheek, still a little miffed, I think. "Bye-bye, balls," she says, unapologetically, grabbing an open seat in the waiting room. I leave her to watch ESPN break down today's basketball games with the eight other wives.

1. I, the undersigned, request that Empire Ridge Urology, Inc. perform a vasectomy on me. It has been explained to me that this operation is intended to result in permanent sterility, which means that I would not be capable of fathering a child.
2. I agree to the administration of local anesthetic (medicine to numb the area of the surgery) or other medications before, during, or after the procedure.
3. I understand that vasectomy is not immediately effective and that I must use another method of birth control until a semen test proves that my vasectomy was successful.
4. I recognize that, as with any operation, there are risks, both known and unknown, associated with vasectomy, and that no guarantee has been given to me as to the results of this operation. Possible complications include, but are not limited to, the following:
    a. Inflammatory reaction in the epididymis or vas deferens (5%)
    b. Excessive bleeding into the scrotum (hematoma)
    c. Painful nodule or scar (sperm granuloma, neuroma)
    d. Infection
    e. Allergy or adverse reaction to an anesthetic or medication
    f. Emotional reactions that could interfere with

>     normal sexual function
>   g. Impaired blood flow resulting in loss of a testicle
>   h. Failure to achieve or to maintain sterility
> 5. I understand and accept that these or other conditions may necessitate further treatment, tests, another operation, procedure, and/or hospitalization, at my own expense. I request and authorize Empire Ridge Urology, Inc. to perform such treatment or procedures as required.
> 6. I have read and understand the contents of the Informational Booklet, including the alternative forms of birth control for both men and women. I understand and will abide by the instructions for care after vasectomy, and I have received a written copy.

I hand Lang my signed consent form. "Excessive bleeding into the scrotum? Loss of a testicle? That's comforting."

She tries not to laugh. "Those are extreme worst-case scenarios, Hank."

I'm trying to make small talk, given that I'm pants-less and Lang has just dropped to her knees and is about to grab my balls. It's all I can do to not get an erection, but the mental image of my scrotum bleeding excessively helps.

"This should only take a second," Lang says. She grabs the can of Barbasol off the counter with her right hand. She squirts a dollop of shaving cream in her left palm. She gently massages my scrotum with the shaving scream.

Memo to any guys considering a vasectomy: Make sure your urologist has a hot nurse, and shave poorly.

"Soooo . . ." I say, "is Lang a family name or something?"

Her face only inches from my junk, Lang shaves with a deft touch. "It's a Vietnamese name."

"Meaning what?"

"It's a little embarrassing."

I look at my balls and then at Lang. I arch my eyebrows. "Uh, *you* are worried about being embarrassed?"

"Good point," Lang says. She rubs my bare balls with a wet, warm towel. "All done."

"So I can go?"

"Don't you wish."

There's a knock at the door. The door to the exam room opens. A big black man in a small white coat enters. His nametag says, almost unbelievably, *Dr. Balzac*.

The doctor nods at us both. "Nurse Lang, Mr. Fitzpatrick."

"Good morning, doctor," we chime in unison.

"Let's get to it, shall we?" He reaches his open hand out to Lang. Lang hands him a syringe. He points the syringe at my balls. "You take a Valium before you got in here?"

I nod. "Two of them."

"Oh boy," Lang comments.

"This is the lidocaine," the doctor says in a monotone voice. "Just some local anesthesia to numb the skin and vas deferens. You're going to feel a tiny prick."

"That's what she said," I say.

Lang laughs. The doctor doesn't.

"Fuck me!"

"Sorry about that, Mr. Fitzpatrick. Did I get you?"

"That was more than a little prick," I say. Suddenly, I feel short of breath. My chest is tight. I'm sweating.

Lang notices immediately. "Hank, what is it?"

My eyes are open wide. The room is shrinking. "I think I'm having a heart attack."

"Nonsense," the doctor says nonchalantly. "Probably nicked a blood vessel. You're just getting a small dose of adrenaline in your heart right now. It'll pass."

I'm scared. "Please . . ." I say, grabbing Lang's hand. "Just talk to me."

"Sweet potato," Lang says.

"What?"

"Lang is Vietnamese for sweet potato."

I nod. "Keep talking."

Lang wipes my forehead with a towel—a fresh one, not the one that was wrapped around my bag five minutes ago. "My mother's parents were sweet potato farmers just outside of Saigon. My father was a US Marine. He was married to my mother in the US Embassy the day Saigon fell."

"Wow, that's kind of awesome."

"Yeah, it is."

"I'm feeling better now, save for the fact the ceiling looks like it's made of Jell-O."

"That's the Valium kicking in."

"Cool," I say. And then it hits me: the urge to sing. *"They're called Bui-Doi . . ."*

Lang shakes her head. "Here we go."

*"The dust of life! Conceived in hell! And born in strife!"*

"Nurse Lang?" Dr. Balzac says.

*"They are the living reminder of all the good we failed to do . . ."*

"Sorry about this, doctor," Lang says. "Hank is on a little bit of a Valium bender right now. Apparently my Vietnam story has him singing the big emotional anthem from *Miss Saigon,* the one about the lost generation of

Vietnamese children conceived from Vietnamese women and US soldiers during the war."

*"We can't forget, must not forget that they are all our children, too!"*

I think the doctor actually smiles this time, although to be honest the whole world looks like it's smiling at the moment. "Well . . ." he says, "that's different."

Lang wheels me out of the exam room in a wheelchair. Beth is standing there waiting for me near the exit door.

"How did it go, honey?"

I throw a thumb over my shoulder. "I got my balls shaved by this sweet potato!"

Beth puts her finger to her pursed lips. "Shhhhhh . . ."

"What?"

"You're screaming, Hank."

"My urologist's name was Doctor Ballsack! Can you fucking believe that?"

Beth looks at Lang. "Is he going to be like this all day?"

"Ballsack!"

Lang shakes her head. "He's been hallucinating a bit from the anesthetic. It should wear off soon."

"Thanks, Miss . . ."

"You can call me Lang, Beth."

"Have we met?" my wife says. "You look familiar."

"Just in passing," Lang says. "I'm your neighbor."

"Get out of here."

"No, really."

"Ballsack!"

"I can't imagine why we haven't crossed paths yet." Beth laughs without a trace of earnestness in her voice.

"Oh, oh, oh, I know," I say, sticking my hand in the air like Arnold Horshack from *Welcome Back, Kotter*. "It's because you're too insecure to have friends who are hotter than you."

An uncomfortable, almost standoffish silence hangs in the air between Beth and Lang. If I could feel my tongue, I'd probably try to articulate some sort of mediation. What the hell, I'll give it a try:

*"They're called Bui-Doi! The dust of life! Conceived in hell! And born in strife!"*

"Uh . . ." Beth says. "What's going on?"

Lang smiles. "I find it's best to just let him finish."

*"We owe them fathers and a family a loving home they never knew. Because we know, deep in our hearts, that they are all our children, too!"*

# Chapter 34

"Ty Detmer is the least-deserving winner of the Heisman Trophy in the history of college football. That's a fucking fact, Gillman!"

"Hank, language!"

"My car, my rules."

My stepfather and I sit in my Subaru, arguing as we drive up Highway 31. We're attending the Notre Dame-Michigan together. Last week, Gillman hosted a viewing party for Notre Dame's opening game in the 2004 college football season because they were playing his alma mater, Brigham Young University. They were playing BYU in Provo, I got tired of Gillman harping on about BYU's supposed "tradition," and at some point during the game I declared, *"You want to see tradition, Gillman? Tell you what, if the Cougars beat the Irish, I'll buy us tickets to next week's Michigan game and personally drive us up to South Bend. Just you and I taking an old-fashioned father-and-son road trip."*

Final score: BYU 20–Notre Dame 17.

"Rocket Ismail better than Ty Detmer?" Gillman says. "Is that a joke?"

"Ty was just another overrated stats machine destined to flame out in the NFL, while Rocket was probably the most electrifying player of the decade."

"Says you, Hank."

"Says me and everyone who doesn't live in Utah. And what happened to Detmer the first game he played after winning the Heisman?"

"Oh no, here we go."

"Two broken arms, Gillman!"

"It was two separated shoulders, actually."

"Whatever," I say. "If that isn't God coming down and smiting him, I don't know what is."

"So your theory is that Ty Detmer's shoulders were not separated by a Texas A&M defensive player, but rather by God as vengeance for Rocket Ismail not winning the Heisman Trophy?"

I shake my head, my left hand on the steering wheel and my right pointing at Gillman. "You've got a lot to learn about Notre Dame football."

Gillman and I walk just past the northwest entrance of Notre Dame Stadium. "And right here was where I stood as an extra when Ned Beatty got off the bus. I remember he had on a faded brown trench coat and dark brown cap pulled over his ears and tufts of silvery-gray hair poking out of the bottom of his cap that made him look like my Grandpa George."

"So you were here when they filmed *Rudy*?"

"For some of the scenes, yeah."

"That's quite a memory, Hank."

"It's kind of hard to forget that season."

"What year was it?

"1992."

"Oh, sorry."

"Yeah. Me, too."

"We don't have to talk about it if you don't want to."

"I don't mind. After Dad died in October, Mom decided not to renew his tickets, so it was our last year as season ticket holders. She gave me two tickets for each of the remaining home games. I missed the Stanford game because of the funeral, but I went to BYU, Boston College, and Penn State.

"Dad had told me the *Rudy* story a hundred times before Hollywood ever got a hold of it. An old classmate tipped him off that they were going to be filming most of the campus scenes during the BC and Penn State games. I remember he had the dates, November 7th and November 14th, circled on his office calendar. I brought Jack with me to the BC game, but he was four years old and didn't know what was going on. We made it to our seats right before kickoff, but we missed all the pageantry: the gold helmets coming out of the tunnel, the band's high-step routine to *Hike Notre Dame,* the *Notre Dame Victory March,* even the national anthem and *America the Beautiful.*"

"Your father would have been pissed."

"Totally," I say. "At 6–1–1 Notre Dame was ranked number eight in the country. They had tied Michigan back in September and lost to Stanford the Saturday after Dad was killed. BC came in with a 7–0–1 record and a number nine ranking. It was the highest both teams had ever been ranked when facing one another. I saw a guy holding a poster that said *The Pope Needs Four Tickets*. ND won the coin toss, deferred to the second half, and Boston College chose to receive. The Irish defended the south goal, and I expected a great game."

"And did it meet your expectations?"

"Depends on what my expectations were."

"A win maybe?"

"Maybe," I say. "Two BC fans arrived late, toward the end of the first quarter. There was a TV timeout on the field, so the teams were huddled on opposite sidelines. The two BC fans sat down next to Jack and me, and one of them complained that he didn't realize there was an hour time difference between Chicago and South Bend. He asked me, 'What did we miss?' and I pointed to the scoreboard. It was 21–0 Notre Dame with four minutes still left in the first quarter."

"Ouch," Gillman says. "Still, it had to be a fun day with Jack."

"Like I said, he really didn't know what was going on. The highlight of the game for me was halftime. A bunch of extras in vintage 1972 Notre Dame and Georgia Tech football uniforms stormed the field. They executed about a dozen plays, we were given cues to cheer, and at the end, the Notre Dame players carried Sean Astin off the field."

"So you get to see that scene essentially replayed every time you watch *Rudy* now?"

"Yeah, I guess I do. But that game was bittersweet. Not just the circumstances of why I was there, but the game itself. The whole day left a bad taste in my mouth. Coach Holtz called a fake punt when the Irish were leading 37–0. They won 54–7, and no part of me felt good about rubbing it in BC's face. It was like Notre Dame had become as ugly and embittered as I felt. When I got home, I pulled out my shoe box of Notre Dame ticket stubs dating back to the first game I ever attended."

"Which game was that?"

"Georgia Tech 1978. Vagas Ferguson ran for a school-record two hundred fifty-five yards."

"Don't tell me you threw out all your tickets."

"Nope."

"Good."

"I burned them."

Gillman and I half-sprinted across the west side of campus. He watched as I crossed myself beneath Touchdown Jesus. As I patted Number One Moses on the head. As I saluted Fair Catch Corby. As I crossed myself again at the steps of the administration building and Our Lady atop the Golden Dome. By the time we got to the stone steps behind Sacred Heart Basilica, Gillman was hyperventilating.

"You okay, old man?"

We reach the bottom of the steps. Gillman hunches over, panting. "I sure hope . . . this was . . . worth it."

I pat my front pocket. "These things have to be done right."

Tucked in a small hillside just behind Sacred Heart, the Grotto is a one-seventh scale replica of the original Grotto of Our Lady of Lourdes, France where the Virgin Mary is said to have appeared to St. Bernadette. Dozens of white votive candles are perpetually lit inside the cobblestoned sanctuary, with that number hovering closer to a few hundred today, given that we're playing those Godless, Catholic-hating secularists known as the Michigan Wolverines.

I light a candle and drop a dollar in the collection box. A kneeler and a wrought iron fence run the full width of the Grotto. I wait for a small, elderly nun to vacate her spot and kneel in her place, assured that the kneeler will of course retain a little extra Catholic mojo.

I pull the rosary out of my pocket. It belonged to Grandpa George. He carried it with him during the war. Oxidized brass links connect fifty-nine beads of black onyx. Fifty-four of the beads converge into a brass Sacred Heart pendant, from which hangs the remaining five beads and a brass crucifix. I wrap the rosary twice loosely around my left hand. Using my right hand, I hold the crucifix in between my index finger and thumb. I recite the Apostles' Creed.

"I believe in God, the Father almighty, creator of heaven and earth. I believe in Jesus Christ, His only Son, our Lord. He was conceived by the power of the Holy Spirit and born of the Virgin Mary. He suffered under Pontius Pilate, was crucified, died, and was buried. He descended to the dead. On the third day he rose again. He ascended into heaven and is seated at the right hand of the Father. He will come again to judge the living and the dead. I believe in the Holy Spirit, the holy Catholic Church, the communion of saints, the forgiveness of sins, the resurrection of the body, and life everlasting. Amen."

I grab the larger bead just above the crucifix. I recite the Our Father.

"Our Father who art in heaven, hallowed be thy name. Thy kingdom come, thy will be done, on earth as it is in heaven. Give us this day our daily bread, and forgive us our trespasses, as we forgive those who trespass against us, and lead us not into temptation, but deliver us from evil. Amen."

I grab the second smaller bead. I say a Hail Mary.

"Hail Mary, full of grace, the Lord is with thee. Blessed art thou amongst women, and blessed is the fruit of thy womb, Jesus. Holy Mary, Mother of God, pray for us sinners, now and at the hour of our death. Amen."

I grab the next bead and repeat the Hail Mary prayer.

"Hail Mary, full of grace, the Lord is with thee. Blessed art thou amongst women, and blessed is the fruit of thy womb, Jesus. Holy Mary, Mother of God, pray for us sinners, now and at the hour of our death. Amen."

One more time.

"Hail Mary, full of grace, the Lord is with thee. Blessed art thou amongst women, and blessed is the fruit of thy womb, Jesus. Holy Mary, Mother of God, pray for us sinners, now and at the hour of our death. Amen."

I move to the fourth bead.

"Hail Mary, full of grace, the Lord is with thee. Blessed art thou amongst women, and blessed is the fruit of thy womb, Jesus. Holy Mary, Mother of God, pray for us sinners, now and at the hour of our death. Amen."

And finally, I throw in a Glory Be at the fifth bead.

"Glory be to the Father, and to the Son, and to the Holy Spirit, as it was in the beginning, is now, and ever shall be, world without end. Amen."

I stop. Shoving the rosary back in my pocket, I know this is all I have in me. There are people who make it through a full rosary every day, and that's not just one time around. A full rosary is three rotations. It comes out to something like seventy-five Our Fathers, one-hundred-and-fifty Hail Marys, and another seventy-five Glory Bes. Grandpa George tried making me sit through a whole rosary just once. I got about halfway before my knees went numb and I had to pee. Glory be to the Father, and to the Son, and to the Holy Spirit for eight-year-old bladders.

"About an hour until kickoff." Gillman whispers from behind, hushed and respectful. "Probably should think about making our way to the stadium."

"I'm ready, Gillman." I stand, offer my kneeler to another nun—for bonus points, of course.

On our way back across campus, the Young Republicans talk us into bratwursts in front of Doyle Hall. Gillman hands me the mustard.

"Thanks," I say.

"No, Hank, thank you."

"For what?"

"For sharing today with me. I know Notre Dame games were you and your father's thing."

"That they were, Gillman. But don't start getting soft on me. You're a decent guy and all, and you're real good to Mom and Jack, which in the end is all that matters to me. But I still think you're a total whack job."

"I'll take that as a compliment."

"You would."

"Well, Hank, you're one to talk."

"What do you mean by that?"

"For someone who isn't the biggest fan of all the pomp and circumstance of organized religion, that was a quite a show back there at the Grotto."

"I'm a fan of organized religion, Gillman. Just not *your* organized religion."

"You're a true believer, my friend. Against every impulse in your body, you have faith. Just admit it."

"Faith?" I finish off the last bite of my bratwurst and discard the wrapper. "The only goddamn thing I believe in is Notre Dame football."

"Hank, language!"

"My campus, my rules."

# Chapter 35

The rain is cold and ferocious. I can't see out the front of my Subaru. The water veils my station wagon in a sideways sheet of foreboding. Jack is standing outside, waiting for me. He runs to my car, his clothes soaked through to his wiry teenage frame.

"Need a ride?" I say, opening the door.

Jack slides into the car, shuts the door. He runs his hand through his wet hair and pulls his Prep letter jacket around his face, trying to shield his bloodshot eyes from me. "Can we just go?"

"Where?"

"Somewhere, anywhere."

Jack is about an inch taller and twenty pounds lighter than me. Fifteen years old, a month and a half into his sophomore year in high school, his jacket bears his athletic accomplishments: a block-letter $P$ on his left chest; two chevrons, one in soccer, one in golf; a couple all-conference recognition patches in each sport.

"Where are Mom and Gillman?" I say, shifting the car into reverse.

"They went to Brown County for the weekend."

"Car still in the shop?"

"Yep."

In the great Fitzpatrick tradition, Jack's car seems to spend more time in the body shop than on the road. He only has his permit, and he's already wrecked his car twice.

"So how stoned are you?"

"Whatever happened to 'no questions asked'?"

"I guess I forgot about that after I picked up my brother standing in a monsoon in front of a strange house with liquor and marijuana on his breath."

"You can smell all that?"

"I'm guessing Jim Beam and a couple rounds of bong hits in a small enclosed room."

"How the hell did you—"

"The Beam was easy," I say. "Cheap bourbon has a fairly distinctive smell, and I still drink it enough to recognize it almost immediately. As for the bong hits, your eyes are redder than Ben Johnson at the '88 Seoul Olympics, and the cannabis smell coming off your skin, clothes, and hair is way too strong to be delivered by just a joint or bowl."

"Who's Ben Johnson?"

"Shut up, Jack."

Man, I'm getting fucking old.

We head to Wagon Wheel, the late-night greasy spoon on Central Street that's frequented by no one under the age of seventy-five. I used to take Grandpa George here when I was a teenager, a few months before I learned it wasn't cool to hang out with your grandfather in public and a few years before his death taught me I was a dipshit. The waitress brings us two plates of biscuits and gravy.

"Not hungry," Jack says, pushing his plate away.

"Like hell you aren't." I push his plate right back at him. "Now eat and talk to me."

"I can't do it anymore, Hank."

"Can't do what?"

"Live under the same roof as Gillman."

"Come on, Jack. He means well."

"Does he?"

"So he's a little controlling."

"Last night he found a couple of those little travel bottles of whiskey in my nightstand."

"And I assume he grounded you, which is what parents are supposed to do."

"He grounded me all right. He said when he and Mom get back from Brown County I'm losing all cell phone privileges for the rest of the semester."

"Damn!" I say. "That's like cutting off a dude's arm."

"I know, right?"

"I'm kidding, buddy." I sip my black coffee, slowly and with intent. I return my coffee cup to its saucer. I have to get these words right. I'm more than his big brother, and I need to start acting like it. "Look, as much as I want to back you up, I've gotten to the age where I'm not allowed to be on your side sometimes. Does that make any sense to you?"

"No."

"I didn't think it would, so tell me, what's *really* bothering you."

"What do you mean?"

"Saying you have problems with Gillman is like saying the sky is blue. We all have problems with Gillman. He's a dick."

"What happened to 'he means well' and he's just 'a little controlling'?"

"I was being nice. So come on, fess up. You having problems at Prep?"

"No, Prep is awesome. The Ridge sucks, dude."

"Excuse my French, little brother, but fuck you."

"Ha ha." Jack's first smile of the night. "I love getting you all amped up."

"Well, it's working."

"Like I said, Prep is cool. I just had an issue tonight, at the party."

"What kind of issue?"

"It's a little embarrassing."

"Try me."

"There's this game kids at Prep and the Ridge are really into right now. It's called a lipstick party."

"Never heard of it."

"It's big in New York and LA, I guess. Last year somebody transferred in from Culver and brought the game with them."

Culver is a military academy in northeastern Indiana that could have been ripped right out of a Bret Easton Ellis novel. An oasis of old East Coast money, its alumni include George Steinbrenner and Roger Penske. I took a weekend tour of the campus when I was a sophomore in high school and saw somebody snort cocaine out of a girl's cleavage at a party involving a lot of old-money kids with Roman numerals at the end of their names. Whatever a lipstick party is, if it came from Culver, it can't be good.

"I'm listening, Jack."

"A lipstick party is when a bunch of girls put different colored lipstick on their mouths and then give guys blowjobs in the dark. When the lights are turned back on, the guys try to guess which girl gave them the blowjob."

"You got to be kidding me."

"Nope."

"That's not just a plot for a bad TV show on Fox or an exploitative YA novel?"

"It's very real, Hank."

"So you were at one of these lipstick parties tonight?"

"Yes."

"And what did you do?"

"What do you mean, what did I do? I chickened out."

"And?"

"And everyone is going to make fun of me at school on Monday."

"Not everyone."

"You don't know, Hank."

"Don't tell me what I don't know. In fact, I'd be willing to bet almost no one makes fun of you."

"I don't believe you."

"What I'm telling you is not for you to believe or disbelieve. It's a fact. There will be a couple douche bags who give you a hard time, but high school is like an all-you-can-eat douche bag buffet. And sure, maybe a few sluts will no longer look your way at a party. But is empty validation and a sexually transmitted disease really something to lose sleep over? Trust me when I say there will be a lot of girls who are going to respect you more for doing what you did, and out of those girls, you're going to find one who will run through fire for you. Maybe you don't find her tomorrow, or even next year. Maybe you don't find her until college. Or maybe you find her, and for whatever reason the timing just isn't right for you two. But when you do find her, and when the timing is right, hold on to her. A real man only needs one tube of lipstick."

"Why would I need a tube of lipstick?" Jack asks. "I'm not gay."

"You know, little brother, you really suck at metaphors."

"And you, big brother, seem to think everything in life needs one."

# Part VII
# 2005

# Chapter 36

A family road trip from Indiana to North Carolina with a nine-year-old and two five-year-olds: What were Beth and I thinking?

The Southern Outer Banks are about eight-hundred miles away from Empire Ridge. Our Honda Odyssey minivan's DVD player kept the kids occupied nearly all the way to Raleigh, but at this point, as we pass over the White Oak River Bridge in Swansboro, I'm halfway considering chucking all three of them into the White Oak River.

"Daddy," Sasha says.

"Yes, honey?"

"The boys keep farting, and it stinks back here."

"Then open a window."

My wife had tried to put this drive off as long as possible. Stan still owns his pediatric practice in Empire Ridge, but he's pretty much retired at this point, spending eight months of the year at the pink beach house, which he got in the divorce. This is the first time we've brought the kids back to the place since Stan and Joan separated, and we're worried how they'll react. During the holidays, Beth's parents are acutely skilled at pretending they like one another—"I've had decades of practice," Joan told me last Christmas—so up to this point, the kids really haven't been affected by the situation.

"I tried opening a window," my daughter says. "It doesn't work."

"Boys," I say. "Stop it."

"Stop what?" Johnny says.

"You're suffocating your sister."

"What's suck fuck kating?" Burke says.

Johnny giggles.

"Burke said the f-word, Daddy."

"I know what he said, Sasha."

"You have to give him one squirt. Those are the rules."

Burke starts crying. "It was an accident, Daddy. No squirt! No squirt!"

I notice my wife eyeing the glove box. "No, Beth. Like he said, it was an accident. And it's vacation."

"Don't complain to me," Beth says. "You made the stupid rule."

Sasha and Burke are referring to the most feared weapon in our parent arsenal, the doomsday device: a squirt of liquid hand soap. We keep the bottle of orange retribution in the glove boxes of both vehicles. One cuss word equals one squirt on your tongue. Like Tina Turner telling Mel Gibson as he entered Thunder Dome, "Two men enter, one man leaves," the squirt is the law.

"Bust a deal, face the wheel," I say to my wife.

"What's that mean?"

"You know, *Mad Max: Beyond Thunderdome*?"

"That post-apocalypse movie with Mel Gibson?"

"Yes!"

"Never seen it."

"What? So when someone says to you, 'This is Thunderdome, death is listening, and will take the first man who screams,' that means nothing to you?"

"Up until just this moment I have never heard those words used in a sentence together, and I've certainly never heard that bad of a Tina Turner impersonation."

"It was good enough that you recognized it."

"This isn't Thunderdome, Hank. It's a Honda Odyssey."

"I know that, Beth." I look at my red-eyed son in the rearview mirror. "Hey, Burke, bust a deal, face the wheel."

He wipes his nose. "What?"

"If you break the agreement we had for cuss words, I get to choose another punishment."

"What's my other punishment?"

"Well, that's not really in the spirit of the agreement, but I'll go easy on you. Your choice is either to eat soap or be nice to your sister for the entire vacation."

Burke looks at me in the rearview mirror. Looks at his sister. Looks at me again. He closes his eyes and sticks out his tongue.

Burke is on his third juice box in as many minutes, trying to get the hand soap taste out of his mouth. We're about through Emerald City and nearing Stan's place in Salter Path.

"Promise me something, Hank?" Beth both says and asks simultaneously.

"Depends on what that 'something' is."

"No working vacation this week. I want my husband off the clock."

"You know I can't promise that. I have a lunch with Margaret on Wednesday that I can't miss."

"A lunch appointment? Since when?"

"Since we booked this trip."

Margaret is Margaret Maron, the author of the North Carolina-based

Judge Deborah Knott mystery series. I've been trying to woo her away from her print publisher Mysterious Press for years, but Random House has given College Ave increasingly less acquisitions money to work with. I have it on good authority Margaret has already re-upped with Mysterious—well, her agent just flat out told me—and that Margaret is taking this lunch with me more out of guilt. I figure the least I could do is put a couple bottles of red wine and some shrimp and grits on my Random expense account.

It's not that my relationship with Random House hasn't been fruitful. Far from it. I've made a lot of money off being more lucky than good. I was gifted Lila's book, *Sperm Bank Messiah*, which she managed to stretch into a trilogy. Each successive book in the series—the middle volume, *Mrs. Jesus*, and the finale, *Viva Leviticus*—was more critically panned while at the same time more commercially successful than its predecessor. And then, just last year, a flavor-of-the-year graphic novelist at Comic-Con agreed to adapt one of my own short stories, "Plaid & Plasma," into a tongue-in-cheek fusion of contemporary vampire fiction and Scottish Highlands romance called *Blood, Sex and Kilts* that hit the *New York Times* bestseller list and was optioned by FX for a television series.

"You got one lunch," Beth says, holding up her left index finger. "But if at any other point in the week I see you bust out that stupid laptop, I'm chucking it in the ocean. Deal?"

I grab her hand and kiss it. "Deal."

We pull into Stan's driveway. The pink paint on the cedar shake has faded to salmon. A white sign hangs over the front door with the words *Little Pink House* burned into its surface.

"Let's unpack later," my wife says. "Dad hasn't seen his grandkids in months."

We unharness Sasha and the twins. Beth leads the way. A wind chime serenades us as we walk across the white-railed front porch and into the house. My wife walks in without knocking.

Busted.

"Dad!" Beth shouts. With her left hand she covers Sasha's eyes, with her right forearm she shields the eyes of the twins.

A tanned woman in a white bikini, a little older than Beth but not by much, is in the kitchen with Stan. She's on her knees, giving my father-in-law a blowjob.

The woman bolts upright, wiping her mouth.

"You're early," Stan says, pulling up his swim trunks and scolding my wife, as if she's the one who needs the lesson on decorum.

"Apparently not early enough," Beth says.

I reach my hand out to the tanned woman in the white bikini. Much like Jack's old principal, she's more fit than attractive. Upon closer inspection she also looks more midfifties than midthirties. "Hi, my name is Hank."

The woman accepts my gesture. She shakes my hand, outwardly not the least put off by what just happened. There's not even a hint of blushing in her face, although granted that would be hard to see against her leathered, burnt-tan paprika skin. "Hiya, darlin'," she says. "My name is Marilyn, but all my friends call me May-May."

"May-May?"

"Yeah, darlin'. I used to have a twin sister named Margaret, ya see. But she died as a baby, on account of havin' a weak heart. We were born in May, so after Ma lost her, she took to callin' me 'May-May' 'cause she couldn't bear to forget her little Margaret."

"That's . . . interesting," I say.

"You Yankees and yuh manners," May-May says, pulling her hand away from me and backhanding my arm. "It's downright morbid, s'what it is. I just cain't never imagine bein' called anythin' else."

"Well, May-May"—Beth elbows me out of the way—"if you need someone to be rude to you, I can do you that favor."

"Easy, little girl," Stan says, stepping between the two women.

"I'm not your fu—" Beth cuts her expletive in half, realizing her kids are well within earshot. "I'm not your little girl, Dad. But if I were, that would probably be cool, because given her age, May-May and I would probably be into a lot of the same things."

"You think?"

"That's not a freaking compliment!"

"Hey, May-May," I interject. "Can you do me a favor and take the kids out back?"

"Sure thing, darlin'," she says, turning to Sasha and the twins. "Have any of you ever seen a jellyfish before?"

"Is it made out of real jelly?" Burke says.

"No, stupid," Sasha answers.

"Zip it, Sasha," I say. "Just go outside with Miss May-May and your brothers for a few minutes. We have to talk to Grandpa about something."

"Children, y'all can call me Aunt May-May."

"No, *y'all* can't," Beth says.

In between yelling at her father for the last twenty minutes, my wife has consumed a pitcher of margaritas. I'm standing on the periphery, a bottle of Carolina Blonde Ale in my hand as I watch my own Carolina blonde pace between the kitchen and living room, still pissed as hell.

"I'm sorry for what you saw," Stan says to his daughter.

"Apology not accepted."

"Who's apologizing? I'm not sorry for it happening. I don't owe you an explanation for being in a relationship."

"A relationship?" Beth points out the back window. "Is that what you call that tanned dick sucker out there?"

And there's my cue. "Come on, babe. That's a bit harsh."

Beth sends me another slightly more obvious cue. "You stay the fuck out of this, Hank."

"Baby doll, please," Stan says. "We're not going to fix this today. Just tell me what you want from me."

"What do I want from you?" Beth wipes one lone tear from her right eye. I have a feeling that's all she's giving him today. "I want my dad back."

"But I haven't gone anywhere."

"You know what I mean."

"How about if for now I just ask May-May to go home?"

"How about if you just ask her to go to hell?"

"Home is good for now, Doc," I say.

Stan walks out the back door. Beth turns and faces me. "Don't tell me you're on his side."

"I'm not on anybody's side. So your dad has a girlfriend. There are worse things in the world. Quite frankly, I'm a little put off by your behavior at the moment."

"What did I do?"

"Not that I'm surprised, but you seem more possessive and jealous about your father than you ever are with me."

"You're not barking up that tree again, are you?"

"You kind of invite the barking."

"A woman half his age was giving him head in his kitchen!"

"First off, last time I checked your father isn't a hundred years old. Secondly, good for him. He's starring in his own rom-com."

"His own what?"

"Romantic comedy. There's you, the daughter, losing touch with her femininity under the heavy burden of motherhood while dealing with the broken marriage of your empty-nester parents. There's Stan, the exiled father, rediscovering his masculinity in the arms of an attractive and confoundedly endearing woman."

"Confoundedly endearing?"

"I know you don't see it, Beth. But May-May is ripped right out of a screenplay. She's like Bess Armstrong in *The Four Seasons* and Sarah Jessica Parker in *LA Story*."

"Or like Natalie Portman in *Beautiful Girls* and Mena Suvari in *American Beauty*."

"Jesus Christ, it's not like your father is pining after Lolita. He and May-May are two consenting adults. They just want to have a little—"

Beth raises her hand. "Let me stop you right there, hubby."

"What?"

"When I say 'stop,' that means stop talking. You know how you like to do that thing where you distill a scene into something insightful or clever, as if you have an invisible audience watching you?"

I don't respond.

"Uh, hello?"

I shrug my shoulders, still silent.

"You can nod your head, smartass."

I nod my head.

"Well, I fucking hate it."

"Sorry."

"No you're not," Beth says. "Now wipe that faraway look off your face and stop thinking about Natalie Portman in *Beautiful Girls,* you pervert."

Busted.

# Chapter 37

Easter Vigil is the service held traditionally after sunset on Holy Saturday before the sun rises on Easter Sunday. This service engenders wildly disparate reactions in Catholics. The devout regard it as the most important mass of the liturgical year, while the majority of Catholics—i.e., those of us who have two-point-three children because we wear condoms and pop birth control pills like Tic Tacs, think abortions should be rare but legal, and would rather watch *The Last Temptation of Christ* than *The Passion of the Christ*—well, we fucking hate it.

Very simply, Easter Vigil is when the real Catholics get their Jesus on. The service is anywhere from three to four hours long and is an all-you-can-eat sacramental buffet. There are Baptisms, First Communions, Reconciliations, Confirmations, even weddings. Easter Vigil is interminable to the point where in the pantheon of old school Papist rituals I'd rather sit through a Rosary, watch a Mother Angelica marathon on EWTN, or read an entire issue of *Latin Mass* magazine.

The first Easter Vigil service I remember attending was in 1983. We were living in Louisville, Kentucky. Our next-door neighbor was the team doctor for the University of Louisville men's basketball team, a dynastic program of the early eighties. He got Dad and me in to see closed practices in which we met the players, and so names like Milt Wagner, Lancaster Gordon, Scooter and Rodney McCray, Charles Jones, and Billy Thompson supplanted the latest Fighting Irish football players at the dinner table. Granted, Dad and I appropriated the Cardinals more as a temporary distraction from the Gerry Faust era at Notre Dame, but our passion and commitment was real enough to us.

Louisville was playing Houston in the Final Four the Saturday night before Easter. CBS promoted it as "the Doctors of Dunk versus Phi Slamma Jamma." Dad had the bright idea to go to church on Saturday afternoon so we could stay up late and watch the game while not having to worry about getting up early for church. We attended Holy Trinity. An eighteen-year-old parishioner by the name of Mary T. Meagher was the cross bearer, still a year away from winning gold in the pool at the Summer Olympics in Los Angeles. We missed almost the entire game, although about halfway into the four-hour Vigil service, Dad excused himself to go to the restroom, never to return. Just as my feet and knees had gone numb and I shouted my first "Alleluia!" in forty days, Dad was in the car screaming at his radio, "Crum, get a body on Olajuwon!"

Today's Easter Vigil service is passably tolerable, as I have a vested interest. For one, my old friend Father Fisher Kelly presides over today's Easter Vigil. For another, Beth and Sasha are receiving the sacrament of First Communion together. Father Fish wears the traditional Roman Catholic alb, a white linen liturgical vestment with tapered sleeves. The stole around his neck is reversible, purple on one side and white on the other, which allowed him to symbolically flip it from purple to white at the beginning of the service to symbolize the progression from Lent to Easter. He stands behind the altar. A large ceramic bowl of communal wafers sits to his left, a gold chalice of wine to his right.

"Blessed are you, Lord, God of all creation," Father Fish says. "Through your goodness we have this bread to offer, which earth has given and human hands have made. It will become for us the bread of life."

The congregation responds, "Blessed be God forever."

"Blessed are you, Lord, God of all creation," Father Fish says again. "Through your goodness we have this wine to offer, fruit of the vine and work of human hands. It will become our spiritual drink."

We again respond back to him, "Blessed be God forever."

Father Fish walks us through the requisite rituals: the singing, the bell ringing, the bowing, the reaffirmations we say by rote more than faith. After about ten minutes, Beth and Sasha approach the foot of the altar with the other catechists. My wife wears a sheer black dress, my daughter a floral print that, because she's nine years old, I can still get away with calling cute instead of pretty. An altar boy stands in front of Father Fish, holding open a leather-bound book. Father looks down intermittently at the book, but the way he maintains eye contact with the congregation tells me he isn't reading it.

"The holy Eucharist completes Christian initiation," Father Fish begins. "Those who have been raised to the dignity of the royal priesthood by Baptism and configured more deeply to Christ by Confirmation participate with the whole community in the Lord's own sacrifice by means of the Eucharist.

"At the Last Supper, on the night he was betrayed, our Savior instituted the Eucharistic sacrifice of his body and blood. This he did in order to perpetuate the sacrifice of the cross throughout the ages until he should come again, and so to entrust to his beloved spouse, the Church, a memorial of his death and resurrection: a sacrament of love, a sign of unity, a bond of charity, a Paschal banquet in which Christ is consumed, the mind is filled with grace, and a pledge of future glory is given to us."

*Making Out with Blowfish*

This is the part about the Eucharist that usually freaks out non-Catholics. Protestants regard the consumption of Jesus's body and blood as symbolic, while Catholics are supposed to believe in a process called transubstantiation, by which the bread and wine are mystically transformed into the literal body and blood of Jesus. That's right, Catholics are actively practicing cannibals. The doctrine is disgusting, but the truth is most Catholics don't obsess about it too much; with all due apologies to Pope John Paul II and Mother Angelica, we don't buy into it any more than our Protestant friends.

Father Fish continues. "The Eucharist is the source and summit of the Christian life. The other sacraments, and indeed all ecclesiastical ministries and works of the apostolate, are bound up with the Eucharist and are oriented toward it. For in the blessed Eucharist is contained the whole spiritual good of the Church, namely Christ himself, our Pasch.

"The Eucharist is the efficacious sign and sublime cause of that communion in the divine life and that unity of the People of God by which the Church is kept in being. It is the culmination both of God's action sanctifying the world in Christ and of the worship men offer to Christ and through him to the Father in the Holy Spirit.

"Finally, by the Eucharistic celebration we already unite ourselves with the heavenly liturgy and anticipate eternal life, when God will be all in all. The Eucharist is the sum and summary of our faith: Our way of thinking is attuned to the Eucharist, and the Eucharist in turn confirms our way of thinking[1]."

If the Lord works in mysterious ways, the fact Beth came around to "our way of thinking" is as mysterious as it gets. How does the wife of the world's worst Catholic, not to mention the daughter of a divorced atheist, decide that a world of rhythm methods and fish fries is the smart move? In the decade prior to Beth starting catechism, I could count on one hand the number of times we'd been to church that didn't involve a holiday, wedding, or funeral.

Sasha is mostly to blame. Firmly ensconced in the Empire Ridge Public School system, she's now more than two years behind her Catholic friends who received their First Communion at age six or seven. It got to a point where we didn't go to church just to avoid explaining why she was the only one her age required to approach the altar for the Eucharist with crossed arms and a closed mouth. Barring that, we've deferred to the ultimate rationalization of thirtysomething closet agnostics that, our intellectual faculties be damned, we're giving Sasha "a good foundation." Like most parents in their midthirties, Beth and I have talked ourselves into believing that in lieu of relying on our own reasonably competent parenting skills, it

---

[1] Catechism of the Catholic Church; Part Two, The Celebration of The Christian Mystery; Section Two, The Seven Sacraments of the Church; Chapter One, The Sacraments of Christian Initiation; Article 3, The Sacrament of the Eucharist.

is up to an imaginary bearded old man in the sky to teach our kids right from wrong. Furthermore, he's not even teaching them right from wrong; rather, he's teaching them there's no point in worrying about right or wrong as long as you bathe in the soul-cleansing afterbirth of his kinda-but-not-really-dead son.

Like I said, I'm the world's worst Catholic.

"Welcome to the fine young cannibals."

"Aren't they a band?" Beth asks.

"Or so you thought."

Sasha looks up at me. "Daddy, why do grownups drink wine? It tastes horrible."

"Check back with me in about ten years."

Beth wraps her arm around my waist. "If we're that lucky."

"I thought that was you," Father Fish says from behind us. Before I can even turn to face him, he has me in a full bear hug.

"Been a while, Father," I say.

Father Fish grabs Beth and Sasha and brings them into the hug. "Too long."

"I can't breathe," Sasha says.

We stand back for a few moments, allowing Father Fish to reacquaint himself with the polyester brigade exiting the church, the procession of retirees who still regard him as their pastor and will see to it that Father never pays for a meal, eighteen holes of golf, a ticket to a Notre Dame football game, or a car. If Dad were alive, he'd be their ringleader.

The narthex empties. Sasha is busy playing in the baptismal font. Beth and I again approach Father Fish.

"What are you doing here?" I say. "I thought you're retired."

"Semiretired," Father says. "I've been doing missionary work in Central America for the last three years and just needed some time to recharge the batteries. With Father Liam on sabbatical in Rome, I thought I'd come back to my old stomping grounds for Easter. I assume you're going to be at the birthday party in a few weeks."

"Birthday party?"

My master scheduler pipes up behind me. "Jack's 'Second Sixteenth' party, husband."

"Oh, that," I say. "You mean the birthday party Mom is throwing for Jack two months after the fact because she was too busy skiing in Salt Lake City in February."

"Be nice," Father says. "She's the only mother you have."

"Don't remind me."

"Hank!" Beth says, smacking my shoulder.

"I'm kidding," I say. I rub my shoulder, looking at Father Fish. "Of course I'll be there. I take it Mom invited you, Father?"

He flashes me his toothy white grin. "Not really. I kind of invited myself.

I have a little surprise for Jack."

"What is it?" Beth and I say in unison.

A liver-spotted wrinkly hand squeezes my shoulder. I notice out of the corner of my eye that Father still wears a gold claddagh ring on his left ring finger, the heart turned inward as a sign of his commitment to the Lord.

"Your guess is as good as mine," Father says.

# Chapter 38

It's Friday night, April 22. Although Jack's birthday was technically in February and mine was yesterday, Mom decided to throw Jack a "Second Sixteenth" party after missing his actual birthday. With Father Fish here and Jeanine in town from Portland after kicking Marcus out of her condo, Debbie was conveniently rewarded for being a shitty mother. As for me, well, I'm left with a quieter thirty-fourth celebration over Sunday brunch.

My passive-aggressive behavior toward my mother notwithstanding, I have to admit sobriety suits Mom. She's managed to throw quite a party tonight, rounding up conceivably everyone who's ever met Jack. As I look around the backyard, it's a who's who of our family history. Gillman sweats over the charcoal grill, flanked by Lila and Chris. Mom sips on a glass of sparkling water while chatting up Aunt Claudia and Aunt Ophelia. Uncle Howard and Father Fish try to make small talk, pretending they have anything in common. Jeanine stands next to them, just in from Portland and newly single after her long engagement to Marcus ended with him taking a Euroleague front office job in Barcelona with Winterthur FC Barcelona. Nancy Friedman, Jack's old babysitter and surrogate mother, nibbles on a plate of cheese and crackers. Aaron Rosner is down from Ann Arbor with a Monster Energy Drink supermodel on his arm. Hatch and Claire stand on opposite sides of the yard from one another, still happily married, although in typical Hatch and Claire fashion, you'd think they barely like one another. Beth's parents, Stan and Joan, are also on opposite sides of the yard, not having to pretend. And of course there's my brood, Sasha and the twins. They are playing a game of girls versus boys touch football, with Jack and the twins on one side and Beth and Sasha on the other.

The party has already had its requisite awkward moments. Gillman judged Chris with his eyes whenever she touched Lila in an affection manner, after which he caught me with a bottle of Miller High Life and gave me his "not in my house" speech. Stan and Joan tried and failed to not hate one another with Beth as the conscripted referee. Aunt Ophelia remained firmly entrenched in her tenth year of stonewalling me, somehow convinced I'm partially to blame for that pedophile rotting in the ground with a hole in his head. Claire relentlessly flirted with Jack—well, at least to the point where Hatch subbed for Beth in the game just so he could "accidentally" nail Jack in the balls with the football.

"Burgers are up," Gillman says.

"About time," I say, the ice rattling as I sip the soda from my red plastic cup. Rather than endure Gillman's Mormon wrath, I stashed the High Life, but the joke is on him. I'm still making do with a hip flask of Jim Beam, which I use to top off my Diet Coke, and the eleven-pack of High Life sits wrapped in a bow in the mini-fridge in Jack's room.

"Boys rule, girls drool!" the twins shout.

Their sister doesn't appreciate the gloating. "Mom let you win, you dummies."

Beth taps her on her shoulder.

"What?" Sasha says.

"No dessert for you."

"Mom, but there's cake."

"I know."

"But that's not fair!"

"It's fair for sisters who call their brothers dummies."

Beth and the kids enter the house. I hang back with Jack. He seems leaner than usual, although all I have for a control group is my former sparkplug wrestling build.

"Soccer start up yet?" I ask.

"Just finished the indoor season," Jack says. "I'm taking a few weeks off. Prep tryouts are in June."

"Tryouts? I thought you were hoping for team captain."

"I am. Coach has everyone try out just for appearances. No individual player is more important than the other. You know, all that team-building rah-rah shit."

"Don't let Gillman catch you with that mouth."

"Fuck Gillman."

"You got some game out there."

"Where?"

"Out there, with Beth and the kids. You got some moves. Quick feet. You throw a nice, tight spiral. Why didn't you ever try out for the football team?"

"No offense, but I was playing against a nine-year-old girl and a middle-aged woman."

"If you call Beth middle-aged to her face, she'll do worse than what Hatch did to you."

"What's with that guy?"

"Maybe stop making googly eyes at his wife."

"Claire was coming on to me."

"She just loves the attention, and she especially loves getting under

Hatch's skin."

"So he's not a dick?"

"Nah," I say. "He comes on a little strong, but he means well."

"Did he mean well when he threw me in the lake when I was three years old and didn't know how to swim?"

"You still remember that?"

"I remember Dad wanted to kill him."

"Yeah, buddy, that narrows things down to roughly two dozen moments in Hatch and Dad's relationship."

"They had a relationship?"

"More parasitic than symbiotic."

"More what?" Jack asks.

"Never mind," I say. I open the back door, ushering Jack inside the house. "Like I said, he means well."

Between the Beam and Cokes, what I estimate to be a half of a cow, and the red velvet birthday cake made with butter cream icing, I need a nap. Sitting at the patio table on the back porch, surrounded by his loved ones, Jack seems pleased if not overwhelmed by his second round of gifts in the last eight weeks. Mom and Gillman got him an Indiana University soccer jersey to go with the week of summer soccer camp, which disappointed me. I gave Jack a secret "present" earlier in the day: my driver's license that I had claimed as missing to the Indiana Department of Motor Vehicles. I said to him, "On the record, I strongly discourage underage drinking, and if you get caught with this I'll claim you stole it. Off the record, if you can find an out-of-the-way, hole-in-the-wall liquor store, this should do the trick." Officially, however, Jeanine and I already went in together on a used Trek road bike we found on eBay. To go with the roundtrip ticket to New York they bought him in February, Lila and Chris bought Jack box seats and backstage passes to the musical *Rent*, a gesture Gillman seemed not to appreciate. Everyone else left it up to Jack, giving him a mixture of cash, checks, and gift cards.

"Is that it?" Jack asks.

"I guess I'm up, then." Father Fish stands up from his chair and walks across the back porch to Jack. He's wearing a red cardigan sweater and underneath that the standard black-on-black attire of a Catholic priest, his white clerical collar showing at the neck.

"Father, you didn't have to get me anything."

"I didn't." Father Fish reaches into his sweater, pulling out a manila envelope. "This is a letter, from your father."

"What?" Jack says, as shocked as we all are. The backyard suddenly feels a whole lot smaller. Everyone has stopped eating, drinking, talking, or even breathing.

"I guess an explanation might help," Father says.

Jack leans over in his chair. He rubs his mouth with his hand. "Uh, it wouldn't hurt."

"When you were about two years old, your father came to see me in my office." Father looks at Mom. "You remember that, Debbie?"

"I think so," Mom says. "That was after the motorcycle accident, right?"

"Exactly."

Something Mom neglected to tell us until just recently was that three years before he was killed, Dad almost died in a motorcycle accident. Back in '89 Dad was out riding motorcycles with a couple of his buddies. It had started raining, they were on a bridge, and the semi driver never saw them. My father barely avoided the truck only to see one of his best friends crushed between the trailer and the side of the bridge. The guy died in Dad's arms.

Dad's motorcycle phase was brief. His bike was a royal blue Suzuki with white trim. Dad agreed to teach me how to ride it, but only if I promised not to tell Mom about it. I can still smell the collusion of father and son in the air, a mixture of sweat, exhaust fumes, and Aqua Velva aftershave. I still have a scar on my right calf from burning my leg on the Suzuki's exhaust pipe.

Dad let Uncle Mitch drive the Suzuki once. I can still remember Dad handing him the keys and Uncle Mitch sneaking one last drag off his Merit before flipping the cigarette into our front lawn. He had only completed one lap around the neighborhood when he took the last turn right before our driveway a little too fast. He panicked, gunned the engine. The Suzuki spun out, slid sideways a good five or six feet, throwing Uncle Mitch face-first onto the concrete. Everyone cried but me. Uncle Mitch managed to escape with only a busted lip. For a raging closet pedophile, the guy lived quite the charmed life.

Dad sold the Suzuki three days after the bridge accident to one of our neighbors, Calvin Franks. Mr. Franks had a miniature schnauzer, six saltwater aquariums, and two cockatiels. He liked to drink Pepsi, build radio-controlled airplanes, and light illegal fireworks on the Fourth of July with his cigarettes.

"John was white as a sheet," Father recounts. "He told me about the accident, how he kept having nightmares, premonitions even."

"Premonitions?" Jack says.

"That he would die young."

"Oh my God," Mom says.

I stand up, waving my arms. "Okay now, take it easy. Let's not make this out to be anything more than what it really is."

Mom looks at me, her mouth still agape. "And what's that, Hank?"

"A random coincidence," I say. "Please, Father, continue."

"Very well," he says. "So John tells me that he isn't afraid of dying—rather, he's afraid of not getting to grow old with Debbie and most of all not getting to know Jack. He felt like he was so busy with getting into the car business that he missed Hank and Jeanine growing up. He saw Jack as his second chance, his new lease on life, his blank canvas, and he was afraid he wouldn't be there to help paint it."

"So he told you all of this?" I say.

"Every word of it." Father slides the manila envelope across the patio table. Jack stops it with his hand. "Inside that envelope is a letter from your dad, Jack. I was instructed by John that if he died prematurely, I was to deliver it to you on your sixteenth birthday. Well, here I am. Granted, I'm a couple months late."

I shoot Mom a look. "His excuse was missionary work in Third World countries. What's yours?"

Jack grabs my arm, shaking his head at me. "Some other time, Hank."

"Agreed," Father Fish says. "Anyway, there's your letter. May God bless you."

The wise old priest turns on his heels and walks toward the house to leave.

"Wait, Father," Jack says. "You don't want to know what he had to say?"

Father closes his eyes, purses his lips, and sighs. He opens his eyes. "Jack, that picture is for you and your father."

Almost everybody gets the hint. We spend about a half hour saying our goodbyes and thank yous. Gillman leaves with Lila and Chris on an evening drive. (Mormons do that a lot.) Joan and Stan take the grandkids out to see a movie. Jack asks Mom, Jeanine, Beth, and me to stay.

He has yet to move from the patio table. We sit down next to him. I stop the pretense and bring up the Miller High Life from the mini-fridge, sitting it on the patio table.

"Where'd you get that?" Mom asks.

"Jack's room," I say.

"Young man!"

"It's not my beer, Mom."

"Relax, Debbie," I say, unscrewing a cap off the fluted beer bottle. "They're mine."

"Well . . ." my sister says, taking one of the beers and handing another to Beth. "Are you going to read it or what?"

"I can't," Jack says, his eyes welling up with tears. "Hank, you read it for me."

"I-I don't think I should, buddy."

Jack slides me the manila envelope. "Either you're reading it or no one is."

I take the envelope in my hand. Straightening the clasp through the hole, I run my finger under the flap. "You sure about this, bro?"

"No," Jack says. "But do it anyway."

Slowly, I peel back the flap, careful not to rip the envelope. I pull out the white unlined letter. It's written on Fitzpatrick Oldsmobile-Cadillac letterhead and dated February 11, 1991, Jack's second birthday. The handwriting is unmistakably Dad's, his capital letters sweeping, confident, and nearly illegible. It's probably best I'm doing the reading, as I was one of the only people I knew who could ever translate Dad's Sanskrit.

I begin to read.

> Dear Jack,
> If you are reading this letter, it means I am no longer in your life, and for that I am profoundly saddened. The circumstances of why I'm not there are irrelevant to me, but know that I am sorry and that if it were in my power I would never leave you.
> I love your brother and sister, but I feel like I missed their lives. While their mother taught them how to do things like walk, talk, tie their shoes, write in cursive, do long division, and not pee their pants—granted, Hank is still working on that one—I was working sixteen-hour days selling Oldsmobiles and Cadillacs. The fact I missed both Hank and Jeanine say their first words and take their first steps just so Mr. Spangler would be happy with his Coupe DeVille sickens me. If I had to do it all over again, I would have stayed a music teacher.
> You were my reset button, Jack. You were my chance to make things right. I saw you take your first steps. I taught you how to walk and how to tie your shoes. When you took your first big-boy poop in the potty, I was there cheering you on harder than if Notre Dame had won another national championship. You were the only Fitzpatrick whose first word was "Daddy" instead of "Mommy." While your mother still gets credit for teaching you cursive and advanced mathematics—two skills I admittedly lack—I feel like you were really and truly, more than Hank or Jeanine, all mine.
> Choosing to reverse my vasectomy and try for a second family was the craziest and most wonderful choice I ever made in my life. While it did not give me or Debbie the gift either of us expected, it did bring us to you. You may not be of me, but you're of us, and that is more than enough. It is more than I deserve. And I will always call you my son.
> I almost forgot. Happy sixteenth birthday, and here's to many more. Don't be too hard on Hank. I fear this fatherhood thing won't come easy to him, but I know in my heart he'll be a great dad to you.
> Love,
> Dad

I don't know why I read the whole letter. It's not like I hadn't already looked ahead and knew what was coming. Maybe I let it happen. Like a subconscious switch, my brain just shut everything down and said, *"Fuck it, let's finally get this over with."* I've told Beth more than once I was tired of carrying this burden. But that's not the point. The point is that, just like with Uncle Mitch, it was my burden to bear and my burden to relinquish. Right or wrong, these were my choices to make. Yet here I stand again, outed from the fucking grave by my goddamn father.

"Please," I say. "Let me explain."

"No!" Jack, my brother no longer, stands and walks around the table. He rips the paper out of my hand and holds it in front of my face. He screams through his tears. "This isn't possible."

Though galactically inappropriate, an *Empire Strikes Back* allusion sneaks into my brain. I try to snuff it out, but the Beam and the High Life don't let me. It's the only thing I can think to say. "Search your feelings, Jack. You know it to be true."

Jack pushes me to the ground. I fall hard, the back of my head hitting the patio floor. Jack stands over me with his fists clenched, the letter balled up in his right hand. "Fuck you . . . *Dad*. Out of my way, Grandma." Jack throws the letter in Mom's face, giving her a forearm to the chest as he brushes by her. He walks out the patio gate that opens directly to the front yard.

"Where are you going?" Mom shouts after him.

"Let him go." Still seated on the ground, I rub the back of my head and then look at my hand. "Nothing we say right now is going to help."

Beth sees the red smear on my fingers. "Holy shit, Hank. You're bleeding."

"I'll be fine."

Mom makes toward the patio gate. "We have to stop him."

I stand up, a little wobbly. I catch up with Mom, grabbing her elbow. "Don't make a bad situation worse."

"But you don't understand."

"I think I understand plenty."

That's when I hear it: the throaty growl of a Big Block 455 Rocket V-8.

"The Beast?" I say, releasing Mom's elbow. "But she was in storage. We haven't been able to get her started in years."

"It was Gillman's surprise. He rebuilt the engine himself. Did you really think I was just going to get Jack the same old soccer camp gift for his sixteenth birthday?"

"Of course I thought that, Mom. You're not a considerate person."

"You have to go after him, Hank."

"I'm not going anywhere."

"The hell you aren't."

"I'm drunk," I say, sitting in Jack's recently vacated chair. "Besides, I have an idea where he's going. He'll be fine."

Mom starts crying. "You don't know that."

"The hell I don't," I say, purposely snickering for effect. "Jack has about twelve years' experience making it on his own."

*Making Out with Blowfish*

# Chapter 39

Beth and I took the kids home after the party. Later that night, we had wildly inappropriate but erotic sex, first in the hot tub, then in the shower, and finally in front of the standing mirror in the corner of our bedroom. On second thought, it was very appropriate; it was like makeup sex even though we weren't the ones who had the fight. I got maybe four hours of sleep before jumping in the old Subaru Outback for the drive north.

If Hansel and Gretel left bread crumbs for their father, Jack is leaving loaves of bread for me. He picked up a twelve of Natural Light and a pack of Parliaments in a dive bar in between Hope and Shelbyville. I found the empty twelve-pack and the nearly untouched nineteen-pack of cigarettes—Jack doesn't smoke—in a rest area in Greenfield.

Later, sometime around two in the morning, Jack went to the Hiphugger strip club in Kokomo. The Hugger's longtime bouncer—a soft-spoken, smiling giant of a man by the name of Pappy—turned him away at the door. "Gotta love the balls of a sixteen-year-old trying to pass himself off as a thirty-four-year-old," Pappy told me. "But he might want to check beforehand and make sure the original owner of the driver's license didn't spend most of the early nineties in this bar."

Like I said, Pappy has been there a long time.

At some point after striking out at the Hugger, Jack doubled back to Tipton. He booked the Jacuzzi Suite with some of his birthday money at the Flamingo Motel. In the morning, he went to Sherrill's, the diner and gas station right off US 31 with the famous marquee that reads *Eat Here And Get Gas*. He tried to buy everyone in the diner breakfast, but Sherrill thankfully refused the gesture.

I knew where Jack was going the moment he left Mom's house. He's a Fitzpatrick, and there's only one place we drop everything to visit in the middle of April: the campus of the University of Notre Dame, for the Blue & Gold Game spring scrimmage.

The Notre Dame Stadium usher hands me my ticket stub. "You might want to buy some gloves and a hat at the bookstore," he advises me.

"They're saying this is the coldest Blue and Gold Game ever. Game time temps in the thirties, thirty mile-per-hour wind out of the northwest, maybe even some snow."

"I'll take that under advisement," I say.

After a couple false positives, I find him. Jack is sitting by himself, about two-thirds the way up in Section 23, corner end zone, the section that had a front-row seat to Pat Terrell batting down number one Miami's two-point attempt in '88. To the west he's afforded a clear view of Touchdown Jesus. He's decked out from head to toe in brand-new ND gear, the campus bookstore apparently the beneficiary of his remaining birthday funds.

Jack doesn't notice me until I'm three rows away from him. "How did you know that I would—"

"Give me a little credit, Jack." I sit down next to him but not too close. "I may not be your favorite person right now, but I know you better than just about anyone on this planet."

He doesn't respond. The silence is uncomfortable.

"Montana and Zorich honorary captains for the Blue team?" I ask, trying to make small talk.

"Yep," Jack says, trying to make it even smaller.

"And Theismann and Timmy Brown are captains of the Gold team?"

"Yep."

"Brady Quinn looking good?"

"Sure."

"Darius Walker running well?"

"Yep."

"Come on, Jack, talk to me."

"Isn't that what I'm doing?"

"I mean really talk to me."

"What do you want me to say, Hank? What do you consider the proper reaction? You've let me believe my father was dead for sixteen years."

"Technically, ten years."

"What?"

"I didn't know you were my son until you were four-and-half years old. Mom kept it from me, too."

"And I'm supposed to believe that? How could you have not known?"

"My girlfriend lied to me. She and your mother—or should I say, she and your grandmother—faked the abortion, and then Debbie adopted you."

"Wait a second," Jack says. "My mother is your high school sweetheart, Laura Elliot?"

"Wow, you put two and two together pretty quick. How'd you know about the so-called abortion?"

"Jeanine told me that summer I visited her in Portland."

I run my hands through my hair, shaking my head. "Of course she did."

"And Dad—Grandpa, whatever the hell I'm supposed to call him—he knew all about this?"

"Yes," I say. "He was initially reluctant, but considering that aborting his grandson was the only alternative, he went along with it. After a while the deception got easy for most of us, but in hindsight I don't think it ever got any easier for Dad."

"He was just never wired that way," Jack says.

I sigh, my mind on rewind to that moment in the hospital I told Mom about Uncle Mitch's deception, right before she doubled down on the lies. "It was after Dad died that things started spiraling out of control. In the end, I think he gave his family way too much credit."

"Credit for what?"

"For doing the right thing."

"What makes you say that?"

"You don't have to suddenly pull punches for my benefit, Jack. The tone in Dad's letter was pretty obvious, especially those last few paragraphs. He just assumed we would have told you by now. I feel like I let him down again."

"Look, Hank, uh, I mean Da—"

"Please, don't start calling me that. I don't deserve that. I might never deserve it."

"Okay, whatever . . . Hank. Can you just give me some time to process this?"

"Take all the time you need."

"It's not that I'm letting you off the hook for this, because I'm not."

"I don't expect you to."

"But really, at least with you, what are we talking about here? A debate over semantics? You've basically been my father since I was four years old, since before you even found out I was your, you know, your so—"

"Yeah, you don't have to use that word in conversation either."

Jack flirts with smiling. "Thanks," he says.

"You're welcome, bro." Jack looks at me. I say "bro" out of habit, but for the very first time, the word feels strange in my mouth.

"Hank, I have a lot of questions. I don't even know where to begin."

"How about at the beginning?"

"Okay," Jack says, his eyes starting to water. "Can you tell me about Laura? What was my mother like?"

"Jack," I say, standing and patting him on the shoulder. "Let's get out of here."

"Where we going?"

"I'd rather not associate any of this with Notre Dame Stadium."

"Good call. Where to?"

"How about we have this chat over beer and wings at Hooters and go watch the NFL Draft on some big screens?"

"Beer?" Jack says.

"Why not? We're just two thirty-four-year-old dudes knocking back a few pitchers of brew."

"A *few* pitchers?"

"You got somewhere you need to be?"

"Well, there's your birthday brunch tomorrow."

It's hard to resist the way Jack's eyes suddenly light up, reminding me he's still like any sixteen-year-old boy—ready and willing to break the law for little more than a mild buzz. And today at least, I'm more than happy to oblige him.

"You know what, Jack?"

"What?"

"Fuck 'em."

# Chapter 40

Jack and I ended up getting too drunk to drive. We spent the night sleeping in our cars in the Hooters parking lot, but we made good time this morning on the drive back from South Bend.

I pull into my garage. Jack parks the Beast behind me in the driveway. He steps out of his car. "So you're really not going to your birthday brunch?"

"Are you going?" I ask.

"Hell no."

"Then that makes two of us."

Jack points to the empty stall next to the Subaru. "Where are Beth and the kids?"

"At church."

"Church? Since when?"

"Since about a year ago."

"Any particular reason?"

"Don't think I need a reason to be closer to God."

"Hank, this is me you're talking to."

"Yeah, so?"

"I know you're trying especially hard to set a good example for me right now, but you finding religion is like waking up with a vagina instead of a penis. It just ain't natural."

I can't help but laugh. "Okay, you got me. We're doing it for Sasha."

"Ah, yes. Giving her that good foundation."

"Bingo."

"I guess it beats having your ass dragged to a Mormon service."

"Gillman do that to you?"

"Every Sunday. Three hours of hell on earth."

"Sounds like Easter Vigil."

"What?"

"Nothing," I say. "Go on."

"It isn't so much the length that bothers me. The last couple hours are usually just Sunday school and administrative stuff. Debbie and I skip that a lot."

"Debbie?"

"You call her that when you're pissed at her, so I think I've earned the right to call her that for eternity."

"Fair enough."

"Anyway, it's that first hour that always wigs me out. The bishop invites members to come up and testify in front of the congregation. Kids my age come up, but sometimes there are even nine- and ten-year-olds who do it. They start talking about their love for the Lord, all this holy roller shit, and they are bawling their eyes out. We're talking full rapture mode."

"Sounds like you're a few venomous snakes and a mason jar of strychnine away from a genuine End Times party."

"I know, right?"

I point at my face, trying to be stoic. "See this, Jack?"

"What?"

"This is me not looking surprised."

"Well played," Jack says. He approaches the garage. "So, we done for now?"

"Done?" I slide open a small panel to the left of the garage door, type in the security code. The door begins to shut as I walk back out onto the driveway. "We're just getting started."

"Why am I not liking the sound of that?"

"If the lies are going to end, then let's end them all." I walk to the passenger-side door of the Beast. "But you're driving."

Jack walks around to his side of the Oldsmobile, opening his door. He looks over the roof at me. "And to where exactly am I driving?"

We slide into the car, shut our doors. I adjust my lap belt, as the '73 Cutlass Supreme did not come equipped with shoulder straps. "You sure you don't just want to be surprised when we get there?"

Jack starts the car. "I think I've reached my quota on surprises."

"Fair enough," I say. "We're going to go visit your grandma."

"Debbie?"

"No, Tammy. Laura's mother."

Tammy has company, and it's the worst kind of company. A white Suburban with Pennsylvania plates sits in her driveway.

"Stay in the car," I say to Jack.

"But why?"

"Something is up. Laura is here. I'm just afraid things might get a little ugly early on. I'd rather keep you out of the line of fire."

"Roger that," Jack says.

I knock on the front door. Three little mounds of curls, each of varying heights, peek out the picture window to the left of the door. They look at me, stick out their tongues, and then scurry away giggling wildly to one another. I knock on the door again.

Someone fiddles with the lock as the doorknob starts to rotate. The door swings open.

"May I help you?" the man says.

He's a little taller than me and a whole lot heavier—not morbidly obese, more your typical middle-aged thickness around the face and torso, like Kevin James in *The King of Queens*. Much like Doug Heffernan did with the sassy-hot (cue *Saved by the Bell* reference) Stacey Carosi, this guy outkicked his coverage by landing Laura Elliot. He's what we used to call in high school and college "OC," as in "over-cheeving."

"I'm guessing you're Ian Powell," I say, offering my hand.

To Ian's credit he accepts my gesture. His large flesh mitt swallows my childlike hand. "I don't have to guess who you are, Hank."

I shake off his hand. "Look, if we came at a bad time—"

"You most certainly did."

"Ian, behave!"

Her voice is like an emollient, instantly diluting the testosterone in the room. She comes around the corner, steps around Ian's left side, and gives me a hug.

"Hi, Hank."

Laura's curly hair is pulled back in a tight ponytail, so her bare cheek brushes upside mine as she pulls me in. I put my chin on her right shoulder. I could swear her sweater smells like movie theater popcorn. As appropriate as it might be for me to respond with one of those long, swaying, eyes-closed hugs in which both people exhale audibly as if they've been holding their breath waiting for this one embrace, I can't help but notice Ian is still staring me down. This pisses me off. In retribution, I decide to cop a little bit of a feel. With my right hand hidden from Ian's view, I give a quick squeeze just above Laura's waistline—partly to make sure she's done her best to keep off the back fat but mostly so I can reach down and sneak my pinky finger just inside the rim of her jeans. As I pull away, with Ian still staring me down with his oblivious, bloated face, I brush my index and middle fingers subtly underneath the curve of Laura's left breast.

"Hello, Laura. What are you doing here?"

"Ian and I just got back from seeing *Robots* with the girls. Good movie."

This at least explains the popcorn smell. "That's not what I mean. What are you doing *here*, in Empire Ridge."

"Wait," Laura says. "You haven't heard?"

"Heard what? It's not like you and I are pen pals."

Laura's voice cracks. "It's my mother, Hank. She died last night."

"B-but how?"

"Cancer."

"Not leukemia?"

"Yes."

"But I thought she beat the disease way back when you were a kid."

"You remember that?"

"You told me she went into remission when you were like twelve years old."

"That's right. But it came back. It was too fast this time, too strong. She just couldn't fight it. We didn't even get here in time to see her conscious. She was on a ventilator, and my brother is stuck in China on a jobsite."

"Oh God, Laura. I'm so sorry."

"I was the one who took her off life support. I was the one who had to pull the . . ."

Laura buries her face in her hands, sobbing. My instinct is to comfort her, but I step back, conceding her personal space to Ian. He nods in appreciation, wrapping his arm around her shoulder. Laura turns her face away from me.

"Maybe come back later, Hank?" Ian says.

I nod. "Uh, yeah. That's probably best."

Ian shuts the door behind me. I see Jack in the car. He looks at me, shrugging his shoulders with a typical teenage what-the-fuck expression.

The front door opens. "Hank, please, wait!"

I turn to her. "Now is not the time for this, Laura."

"For what?" she says, grabbing my arm. "You came here to see my mom. Why?"

"It can wait."

"Until when? She rises from the dead?"

"I didn't really come here for Tammy's benefit. I came here for—"

"Jack!"

"What?"

"Is that my . . ." Laura's left hand is on her mouth, her right hand pointing at the sixteen-year-old boy now standing behind me in front of the car. "Are you, Jack?"

I lean in toward Laura, my chin tilted. "He knows," I whisper.

Laura shoves me out of the way, practically bounding toward Jack. But then she stops suddenly. They stand there, face-to-face, neither talking nor making eye contact. This moment is exactly as awkward as I imagined it would be.

I step between them. "Jack, this is Laura. Laura, this is Jack."

Jack reaches out with his right hand. Laura grabs it with both of her hands. She looks at Jack's hand, rotating it like an archaeologist carefully studying a lost artifact. She continues looking at his hand, then his face, then his hand again.

"It's wonderful to meet you . . . Jack."

"Uh, uhhh . . ." he mutters. "Same here, Mrs. Powell."

"Can you at least call me Laura?" she says, wiping away her tears.

"Depends," Jack says.

"On what?"

"Can you give me my hand back?"

Laura laughs. She releases his hand. "You came at a difficult time, Jack.

My mother, your, uh . . ."

"My grandmother?"

"Yes. It's just that . . . well, we lost her yesterday. It's been a rough twenty-four hours on us."

"I'm sorry."

"You and Hank want to come inside for a little bit?"

"Oh no," Jacks says, shaking his head. "I don't . . . I-I don't want to impose."

Laura looks at me, then back at Jack. "Jack, I think you've earned the right to be an imposition for a very long time. Besides, I want you to meet a few people."

Jack steps back cautiously, his hands in the air like someone is holding a gun to his back. "Look, Laura, this is all happening a little too fast for me. Like you said, it's been a rough twenty-four hours. I don't think I'm ready to jump right in and chat up your relatives just yet."

"I totally understand and respect that," Laura says. "All I'm looking for is a guy who'll wear a dress and drink some tea."

"Excuse me?" Jack says.

Laura nods toward the front door. "You got three half sisters in that house who are going to love you."

# Chapter 41

"This is the worst idea in the history of ideas."

"Oh shut up and paddle," Beth says to me.

Jack was the one who suggested the canoe trip the day after Tammy Eliot's funeral, and of course nobody was in a position to tell him, "No way in hell!" or "Are you fucking insane?" A seven-mile combined Fitzpatrick and Powell family float down the Sycamore River. Two husbands who can barely stand to be in the same zip code as one another. Two wives who've hated one another for going on two decades. What could possibly go wrong?

The twins and Laura's two youngest daughters were deemed too young for the trip, so we left them with Mom and Gillman. Our flotilla comprises four canoes. Beth and I lead the way, followed by Laura and Ian, Jeanine and Sasha, and then Jack and his half-sister Cassie. Cassie is the same age as Sasha. With their sandy-blond hair and gymnast builds, they could pass for cousins if not sisters. Jeanine and Jack have paddled a good half hour ahead of us by now; probably already out of their canoes and raiding the picnic baskets.

"Hey, Hank, when you taking your skirt off?"

We've covered about five of the seven miles. Ian has been harassing me since about mile two. He started the trip with a twelve-pack of Yuengling and just cracked open his eleventh lager.

"You got me, Ian. I'm obviously a woman."

"Seriously," Ian says. "Who goes canoeing without drinking beer? That's like cookies without milk, or a Philly steak and cheese without cheese."

"Or Pennsylvania without assholes," I say under my breath

"What did you say?"

"I said, 'I think I see some tadpoles.'"

"Hey now," Beth says, splashing me with her paddle. Some of the water runs down the small of her back. Although it's spring and there's still a chill in the air, she's wearing denim shorts and a bikini top. The goose bumps on her skin are incredibly distracting. "You need to behave."

"If you only knew," I say, grinning more than smiling.

We round the bend just northeast of the canoe livery. Thirty feet up, the rusted iron-truss bridge casts a stern, judgmental shadow over the rippling echoes of my past sins. I feel like it's even mocking me a little.

Then again, that might just be Ian's drunk ass.

"This bridge is sweet!" he says. "Anybody ever jump off it?"

"It's illegal," I say.

"That's not what I asked."

"Plenty of stupid kids have jumped off the thing."

"You ever see it?"

"I've done it."

"No way. Your scrawny little ass has jumped off those train tracks?"

"Not the train tracks."

"That's what I thought."

"I jumped off the very top of the bridge."

"Stop it, Hank," Laura says. She's also wearing denim shorts but with a one-piece bathing suit sans the distracting goose bumps (thank God).

"Stop what?" I say.

"Encouraging him."

"Who's encouraging him? I do believe I explicitly said that jumping off this bridge is stupid."

A giant splash interrupts our argument as Ian swims for shore.

"Ian, no!" Laura says.

"Do something," Beth says to me.

"What do you want me to do?"

"Go after him."

"I'm not jumping in there. It's April. South Bend was still having snow flurries *last week*. If Ian wants to get hypothermia, that's his business."

Beth points up at the bridge. "Hypothermia is the least of his problems."

Ian stands on the bridge, already at the level of the train tracks.

"Just jump from there, buddy," I shout.

"You'd like to see me do that, wouldn't you? That way you can always say that you were the one who made the real jump while I pussied out."

"You think this is a contest? Really?"

"Well, isn't it?"

"Step into my world, Ian. My life has sucked—a lot. It's getting better now, and I'm not wasting my time getting in a pissing contest with you or anyone else. I'm fine with the cookie-cutter house in the suburbs and the minivan. I'll fucking hit from the green tees all day long and not give a shit. Hell, come down here, let's drop our pants and just whip it out. You'll probably have a bigger dick than me. You don't need to prove anything."

"You don't get it."

"Then tell me—what am I missing?"

Ian stands on the edge of the tracks, looking down at the water thirty feet below. "I don't need to prove anything, huh? Step into my world, Hank. For sixteen years my wife has had a son by another man. Up until a month ago I thought she had given the baby up for adoption, not shipped him off to her high school sweetheart's mother for safekeeping."

I turn to the other canoe. "What is he talking about, Laura?"

She ignores me. "Please, honey, just come down from there!"

"You didn't tell him who Jack's father was until *last month*?"

"Surprise!" Ian shouts. He moves quickly up the ironworks. The rivets and joints give secure footing all the way up. He reaches the top. "But that's not all. Hey, Roddy, tell our contestant what he's won. Well, Bob, in addition to Ian's wife never telling him about her little bastard, she's also still carrying a torch for the birth father."

*Holy shit.*

Laura looks mortified. Beth looks like she wants to rip Laura's mortified face off. And here I am, my hands cupped around my mouth, still trying to talk down this sauced idiot.

"Ian, shut the fuck up."

"What did you say to me?"

I sneak a glance at my audience. Laura has her face in her hands, hiding from the world. Beth is still staring daggers into the back of Laura's head. Looks like I'm on my own.

"I said, shut the fuck up. First off, if you ever call Jack a bastard again, I'll drive my fist so far down your throat you'll be shitting my fingernails. Secondly, you have a wife who loves you, and three beautiful daughters. Is it worth throwing all that away doing some drunken stunt just because you got your feelings hurt?"

"Didn't you hear what I said, Hank? She still loves—"

"I heard what you said. So fucking what? Newsflash—she's got no shot with me. But there are three girls out there who love their mommy and daddy, who love their family. Answer me this, Ian—do you love your wife?"

"With all my heart."

"Then get down here and tell Laura to get over herself."

"It's not that easy."

"It's not that hard either."

Ian stands in silence atop the bridge.

"How long has he been up there?" Laura says.

I look at my watch. "Ten minutes."

"I can't just sit here. I need to do something."

"I think you've done plenty," Beth says.

"Stay out of this," Laura says.

"Make me, you stupid—"

"Ladies, please. Not that I haven't dreamed about you two getting in another half-naked catfight, but now is not the time." I cast my eyes upward, nodding. "Besides, look."

Ian has backed away from the edge. "Hey, Hank," he says.
"Yeah, Ian?"
"I'm sorry. Jack is a great kid."
"Apology accepted, and I know he is."
"I'm also sorry this got so out of hand."
"It happens."
"I think I'm coming down now," Ian says.
"Good to hear." I take off my hat and run my hands through my hair. Closing my eyes, I let out an exhausted sigh.
"Hey you," Beth says.
I open my eyes. She stands above me, having somehow traversed the length of our canoe undetected. I bury my face in her cleavage, wrapping my arms around her waist and clasping my hands behind her. She kisses the top of my head.
"Hey you," I say into my wife's breasts.
"I think your dick is probably bigger," she whispers.

# Chapter 42

"I mean, really, who stays married for ten years?"
"Apparently we do."
I dip Beth on the dance floor. After surprising her at St. Benjamin with a vow renewal ceremony—highlighted by Father Fish, our entire wedding party, and Joan and Stan being nice to one another—I rented a limo and took everyone up to Indianapolis for the night.
We're partying at the Rathskeller, a pseudo-German *biergarten* tucked on the backside of the Athenaeum Building, which was designed and built in the nineteenth century by Kurt Vonnegut's grandfather. We've had a lot of beer to drink and even more food, the latter of which has adhered to the four main Bavarian food groups: breaded meat, sausage, potatoes, and gravy. Tonight's band is Polka Boy, a bunch of middle-aged white dudes armed with accordions, trumpets, keyboards, guitars, bass players, and drums that do a polka twist on just about every conceivable music genre. At this moment, fulfilling my request, they're muddling through a bizarre rendition of Hootie and the Blowfish's "Hold My Hand."
"Ugh," Beth says. "I don't think I can look at another schnitzel for the rest of the night."
I twirl her away from me, then back. "Hopefully you'll change your mind when we get to the hotel room."
She kisses me. "I'm a sure thing. You know that, right?"
I smile. "Now I do."
"Did you see my mom and dad earlier?"
"You mean the laughing?" I ask.
"The laughing, the flirting."
"What's going on there?"
"I don't know, but they need to cut that shit out."
"Why is Joan and Stan's being nice to one another such a bad thing?"
"You don't understand, Hank. I've *never* seen them like this. Remember our therapy sessions?"
"Do I have to?"

"You said my parents were nothing but glorified roommates. I hated you for saying it at the time, but you fucking nailed it."

"I'm sorry, babe. I didn't mean to—"

Beth douses my lips with a kiss. "No, no. You were right. Don't apologize. I blame them for a lot of our problems, for not knowing how to love you."

We ease into our customary slow dance position, my left hand holding her right hand against my left shoulder, my right hand guiding the small of her back, her torso swaying in unison to mine. Every third or fourth beat of the song I pull her a little closer, bending at the knees just enough for my unabashed erection to rub between the insides of her thighs.

"So, what you're saying is, all our problems are your fault?"

My wife raises her knee into my crotch. "So what you're saying is, you don't want me to eat your schnitzel when we get back to the hotel room?"

I move my hand from her back to the bottom crease of her ass, pulling her up onto her toes and into me. "You've been quite the minx lately."

"To be fair, you've been quite the good husband."

"You're rewarding me, then?"

"No," Beth says. "You're rewarding me."

"You know my motto."

"What's that?"

"Ladies first."

Beth eases back down to the balls of her feet. "I know and very much appreciate your motto."

"Okay, lovebirds, break it up." Claire separates us with her arms like a referee in a prizefight. "I swear, whatever you two have going on here, you need to bottle and sell it."

"Where's Hatch?" I ask.

"He just got here," Claire says. "In fact, he's right behind—"

"Hank, my boy!" Hatch grabs me from behind, lifting me at the waist. "Good lord, man. Fucking eat something. What do you weigh now?"

"A lot less than you."

"What's your secret?"

"Still just running with my dog."

"How old is Chef these days?"

"His name is Chief, not Chef. And he just turned nine."

"That's getting up there for a big dog."

Beth gives a frantic slashing motion, her hand palm down and waving horizontally beneath her chin.

"What?" Hatch hunches his shoulders. "What did I say?"

"You broke rule number one in the Fitzpatrick household," I say.

"What's that?"

"We don't talk about Chief getting old."

"My bad," Hatch says. "Here, take this. Maybe it will put some fucking weight on you."

Hatch hands me a pint glass filled to the rim with a dark amber beer. I hold it to my nose, catching a strong smoked meat scent.

"What is this?"

"Bartender called it *rauchbier*, which literally translates as—"

"Smoke beer, I know. My four years of high school German weren't completely useless. What's in it? Smells like bacon."

"Evidently all beers used to smell like this. The kilns would dry the green brewer's malt over open fires, and so the grains picked up the smoky flavors of the wood and passed them on to the beers. Nowadays the process is much more controlled and breweries tend to just use clean malt. *Rauchbier* is such a lost art that only one town in all of Germany—Bamberg—brews *rauchbier* anymore."

"And you just learned all that from the bartender?"

"Learnin' ain't nothin' but listenin', Hank."

"Which is why I'm surprised."

"Surprised?"

"Hatch, if you ain't talkin', you ain't listenin'."

"Drink your beer, asshole."

"Don't mind if I do." I hold the pint glass just under my nose. "There's more than just bacon going on here. There's beech wood and charcoal, various cooked meats—bacon of course, but also grilled hot dogs and smoked sausage."

"Hey Hank, are you going to drink it or fuck it?"

"I'm getting there." I lift the glass to my mouth, letting the amber liquid slide down my tongue. Like most quality beers, it's served and tastes better at a temperature more cool than cold.

"Well?" Hatch says.

"I like it, a lot."

"What do you like about it?"

"It's a deceptive beer. The meat smells are not nearly as pronounced in the mouth. The finish is surprisingly clean and almost a little too thin, especially for a beer that initially portends something closer to an Islay Scotch."

"What's that like?"

"It's like a campfire, a dense, barley-infused smoke bomb."

"And you smell all that in the beer?"

"Initially, yes. But for all that smokiness that hits you upfront, the flavor profile on the backend is actually very accessible."

"Good to hear."

"Why? Do you owe the bartender a full report?"

"No," Hatch says. "I just like to know that my company is brewing good beers."

Beth sits naked on the executive table, sipping a glass of champagne. It's four in the morning. We've had sex twice, and we're contemplating a third time.

Our next-door neighbor down in Empire Ridge—Lisa, the retired Colts cheerleader turned divorcée turned Hilton regional manager—hooked us up with the employee discount on the corporate suite. It's a three-room suite, with a large main room flanked by two bedrooms. The front of the main room is the lounge area, with a wet bar, a television, a couch, a loveseat, and two Barcaloungers. The back part of the main room is dominated by a long executive table surrounded by eight chairs, and a floor-to-ceiling picture window overlooking Monument Circle and downtown Indianapolis. I feel we're going to need to tip the maid service some serious cash, because we have really fucked this place up. Beth spilled almost an entire bottle of red wine while dancing on the boardroom table to the Black Eyed Peas' "My Humps." We broke one of the Barcaloungers when we rented *Ass Worship 7: Assphyxiation* on pay-per-view and tried to mimic some of the moves. And the executive table is covered with a thin layer of edible, Creamsicle-flavored massage cream.

"Now take me through this," Beth says between naked sips of champagne. "Hatch and his father, both of them alcoholics, went in together on a microbrewery up in Indianapolis?"

"You got it." I walk over to the executive table, similarly naked. Beth hands me a glass of champagne. "They're more like silent partners really."

"What happened to the Navy? I thought he was looking at being a career officer."

"He was, up until about six months ago. Says he saw some things he wasn't supposed to see over in Afghanistan, and the Navy paid him a lot of money to shut up and be honorably discharged."

"And that's all he told you?"

"That's all I wanted to hear."

Beth jumps up from the executive table, her breasts bouncing. She stumbles forward, spilling her alcohol, again. "How about a toast?"

"To what?"

My wife of ten years raises her champagne flute. "To no secrets."

"To no secrets."

"I love you, Hank."

I sip my champagne, the bubbles tickling the back of my throat. I start to return the affirmation, but apparently there's a disconnect between my brain and my mouth.

"Right after we got engaged, I made out with Lila on the Mineshaft dance floor, but it didn't mean anything. Before the twins were born and you hated me, and I hated you, I had a Bloody Mary with Angelina Valerio when she had a layover at Indianapolis International Airport. Nothing happened, and it was a stupid thing for me to do. I also kissed Lila once more when I was living in New York when you and I were separated, but I didn't really like it, and all I thought about was Sasha sitting on the end of the bed."

"Hank, what the fuck?"

"Hey, it was your toast. You said no secrets. Do you have anything you want to say to me?"

"No!"

"Nothing at all?"

"You know I have a lot of eyes and ears in Empire Ridge, right?"

"Good grief," Beth says. "It was like two or three horrible blind dates when I thought we were getting divorced."

"Two *or* three?"

"Three."

"You sure about that?"

"Yes."

"So we're done here?"

"I don't know," Beth says. "Are we?"

"I'm getting conflicting vibes."

"What are they telling you?"

"One vibe says we're sleeping in separate bedrooms tonight, the other says I'm supposed to bend you over that executive table and fuck your brains out."

Beth finishes her sparkling wine and throws the empty glass over her shoulder. It shatters against the wall. She grabs the freshly opened champagne, taking a generous pull straight from the bottle.

"We've been married for ten years," she says, wiping the champagne from her lips with the back of her hand. "Figure it out."

# Part VIII
# 2006

# Chapter 43

"Maybe we should slow down," Jack says.
"Slow down? We're like five blocks from home."
"But Chief isn't looking so great."
Jack and I are in the homestretch of a brisk five-mile run. As always, Chief is at my side, his once jet-black coat now flecked with bits of silver and gray, his tongue hanging out of his mouth. The dog tags on his hemp collar—handmade by Jeanine for his tenth birthday in the spring—clang together like sleigh bells to the rhythm of our run. I look down at my friend, giving a tug on the leash to get his attention. "Hey, Chiefy, you okay, boy?"
He turns to the sound of my voice. His dark eyes are expressive, humanlike. He started limping about a mile ago, and he's tired.
"Okay," I say. "Let's walk."
"Good call," Jack says. "Gotta give the old man credit for hanging that long."
"You talking about Chief or me?"
"Thirty-five years old, Hank. That's getting up there. Did you know you're closer to seventy than you are to the day you were born?"
"Well, I do now, asshole."
"Ha!"
"But at least I can take my wife to see an R-rated movie without having to show identification every time."
"Barely," Jack says. "What is up with that anyway?"
"With what?"
"Our baby faces. You're approaching forty and still getting carded for booze."
"Chalk it up to good genes and large pores."
"Huh?"
"That oily skin and bad complexion you hate right now is a gift."
"A gift from whom? The Devil?"
"Oily skin now equals fewer wrinkles later. All the Fitzpatrick men looked fifteen to twenty years younger than they really were, at least in the

face."

"I wish I could say the same for Chief."

"What's wrong with Chief?"

"Come on, Hank. We've all seen it. He's going downhill fast."

"Says you."

"Says your vet. How much that last knee surgery set you back?"

"Couple grand."

"So, between having his stomach cut open and his two ACL tears, what are we talking?'

"It's just money."

"Four thousand?"

"Closer to five."

"You know I'm going to college next year, right?"

"Yeah, so?"

"How you going to be able to help me out when you're dropping five thousand dollars on your pets?"

Jack moved in with us late last summer, several months after everything went down at his sixteenth birthday party. It was Beth's idea, but our transition from siblings to something else was surprisingly seamless.

My wife has been very supportive, and not just because we have a full-time free babysitter. And by "free" I mean I slip Jack money when Beth isn't looking. We still haven't quite figured out how to tell Sasha and the twins that "Uncle Jack" is actually "Half Brother Jack," so we haven't told them. Debbie and Jack are still struggling to define their new mom-turned-grandma/son-turned-grandson relationship. He only just started talking to Mom again about a month ago.

Gillman, for all his LDS quirks and fundamental flaws as a human being, has actually been my go-to mediator in this. He was the one who suggested that, with Jack now less than a year from being of legal majority age, we just keep a lid on everything. "Your choice, Hank," he said to me. "Sue your mother for paternity rights and make the next year a living hell for everyone you know, or just be quiet for twelve measly months and Jack is yours anyway." I think I might need to send Gillman a gift basket.

Jack and Laura have grown close—or at least as close as the distance between them will allow. Ian took their daughters back to Pennsylvania a couple weeks after the funeral while Laura spent some time in Empire Ridge settling up her mother's affairs and getting to know her son. She went back to Pennsylvania a couple months ago. Ian has a new job with PNC Bank in Philadelphia. Last I heard, he and Laura were in counseling and doing well. Jack says they've moved into an eighteenth century townhouse in in the Old City district that they're restoring, and that it has a spare bedroom for when he visits.

I'm not particularly happy at Gillman being a confidante in family matters or Laura managing to forge a connection with our son by being little more than goddamn instant messenger buddies for a few months, but

I've kind of lost the right to bitch about it. Chief, on the other hand, is my family. Not Gillman's. Not Laura's. Not Jack's.

"Let's get something straight, son."

"Hey, I haven't signed off on you calling me—"

"Shut up."

"Now wait just a second."

"No, Jack. I mean it, shut up. Chief isn't just a pet. He's a Fitzpatrick. If I want to spend ten thousand dollars on him, then I'll spend ten thousand dollars."

"Okay, sorry."

"You better be. Now, as far as that helping you out with college thing, since when has that been part of the master plan?"

"Oh, I don't know, since you stuck your penis inside Laura's vagina?"

"Bitter much?"

"You were the one who asked."

"I doubt you're going to need my help. When was the last time you got anything less than an A-minus on a report card?"

"The second grade."

"And how much money is coming to you via the annuity settlement with the auto auction?"

"Twenty-six thousand dollars a year until I'm twenty-six years old."

"After taxes?"

"Yes sir."

"Hell, I'm the one who's going to be hitting you up for a loan."

We approach our house. Beth is pulling out of the driveway. She rolls down her window. "Good run, boys?"

"Yeah," I say. "Although I think it might have been Chief's last."

She looks down at the dog. "I'm sorry."

"Don't be." Jack jumps in. "Chief might not be a runner anymore, but he's got plenty of years of couch potato left in him."

I nod, giving a smile of recognition and gratitude. "That he does, Jack. That he does."

"I'm dropping the kids off at school," Beth says to me. "See you for lunch?"

"Not today, honey. I have to drive up to the Indy office."

"I thought you were working from home this week."

"I wish. The boss is flying in from New York this afternoon. He's really on my ass about hitting my numbers this year."

"What are your chances?"

"Slim to none. As they say in publishing these days, down is the new up."

"Well, good luck, babe."

"Thanks."

Beth rolls up her window. Just as the window is about to seal shut I hear her shout, "Stop licking your sister!" She backs the minivan into the street, then drives away.

"Let's go inside and get some coffee," I say to Jack.

"I still don't like coffee."

"Oh, sorry. Just distracted, I guess."

"I could go for a hot chocolate, though."

We walk inside the house. I start some water in the kettle for Jack's hot chocolate and pour myself a cup of coffee. Chief crawls more than walks to his corner of the family room. His descent to the floor is slow and deliberate, and I can tell it hurts.

"You worried?" Jack says.

"About work?"

"No, about Chief."

"Of course I am. I never had a dog growing up. Chief is my first, my one and only. He came into our house before Sasha or the twins. Beth and I went from being a couple to being a family because of that stupid dog."

"Too bad Dad, I mean Grandpa, never let you have a dog in the house."

"What are you talking about? The no dogs rule was Debbie's doing."

"No, it wasn't."

"She hated animals."

"That's what she wanted you to believe. It was John's rule."

"I can't imagine Dad hating anything."

"I didn't say he hated animals. In fact, he loved them, and he loved dogs most of all."

"Then why didn't I ever have one growing up?"

"You didn't have one, but he did."

"Excuse my language, Jack, but can you stop being so fucking obtuse?"

"I don't even know what that means."

"Just get to your point!"

"Well, the thing is, Dad, Grandpa, John—that guy—he had a beagle as a kid."

"I never heard about any beagle."

"You haven't?"

"No."

"Debbie has told me this story a bunch of times. His name was Snooper. Grandpa George used to go foxhunting with him."

"Foxhunting? Are we talking about the same Grandpa George? I can't imagine—"

"Do you want me to tell you the story or not?"

"Sorry," I say. The kettle starts to whistle. I scoop a generous portion of cocoa into a stoneware mug. I pour the steaming hot water into the mug, stirring as I pour with one of the twins' baby spoons. "Here's your hot chocolate. Continue."

"Thanks," Jack says. "As I was saying, Grandpa used to go foxhunting with Snooper, but as it turned out, the beagle sucked at foxhunting. Still, he was a great family pet and fiercely loyal to John. One day John came home after school with two black eyes and a missing front tooth. He had got in a fight on the playground."

"Dad in a fight?" I say. "Okay, now I know you're making this story up."

"He was eleven years old, and at recess he saw three teenage boys ripping off a black girl's dress behind the school. He stopped them and probably saved the girl from being raped or worse. While they roughed him up pretty bad, he managed to get in a few good shots. Ripped out a chunk of one of the kids' shoulders with his teeth and partially tore the testicle of another. John walked home from school. Two of the three teenage boys left school in an ambulance."

"Nice!"

"Yeah, all four boys got suspended."

"When's the dog come back into this story?"

"I'm getting to that part," Jack says. "So John got home from school and told Grandma Eleanor what happened."

"Where was Grandpa George?"

"Out of town at an American Legion function."

"And what did Eleanor do?"

"She took John out back underneath the willow tree."

"Not the switch."

"You know about that?"

"Dad had permanent scars on his back. He was pretty careful about hiding them. Can we skip the gory details?"

"The details are important to the story."

"Very well."

"Grandma Eleanor tied her son's wrists to the willow tree and started whipping his bare back. He was screaming and bleeding, and at one point she hit John so hard she broke a switch in half and he nearly passed out from the pain. Just as Eleanor was about to lay into him again with a new switch, Snooper broke through the screen door on the back of the house. He had been locked in a kennel in the basement, and when he heard John's screaming, he ripped the metal door off the hinges of his kennel. He broke all four canine teeth in the effort."

"Holy shit!"

"Imagine this ball of fury charging Grandma Eleanor, his face covered in blood from his busted teeth."

"Cujo to the rescue!"

"You better believe it. Those busted teeth clamped down on Grandma Eleanor's arm, the one holding the switch. So, with her free hand she grabbed a baseball bat lying in the yard and hit Snooper in the head. She knocked the dog unconscious, but she didn't kill him."

"Jack, I don't think I want to hear any more."

"Well, you're gonna. Eleanor untied her son and went into the house. John ran to Snooper. He put his ear on his muzzle and was relieved to hear him breathing. That's when Eleanor came outside with Grandpa George's

shotgun."
"She did not shoot Snooper and make Dad watch."
"No, she didn't."
"Thank God."
"She made John shoot him."

# Chapter 44

Deer Creek is the oasis of my youth, a sprawling outdoor amphitheater north of Indianapolis that used to stand alone among acres and acres of farmland. That iconic photo of Jerry Garcia standing in a wheat field, wearing all black and holding a guitar with his head bowed? That was taken at Deer Creek. I've seen at least three KISS "farewell" tours here and more than a dozen Buffett concerts, none of which I was sober enough to remember. The best live show I ever saw here was Metallica's '94 Shit Hits the Sheds tour, and the worst by far was Coldplay's Twisted Logic tour last year. The younger kids call the place by its shiny new corporate name, Verizon Wireless Music Center. All the farmland has long since been paved over. Deer Creek is now merely the "you are here" dot near the top of the Hamilton Town Center map. And Jerry Garcia's wheat field is a Bed, Bath & Beyond parking lot.

Hatch pulls the minivan into the Deer Creek parking lot. We're here for the Journey-Def Leppard concert, and Hatch is the only sober one in the vehicle. The rest of us—Claire, Beth, and I—are both drunk and stoned. We've been passing around a half gallon of Jim Beam and a two-liter of Diet Coke for the entire ride up from Empire Ridge. Claire fired up a joint just south of Indianapolis, which we proceeded to smoke before we even got to the Marion-Hamilton County border. Hatch is in the middle of trying to give me a music history lesson.

"I'm telling you 'Song and Emotion' by Tesla was a tribute to Def Leppard guitarist Steve Clark."

"Bullshit," I say. "You just love Tesla because they remind you of that sappy mixtape you made for my wife."

"Fuck you, Hank!"

"Okay, boys," Beth says from the backseat. "Let's settle down."

"When do we eat?" Claire shouts.

Hatch turns the car off and reaches for the door handle. "You guys have got to get it together."

"What are they gonna do?" his wife snaps back at him. "Arrest us for being hungry?"

"Just bring the volume down is all."

"That's hilarious," I say.

"What?" Hatch says.

"You asking someone else to watch their volume."

A few words about Journey and Def Leppard.

Like many adults in their thirties and forties, I regard these bands as two of our generation's touchstones. I associate songs from both their catalogs with various seminal moments of my youth. Journey's weepy ballad "Open Arms" reminds me of two things. One is the night I first got my hand up a girl's shirt during a slow dance. Her name was Molly Alden, my favorite partner in our sixth-grade evening cotillion class. I snuck my hand up the back of her sweater to "Open Arms," and my hand stayed there for both Neil Diamond's "Heartlight" and "Up Where We Belong" by Joe Cocker and Jennifer Warnes, the latter of which, just as an aside, never fails to induce a flashback of Richard Gere boning the shit out of Deborah Winger in *An Officer and a Gentleman.* The other event I associate with "Open Arms" is when I snuck down to my grandparents' basement to watch *The Last American Virgin* on HBO just because it was rated-R and had *virgin* in the title. I woke up the entire house crying when Diane Franklin's character —spoiler alert!—ends up back with the asshole that got her pregnant, while the sweet-natured nerd who loved her and nurtured her through her abortion is left broken and defeated just as the movie ends with both his tears and the credits rolling in parallel lines down his face. Saddest ending to a movie. Ever.

"Wheel in the Sky" reminds me of my Uncle Mitch's peach and custard pie.

"Any Way You Want It" reminds me of the first time I saw *Caddyshack.*

"Send Her My Love" reminds me of my seventh-grade girlfriend's breasts.

"Only the Young" reminds me of Linda Fiorentino's ass.

"Separate Ways" reminds me of bad tank tops.

"Don't Stop Believin' " reminds me of Dad's smile.

As for Def Leppard, there were a few specific moments. The first time I ever got stoned was to a scratched LP of *High 'n' Dry*, which I still consider to be the band's best album. I got a *Pyromania* Velcro wallet as a Confirmation gift—oh, the irony—and later that year for Halloween I wore a white scarf and sleeveless Union Jack T-shirt and dressed like lead singer Joe Elliott in the "Autograph" video. The morning after the *Hysteria* concert—Tuesday, October 27, 1987 to be exact—at least half of Empire Ridge's student body showed up to school with Def Leppard concert tees reeking of sweat, tobacco, and pot. Beyond that, however, Def Leppard was bigger than any single moment. While ostensibly more meaningful bands like The Police, Talking Heads, or U2 vied for a mere sliver of my memory, I was hard pressed to remember a day in the 1980s when I didn't hear at least one Def Leppard song on my radio or cassette deck. Whether in my car playing air guitar with Hatch or in my room masturbating to Dad's *Playboys*—the volume always surreptitiously turned up to mask my moaning—the arena rock kings from Sheffield, England defined my teenage years. Okay, co-defined. Bon Jovi's *Slippery When Wet* album was a big fucking deal, too.

I stopped listening to Def Leppard in the nineties, partly because Steve Clark died, but mostly because the band became incapable of making music that didn't suck. I ostracized friends who thought *Adrenalize* was anything more than a steaming pile of shit, including a girl I had sex with several times—her name escapes me at the moment—who included "Have You Ever Needed Someone So Bad" on a mixtape she made for me.

"Hank?" Beth says. She grabs my hand as we walk across the parking lot toward the amphitheater. Claire and Hatch are about ten yards behind. Claire is mad because Hatch didn't let her bring the other joint into the concert. Hatch is mad because it's an hour before the show and his wife is already a puddle.

"Yeah, babe?" I say.

"What are you thinking about?"

"Sweet potatoes!"

"Huh?"

"Nichole Chase was one of my college flings, back in my wilder days. About three years after we stopped fooling around, she heard my dad died and sent me a mixtape. I liked most of the songs on it except for that shitty fucking ballad 'Have You Ever Needed Someone So Bad.' "

"Uh, so?"

"Sorry, I just couldn't remember her name."

"Why did you need to remember her name?"

"Because of Def Leppard, of course."

"Then why did you scream out 'sweet potatoes'?"

"Because of the giraffes at the circus."

"Uh, how much dope have you smoked?"

"Who the hell is that?" my best friend shouts in the middle of "Lovin', Touchin', Squeezin'." "Where the hell is Steve Perry?"

Our seats are in the lawn. Claire proceeded to smoke the joint by herself before Journey even came on stage. She's passed out right now, fetal and sweaty at her husband's feet.

"You know, Hatch," I say, dry-humping my wife—because come on, "Lovin', Touchin', Squeezin' " demands that you dry-hump the closest available female with a grindable ass. "For being sober, you're a real fucking idiot sometimes."

"What do you mean?"

"Perry hasn't been with the band since like the late eighties. That's Steve Augeri up there. Looks and sounds just like Perry."

"That guy looks nothing like Steve Perry."

"You're both wrong," Beth says into my shoulder. "Perry rejoined Journey for some reunion gigs in the nineties then left the band for good in 1998, which is when he was replaced by Steve Augeri."

I smack Hatch's arm with the back of my hand. "See, I was right. That guy up there—"

"*Isn't* Steve Augeri," Beth says, preempting my boast. "He dropped out of the band before this tour with some chronic throat problems. That mop-headed guy up there on stage sounds like Perry and Augeri, but he doesn't look anything like them. His name is Jeff Scott Soto."

"Who the hell is that?" I ask.

Hatch smacks my arm with the back of his hand. "Journey's lead singer, dumbass."

I convinced Hatch and Beth to leave before Def Leppard started into their encore. Being thirty-five years old, I hate bad traffic more than I like a good show. With the exception of Guns N' Roses' original lineup reuniting or Roger Waters fronting Pink Floyd again, there's no band on Earth that justifies me stewing in a car for two hours at the mercy of rent-a-cops and traffic cones.

"Who's ready to party?" Claire shouts from the backseat. She was unconscious for the entire concert. Hatch had to carry her over his shoulder back to the car. About halfway back to Empire Ridge, she woke up. And she's ready to party.

Claire offers me the nearly empty bottle of Jim Beam. I wave it off. "Not all of us napped for the last three hours, Claire Bear."

"You're no fun, Hankie," she says to me in her usual shamelessly flirty tone, which Beth immediately shuts down.

"Claire?" Beth says.

"Yeah?"

"Shut up."

"Mrs. Hatcher, I don't think I should."

Claire found an old New Year's bottle of unopened champagne in the back of the refrigerator. She's cornered Jack in the kitchen with booze and estrogen.

"Oh poo, Jack, have a sip. And call me Claire. When I hear someone say 'Mrs. Hatcher,' I look around for my mother-in-law."

"Lay off the kid," I say, stepping between them.

"The kid can handle himself," Hatch shouts from the living room.

"It's not the kid I'm worried about," I shout back. "Hey, Claire, go torment your husband instead of my seventeen-year-old son."

She shakes her head. "That's still so weird to hear you call him that."

Claire exits the kitchen. I hand Jack a couple twenty-dollar bills. "How were the kids?"

"Twins were demons, Sasha was perfect."

"Typical."

"Yep," Jack affirms. "Did I hear you were going to brunch with Mom tomorrow?"

"With Debbie, you mean?"

"So that's her name for good now?"

"Well, it ain't Mom, and she certainly doesn't deserve Grandma."

"At least you're talking. That's a start."

"I suppose so."

"You can go to bed now," I say. "Thanks for watching the brood."

Jack leans in and hugs me. "Thanks for letting me . . . Dad."

The hug suddenly goes from sweet to suffocating. "Look, you don't have to call me—"

"Just trying it on for size," Jack says.

"How does it fit?"

"Like a youth small T-shirt on a fat guy."

*"Black bandanna, sweet Louisiana, robbin' on a bank in the state of Indiana!"*

It's approaching two o'clock in the morning. Beth and Claire are standing in the middle of the hot tub. They're drunk, dancing and singing to the Red Hot Chili Peppers.

Hatch plugged his iPod into the stereo and is running through his "Indiana mix"—i.e., a shitload of John Mellencamp and any song that uses the word "Indiana" in the lyrics. The mix began with Mellencamp and India.Arie coming up from Indiana down from Tennessee, which when you think about it doesn't make any fucking sense. Next up was the Jackson Five's "Goin' Back to Indiana," which segued into Tom Petty telling us all about Mary Jane growing up in an Indiana town with Indiana boys and Indiana nights. I almost bailed on the mix entirely when it took a dreary turn with Melissa Etheridge's "Indiana," but Hatch rallied with the Dixie Chicks talking about their brothers finding work in Indiana and now the Chilis.

There's something melodic and soulful about the word *Indiana*. Four syllables flowing into one another, almost like a poem contained within a single word. The state itself might not be much to look at, but she has a beautiful singing voice.

Beth had offered Claire a swimsuit. Claire being Claire, she winked and said, "I couldn't possibly fit into one of your suits," when what she really meant was, *Bitch, please, I'm so much skinnier than you.* With her best friend reasonably demoralized, Claire then just stripped down to her bra and panties and jumped right in.

Hatch and I sit off to the side of the tub in two Adirondack chairs. I'm nursing a High Life, my best friend a cup of decaffeinated coffee.

"About time to shut this down," I say.

"Why?" Hatch sips his coffee. "You don't like the view?"

It's hard not to stare. Beth and Claire have two different body types—one petite and muscular, the other tall and lean. They complement one another very well, though, especially when half-naked and wet. I'm reminded vaguely of the lesbian sex scene between Anne Heche and Joan Chen in the underappreciated soft-core flick *Wild Side*.

You would think after sleeping with the same woman for thirteen years that broaching sexual intercourse would be old hat.

You would think.

The hot tub dance party lost its mojo quicker than I expected. By 3:00 a.m. Hatch and Claire headed down to the basement for the night. Before she crawled into bed, Beth changed out of her swimsuit into an old shirt and cotton pajama pants—the official bedtime uniform of middle-aged married women who no longer give a shit. But I'm not giving up that easy. Not tonight. Not after watching my wife dirty dance half-naked with the Hottest Girl I Never Tried to Sleep With.

And so begins the dance. After Beth turns off the lights, she always tries to first fall asleep on her back. If that happens, then the dance is over. Posted no fishing.

Beth rolls to her side facing away from me. Step one accomplished. *It's on!*

I slide across the bed behind her for step two, the spooning. This is the toughest step in the dance. It can make or break the deal and must be exercised with patience and care. Move too slowly, and she grabs your arm and pulls it tight around her for the all-night cuddle. Move too fast—say, go immediately for a boob squeeze or let your fingers do the walking straight to the clitoris—and it's the dreaded shutdown: not only no sex tonight, but also likely some lingering resentment that will keep you out of the T & A trade at least through her next menstrual cycle.

To avoid this confrontation, you move to step three, the foot test. While fully spooned and your hand placed casually on your partner's waist or the side of her thigh, you slide the top of your foot lightly against the arch of her foot. There's potential for disaster even with this innocuous move. Tread too lightly, and by the time you've mustered the courage to move to step four, she's in full REM sleep. Tread too aggressively, and you end up tickling her, which annoys her and sends you back into the whole lingering resentment shame spiral.

Beth pushes gently back on my foot. *Green light!*

The foot push isn't a guarantee, so it's usually best to go to step four just for confirmation. There are a couple options. One, slide the hand under the shirt and do a finger swipe beneath her breasts. Or two, slide your hand inside the back of her panties and give her cheeks a good squeeze. I'm an ass man, so I think I'll—

"You going to fuck me any time this century?" Beth says.

"Wait a second. You're awake?"
"Kind of hard to sleep with your erection stabbing me in the back."
"But you put on PJ pants. I thought that meant you didn't want to—"
"I didn't."
"But now you do?"
"I could easily be talked out of it."
"I don't want your pity."
"You want something that starts with a *P*."
"You're a cruel woman, Beth."
"A cruel woman with an awesome rack."
"Well, yeah."
"And I noticed."
"Noticed what?"
"You looked at me in the hot tub."
"Of course I did."
"No, you looked at me *instead of* Claire."
"I did?"
"Hank, I love Claire to death, but we both know she sucks the air right out of a room. You had tunnel vision tonight, and I just wanted to say I appreciated you appreciating me."
"So we *are* having sex tonight?"
Beth reaches down, pulling her PJ pants and panties down to her knees. She reaches her hand into the slit of my boxers. "Would you prefer an all-night cuddle?"
"Only if it involves my dick inside you."
"You almost don't deserve to get some after that pickup line."
"Hey, you're the one with my dick in your hand."
"And don't you forget it."

# Chapter 45

Lila and Chris broke up, again. Lila is still in New York, living right now with a friend from work in the West Village. I'm in town for a week of meetings at the Bertelsmann building, so Lila asked me to meet her at Sweet Revenge, a cupcake, beer, and wine bar on Carmine Street.

Lila is already at the bar when I arrive. I can tell something is up the moment I walk inside. She stands up, kisses me on the cheek, and exhales right when we hug, as if she's been holding her breath for just that moment.

"Hey, girl," I say, kissing her on the cheek. "Everything okay?"

Lila smiles. "It is now."

We order a couple peanut butter cupcakes, which our waitress advises to pair with a glass of Malbec.

I reach over and squeeze Lila's hand. "You up for some red wine this early?"

She squeezes back. "Already a glass ahead of you."

I nod to the waitress. "Red wine it is, then."

I'm on my second glass, Lila her third. The cupcakes—peanut butter cake with a ganache center and peanut butter fudge frosting—were so decadent that we ordered two more.

"Sorry to hear about Chris," I say, taking a bite of cupcake.

Lila reaches over with her napkin, dabbing at the frosting on my upper lip. "What's to be sorry about, Hank?"

"I know you loved her."

"I loved the idea of her, but let's face it—Chris was an exhausting girlfriend."

"True, but still, you two were a couple for a long time. That's not something where you just turn the page and move on."

"Who's turning the page?" Lila says. "I walked in on her doing a nineteen-year-old Columbia coed with a strap-on. That's not an image I'm forgetting anytime soon."

"Wow. I-I'm sorry."

"Oh shut up, Hank."

"What did I say?"

"You didn't have to say anything. I can see it in your expression."

"What can you see?"

"Your conscience wrestling with whether or not you should be sympathetic or turned on."

I hide my guilt in an aggressive swallow of wine. I place the empty glass on the table. Lila smiles. I smile back. "You ever wonder what would have happened with us if our parents never got together?"

"I don't follow," Lila says.

"I don't know. It just seems like, well, we've always been so compatible."

"Don't kid yourself."

"Why do you say that?"

"I love you to pieces, but we are *not* compatible."

"That's a little harsh."

"Is there chemistry? Sure there is. But true compatibility? No offense, Hank, but the idea of waking up every day with you and wrestling with all your psychological repression, sexual dysfunction, and emotional transference just sounds exhausting. Beth deserves a medal, not a fucking ring."

"Speaking of emotional transference," I say, "I'm not, Chris. You know that, right?"

"Sorry, Hank." Lila rubs my arm. "That just all kind of came rushing out."

I respond to her gesture by grabbing her hand. I rub it between my thumb and index finger. "Maybe you just need to get out of here for a while. Get away from the New York scene."

"No arguments from me."

"You've done all you can do here: the editing thing, the writing thing . . ."

"The lesbian band aid thing."

"Yeah, that too."

"Funny you should say that." Lila pulls an envelope out of her purse. She hands the envelope to me. It's addressed to her, and the top line of the return address reads *Brigham Young University–Hawaii*.

"What's this?"

"You don't want to read it?"

"I'm sorry, have we met? Why would I want to read anything from BYU?"

"They've offered me a teaching position in the English department. Full benefits, and I could get tenure as early as seven years."

"But it's a Mormon university, in fucking Hawaii."

"I've made my peace with my church after those wretched books I wrote."

"Wretched? Those things put food on both of our plates for the better part of the last decade."

"Money and notoriety isn't everything, Hank. I want stability. I want to put down roots. BYU–Hawaii is offering me all of that and more."

"Why do I suddenly feel like you're telling me this is happening as opposed to asking if I think you should do it?"

"Because you know me, and we're compatible."

"See, I knew it!"

"Come on, Hank. Be happy for me."

"I am, Lila."

"You are?"

"If this is what you want, I'm ecstatic."

"Thanks. Now what about you?"

"What about me?"

"You seem to be losing your steam at College Ave."

"Is that what you call it?"

"What do you call it?"

"I call it tired of being a figurehead for a shitty list. I'm not an editor anymore. I'm just a paper pusher."

"Then do something about it."

"Like what?"

"I think you know that answer."

"Right now, I'm having a hard time even figuring out what the fucking question is."

"You need to be a writer, Hank."

"Are you insane? I have three kids and a mortgage."

"So?"

"Now isn't exactly the opportune time to explore a hobby. Besides, what the hell am I going to write about?"

"Tell *your* story."

"My story?"

Lila stands up from the table, closing her eyes. " 'My morning gets off to its usual start,' " she recites. " 'I wake up. Masturbate. Eat some bacon and eggs. Drink a cup of creamed and sugared coffee. Have a frank discussion with my father about his testicles.' "

"How in the hell did you—"

"I read it on your laptop one of those various nights you passed out on my couch."

"So you're suggesting I write a memoir? Uh, hello, welcome to 2006. Did you see James Frey on *Oprah* back in January? It's not exactly a growth industry in publishing right now."

"Hank, I'm not telling you to quit your day job or pen the next great memoir. I'm just telling you to write. Just sit down with your computer, a pad of paper, whatever, and write something. All that shit that's in your head? Just let it out. There's a story there. I know there is. I can feel it wanting to come out."

"Problem is there are a lot of people who would probably prefer that this story stay in my head."

"Fuck 'em."

"Debbie would certainly need to take a long hard look in the mirror."

"And that's her problem, not yours. Besides, what's Debbie care now that she and Dad are essentially abandoning you?"

"What do you mean by that?"

"You know, with the move and all. I mean, converting to LDS is one thing. I pretty much saw that as inevitable with your mother. But actually moving to Salt Lake City? Debbie is in for one hell of a culture shock."

I prop my elbows on the table, burying my forehead in my hands. Grinding my teeth, I look up and hold my right index finger in the air. "Waitress, we'll take our check now."

"Wait," Lila says, finally picking up on my body language. "You didn't know?"

I shake my head. "That's a negative, Ghostrider."

# Chapter 46

Mom invited Jack and me over for dinner. I brought a box of red wine, mostly just to piss Gillman off. He invited me to say grace prior to the meal, but I declined. The four of us sit around the long Amish table Mom found at an antique store in Gnaw Bone, a peculiarly named Indiana zip code halfway between Nashville and Columbus.

"What exactly are we eating here?" Jack asks me under his breath.

I eye the spread: cubed steak, Spanish rice, and green beans stewed in bacon grease. "It's a Fitzpatrick specialty."

Jack shakes his head. "No it isn't."

"Yes it is," Mom says. She ladles mushroom gravy over the cubed steak on Jack's plate, following it up with the rice and green beans. "This meal was an old staple when Hank was a kid. Try it. You just might like it."

Jack sticks his fork in the Spanish rice, dissecting it more than eating it. He eats a small bite.

"Well, what do you think?" Mom says.

"Isn't this just white rice mixed with tomatoes?"

"Eureka!" I say. "Someone has finally cracked the code. Four-star restaurants everywhere are now doomed to irrelevance by this 1970s culinary masterpiece."

"Give it a rest, Hank," Gillman says. "Your mother made this meal especially for you."

"Yeah, I kind of assumed that." Grabbing the napkin from my lap, I reach up and wipe my mouth. I place the napkin to the side of my plate. "Truthfully, though, I don't really have an appetite right now."

"You sick or something?" Mom asks.

"Or something," I answer. "Can we just get on with this?"

"Get on with wh—"

"Utah, Mom?" I say.

"Oh."

"Fucking Utah?"

"What about Utah?" Jack says.

I nod in my mother's direction. "Your grandma is moving with Gillman to Salt Lake City."

"It has the highest quality of life of any major metropolitan area in the continental United States."

"Says who, Mom? Your oh-so-impartial husband?"

"Says a Gallup poll for the fourth year in a row," Gillman chimes in.

"Gillman, shut the fuck up."

"Hank, you will not talk to your stepfather like that in front of me."

"I think I just did, Debbie."

"It's just time."

"Time for what? To run away?"

"I don't see this as running away from anything," Mom says. "I see it more as running *to* something—to a new life, to some place where I'm wanted."

"Oh bullshit. You're not just moving to another state. You're moving to another planet. A planet of weird white people, weird white gods, and weird white underwear. You're moving to fucking Honkeytown."

I back away from the table. Standing, I turn and walk into the living room, my back to the kitchen. Gillman follows me.

"When was the last time you really included your mother in anything, Hank?"

"What are you talking about? I include her. We see each other for the holidays, and I always take her out for a birthday dinner."

"What about the other three hundred sixty-odd days of the year?"

"I call Mom all the time."

"You call Debbie for three things . . ." Gillman says. He moves close to me, now nose to nose, holding up three fingers. "You call her when you need a last-minute babysitter, on your father's birthday, and on your parents' wedding anniversary."

"That's not true."

"It is true. In fact, that's one of the reasons we're moving. It's time to lay John Fitzpatrick to rest."

"Fuck you!"

Gillman sticks his finger in my face. "I think I've earned the right not to stand in his shadow anymore."

"Careful, Gill-MAN."

"I'm tired of being careful, HEN-ree. I'm tired of hearing about the perfect John Fitzpatrick. He was a flawed person who struggled at being a husband, a father, and a man just like you and me."

"I would seriously shut your piehole right about now if I were you."

"Heck, Hank. Far as I'm concerned, John failed you. He shielded you from the truth about his abusive mother. He lied to you about Jack. When Uncle Mitch abused you all those years, it was on John's watch. His death didn't mess you up. His life did."

Because of the way Jack is positioned at the kitchen table, he's the only one who has a clear view of my right arm, which is partially hidden behind my back. He sees me clench my fist, but by the time he stands up he's already too late.

I underestimate Gillman's substantial gut. I land a solid punch into his midsection that I assumed would knock him off his feet. Instead, he's merely doubled over and gasping for air.

"Gillman!" Mom shouts.

"I'm okay, Debbie," Gillman says, waving her off with one hand, his other hand on his knee.

"Holy shit, Hank!" Jack says, trying not to laugh. It's just the distraction Gillman is looking for.

A word about my stepfather. He was an all-state linebacker in high school and walked on at BYU before blowing his knee out.

Gillman crouches low, his feet shoulder-width apart. He slides his head to the side of my waist and reaches his arms around my thighs. He wraps my legs, raises me up in the air, and slams me through the coffee table. It's a textbook form tackle.

My wrestling instincts kick in about halfway through the spray of glass and splintered wood. Right before I hit the ground, I turn my right shoulder in just enough so I won't get caught on my back. I secure Gillman's right arm with my left while bringing my right elbow down on his right ear. His grip grows slack from the blow, his ear bleeding profusely. I slide out from under him, staggering to one knee. I raise my right fist for another shot.

"Dad, stop!"

Jack's hand squeezes my wrist, my fist hovering inches in front of Gillman's face. I think Jack might be stronger than I am, although I'm not going to admit it to him anytime soon.

"Please," Jack says to both of us. "No more."

Gillman and I are at a standoff. If I punch him, he'll punch me right back.

Mom helps Gillman to his feet. She leans his head over the kitchen sink, cleaning his ear with a cold washcloth.

Jack offers to help me up, but I refuse. "I can take care of myself."

"I know you can," Jack says. He still grabs my elbow, steering me toward the couch. We both sit down.

"Nice move," I say.

"What move was that?"

"Calling me 'Dad.'"

"Snapped you out of your fucking 'roid rage, didn't it?"

"That it did."

"Hank?" Gillman says, walking up to us.

"I think we've said all we need to say to one another."

"I just wanted to let you know I didn't mean what I said. I'm sorry."

"Fuck you and your apology."

"I suppose I deserved that."

"Come on, Hank," Jack says. "Be nice."

"Be nice?" I stand up, walking into the kitchen where Mom sits stone-faced and silent at the Amish table from Gnaw Bone. "Someone just accused my dead father of enabling a pedophile. You call that being nice?"

"I said I was sorry, Hank."

"And I said fuck you and your apology, Gillman."

"Just get out of here," Mom says, tears now running down her face.

"What?" I say.

"I think you and Jack probably need to leave now," she reiterates. "Some of the things Gillman just said to you were cruel and unnecessary, and I'm sorry for that. But his heart is in the right place. I love you and Jeanine and Jack more than life itself, but I also love Gillman. And for him and for me, I can't be Mrs. Fitzpatrick anymore. It's time for me to be Mrs. Prestwich."

"But Mom, you can't go."

I don't say these words. They come from the family room—from Jack.

He runs across the room crying and into Mom's arms, just like when he was a little boy and the tornado watch would flash across the television.

"There, there," Mom says. Jack sits in her lap. She strokes her seventeen-year-old boy's hair. "You know the difference between a tornado warning and a tornado watch, right?"

"Yeah, Mom," he answers. "A warning means a tornado has been spotted in the area, and a watch means the conditions are right for a tornado."

"So when there's a watch?"

"There's no tornado."

Mom kisses Jack on the forehead. "And when there's a warning?"

"It doesn't matter, because you'll always keep me safe."

# Chapter 47

Jack and I are in the driveway playing a game of H-O-R-S-E that's just recently morphed into a game of S-T-U-P-I-D.
"How late is she?"
"About three weeks," Jack says.
"What's her name again?"
"Her name is Caitlin."
"Of course it is. And she isn't sleeping with anyone else?"
"No! We're in love."
"Oh, I'm sure you are."
Whenever you hear someone characterized as a "player's coach," it's really a pejorative cloaked in a superlative. The players love him because he "speaks their language" and because "he's a mentor first and a coach second" who "knows how to put them in the best possible position to succeed both on and off the field."
Translation: He's a shitty coach that loses a lot of fucking games.
I think that as a father, I make for a great player's coach. A player's coach who at the moment is trying to wrap his head around the fact that exactly seventeen years after his own conception, Jack has apparently decided to double down.
"I feel like I gave you the information you needed so you wouldn't get into a situation like this."
"You did."
"So what happened?"
"I don't know," Jack said. "I guess we just got caught up in the moment."
Statements like this should scare the living shit out of parents, because in the nearly two decades since I was Jack's age, nothing has fucking changed. Sex education still usually devolves into on-the-job training. All those parents, teachers, and taxpayer dollars assailed against the ignorance of youth, vanquished in one split second because *I guess we just got caught up in the moment.*
"What are you going to do?" I ask.

"Caitlin is taking a pregnancy test today, so we'll cross that bridge when we come to it."

"You're not thinking about keeping it, are you?"

"What if I was?"

"Then you're a dumbass."

"Gee. Love you too, Dad."

"What's that supposed to mean?"

"So you regret that Laura didn't abort me as planned?"

"Apples versus oranges, Jack."

"All I see are fetuses versus fetuses, Hank."

He still bounces back and forth between "Hank" and "Dad" as the mood suits him: the former if we're having a bad day, the latter if we're having a good one. It doesn't take a player's coach to figure out where this day is heading.

"Can I give you one piece of advice?"

"Go for it."

"No matter what happens, you let this be her decision."

"I think I have the right to—"

"You have the right to keep your mouth shut."

"But that baby inside Caitlin is half mine."

"And a dude presuming a prenatal fetus to be 'half his' is like the guy who sold paint to Leonardo da Vinci being called the cocreator of the *Mona Lisa*."

"I dispute that analogy," Jack says.

"It's not an analogy for you to dispute. It's a fact. You're not the one carrying another living organism inside you for the next nine months. You're not the one whose body is going through a physical and chemical metamorphosis. You're not the one who has to fight the stigma of being a pregnant teenage girl day after day. Look at Caitlin as the owner of a bank and you as a depositor who will never be allowed to own a bank. All you did was deposit your money in the bank and walk away. And if I'm not being clear enough, the bank is Caitlin's vagina."

"Uh, yeah, I got that part."

Jack's phone vibrates in his pocket as he shoots the basketball. It ricochets off the back of the rim to give me the undisputed H-O-R-S-E driveway title yet again.

"You going to get that?"

"Yeah." Jack reaches inside his pocket. He flips open his phone, reads the text message.

"Well?" I say.

# Chapter 48

I offered to help, but Jack insisted on paying for the abortion. He gathered some items from the attic and sold them on eBay. Most of the items were mine—one complete collection of late seventies Mattel Shogun Warriors, one unopened 1980 Kenner Star Wars Droid Factory, one well-used Atari 2600 game console—but I didn't make a big deal out of it. He was up to two hundred seventy-five dollars, still twenty-five short of where he needed to be, with nothing but some old comic books—also technically mine—left to his name.

We pull into the parking lot at Sal's Comic Barn, a giant aluminum-sided box in Beech Grove. Empire Ridge is just too damn nosy for something like this. Local boy tries to unload some things in a pawnshop, and people talk. Here in Beech Grove, Jack is just a nameless kid trying to scrounge up petty cash.

The comic books are individually wrapped in clear vinyl sleeves. We each tuck a stack under our arms and then enter the store. Sal sits behind the counter, a middle-aged paradox with an old-man comb-over and teen-profuse acne.

Sal's Comic Barn is a familiar place to me. I was an avid comic book collector beginning in second grade and ending in puberty. My last two years of collecting in the seventh and eighth grade were largely spent arguing with Sal, his store only two blocks away from Our Lady of Perpetual Help.

"Hank Fitzpatrick?" Sal says, brushing the remnants of his barbecued pork sandwich off his face. He sticks a toothpick in his mouth. "Is that you?"

"Been a while, Sal."

"Twenty years if it's been a day. How's it going?"

"My son here is just looking to unload some comics."

"Your son?" Sal says, looking at Jack, then at me, then at Jack again. "Looks to me like he could be your brother."

"Yeah," I say. "We get that a lot."

I nod to Jack. He nods back and places the comic books on the counter. Sal eyes them one by one. He retrieves one book, then another, and another. He slides seven of them back across the counter.

"How much for these?"

I grab the comic books, shuffling them as I pretend to assess their worth when I already know their value down to the penny. "Detective Comics numbers three hundred thirty-seven through three hundred forty-three. Good picks, Sal."

"They're okay, I guess." He shrugs. "I'll give you twenty bucks for all of 'em."

"Twenty bucks?" I say. "How stupid do you think I am?" I drop the comic books on the counter one at a time, smacking them with the back of my hand to emphasize each point.

"The first appearance of Martian Manhunter." *Smack.*

". . . winner of six awards for comic book excellence." *Smack.*

". . . both Archie Goodwin and Walter Simonson were recognized for their work in this series." *Smack smack.*

". . . the artwork, some of Simonson's earliest stuff, continues to be hailed as a masterpiece of page layout and storytelling." S*mack smack smack.*

"Yeah yeah yeah." Sal waves a dismissive hand. "Take it or leave it."

We could have easily got fifty for them if we had the time or inclination, but like most seasoned comic book collectors, Sal's superpower is smelling desperation.

"Come on, Sal. Can you at least come up to thirty? For old time's sake?"

"I'm running a business here, not a charity." Sal rubs his patchy attempt at a goatee. He cracks a smile, a barbecue-stained row of what I like to call "summer teeth": some are here, some are there.

"Then how about twenty-five?"

"Deal!" Sal says with shamelessly obvious haste, as if to let me know he fucked me over. He throws the money on the counter. "Nice doing business with you, Hank. Try not to be such a stranger."

"See you in twenty years, Sal."

He laughs us out the door.

# Chapter 49

We picked Caitlin up at 8:00 a.m. The hour-long drive north to the clinic in Indianapolis passed in complete silence save for *The Bob & Tom Show* on the radio. I tried to laugh at some of the jokes. Jack and Caitlin didn't.

Ours is only the third car in the parking lot. Save for the nearby hum of morning rush hour on the interstate, there's an eerie quiet to the place. With its mustard-painted vertical siding and faux fieldstone, the clinic reminds me of our family pediatrician's office. Jack only switched from his pediatrician to a general practitioner last year. Babies having babies.

I open the door for them both. The inside of the clinic is also like any other doctor's office. The required minimum six tropical plants. A faint antiseptic odor. Old copies of *Glamour.*

"Are you eighteen years of age, miss?" the nurse at the front desk asks. I can hear her voice just above the din of Christopher Cross's "Sailing" that crackles out of a blown speaker on the ceiling. The nurse has a large jaw and big breasts, with wide hips perched on oddly lean legs, kind of like Sally Spectra in *The Bold and the Beautiful.*

"Yes, I'm eighteen," Caitlin says. She produces her driver's license from her back pocket. With her free hand she reaches over and gives Jack's hand a squeeze. Jack tries to give her a reassuring smile, but he doesn't quite get there.

For a few seconds, I see myself in Jack's place. Laura standing at the counter handing the nurse her identification. The nurse giving her a clipboard of papers and saying, *Thank you, Ms. Elliot. I'll go make a photocopy of this. You can have a seat and fill out these papers.*

"What is all this?" Caitlin asks.

The nurse points to the clipboard. "The top two sheets are your patient history and your written consent to perform the procedure. The third is the consent to administer anesthesia, which you'll take in with you and sign after the anesthesiologist explains everything to you. They'll call your name shortly."

Caitlin fills out the forms, Jack sitting beside her. I flip through a worn issue of *Glamour* with Britney Spears on the cover. Between the how-to pictorials on breast exams and the underwear ads, I used to find *Glamour* to be a surprisingly adequate visual aid.

"Caitlin," the nurse says from a cracked-open door to our left.

"Yes," she says.

Caitlin stands up, squeezes Jack's hand one more time. He wants to go with her, but he knows that is impossible. His eyes start to well with tears. When it matters most, he can't be there for her, and it's breaking his heart. Jack seems to have figured out the part of the equation I was always missing as a teen: the part about how to do a little more honoring and a little less coveting.

Caitlin lets go of his hand, disappearing behind the door. The nurse sits back behind the front desk. "Sir," she says to Jack.

"Sir!" she says again, louder this time.

"Huh?" Jack says. He looks down to realize he's standing there with his hand on the doorknob.

"You can't go back there."

"I wish I could."

"No you don't."

"It'd be nice if someone would at least tell me what was going on."

I stand up from my chair. "You mean you don't know, Jack?"

"Not a clue."

The nurse shakes her head. I look at her. "Can I have a copy of that third form you handed Caitlin?"

"Why?" she says.

"Do I need a reason?"

She hands me the form. I hand it to Jack. "Sit down and read this."

I sit next to Jack, looking over his shoulder. I try to imagine what Caitlin is going through. Is this what Laura would have gone through had she not chosen to deceive me? Dear God, how can I be mad at her now? She didn't betray me. She saved me.

```
CONSENT FOR ABORTION
    I  hereby  direct  and  request  the
    physician from Women's Freedom, LLC to
    perform  a  suction  aspiration  abortion.
    If  any  unforeseen  circumstances  arise,
    or  are  discovered  during  the  course  of
    the  abortion,  which  call  for  procedures
    in  addition  to,  or  different  from  those
    contemplated,  I  further  request  and
    authorize  the  physician  to  take  whatever
    measures    he/she    deems    medically
    necessary.
```

I assume the first thing Caitlin does when she enters the operating room is take off her clothes.

> I understand that the purpose of the procedure is to terminate my pregnancy, but that no guarantee has been made to me regarding the outcome of this surgery.

Caitlin is repulsed by her own body. More than that, she thinks to herself as she rubs her ever-so-slight pooch belly, it has betrayed her.

> It has been explained to me that, in rare instances, the pregnancy is not terminated and, if that happens, further treatment may be necessary at my expense.

The anesthesiologist enters the room. *Hello, Caitlin,* he says. He offers a limp-wristed handshake, an empty gesture on behalf of a palatability this situation can never have. He explains what he's about to do to her. She signs the consent form, hands it to him.

> I understand the procedure is done by suction aspiration of the uterus.

Ten minutes later, the doctor and the nurse from the front desk enter the room. *Good afternoon, ma'am,* he says to Caitlin, dispensing with the pleasantries and getting right to it. *This will be a lot like a pelvic exam or Pap test, so I need you to lie down on the exam table, please.*

> I understand that the risks involved include, but are not limited to perforation of the uterus with possible damage to abdominal organs . . .

*Just relax, ma'am. I'm inserting a spectrum inside your vagina.*

> Hemorrhage . . .

*I'm now going to clean the vagina and cervix with an antiseptic solution.*

> Blood clots in the uterus . . .

*You should be feeling the effects of the local anesthetic that was administered.*

> Allergic reaction to the local anesthesia . . .

*You will notice a numbing sensation in your cervix.*

> Cervical tear . . .

*And the Misoprostol should be kicking in any second now to dilate your cervix.*

> Infection . . .

*Okay, ma'am, I'm inserting a thin, hollow tube into your cervical canal.*

> Hysterectomy . . .

*The cramping is unavoidable, but it'll all be over shortly. I promise.*

> Sterility . . .

*Your cramping should gradually subside now that the tube is out. What's that? You need to throw up? Nurse! Please help this young lady.*

> Emotional reaction, both long and short term, to the termination of my pregnancy . . .

*Feeling better, ma'am? Let's run through our recovery checklist.*

> If I experience any complications that require emergency medical care, I understand that I am financially responsible for the cost of said care.

*You'll have irregular bleeding and more cramps for the next two to three weeks. You should only use sanitary pads for the first week. No tampons, got it?*

> I agree to see additional care promptly, if advised to do so.

*You're welcome to take ibuprofen or acetaminophen for the cramping and the pain, but absolutely no aspirin.*

> I have been told that, as an alternative to abortion, I may choose to continue this pregnancy and either parent may have custody of the child or elect adoption.

*No sex for one week.*

> I agree to read the aftercare instruction sheet and contact Women's Freedom, LLC if I experience any of the symptoms listed on said sheet. I further consent to the disposal of any tissue removed from my body during the abortion.

*Other than that, I think we can agree that this was a fairly painless procedure, right?*

> I hereby release the physician and staff from any and all claims arising out of, or connected with, the above procedure or any resulting complications and expenses.

*Have a nice day, ma'am.*

> I certify that I have read and fully understand this consent. I further state that consent is given without coercion or duress.

*Bye now.*

Caitlin is wheeled out the door in a wheelchair. How long has it been? Twenty minutes. She's hunched over, limp, like she's been poured into the wheelchair.

Jack pushes the wheelchair to the car. I open the rear passenger-side door and offer my hand to her. She grabs my hand and stands, her knees wobbling. She steadies herself and looks over her shoulder at Jack.

"Paperwork," she says.

"What's that?" Jack says.

"Forgot to fill out the paperwork. Gotta go back. The receptionist said I need to fill out something else."

"You two get in the car," I say, stern-faced. "I'll take care of this."

I throw open the door to the clinic. The nurse is standing there with a piece of paper in her hand, evidently expecting me. "I apologize for the inconvenience, but we need to just—"

"Inconvenience? That's what you call this bullshit?"

"Please, sir, calm down."

"Listen, lady, I don't need to calm the fuck down. I want to know why it is you want that young woman out there to fill out more goddamn paperwork."

"We don't need her to fill out anything."

"You don't?"

"No."

"Then what's this about."

"It's her blood type. Ms. Caitlin is Rh-negative, and so we had to administer a shot of RhoGAM after the procedure."

"Roe what?"

"RhoGAM."

"What's that?"

"It's short for RHO immune globulin. We administered it to Caitlin because the fetus was Rh-positive. If some of the red blood cells of the fetus leaked into her system, her body could produce antibodies to the Rh D factor—a condition called sensitization. Without the RhoGAM shot, these antibodies would cross the placenta and potentially destroy the red blood cells in the next Rh-positive baby she has, killing the child."

"Look, I just want to get out of here. What do you need from me?"

The nurse hands me the invoice. "I'd prefer to just bill Ms. Caitlin and not bother her about this today, but she won't give us a mailing address."

I look at the invoice. "So basically you need fifty more dollars."

"Yes," the nurse says. "That covers the cost of the RhoGAM shot."

I pull out my wallet, extracting two twenty-dollar bills, a five-dollar bill and five one-dollar bills. I slam the money on the counter. "Take it."

Caitlin is the second person I know with an Rh-negative blood type. The other person is my mother. Mom discovered her blood type on the day I was born; Caitlin discovered hers on the day someone wasn't.

# Part IX
# 2007-2008

# Chapter 50

When I was a child, Dad kept a Laser in our garage. It wasn't the five-megawatt weapon of mass destruction like the one invented by Chris Knight and Mitch Taylor in *Real Genius,* the greatest Val Kilmer movie no one remembers; rather, it was a small fiberglass cat-rigged sailing dinghy. Dad taught me to sail when I was six years old, and for one perfect summer, we went out at least twice a week on Eagle Creek Reservoir, the long and narrow man-made lake on the west side of Indianapolis that had strict horsepower limits, which kept all the powerboaters away.

Later, that following spring, Dad took the Laser down to the Gulf of Mexico for our family's spring break. We went out sailing one day on the front end of a storm. Mom watched as Dad and I came flying into a lee shore, the shore that was facing into the wind. The storm front was closing, wind and salt spray roaring over our backs. A wave caught the bow just right, pitchpoling our boat. The Laser flipped end over end, the aluminum mast snapping in half after getting stuck upside down in a sandbar. I nearly drowned. When we drove back to Indiana, the boat—and Dad's nascent hobby—stayed in Florida.

A lot went through my mind when I saw my gay neighbors Oscar and Marshall park the beat-up sailboat in their driveway with a For Sale sign. What were two gay guys who were both afraid of the water doing with a sailboat? What was the over-under on how long it took the HOA to send them a strongly worded warning letter? Was she seaworthy? And most importantly, how pissed was Beth going to be after I bought her?

As it turns out, Oscar and Marshall were selling the boat for a friend. The HOA waited a whole two business days to send the letter, which when you factored in the time it took to actually mail the letter meant it was sent out almost the instant the boat appeared. Not only was she seaworthy, she sailed beautifully. And yes, Beth was way fucking pissed.

The boat is called a Highlander. Twenty-feet long, with about two hundred seventy-five square-feet of sail between the jib and main, plus a three hundred-square-feet spinnaker, she's a lot beefier than Dad's old four-meter, one-sail Laser. I named her *Heather*—after Connor MacLeod's first wife in the movie *Highlander,* obviously.

I've been trying to turn Beth into a sailor, but she's having none of it. We're a month into the summer. This is already our third weekend on the water, and I think it might be Beth's last. I'm skippering the helm at the moment, doing my best to guide my first mate.

"What do you mean, grab the sheet?" Beth says. "The only sheets I see are the sails."

I point to the left side of the boat. "The jib sheet to port. Just cleat it off."

"What side of the boat is port again?"

"The left side," I say. "Remember, port and left have the same number of letters."

"Oh yeah."

"So grab the sheet already!"

"*What sheet?*"

I take my hands off the tiller and grab the line running from the clew of the jib back into the cockpit. I attach it to the portside cleat. "This sheet."

"You mean the rope?"

"Sailboats have lines or sheets, not ropes."

"Hey, Hank."

"Yes, honey?"

"Nautical douche bag know-it-all is not a good look on you."

The wind died, as it's prone to do in the summer in Indiana. Beth yelled at me for not bringing along the electric trolling motor. I said something about being a sailing purist and quoted Joshua Slocum's *Sailing Alone Around the World.* She called me a douche bag again. As we crawl into the marina, I see Jack sitting on the edge of the dock, his shoes off and his feet in the water.

Mom and Gillman came back to Empire Ridge last month for his high school graduation. It was the first time they had been back since they moved to Utah a year ago. Jack's grades fell off a little during the tail end of high school, but he still made the National Honors Society and graduated in the top five percent of the Prep Class of 2007. He broke up with Caitlin after the pregnancy scare, got back together with her, then broke up with her again. I still rarely see them apart, although Jack insists they're just casually dating, which I take to mean they're still casually having sex with one another. *With all due respect, son, this isn't my first rodeo.*

"Look what the cat dragged in," I say, throwing the line at Jack.

He catches the line, cleats me off at the dock. "How's the sailing today?"

Beth rolls her eyes. "Ask Captain Douche Bag."

"Ha!" Jack laughs. He offers Beth his hand. "Milady."

My wife accepts the offer, stepping out of the boat and onto the dock. She kisses Jack on the cheek. "At least one of the Fitzpatrick men knows how to be a gentleman."

"Where are you going?" I ask. "We still need to break the boat down."

"I'll leave that to you two," Beth says. "If you need me, I'll be up at the marina bar drinking margaritas."

I shake my head. *Prima donna*, I mouth silently to Jack.

"I heard that," Beth says.

Jack laughs. I squeeze his shoulder. "Ain't love grand, buddy?"

"Don't be so hard on yourself," Jack says. "You two make it look easy. How long has it been now?"

"Married twelve years this August. Next year it will be twenty years since we first, uh . . ."

"Kissed?"

"Exactly."

"You ever talk to Laura anymore?"

"Huh? What kind of a question is that?"

"I don't know. Just thought I'd ask."

"I know you two have been talking."

"You do?"

"Yeah. I see the letters in the mail and the occasional text on your phone. Just because I do a lot of idiotic things, doesn't mean I'm an idiot."

"So you're not mad?"

"Why would I be mad? She's your birth mother."

"That's good to know. In fact, it's kind of the reason I came out here today." Jack hands me an envelope. It's addressed to him, and the top two lines of the return address read *University of Notre Dame, Admissions Office*.

"What's this?"

"You don't want to read it?"

"I'm sorry, have we met? Hell yes, I want to read it!"

I unfold the off-white paper. Before I read the letter, I hold it to my nose. It carries with it the smells of expectations: fresh-waxed floors, leather chairs, a professor's aftershave, the mustiness of an old textbook tempered by the chemical-sweet note of the book glue binding its pages together. Where's the *Rudy* soundtrack when I need it?

"Uh, what are you doing?" Jack asks.

"Just give me a moment." I close my eyes, then open them. I begin to read.

Dear Jack,

The Committee for Admissions has completed its review of your application for admission. I am pleased to report that your academic achievement and personal qualities have earned you a place in Notre Dame's 2007 Freshman Class. I trust that you will view this offer of admission as a special recognition of your accomplishments during the past four years and as a vote of confidence in your potential for success during your college years.

To confirm your enrollment at Notre Dame, please follow the instructions on the enclosed sheets, noting all the important dates and deadlines. If you have not already done so, please forward a copy of your final transcript when it is available. If you have any questions or need some personal attention, please call us and ask to speak with one of our counselors.

Those who love you must be proud of you—who you are and what you have accomplished. We at Notre Dame are eager to have you with us because your intellectual and spiritual growth will continue here.

Sincerely,

Sister Vivian Rose Morshauser, O.S.F.
Assistant Provost for Enrollment

"Are you fucking kidding me?" I grab Jack in a bear hug, heaving him up in the air. "You did it!"

"I take it you're excited, then?"

"Best day ever."

"Come on, really?"

"Okay, there's the day Mom brought you home, the day I married Beth, and the days Sasha and the twins were born, but this has to be a solid number five on that list."

"Wow."

"You don't understand, Jack. This was Dad's dream for me, and I let him down. I never even filled out the application. He's up in Heaven right now looking down at us with the biggest ear-to-ear grin, and I bet Grandpa George and Grandpa Fred are right there with him."

"What about Grandma Eleanor and Grandma Louise?"

"Yeah," I say, folding the letter carefully into the envelope and handing it back to Jack. "I think those two might be living the afterlife in a different zip code."

"I'm glad you're happy, Dad."

"Aren't you?"

"I guess so."

"You guess so?"

"It's just that, well, Notre Dame was . . . like you said. It was Grandpa John's dream for you, and it became your dream for me. But it's never been my dream."

"Then make it your dream, Jack. Opportunities like this don't come around every day."

"I realize there are a lot of rare opportunities in life."

"Good."

"And that's why I'm not going to Notre Dame."

"Wait . . . what?"

"You heard me. I'm not going to Notre Dame."

"Slow down, son. Let's not rush things."

"That's just it. I've been thinking about this all year, during the entire college application process. Laura has really been there for me. She's talked me through it."

"Oh no."

"I was hoping the Notre Dame Admissions office would make my decision a little easier by declining my application. I purposely slacked off a little over these last two semesters just to stack the odds against me."

"This isn't happening."

"I'm going to attend Temple University in Philadelphia. Laura and Ian live within walking distance of campus, and they have a spare bedroom."

"Jack!" I shout.

"What?"

"I need you to stop talking."

We break down *Heather* in silence. I make sure she's tied fast to the dock and her rainfly fits snug over the cockpit in anticipation of some rain later in the week. I finish the breakdown by buffing out a couple of scuffmarks on her stern with a small shoeshine cloth.

"*Heather* . . ." Jack says, watching me. "Where'd that name come from again?"

"*Highlander.*"

"Second-greatest movie ever?"

"That's right. Second only to?"

"*Road House*, of course."

"Of course."

We both smile, the tension subsiding.

"Dad."

"Yeah, son."

"You know this isn't about you, right?"

"I wish I could believe that."

"You'll always be my number one—my teacher, my friend, my dad. But this is about building a relationship—building at least something—with Laura. You've had me to yourself for eighteen years. She deserves to get to know me. I deserve to get to know her."

"Not to mention those three sisters of yours."

"I know, right?"

"Good luck with that."

"Their boyfriends don't stand a chance with me."

"I would expect nothing less." I stand up, shove the shoeshine cloth in my pocket. "When did you get to be such a grown-up man?"

"I had a great teacher."

"Can I meet him?"

"Get in line. There's a lot of people who love him, so I'd have to check and see if he could fit you into his busy schedule."

Reaching across to Jack, I grab his arm. "Thanks for that."

He returns my gesture, squeezing my opposite arm. "I still don't get it."

"Get what?"

"Why *Heather*? Why not something cooler from the movie like *Ramirez* or *MacLeod* or even *Kurgan*?"

"You don't name your boats after guys."

"Why not?"

"Some people say it's bad luck. I don't really know. That's just the way it's always been. When you're ready to take a boat out, you'd never say, 'Let's take *him* out,' would you?"

"No, I suppose not."

"I guess there's just something inherently feminine or maternal about a boat. It's comforting to know *she* is there for you when you're out at sea and all alone."

"So a sailor is just a boy who needs to be by his mother?"

*Mom watched as Dad and I came flying into the lee shore, the shore that was facing into the wind. The storm front was closing, wind and salt spray roaring over our backs. A wave caught the bow just right, pitchpoling our boat. The Laser flipped end over end, the aluminum mast snapping in half after getting stuck upside down in a sandbar. I nearly drowned.*

*A father and son obliviously living in the moment. A mother not caring about the moment, wishing nothing more than for them to be safe and in her arms.*

"Yeah, Jack," I say. "That's exactly what a sailor is."

# Chapter 51

I hate my fucking boss.

Dean Zacharias is one of the lingering legacy hires at Random House. A direct descendant of Frank Nelson Doubleday, the nineteenth century founder of Doubleday Books, he still brandishes the staunch Roman Catholicism of the Doubleday family like a badge of honor. He's the guy who gives good Catholics a bad name: writes large checks to Opus Dei, watches the Eternal Word Television Network, subscribes to *Latin Mass* magazine. A poor man's Mel Gibson. He's a raging misogynist who is grossly underqualified for his job. He doesn't read. He thinks all librarians and women writers—save for Ayn Rand and Ann Coulter—are lesbian socialists and that the Crusades were invented by the liberal mainstream media. He's the worst kind of manager, the type who is so small-minded and unintelligent that the only thing he can do for validation is micromanage menial tasks. His favorite ritual is to bring employees into his office and yell at them about their To Do lists. Never mind the fact that you've managed the only imprint under the Random House umbrella to stay in the black every quarter for the last decade, because you e-mailed him your To Do list three minutes late, you're a lazy, uncommitted employee.

I'm sitting in Dean's office. Random House flew me in this week with no explanation, other than it was urgent. We're in the midst of our sixth reorganization in as many years, a bloodletting I've managed to avoid by being profitable while most other New York publishers stare down the barrel of a once-in-a-lifetime recession that is shrinking wallets and shuttering bookstores.

"The problem with you, Hank, is that you got no clangers."

"Excuse me?"

Dean stands up. He grabs an unlit cigar out of the ashtray on his desk, sticks it in his mouth. He quit smoking ten years ago, but he still chews through a box of cigars every month. A woman hater with an oral fixation: yeah, like that's a fucking surprise.

"You got nothing swinging down there between your legs." Dean points at my midsection. "No fucking balls!"

"I don't know what you're getting at, Dean, but I don't think this is an appropriate conversation to be—"

"What's with all these books you're buying?"

"What do you mean?"

Dean grabs a hardcover novel off one of his shelves. He throws it on his desk. "Like this garbage."

I pick the book up and read the title aloud. *"Teaching Yoga in Belize."*

"What the fuck is that?"

"It's a great memoir. Won a lot of awards."

"I'm sure it did. I'm sure a bunch of intellectuals got in a room and agreed this book was the next *Atlas Shrugged.*"

"Dear God, I hope not."

"See, that right there is what I'm talking about. No fucking balls."

Dean's rant continues. I tune him out, flipping through the first few pages of *Teaching Yoga in Belize.* I lean my face into the book, smelling the rough-cut pages. This particular copy carries some unusual notes—freshly ground coffee buffeted by something almost familiar and intimate. It reminds me of that oily-haired smell of the inside of my father's baseball hats. I kept a half dozen of them in a cardboard box in my closet for about four or five years after his death. Every now and then, when I had a day that knocked the wind out of me—and I had a lot of those days after Dad died—I'd take out the hats and bury my nose in them. Back then I didn't know where I was going, but I didn't really care. Hell, I was just learning how to smile again. I had the bravado of youth—the unbridled confidence that the road ahead can't be any worse than the one you leave behind.

As I place the book back on my boss's desk, I think about that son who just needed to smell his father's hats.

"Dean," I say.

"Don't interrupt me, Hank."

"Oh, that's okay. I haven't listened to a word you've said for the last five minutes."

"Now you listen here, you disrespectful son of a—"

"Fuck you, you sanctimonious buffoon. I quit."

"What?" Dean says. "Now wait just a second."

"Good luck finding somebody who will keep College Avenue Press in the black for another ten days, let alone another ten years."

I stand up and make for the door. Dean gives chase.

"Calm down, Hank. You're making a rash decision here."

"And that's exactly why I know it's the right decision. There's just one more thing I wanted to say to you."

"What's that?"

I open the door to his office, smiling. "Pope John Paul II is fucking overrated."

# Chapter 52

Beth and I sit in a dorm room in St. Francis Hall on the campus of Marian College. We're playing a drinking game with some nursing students. Beth's mother is babysitting Sasha and the twins for the night.

"Ladies," I say. "Before we're all too far gone to remember, I want to make a toast to my brave and beautiful wife, Beth Fitzpatrick."

After I quit College Ave, things got a little tight, but we managed. I called Joe Mann at Talk Hard, and he hooked me up with a job as the Midwest library sales rep. This past year I've put close to fifty thousand miles on my Subaru Outback, peddling audiobooks to librarians in Indiana, Ohio, and Illinois. It pays the bills, and I still get to be around book people, so I can't complain. I've also started writing again.

Beth is the real story here. Unwavering in her support of my decision to quit my job, she decided to follow my lead and turn her own life upside down. She retired from coaching gymnastics, a career that essentially began when she was thirteen months old in a Mommy & Me class and ended at the age of thirty-seven when she came to the long overdue realization that no amount of money was worth babysitting moody teenage girls—never mind their overbearing mothers—ten hours a day. She enrolled in the accelerated nursing program at Marian College in Indianapolis. Within eighteen months, she had graduated from nursing school, passed her board exams, and accepted a job in hospice care. Depending on my monthly bonus or lack thereof, Beth's take-home pay will be at least as much as mine.

We toast to my wife. Beth wipes a trace of beer off her bottom lip, looks at me. "Drink, Asshole."

If there's an official card game in the state of Indiana, it has to be euchre. But honorable mention, especially when drinking is involved, has to go to Asshole. Numerous variations of the game exist, but we stick to the basics tonight: fifty-two cards, four players, suits are irrelevant, cards are ranked high-to-low two, ace, king, queen, jack, ten, and so on. All the cards are dealt. First one out of cards is President. Last one out is Asshole.

In the first game I am summarily dismissed to the bottom of the Asshole hierarchy, President Beth issues edicts from her throne: "I said drink, Asshole."

I lift my beer to my lips, taking a sip of Natural Light, which thirteen years after my graduation is still apparently the beer of choice of the frugal collegiate drunk.

Each person has to know his place in the hierarchy. As President, Beth can tell anyone playing to drink for whatever reason and is beholden to no one. Each successive player has varying levels of executive authority, save for Asshole, who obeys the whims of all who precede him and inevitably drinks the most.

"Shit!" I throw my cards down on the table in disgust. I'm the last one out. Asshole again.

I've managed to be Asshole for five consecutive hands—a dazzling feat of ineptitude. Beth has been President twice already, VP the other three hands. To Beth's right sits Vicky Elstrom. Vicky is an attractive redhead in her early twenties. Slim-figured, she's been debating getting a boob job and about a month ago was wine-drunk in our hot tub when she asked if she could feel Beth's breasts. Beth said, "Of course," and took off her bikini top while Vicky fondled her for a good five minutes.

This is all hearsay of course, as I was out of town on business. Because God is a fucking dick.

The other coed in the room is average-looking at best, with the personality to match. She has dirt-brown hair, and her name is Susan. Vicky plays two tens on Beth's two eights. Susan plays two jacks, and it's to me. I pass. Beth jumps on the two jacks with two aces. No one can match. Beth puts that pile aside and starts a new deal. She leads with the three cards she has in her hand—three fives—and is out. President once more.

"Shit!" I say.

"Drink for being a sore loser, Asshole!" Beth says.

I do as she commands. Smiling, I put my cup down. I show my cards: three sevens. Hello, Vice Presidency!

I point to Vicky and Susan. "Drink, bitches!"

Beth and I bowed out of the game gracefully, and by that I mean she tried to sit on my lap, slid her leg across my torso, and her right foot knocked a beer over, soaking the playing cards. The entire room, including someone I wrongly assumed was passed out on the bed behind us, screamed, "Party foul!"

Two more beers and a Southern Comfort shot later, Beth and I decide to take a walk across Marian's campus.

"Where we going?" I ask.

Beth points to the northeast corner of campus at the Tudor mansion on the hill. "Allison Mansion, baby. Built in 1911 by automobile magnate James

A. Allison."

"I know that guy. My dad used to talk about him. Cofounded the Indianapolis Motor Speedway and Allison Engine Company."

"That's the one." Beth nods, hooking my arm in hers. "Allison Mansion has been on the National Register of Historic Places since 1970. It has a one-ton German silver chandelier, a staircase built of solid hand-carved walnut, a music room encased on carved mahogany paneling, an aviary lined with white Italian marble crowned by a Tiffany stained-glass ceiling, and a two-story foyer made from now-extinct Circassian walnut that was imported from Czarist Russia."

"Did you memorize all that useless trivia for my benefit?"

"I sure as hell didn't memorize it for mine."

"You really do love me, don't you?" I close my eyes and smile, leaning in for a kiss.

She pushes my mouth away. "It's a dirty job, but somebody's got to do it."

"Now, what exactly are we going to do once we get to the house?"

"Go skinny-dipping," Beth says.

"What?"

"Something else Allison Mansion can claim is the Midwest's first-ever indoor pool. It's in the basement."

"So you're serious?"

"You bet I am."

"How are we getting in? I assume a place that nice is locked up as tight as a drum."

"You would think so."

"Yes, I would."

Beth looks around. We're standing at the bottom of the hill just south of Allison Mansion, still a good two-hundred yards away from the house. She crouches down, feeling around for something. Her arm disappears. "There it is."

"There what is?"

"Our ticket inside." Beth removes her arm from the black hole in the ground. She sits on the ground, scooting her butt toward the hole until her legs suddenly disappear.

"What's going on?"

"It's the tunnel between Allison Mansion and the Alverna Hall student center."

"Why would they have a tunnel between Allison and the student center?"

"The student center used to be the caretakers' quarters for Allison before a group of Franciscan nuns established Marian's campus here in the 1930s. Nobody ever bothered to block the tunnel, so sometimes students sneak into Allison and Alverna after hours."

"Beth, this is trespassing."

"I'd be happy to compare arrest records."

"Funny."

"I thought so," Beth says. She raises her hands in the air. "Now help me down."

"This can't be safe. Plus, there have to be security cameras in the mansion."

"Oh, there are."

"Then what the hell are we doing?"

"In exchange for a really nice bottle of Scotch, campus security gave me one hour."

"Wait, what?"

"You might find this hard to believe, but you're not the only charming person on the planet. Now, help me down."

"Almost there," Beth says. She leads the way with a small pen light attached to her car keys. "There's the entrance to Allison."

"Is it unlocked?"

"Let's hope so," she says, turning the handle on the large oak door.

The door opens to an ornate room dimly lit by security lights. There's a sloping Gothic ceiling of what looks to be carved, pressed leather. The windows on the south side of the room are made from multi-sized and stained bottles set in wrought iron. A large stone fireplace anchors the room.

"What is this place?"

"Looks almost like a basement den or something."

"A den?"

"Yep."

"Sweet," Beth says. "That means the pool is right around the corner."

The smell of chlorine lets us know we've arrived. Beth shines her pen light into the cavernous room and then down at the water. The large tiled pool is rectangular shaped and runs from east to west, with the deeper water in the east end.

"Well, it's full." I reach down, sticking my hand in the water. "And it's fucking cold."

"Oh, don't be a wuss," Beth says, already undressed. She jumps in.

I'm a little more deliberate. I take off my shoes and socks, then my shirt, then my pants, then my underwear. I sit on the edge of the pool, my feet dangling in the water.

"Today, Romeo." Beth splashes me.

Finally I jump in. I swim underwater with my eyes open. The chlorine burns, but I can barely make out Beth's shadowy form in front of me. My hands reach around and find her ass. I pull her toward me. As I start to come up for air, I blow a stream of bubbles between her legs, then up her belly and between her breasts until I finally break the surface.

"Is that better, Juliet?"

"Quiet," Beth says.

"Oh, *now* you're being cautious?"

"Someone's here."

"I thought you said security gave you the run of the place for an hour."

"Not security." Beth points her finger in the air, tilting her head. "You hear that?"

"I don't hear any—"

"Shhh . . ." Beth holds her finger to her mouth. "*That.*"

My hair stands on the back of my neck. I hear the sound of a little girl crying.

"What the fuck, Beth?" I whisper.

"It can't be true."

"What can't be true?"

"Legend has it this pool is haunted by a little girl who drowned here in the 1920s. I never believed it—until now."

"Holy shit," I say, still whispering. The girl's crying is getting louder. "I've tried to talk you into more spontaneous acts of nudity than I can possibly count, and the first time you go out on a limb, you pick a haunted pool?"

"Maybe she'll just go away."

"She's been here for ninety years. I don't think she's going anywhere."

"What are we going to do, Hank?"

"Don't look at me," I say. "This is your show."

"I guess it is, isn't it." Beth smiles. "You can come out now, Vicky."

Vicky walks around the corner, a Coleman lantern in her left hand and a handheld tape recorder in her right. "That . . . was . . . awesome!"

I splash Beth. "You suck."

"Oh come on, honey, you needed that."

"I needed to be scared shitless?"

"In a way, yes. You needed someone to pull that stick out of your ass."

"Well, mission accomplished."

"Hey, lovebirds, you want me to leave the lantern?"

Beth smiles again. "It's a big pool, Vick. Why don't you come join us for a swim?"

"You sure?" Vicky says.

"Wouldn't bother me. How about you, Hank?"

As I try to string together a few coherent words, I notice Vicky already has her pants and underwear off. "I, uh, well, um, it, I guess, uh . . ."

"I'm not sure, Vicky," Beth says, "but I think that's a 'yes.' "

Vicky jumps into the pool.

Okay, God, maybe you're not a dick after all.

# Part X
# 2009

# Chapter 53

Lila sits at the wet bar in my basement. I've just poured her a Beam and Coke. I drink mine on the rocks.

"Cheers," I say.

"Cheers," Lila says, raising her glass. She sips the bourbon, sets the glass down. "Thanks for letting me crash at your place this weekend."

"Don't mention it. When's the wedding again?"

"One thirty tomorrow afternoon."

"Down at the Mormon temple in Louisville?"

"Yep."

"A cousin?"

"A friend."

"Same thing."

"No it isn't."

"Whatever. Normally I'd say one thirty is aggressive, given that you'd be kicking off the party around three, but we are talking a Mormon wedding reception."

"You'd be surprised."

"At what?"

"LDS receptions can get out of hand."

"And by 'out of hand' you mean aggressive square dancing, lemonade bongs, and innocently suggestive love anthems by David Archuleta?"

"Hey now, David Archuleta rocks."

"No, he doesn't rock. What the hell, Lila? Two years removed from being a lesbian band aid, and now you're into Honduran LDS bubble gum pop?"

"Honduran?"

"On his mom's side. I watch *American Idol*. I'm not a fucking communist."

"So you thought the best singer won?"

"David Cook could fart a better song than David Archuleta could sing."

"That's not nice, Hank."

"Whatever," I say. "How much you want?"

"What do you mean?"

"For your lame-ass LDS wedding reception. A bottle of bourbon? A hip flask?"

Lila shakes her head. "I'll take a hip flask."

"And?"

"And the bottle."

"That's what I thought."

"Do you have anything besides Jim Beam?"

"What's wrong with Beam?"

"Nothing, if you're nineteen years old."

"I got this," I say, turning to the glass shelves behind me. I grab a bottle and hand it to my stepsister. "Jameson 18 Year Reserve. I've been saving it for a special occasion, but you're special enough."

"Special *enough*?" Lila says. "I'm flattered you think so much of me."

"Do you want it or not?"

Lila grabs the bottle. "So what's up with you?"

"Nothing really."

"Jack is good?"

"He's great. We don't talk or see one another nearly as much as I'd like, but he loves it out East."

"You okay with that?"

"Laura and Jack deserve all the time they need to figure things out."

"Wow."

"What?"

"That's such an adult thing to say, Hank."

"I'm thirty-seven years old. At some point I need to act the part."

"Is it acting?"

"I hope so," I say, grinning from ear to ear, Cheshire-like.

Lila leans in and kisses me on the cheek. "There's my Hank."

"He makes an occasional cameo."

"Where's your beautiful wife?"

"She and the kids are out shopping for the Christmas party."

"You hosting?"

"Yes, unfortunately. Stan got us a killer deal on the caterers who did his office party."

"He's back in town?"

"More than he has been. He and Joan are actually talking about making another go of it."

"No way."

"Beth is deliriously happy about it."

"And you?"

"I think Stan and Joan are two of the least compatible people on the planet."

"You tell Beth that?"

"Hell no."

"Good boy," Lila says. "And the job at Talk Hard is going well?"
"Well enough."
"I wanted to talk to you about that."
"About audiobooks?"
"About your career. How's the writing going?"
"It's going."
"It is?"
"Sure."
"So you're writing?"
"I'm dabbling," I say.
"Define 'dabbling.'"
"I got about seventy-five thousand words down of a memoir. Signed with an agent about a month ago just based on the first three chapters."
"That's exciting. You got a title yet?"
*"Waiting for the Sun."*
"Oh, I like that. Double entendre, great metaphor for the story of a boy figuring out how to be a man."
"All of the above."
"You could even open with that Doors song."
"I wish."
"Why not?"
"The Morrison Estate is controlled by his dead girlfriend's parents."
"The Meg Ryan character in the movie?"
"Pamela Courson was her name. She died of a drug overdose three years after Jim Morrison, and all rights to Jim Morrison's music passed to her parents. They hated Jim and blamed him for their daughter's death. They consider any advances or royalties related to the Morrison Estate to be their daughter's blood money and subsequently charge exorbitant licensing fees."
"You blame them?"
"I applaud them."
"Thought you might," Lila says. "Hey, what's that noise?"
"The whining sound?"
"I guess."
"That's Chief."
"Chief? Good Lord, how old is he now?"
"Pushing fourteen."
"That's pretty old for a big dog."
"He's got a few miles left on the chassis."
"Where is he?"
"He's upstairs. He pretty much sits by the back door all day. When he starts whining, we have to go lift him by his hips because he can't stand up from a sitting position by himself anymore."
"That's no life, Hank."
"I think Chief is getting by okay, but enough about me. How about you?

Hawaii treating you well?"

"I guess."

"Trouble in paradise?"

"Chris has just been, uh, writing and texting and calling me lately."

"Oh God."

"I miss her, Hank."

"Of course you do."

"What do you mean?"

"She's your Laura. She's your fucking stupid."

"My what? Listen, you pompous ass, my life is not a reflection of yours."

"I didn't say it was. Everybody has a Laura, that one person you have no business being with that you keep going back to until the meat is completely stripped from your bones."

"That's pleasant."

"That's Laura."

"So I should ignore Chris?"

"Hell no."

"What?"

"You gotta let it play out."

"Has anyone ever told you that you're a fucking lunatic, Hank?"

"Pretty much everybody I know. Look, Lila, you're a big girl. My advice to you is to not do anything half speed, good or bad. Half speed equals regrets. Full speed equals results."

"Full speed equals disasters."

"Yeah, but they're awesome disasters."

# Chapter 54

Beth wakes me up.
"What is it?" I say. My head is throbbing. I'm hung over from our Christmas party.
My wife is crying, still wearing nothing but a Peyton Manning jersey from our all-night sexcapades.
"Baby, I said I was sorry about the beer pong with the caterers. I thought we had gotten past that."
"That's not it, honey."
"Then what is it?"
"It's Chief. He's . . ."
"He's what?"
"Just . . . go look."
"Is he dead?"
"No, but I don't know what he is."

I walk into the kitchen, Beth trailing behind me. The smell is overwhelming. Chief raises his head when I come up to him. He wags his tail. He's sitting in a pool of his own urine and feces.
This isn't the first time he's done this, but it's never been this bad. I grab him by the muzzle, shake his head playfully as if nothing is wrong. Now I'm crying too. "You okay, Chiefy?"
Chief wags his tail.
"Help me with him," I say to my wife.
"What are we doing?" Beth asks.
"We're giving him a bath. I'll take him into the vet tomorrow morning, but our big black bear is going to at least leave this world with some dignity."

# Chapter 55

Chief fell down the basement flight of stairs this morning. Not even an hour later, he pissed and shit himself again. If there's one lesson in life my dog has taught me these last thirteen-plus years, it's how to live selflessly. And right now, I'm keeping Chief alive for me, not for him.

Beth and I decided to tell the children after the fact when they come back from school, fearing the trauma will be too much for them to handle. I leashed Chief up and took him outside for one last walk. I pretended everything was normal. I ran into Oscar and Marshall and their seven gay Chihuahuas and let them nip at Chief's ankles. I let Chief raise his leg and piss one last time on Roy and Betty's mailbox. We sprinted full-speed for about a block. It was the most exercise my loyal running buddy had seen in years, and he loved it. His hips were so shot from the effort he just collapsed in the yard, tail still wagging.

I carry Chief to the car. Beth stands in the garage, still in her robe.
"What are you doing?" I say to my wife. "Get dressed."
"I can't go, Hank."
"What do you mean?"
"It's too hard."
*Their collective date of birth was listed as April 1, 1996—April Fool's Day. The puppies were all jet black, save for one. He had a white dot on his head, white paws and a bold splash of white on his chest. Beth picked him up, his brothers and sisters yelping after him, starved for attention.*
*"This little guy is adorable," she said.*
*And with those words, seemingly on cue, the puppy laid his head on my wife's shoulder.*
Beth approaches the car. She kisses Chief on the nose, rubbing his ears. "Thanks for choosing me," she says through a shower of tears.

We arrive at the veterinarian's office. Even after polishing off his third quarter pounder with cheese in the last ten minutes, Chief weighs an anemic eighty-four pounds, a full twenty-five pounds lighter than his previously highest recorded weight.

"This is crazy, Hank," the vet says. Her name is Kimberly. She's in her midthirties, well put together. Athletic in the right places. A pretty face as far as vets go, albeit my exposure to the veterinarian pool is limited.

"What's crazy?" I say.

"You're telling me he only really broke down last night?"

"Pretty much."

"Chief's pituitary gland was already failing. His hormone levels were off the charts during his physical *last year*. There was no medical explanation for him being alive then, let alone now standing in front of me wagging his tail."

The vet's resident white cat Buddy comes running into our room, and Chief, for the briefest of moments, thinks he's a puppy again. Chief's ears prick up, his tail wagging even more enthusiastically. He allows Buddy to cuddle against his leg. He leans down and licks the cat in the face.

"He's got a way with cats," the vet says.

"He's got a way with everybody," I say.

The vet notices me fighting back the tears. "Hank, can I talk to you in my office for a second?"

"Why?" I say.

"Just humor me."

"Okay."

We walk into the vet's office. A hundred-gallon salt water aquarium lines the wall. "Are those blowfish, Doc?"

"Yes, a type of blowfish. The more accurate name is Takifugu or pufferfish. How'd you know?"

"I have some experience with them."

"Look, Hank, I don't want to make this any harder on you than I have to. We can do this quietly and let you be on your way."

"That's not an option."

"What do you mean?"

"Doc, I don't want to unload all my shit on you right now."

"Please, call me Kimberly, and I can take it."

"Oh no you can't."

"Try me."

"Chief has been here for nearly my entire fourteen years of marriage. He was there for the birth of all three of my children. He's my first dog. He's my best friend. He's my family."

"You're not the first dog owner to tell me this story, Hank."

"I'm not finished, Kimberly."

"Sorry."

"My innocence was taken away from me by my godfather. My son was taken away from me by my girlfriend and my own parents. My father was taken away from me not by cancer or by old age, but by a senior citizen driving a repossessed late-model SUV. My life has never been on my fucking terms. It's been one random ball of shit. Everybody takes things from me, and for once I'd like to be allowed to just let something go."

"So you see Chief as a sort of vindication of life, as maybe a chance for you to say goodbye to somebody on your terms?"

"As ridiculous as it sounds, yes. I want to be given an actual choice. I want to believe that life isn't so random and cruel. I want to make out with blowfish and live to tell about it."

"Uh, what?"

"Never mind," I say. "I'm ready now."

Kimberly and her assistant spread a blanket on the floor. They bring Chief into the room and place him on the blanket. I lie next to him.

"This first injection is just a sedative. It will relax Chief and make him very tired before we administer the pentobarbital, which is the euthanizing agent."

Kimberly injects Chief's right front paw with the sedative. He begins to fall asleep almost immediately. I stroke his square, slightly pointed head. I grab him by the ears and kiss him between his now-closed eyes, soaking his muzzle with my tears. He sticks his tongue out one last time and licks my face. His breathing grows shallower and shallower.

The assistant hands Kimberly the second syringe. She pokes Chief. I watch her thumb slowly send the poison into his paw.

"How long does it take?" I say through my sobs.

"I think he might already be . . ." Kimberly trails off with a whisper, placing the stethoscope on Chief's still-warm chest. "Yes, he's gone now."

They told me to take as much time as I wanted, so I stayed with Chief until someone came in and asked if I was ready to leave. It was a privilege I was denied with my father. This time I was there at the end. Chief was not alone, and he knew that he was loved.

I sit inside my Subaru for several long minutes before I start the engine. The car still smells like quarter pounders and dog hair. I can't stop crying.

Sleep well, old buddy. Dream dreams of dirty diapers, Oreo cookies, and large, voluptuous poodles in heat. You will be missed. And if I can find another dog in this lifetime only half as good as you, I'll still have the best dog in the neighborhood.

# Chapter 56

I crawl into bed with Beth. *The Late Show with David Letterman* is on the television.

"How you holding up, babe?" she says.

"Not one of my better days. Didn't expect to feel this sad."

"You said so yourself, Hank. Chief was family."

"I know he was family. And even though I got to say goodbye, losing Chief made a part of me feel powerless all over again, just like I was with Dad's death and with Jack . . ."

"And with Uncle Mitch?"

"Especially with Uncle Mitch," I say. "What's the point of loving something only for it to be taken away?"

"The point is in the loving," Beth says. "Our willingness to endure the heartbreak and to still travel down the road together hand in hand even though we know how it's going to end is exactly what makes life worth living and people worth loving."

And with those words, seemingly on cue, Darius Rucker stands in front of a microphone on *The Late Show*. He settles into the chorus of a country song I've never heard: *"Don't think I don't think about it, don't think I don't have regrets, don't think it don't get to me, between the work and the hurt and the whiskey."*

I try not to smile.

Beth stands up, pulls me out of bed with her.

"One more dance?" she says.

I take her hand in mine. "How about we keep that number a little more open-ended?"

"Forever then?"

"Forever it is," I say.

# Chapter 57

I stand on the front porch of Elias Hatcher's house, knocking on his front door. The door opens. Hatch stands there in just his boxers.
"Do you have any fucking idea what time it is, Hank?"
"About 4:00 a.m. Claire here?"
"She got called in by the airline for a twelve-hour run to Los Angeles. What's that under your arm?"
"Chief."
"Excuse me?"
I'm holding a bronze urn that I picked up yesterday afternoon at a thrift store. I was tired of looking at that container the vet had given me. "It's his ashes."
"Jesus." Hatch reaches out, squeezes my shoulder. "I'm sorry, dude."
"It's okay, really. But now, I need your help."
"Doing what?"
"Figuring out where we should dump them."
Hatch is protective and sentimental toward his closest friends to the point of it being comical. Stick Jimmy Buffett's "A Pirate Looks at Forty" in the tape deck, and Hatch is hugging you and bawling his eyes out—guaranteed. If he seems reluctant to commit any impulsive act, all you have to do is invoke the word *pals*, and he has no say in the matter.
Like tonight.
"It's early, Hank. How about we circle back to this tomorrow, in the daytime?"
"Pals, Hatch."
"Come on, Hank."
"Pals!"
"But I can't—"
"Pals!"
"Ah fuck it." Hatch rubs his eyes. "Let me put on some clothes and find where the hell Claire put my hat and gloves. Got any ideas where we might be going?"

"I was thinking maybe the Falls."
"Perfect choice."
"We'll see."

Bourbon Falls, or simply "the Falls" in Empire Ridge circles, is a sickle-shaped waterfall about ten miles out of town. It's owned and maintained by the Indiana Department of Natural Resources, at least to the extent the DNR can tolerate cleaning up after underage drinkers and meth heads.

Hatch and I walk the steep path toward the falls. If it were daytime, our eyes would be greeted by the twenty-foot plunge of Bourbon Falls framed by southern Indiana in its winter canvas of brown dotted by silver-white sycamore trees.

We reach the water's edge. Hatch suddenly seems less than enthused.

"I don't know about this, Hank."

I can barely hear him over the roar of the falls fewer than twenty-five yards downstream. "What don't you know?"

"It's pretty fucking dark out here."

*Click.* I turn on my flashlight. "No shit."

We step across the dozen or so unevenly spaced stones to the other side of the creek. I shine the flashlight down to reveal a snarled sycamore root.

"Watch your step, Hatch."

"Thanks, buddy."

We cross a small wooden plank bridge.

"Don't remember it being this far," I say. "Do you?"

Hatch nods and points. "It's just up ahead."

He's right. I see it. The jagged limestone edifice is as long and as tall as a school bus. I flash the light on the rock. I set Chief's ashes down at the base of the outcropping.

We follow the beam of light. Generations of initials are carved into the limestone's forgiving surface. I stop the beam of light near the bottom right corner of the rock and shine it on a familiar mathematic equation:

**HF + LE '89**

"It's still there," I say.

Hatch isn't paying attention to me. I hear him counting aloud: ". . . four, five, six . . ."

"Hey, Hatch."

"Yeah?"

"What are you doing?"

"Counting the number of times I see your initials or my initials up here."

"This was your big move, too?"

"Oh, hell yes. Get them out to the rock, and it was a done deal."

I laugh. "Yeah, a done deal."

"What's so funny?"

"We had horrible game back then. How did we ever get laid?"

"Desire and persistence, Fitzy."

"And alcohol."

"That, too," Hatch affirms. He nods at the urn. "So is this the place?"

"I don't think so."

"How about jacking them over the falls?"

"No," I say. "It's not like I brought Chief out here. This wasn't one of our hangouts."

"Well, where did you go?"

"All over. Never really ended up finding one place that was just ours where we could go to get away from the world and toss a ball around."

"That's a shame."

"It is, isn't it?"

"A boy and his dog deserve a special place to toss a ball around, like maybe a field with a single solitary tree just big enough to keep the afternoon sun at bay."

"Wait a second, Hatch."

"What?"

"That's it!"

"That's what?"

"You beautiful fucking bastard!" I grab my best friend in a bear hug and give him a big, wet manly kiss on the cheek.

Hatch seems confused. "What the hell did I say?"

I reach down, grabbing Chief's ashes. "Let's go."

"Where?"

"To the cemetery."

In my humble estimation, one of the most underrated movies from the 1980s is *Stealing Home*. Regarded as little more than a B-side flick on Jodie Foster's staggering résumé and almost universally despised by the critics, it is my favorite movie Foster has ever been in. It's her sexiest, most endearing role, and I don't think anything comes close.

As the story goes, Billy Wyatt, played as an adult by eighties heartthrob Mark Harmon and as a teenager by William McNamara, was once a very talented high school baseball player and minor-league prospect. Now in his thirties, out of work and a bit of a social misfit, he receives a telephone call from his mother revealing that Katie Chandler, as played by Jodie Foster, has committed suicide and left instructions that only Billy can decide what to do with her cremated remains. This mortifies her parents, who want Katie buried in their family plot. Katie is Billy's former child-sitter—and later, in his teens, his first love. The tragedy conjures wonderful and painful memories of the times Billy spent with her, as well as of his own childhood, especially with his father Sam Wyatt, played by John Shea, with whom he had a close relationship, and with his best friend Alan Appleby, played by Jonathan Silverman as a teen and then Harold Ramis as an adult.

The memories become the story, flashing back to Billy's preteen time with Katie as his child-sitter (Katie was in her late teens at the time) and with his father; then to his teens, both before and after his father died in a car accident. Billy and Katie shared a brief time of love together, and Katie was immensely comforting to him after his father died. She then moved out of the country to be with a man she loved, which was the last time he saw her.

Billy, in the present, struggles to know what to do with Katie's ashes. He searches his memories for answers and finds Alan Appleby after many years of having lost touch. They embark on new adventures as adults, with Katie's ashes in tow, until the answer finally comes to Billy. He remembers Katie spoke of something long ago from her own early childhood: a horse in Atlantic City, forced to run full speed down the boardwalk and off the edge into the water. Remembering that she wished on that day that she could fly to a faraway land to find happiness, Billy spreads her ashes into the air off the edge of that same pier. Afterward, he rekindles old relationships and returns to a life of baseball by joining a minor league baseball team.

Even after seventeen years, Dad's monument is still the tallest in this corner of the Whiskeyville Cemetery. We park the Subaru so the headlights illuminate the headstone, a veiny gray and black slab of marble with a giant shamrock carved on the front. Inside the shamrock in big block letters are the words JOHN H. FITZPATRICK, HUSBAND, FATHER AND FRIEND, followed by the dates of his birth and his death, and then the Irish Blessing. The sugar maple that used to stand a good ten yards away now canopies Dad's burial site, protecting him from the elements. Just big enough to keep the afternoon sun at bay

I reach for Dad's headstone, like always tracing the word FATHER with my fingers.

"Want to say it with me?" I say to Hatch.

"Say what?"

"The Irish Blessing."

"That's okay, Hank. You do it. This is your moment."

I read the Irish Blessing aloud: "May the road rise up to meet you. May the wind be always at your back. May the rains fall soft upon your fields, and the sun shine warm upon your face. And until we meet again, may God hold you in the hollow of his hand."

With that, I unscrew the urn and dump Chief's ashes at the foot of my father's grave.

The wind whistles between the sugar maple's bare branches, but I hear something else. The sound is subtle but unmistakable.

"You hear that, Hatch?"

"Hear what?"

"It's a clanging noise, like metal against metal."

"Wind chimes maybe?"

"No."

"Then what?"

"Sounds more like . . . dog tags."

"I think you just need some sleep." Hatch says, looking to the horizon. "It'll be morning soon. We should go."

"Ready when you are," I say.

"Give me ten minutes?"

"Sure."

"Thanks." Hatch nods across the cemetery. "I think my grandpa is a couple hundred yards that way. Been a while since I paid my respects. I'm going to take a walk."

Hatch has been gone for close to twenty minutes now. It's still dark, but the faint pink edges of dawn fleck the eastern sky. I almost nod off while sitting at the base of my dad's headstone.

I hear the dog tags again.

I stand up, look around. Where is that sound coming from? My cell phone vibrates. I pull it out of my pocket. *Seven missed calls,* the display screen warns. Shit. I need to get home. I make my way to the car.

Stood up too fast. Head is spinning. Seeing spots, I fumble with my car keys.

Wait. There it is again. The clanging noise. They *are* dog tags. I'm sure of it now. I look around again. Still no one.

"Hatch," I shout across the cemetery, my hand cupped around my mouth. "We gotta go!"

He doesn't answer back. I slide into my seat and start the ignition. Where the fuck is he? I look out toward the end of the car's eyebeams at my father's grave marker one last time.

A man is standing there with a black dog on a leash.

The man is facing me. He begins to wave, maybe even to smile, when I close my eyes. I reach for the door handle. But do I want to open my eyes? Do I want to get out of my car and confront whoever that is standing out there? Do I even want them to be real?

Deep breaths. Think, Hank. Think.

*Matching Notre Dame hooded sweatshirts. The tobacco farm in Kentucky. Hours at a time spent just sitting in the barn. Dairy cows poking their heads around the barn door to say hello. Tomcats chasing mice across the straw-covered floor. The sweet-scented tobacco leaves curing in the rafters. The flip-flop sound of Dad's sandaled feet in the summer. Dirt and earthworms under his nails after he baited you a hook. His laugh. The scratchy feel of his face against yours when he'd forget to shave for a couple days. His smell. That particular smile he reserved for his sons.*

Those moments in the depths of quietness the world seemed to talk to you more.

That's just it, Hank. Don't think. *Listen.*

His words ride the wind like a plaintive yet hopeful whisper, and I hear them as if he's right next to me, just outside the car window. I start to pull on the door handle again. My nose twitches at the earthy aroma of tanned leather. But then I let go. I don't need to open my eyes. Believing is enough.

*"Thank you, son."*

"You're welcome, Dad."

# Acknowledgements

Moments like these, I feel like that actor stuck holding the golden trophy and staring into your living room without an acceptance speech. Save for trying to make sense of a few chicken scratches on a cocktail napkin—*don't forget to tell your wife you love her, don't forget to tell your wife you love her*—all there is left for me to do is mumble my way through thirty interminable seconds until the orchestra plays me offstage.

All kidding aside, the acknowledgements section in my previous novel ran over a thousand words. It was well-intentioned but admittedly self-indulgent. I do have a new editor this time around, which bears mentioning, as I can be a pain in the ass. Please take a most deserved bow, Erin Morgan.

I would also like to give a special thanks to all my teachers, many of whom continue to pursue their profession while being criminally underappreciated and underpaid. Without them, I would never have learned to appreciate the English language or the writing craft while at the same time so thoroughly despise mathematics.

Lastly, I'd be remiss not to acknowledge my childhood home of Columbus, Indiana, which inspired the fictional town of Empire Ridge in both *Exotic Music of the Belly Dancer* and *Making Out with Blowfish*. It's the type of town in which every child should want to grow up and every adult should want to grow old. While I no longer call Columbus home, it's never too far away from my heart.

Oh yeah. Robin Loheide Sweany, I love you.

# About the Author

Since 2000, Brian Sweany has been the Director of Acquisitions for Recorded Books, one of the world's largest audiobook publishers. Prior to that he edited cookbooks and computer manuals and claims to have saved a major pharmaceutical company from being crippled by the Y2K bug.

Brian has a BS in English from Eastern Michigan University, from which he graduated magna cum laude in 1995. He's a retired semiprofessional student, with stopovers at: Wabash College, the all-male school that reputedly fired Ezra Pound from its faculty for having sex with a prostitute; Marian University, the former all-female school founded by Franciscan nuns that, if you don't count Brian's expulsion, has fired no one of consequence and is relatively prostitute-free; and Indiana University via a high school honors course he has no recollection of ever attending.

Brian has penned several articles for EverydayHealth.com about his real-life struggles to overcome sexual abuse as a young boy. *Making Out with Blowfish* is the sequel to his debut novel, *Exotic Music of the Belly Dancer*, and both books draw inspiration from this experience.

Brian has spent most of his life in the Midwest and now lives near Indianapolis with his wife, three kids, and two rescue dogs. For more details, check out the author's website at: www.briansweany.com.

CPSIA information can be obtained at www.ICGtesting.com
Printed in the USA
BVOW08s1803190814

363446BV00009B/59/P

9 781612 132181